VIRTUE

COURAGE COMPASSION REDEMPTION

Geoffrey Holland

1. Main category—Literature & Fiction › Contemporary Fiction › Romance
2. Other category—Literature & Fiction › Genre Fiction › Political
3. Other category—Romance › Contemporary

Published by: AR PRESS
Roger L. Brooks, Publisher
roger@americanrealpublishing.com
americanrealpublishing.com

PROLOGUE

"**Y**OU OKAY, SIR?"

Greg Hammond glanced at his young assistant, Michael Block, and waved off his concern.

The two of them were in the back seat of a New York City cab, headed uptown in an early afternoon rain. The traffic was snarled and crawling along, adding another dimension of irritation to the nagging pain in Greg's chest.

Michael was still staring at him.

Greg gestured toward the sheaf of documents on Michael's lap and said, in a weary voice that reflected his discomfort, "I'm fine. Let's keep our focus."

Michael turned his attention back to the documents, all of which related to the pending acquisition of NNA, a high-value, Latvian-based internet provider.

Greg had his own problem with focus. The chest pain had been bothering him since the night before. Though it didn't seem serious, it was a nuisance. The private lunch he was just returning from with the Latvian UN Ambassador probably hadn't helped matters. The meal had been too heavy, and the ambassador's English had often been difficult to understand.

Eight minutes later, the cab pulled up in front of the Starling Worldwide Building at 56th and 1st Avenue. Greg exited the vehicle. A gauntlet of security people stayed close as he crossed the building's plaza, passing by the company's massive, brushed-steel emblem, which was set in a fountain of rushing water.

Greg's attention went to a handful of protesters waving a large banner with the Starling emblem painted on it followed by an equal sign and the words *Media Whore.*

The agitators spotted Greg and began chanting, "Chairman of the Whore! Chairman of the Whore! "Chairman of the Whore!"

Greg turned his gaze straight ahead and pretended to ignore them.

Inside the glass-and-steel skyscraper's lobby, the security detail remained behind as Greg and Michael entered an elevator reserved for top executives. The doors closed behind them.

Greg felt the elevator surge upward. The protesters quickly faded from mind as he focused on the deal at hand. Starling's M&A lawyers were in Riga, Latvia, working through a handful of contested line items in the takeover agreement that would give Starling Media control of NNA, the most prominent new internet provider in the Baltic countries. No one would characterize it as a big acquisition, but it did offer a valuable foothold from which Starling could expand its all-important web presence farther into Eastern Europe.

The elevator doors opened on the fifty-third floor. Greg stepped off and headed straight to the reception counter.

"How you feeling, Mr. Hammond?" said Mindy, his longtime executive receptionist.

Greg acknowledged the middle-aged woman with a smile and a little gesture that implied he felt better than he actually did. Then, he said, "Anything from the M&A Team?"

"Nothing, sir."

Greg's expression remained stoic, but he was not happy. His people were the best in the high-stakes game of corporate mergers and acquisitions, and the issues left were little more than formalities. They should've been in touch by now.

He walked into his office, crossed directly to his desk, and slumped into his cushy leather chair. He closed his eyes and tried to block out the pain in his chest. Being CEO of a fifty-six-billion-dollar global media enterprise was a 24/7 high-wire act. He'd endured many symptoms of stress over the years. His current discomfort was just the latest variation. No way was he going to let some kind of transient dyspepsia interfere with his pending deal. He had a track record to maintain.

Over the past fourteen years, through the aggressive acquisition of TV and radio stations, newspapers, magazines, book publishers, and internet-related businesses, mostly in North America, Europe, and Asia, he'd transformed Starling into the third largest media empire in the world. The acquisition of NNA in the Baltic was a small but important piece of the company's expanded focus on internet-based media services.

Greg pulled open a desk drawer and grabbed a bottle of antacids. He'd gone through nearly a third of the container since morning. He dumped several of the chalky white tablets into his hand, then threw them into his mouth. He chewed and swallowed the pills, then closed his eyes again and willed them to work. After several minutes, there was still no relief.

Relax…resist the pain, he told himself. Then he swiveled his chair around until he was able to look into a large mirror hanging behind his desk. He studied the wrinkles at the corners of his eyes and around his mouth while smoothing his brown hair. Though he was only forty-two, he felt, and thought he looked, much older.

Turning back to his desk, Greg put on his reading glasses and gave his attention to the paperwork spread out in front of him. The pain continued, derailing his focus. After another moment, he cursed under his breath and got to his feet. He went over to the rain-streaked windows that lined one side of his office and peered out at the misty April overcast hanging low over the city. He could barely make out Roosevelt Island in the East River several hundred yards distant or the Queensboro Bridge a few blocks north. The gloomy weather seemed appropriate—a muted reflection of his inner turmoil.

There was a knock at his office door. He turned and saw his executive assistant look in.

"Feeling any better, sir?" Michael asked.

Greg waved half-heartedly, implying he was okay.

Michael seemed to know he wasn't getting the truth. "Afternoon meetings?" he said. "You want to reschedule?"

Greg used a handkerchief to wipe a light bead of sweat from his forehead. None of his appointments were urgent, and he didn't want to pretend to be cheery when he didn't feel the least bit that way. He looked at Michael and muttered, "Yeah. Reschedule."

"Some rest might help," said Michael.

Greg ignored his assistant's concern. "What time is it in Riga?"

"After nine p.m.," said Michael.

"We should've heard by now," Greg said.

He felt lousy, and his mind was a swirl of frustration. Discipline and focus had long been cornerstones of his winning personal formula, but at this moment, he sensed he was running on empty. He zeroed in again on the Baltic deal. He wanted an answer, was it on or off? The uncertainty was making him crazy.

He pulled out his phone and began texting the M&A team in Latvia. When he touched the device's small screen in the wrong place, an error message came up. Greg closed his eyes and refocused. He cleared the screen and was about to start over when the discomfort deep under his sternum suddenly erupted like a small bomb. He groaned loudly as the phone slipped from his hand and fell to the floor.

He saw Michael whirl toward the open office door and shout to the receptionist seated outside, "Mindy! 9-1-1! Call 9-1-1!"

The pain was the worst Greg had ever known. His legs grew wobbly and started to buckle.

In an instant, Michael was there, slipping a shoulder under Greg's arm and holding him up. They stumbled toward the sofa across the room.

Greg barely heard Michael's pleas for him to hang on. His chest felt like it was on fire, burning from the inside out. He let out another deep groan, then his legs stopped working. He collapsed to the floor, pulling Michael down with him.

Greg's face contorted, and his body shook with every agonizing breath. The pain was relentless. He glanced about helplessly as more and more staff poured into the office. His past started flashing through his mind. His body convulsed, and he fought to stay alert. He didn't want to die. He fought hard. His vision blurred as his mind went into shock. He fought and he fought…then all went black.

❖

Half a world away, Jack Hammond jogged along the windblown beach at Shamrock, the family's sprawling seaside estate on Kakapo Bay, south of Christchurch, New Zealand. He shaded his eyes with his left hand as the morning sun broke from behind a cluster of cumulus clouds. He turned his focus to the mob of seagulls hovering close overhead, then tossed a piece of dry dog food into the air and watched the squawking birds go after it. They were accustomed to Jack's regular visits.

A young gull caught the piece of kibble in its beak. The others attacked, forcing the winner to drop the prize on the beach. The birds landed atop the morsel and fought for it.

Hap and Randy, the old man's German Shepherds, rushed in, barking. En masse, the gulls went airborne and scattered. The dogs lost interest and went back to chasing each other in and out of the surf.

Interacting with the gulls was a regular part of the retirement routine Jack had long maintained. His shaggy, gray hair blew wildly as he tossed another morsel to the noisy birds. An instant later, he heard a shout and turned as his stout Māori driver, Eddie Ponaruma, rushed toward him from the house. As Eddie drew closer, the old man saw the distress in his face.

"Mr. Jack!" Eddie shouted. "It's Greg! Something's happened!"

"What?"

Eddie handed the cell phone he was holding to Jack.

The old man immediately put the phone to his ear. Greg's assistant, Michael Block, was on the line.

"I'm sorry, sir," Michael said. "We've had an unexpected turn here."

"What?"

"Our Mr. Hammond is in the hospital," Michael said.

An intense, cold chill radiated through Jack's body. "Is it serious?"

"Yes, sir. It seems it is."

"What happened?"

"They thought it was a heart attack," Michael said. "They're saying now that was wrong."

Jack sensed his lower lip trembling. "If not his heart, then what?"

"He's in surgery now," Michael said. "The doctors haven't given us a report yet."

Jack started to feel light-headed and settled on a nearby boulder. The news was devastating. Greg was his only son. He'd half expected a day like this would come, though. For years, he'd been warning Greg about pushing himself too hard.

"When will we know?" Jack said.

"Hold on, sir," Michael said. "I'll see what I can find out."

Jack used the sleeve of his windbreaker to wipe away a tear as he waited for Michael's return. Along with his deep distress about his son, he suddenly felt the huge weight of responsibility for the company. Starling was a massive enterprise. With Greg incapacitated, at the least, Starling was a media empire plowing ahead without a rudder. Though it had long been a publicly traded company, well over half of Starling's voting shares remained closely held within the family. As far as Jack was concerned, it was still a family business. Yes, there were senior executives who could maintain the day-to-day operations, but somebody from the family had to assume responsibility.

Michael came back on the phone. "He's still in surgery, sir. They won't release details of his condition except to next of kin."

Jack struggled to contain his grief.

"I've given them your number," Michael said. "When they can, I'm sure they'll be in touch with you."

The possibility of losing Greg was painful enough without the added weight of the company pressing on him. Though he looked younger, Jack was seventy-two years old. His hearing was bad, and his blood pressure had been a problem for years. Going back to work had never crossed his mind until this moment. The prospect of running a business of such immense size was daunting to say the least, but the only other possibility was his grandson, Andre. That would never be acceptable to Greg. Handing the reins to Andre was not the way to go, at least not now. But Jack saw no other choice. He was head of the family. After Greg, he was also Starling's biggest shareholder.

Michael's voice came through the phone. "Mr. Hammond? Are you still there, sir?"

Jack fought off another wave of emotion. He refused to accept that his son might be lost. "When Greg comes out of it, tell him I'm on my way."

"Should we book plane reservations for you?" Michael asked.

"That would be good," Jack said. "Get me out as soon as you can. This afternoon, if possible."

Sensing something was wrong, the two dogs came up to Jack. Hap pushed at the old man's hand with his cold nose. Jack stroked the big, black-and-brown Shepherd's neck. The dog's concern was a comfort, and it allowed him a moment to compose himself before he spoke again. "Michael, regular reports, please. Every hour, if possible."

"Of course, Mr. Hammond," Michael said. "Every hour. Sooner if there's a change."

Jack was thinking about succession. There was no plan. The assumption had been that Greg was indestructible, that he was firmly in charge at Starling for the foreseeable future. Now, that comfortable illusion was shattered.

"Mr. Hammond?" Michael said, through the phone. "Sir?"

Jack suppressed his grief, then responded, "Tell our people business as usual. We'll sort this out when I get there."

"Yes, sir."

There was nothing more to say, so he ended the call and then stared out at the white-capped waves rolling toward the rocky shore. The morning had begun like so many others, with a carefree jog on the beach. How quickly the tide had turned. He had to pull himself together.

Less than two hours later, Jack was in his bedroom getting ready for his grueling journey to New York. On top of everything else, he had a terrible headache. A double dose of prescription Tylenol had helped but not much.

Jack dreaded the trip. After a short flight from Christchurch to Auckland, it was fourteen hours on Air New Zealand to Los Angeles. Then, after making his way to another terminal, there was another five-hour-plus flight to New York. The journey was daunting even for a young person. No way would Jack embark on such a trip under any other circumstances, at least, not feeling the way he did at the moment.

Jack had spoken with Michael again. Greg was still alive, now in intensive care and hanging on. Still no call from his doctors. For Jack, not knowing if his son was going to live or die was agonizing. At best, he would arrive in New York in time to be at Greg's bedside when he regained consciousness. At worst, he would be there to honor him by escorting his body home to New Zealand for burial.

Jack glanced at his watch—half an hour before heading to the airport. He turned and walked into the bathroom. He stood at the sink and began lathering his face. Then, with no warning, his mind became confused. Dizziness took over. He steadied himself and tried to shake it off. He reached for the safety razor sitting on the sink, but his right arm wouldn't move. The right side of his body felt very strange. Fear and confusion flooded through his mind. He struggled to the toilet and sat down, then tried again to move the fingers of his right hand. He couldn't. He tried calling for help. No words came out. Then he slumped over and fell off the toilet to the floor, still conscious but terrified and seriously incapacitated.

Greg was awake but not alert. He heard voices and smelled the antiseptic air. Gradually, his eyes focused on two nurses standing over his bed, talking to him gently, encouraging him to return to full consciousness.

One nurse held up his head while the other offered him water. He took a few sips and grimaced at the sting in his badly irritated throat. As he became more conscious, he recognized he was in an intensive care facility with an IV in his left arm and monitors displaying his vital signs.

He coughed. The muscles in his chest cramped painfully. He exchanged a few incoherent words with the nurses, then drifted back to sleep.

When Greg awakened again, he found himself propped up in a bed in a private room and still connected to an IV. A digital monitor by the bed showed his pulse, blood pressure, and cardiac rhythm.

"How you doing, sir?" Michael asked from where he was sitting at the side of the bed.

"Terrible," Greg said in a scratchy, barely audible voice.

"You're still here," Michael said. "That's all that matters."

A short time later, a slender man with a shaved head, wire-rimmed glasses, and a stethoscope draped around his neck appeared at Greg's bedside. "Mr. Hammond, I'm Ron Jaynes, the surgeon who operated on you."

Greg managed to smile a little. He clasped the doctor's hand.

"When you came in, it appeared you were having a heart attack," Jaynes said. "It wasn't a heart attack. Fortunately, the team recognized the real problem. Sometimes, more often than we'd like, the correct diagnosis does not get made."

Greg was confused.

"You had a type one aortic dissection," Jaynes said. "That's a rupture of the large blood vessel coming out of your heart."

"How bad was it?" Greg asked.

"Many people don't survive," Jaynes said. He gave Greg a reassuring pat on the shoulder. "You beat the odds."

Greg felt a deep chill ripple through his soul. So close. He'd come so close.

"No need to worry," Jaynes said. "Prognosis is good. Give it six weeks, assuming no complications. Your personal physician will probably recommend some lifestyle changes."

"Thank you," Greg said. "Thank you so much." He reached out and again grasped the hand of the surgeon who had saved his life, then watched him leave to continue his rounds.

Though he felt as helpless as he had ever been in his life, he was grateful to be alive. *Amazing,* he thought. Until now, he'd never taken time to consider he was mortal. He'd been too busy, too wrapped up in himself and his work, to give any real consideration to his own ending.

He looked at Michael. "Does my father know?"

"Yes," Michael said. "He wanted to be here."

Greg sensed something was wrong.

"Your father is in the hospital," Michael said.

What is Michael saying? Poppy is in the hospital? That can't be right. Greg spoke up. "Repeat that."

Michael hesitated, then said, "They say it's not life-threatening."

"What happened?"

"I'm so sorry, sir," Michael said.

"Tell me."

Michael held back another moment, then said, "Your father had a stroke."

Greg was shocked. He'd never known a moment in his life when Poppy wasn't healthy and active. "I need to talk to him," he said.

Michael looked away and said nothing.

Greg sensed the worst. "He can't talk?"

Michael hesitated, then nodded.

Greg gripped his young assistant's arm and began to weep.

"I am so sorry, Mr. Hammond," Michael said. "I'm right here for as long as you need me."

It was almost too much to assimilate. Both Greg and his father struck down at the same time. Poppy was his best friend, the one person in the world he felt comfortable confiding in. He sensed his mind plunging toward panic as he struggled to contain the unmodulated grief ripping through his body.

Here he was in the hospital, having barely escaped the Reaper, and the only person watching over him was a business associate. Michael was the best, exceptionally competent and very loyal. They had a warm and trusting relationship, but Michael was on the payroll. At the end of the day, he was an employee like all the others who worked for Greg. Their association was a business arrangement.

Self-pity surged through his body. It quickly hardened into frustration and anger. He had no family to care for him. His mother had been lost years earlier in an accident with a drunk driver. Other than his father, there was just his older half-sister, Lydia, and her son, Andre. Greg had no use for either of them.

His one and only marriage had soured, ending with no children shortly after he'd taken control of Starling. In the years since, there had been women off and on, but none had lasted. With the exception of his father, Greg had no close personal relationship with anyone.

Here and now, at age forty-two, he had no lover, no children, no relatives, other than Poppy, who truly cared about him. It seemed he was on a slippery slope, perched on the edge of a dark abyss.

Since taking over at Starling, his personal life had been about work. He sensed the corner into which he'd painted himself. He'd defined himself entirely by his business success. He had money. He had power. But for the most part, his life was cheerless. For that, he could only blame himself. He had set his own priorities. He had very effectively shaped and molded the world he lived in. He controlled a massive media empire, but here and now, at this most vulnerable juncture in his life, he was alone. He had no one to turn to. His physical ailment had almost killed him while leaving his heavy emotional armor shattered.

Greg closed his eyes and tried not to weep. The healing of his body would be difficult enough. He also had to face down the heavy burden of uncertainty and self-doubt churning in his mind. He dreaded the recovery ahead.

PART ONE

CHAPTER I

"Ten minutes," Daria Kocánová called out to the classroom.

There were twenty-eight students, all in their third year of studies in Cultural Anthropology at Charles University in the city of Prague in the Czech Republic. The course was titled Gender, Culture, and Human Development. All the students were quietly focused on completing their final exam.

Daria looked up from the open laptop in front of her on the lecturer's desk and smiled as she scanned the classroom. She had thoroughly enjoyed teaching and sharing knowledge with this group. Like her, they had chosen anthropology as the primary focus of their university studies. They were fully engaged in the learning process and eager to understand the human condition.

As her students completed their exams, Daria gazed out the classroom windows at Prague Castle, set high on a hill across the nearby Vltava River. With its turreted ramparts, round towers, and cathedral spires, the sprawling medieval castle complex was mottled by afternoon shadows and bright sunlight. How lucky she felt to live and work in one of Europe's most beautiful and best-preserved old capitals.

A few more moments passed. Daria glanced at her watch, then said, "Please turn in your exam work. Thank you all for your kind attention and enthusiasm over this semester."

The students applauded enthusiastically.

Daria eagerly shared hugs and best wishes with many of her students as they filed by and dropped off their exam papers. The moment was deeply satisfying, not only because her efforts as an educator were being validated by their kind words but also because she felt like she had delivered on the trust extended to her by the curriculum committee of the university's Department of Anthropology. This was the first time an upper-level elective course had ever been assigned to a teaching assistant who was still a student herself.

Now, with her classroom commitment out of the way until the beginning of the university's next semester, Daria had nearly a month to give full attention to her own academic agenda. She slipped her laptop into her shoulder bag and headed for the door. She didn't want to be late for an appointment she'd made with her thesis advisor, Professor Jakob Mittermeier. She was to meet him a short distance away, at the university's faculty lounge.

The campus of Charles University was spread over many blocks of central Prague. As Daria walked along the cobblestone street, her thoughts turned to her own studies. She had more than a year left in her program. Most of it would be focused on completing the thesis required to receive her doctorate diploma. She thought about how her academic ambition had evolved. Nearly seven years earlier, when she had first begun her studies, her intent had been to get her diploma in marketing and business management. That all changed when she took the required course for first-year students in Cultural Anthropology. The lecturer had been a charismatic young woman teaching assistant only a few years older than herself. The lecturer had also been a self-declared feminist, and over the semester, as her classroom narration rolled through the evolution of human development, she had given particular attention to the impact of gender on culture and history.

From the time humans started to evolve away from being nomadic hunter-gatherers toward living in permanent settlements and being dependent on crop-grown plants and domesticated animals raised for slaughter, out went cooperation, in came male dominance. Women were reduced to a form of property, owned and subjugated by men. Recorded history to this point had been shaped almost entirely by the males of the species. The process of human evolution over thousands of years had been defined substantially by aggression, confrontation, and blood-soaked turf wars. Even now, the world remained culturally mired in the same brand of gender dominance.

Throughout most of history, there weren't enough humans in existence at any given time to cause much more than temporary setbacks to order and progress. Now, in the early part of the twenty-first century, that equation had changed fundamentally. Earth was not getting any larger, but more than eight billion humans now traveled together on this one small planet—more than four times the number that existed only a hundred years earlier.

Quite simply, the needs of eight billion-plus humans were pushing the planet's living biosphere to the brink of exhaustion. Climate change, anthropocentric weather extremes, deforestation, the collapse of the world's fisheries, the shrinking of accessible freshwater supplies, the plunge toward extinction of many of Earth's wild plant and animal species, the loss of fertile farmland topsoil, the threat to the world's pollinators caused by chemical-based agriculture—all were driven by too many humans making too many demands on Earth's finite ability to provide.

For Daria, the first-year course in Cultural Anthropology had been an extraordinary, life-altering epiphany. It had inspired her to become a change agent, to assertively turn away from her former expectation of a career embedded in the wheels of commerce.

Over the years that followed, as Daria pursued her studies in anthropology, she took particular interest in the traditional role of women in human society. It was clear enough that education and the empowerment of women, particularly in the least developed nations, was a huge part of the solution to population growth. The research showed that when women were educated and treated as equals, and had ready access to health care and contraception, much more often than not, they choose to limit family size.

Most assuredly, progress had been made for women in Europe and the rest of the world's advanced nations. However, well over half of the planet's women were living in lesser developed nations. In the poorest of places, women were still having lots of babies, and population numbers were still continuing to grow rapidly. In those poor, most-in-need-of-gender-awakening places, tradition still defined the culture. Men were dominant. Women were still largely treated as chattel. Girls were denied education. Life was still constrained by custom.

As she pursued her university studies, Daria had become firmly committed to a life as an educator, dedicated to making the world better, particularly for those of her own gender, who were still culturally bound and oppressed in too many places. Part of her motivation came from her own experiences as a child, growing up in a small village in the Moravian region of post-Soviet era Czechoslovakia. She was the only child of a single mother and had experienced very real hardship in the early years of her life. She could never forget what it was like to be hungry, and to struggle with constant uncertainty.

The academic commitment Daria had made gave her a platform for leveraging her own deep well of compassion. The title of her doctoral thesis was *The Empowerment of Women and Girls Using Language-Specific Interactive Learning Tools*. To be sure, the idea was bold. Just developing it would be expensive.

Daria had to have Professor Mittermeier's approval before she could launch her study. A month earlier, when she had first told him what she wanted to do for her thesis, he'd been skeptical. He had appreciated her passion for the idea but thought the time and effort required to do it right, not to mention the money it would cost, were substantially beyond what was normally expected, even from the most highly regarded candidates for doctoral degrees. He had strongly urged her to moderate her ambition.

Since then, Daria had written a detailed thesis proposal and handed it off to the professor for review and acceptance. There was not a hint of compromise in it.

Now, as she approached the faculty lounge, she knew the make-or-break moment had arrived. The university would not sanction her thesis study without her professor's approval.

Daria walked through the lounge's foyer to the dining room, a remarkable eighteenth-century space with a high ceiling held up by massive carved timbers. Many of the three dozen tables in the room were filled with faculty members dining with colleagues.

Mittermeier was across the room, standing by a table, engaged in thoughtful conversation with another faculty member.

Daria studied the professor as she waited to approach him. He was one of the most highly regarded members of the university academic community. In his mid-sixties, Jakob Mittermeier was one of the world's leading authorities on Iron Age toolmaking and metal forging in Central and Eastern Europe. Clad in jeans and a red pullover sweater, he had a wild mop of gray hair and wire-framed bifocals hanging halfway down his nose.

At that moment, Daria saw Mittermeier glance at her. He exchanged a final word with the faculty member at his side, then gestured for Daria to join him.

A moment later, the two were seated across from each other. Daria's written thesis proposal for *The Empowerment of Women and Girls Using Language-Specific Interactive Learning Tools* was sitting on the table between them.

Mittermeier picked up the proposal. He ruffled the pages, then said, "Very impressive. In my years, I have seen many thesis ideas. Only one other time have I seen one this ambitious. In that case, it never got beyond idea."

"My intent is to meet my diploma obligation and also do something useful for people in need."

"Yes. Your motives are all good," Mittermeier said.

Daria sensed the professor was still not persuaded.

"Imagine how many women could be elevated by teaching tools presented on the net in underserved native languages," she said.

"The UN is already doing some of that."

"Not for uneducated adult women," Daria said. "Not in geographically specific, regional languages."

"What makes you think you can make this work?"

"Every good thing that happens begins with a first step."

"You cannot do it only halfway. You do that, you fail. Your very good idea could be discredited, and so could you."

"I will not be doing it halfway."

"Your budget exceeds one million euros."

"Yes."

"Where will this money come from?"

"I ask you to trust me. Money will not be an issue."

Mittermeier stared at her for a moment, then said, "You are determined to do this?"

"We are already designing teaching videos and net content that can be adapted to language and culture in the places most in need."

For the next twenty minutes, Mittermeier challenged every aspect of Daria's thesis proposal, trying to expose weakness. For every question, she gave him an encouraging, well-considered response.

Finally, the professor seemed satisfied. He studied her quietly for a moment, then asked, "A million euros is a lot of money. Where will it come from?"

"My source asks to remain anonymous."

"I hope your confidence is not misguided," Mittermeier said. He reached out, clasped her hand, and smiled. "You are a good soul, Daria Kocánová. What do you need from me?"

"Your support."

"You have that. What is your next step?"

"I must find a nonprofit that is already working in places that can benefit from the interactive tools we will develop."

"You have someone in mind?"

"I do."

CHAPTER 2

THE NARROW STAIRS OF THE Beacon Hill walk-up creaked under Eric Mun's weight as he ascended with his twenty-four-speed mountain bike on his shoulder. When he reached the second floor of the Boston headquarters of the Equitable Health Alliance, he saw Jessica Leonetti, the organization's executive director, darting about the corridor between their offices. She was picking up loose paper and trash and stuffing it into a waste basket—odd behavior, given that tidiness had never been a high priority in their well-worn workspace.

Jessica stopped and stared at Eric. She looked pissed.

"Is your cell on?" she said.

Eric groaned. He'd forgotten to charge the phone's battery. "What's going on?"

"We're expecting a visitor," Jessica said.

Eric was surprised. Visitors worthy of a sudden flurry of neatness were pretty much unheard of at EHA's 1,300-square-foot, converted walk-up world headquarters.

"When?" Eric said.

"Ten a.m." Jessica rushed to straighten some cardboard filing boxes stacked haphazardly in a corridor.

Eric glanced at his watch—9:47 a.m. No time to waste. He entered his office and dropped his bike in the spot he kept reserved for it amidst the clutter of stacked books, reports, and health-related abstracts.

He called out to Jessica, "Who are we expecting?"

"Somebody with access to big money," Jessica shouted back to him. "That clean shirt still in your drawer?"

Eric went to a desk drawer and pulled out a folded white shirt. He removed the bicycle helmet he was wearing, tossed it aside, then pulled off his sweatshirt and used it to wipe away the sweat glistening on his face and torso.

"Who is this person?" he called out, as he slipped his left arm into the sleeve of the white shirt.

Jessica stuck her head in through his open doorway. "Her name is Daria Kocánová."

Eric didn't recognize the name. "We just found out about this?"

"Got an email two days ago asking for a meeting."

"You tell me about that?"

"Didn't think she was legit."

Eric understood. Little good had ever come from people who approached the organization cold, without an introduction.

"Got here this morning, there's a phone message. It's her saying she's in Boston. She'll be here at ten," Jessica said.

"You're sure it's today?" Eric said.

"Yes. There was another message. This one's from the President of the African Primate Protection Foundation in Berlin. He's calling about this woman. He says I should get back to him ASAP."

Eric was eager to hear more.

"I called him," Jessica said. "He tells me this Daria Kocánová raised a million euros to support their program protecting some endangered primate species I never heard of in the Congo."

"Bonobo?"

"That's it."

"They look a lot like chimpanzees, only smaller and less aggressive," Eric said.

"The guy tells me this woman also raised a million for the Dyak Indigenous peoples in Borneo."

"To do what?" Eric asked.

"Their traditional territories are being clear cut. The money is backing a legal challenge."

"We have to take this lady seriously," Eric said.

"The complete package," Jessica said. "That's how the Berlin guy described her."

Eric was immediately concerned about the impression they would make. Normally, with potential big-money donors, meetings were set up at a restaurant or at the home of a wealthy patron. Eric, as the organization's medical director, and Jessica, as its executive director, were the only paid staffers in the EHA office. There were also a couple of unpaid research interns and about a dozen people who volunteered with the phones from time to time. Everyone was squeezed into a space that took up the second and third floor of a converted townhome in one of Boston's historic neighborhoods. It was cramped. It was cluttered. It was not a place to meet with a potential, deep-pocketed benefactor. Eric sensed that Daria Kocánová, whoever she was, may have purposely wanted it this way. She had not agreed on a mutually acceptable location for a meeting. She'd simply informed them she was coming to their offices. That could be good or bad, depending on what this mystery woman would value more—style, which they had in short supply, or substance, which they had in spades.

Just before 10:00 a.m., Eric heard the bell jingling on the townhome's front door. He joined Jessica in the corridor at the top of the stairway. They saw a young woman tramping up the steps toward them. They both called out, "Good morning."

The woman looked up at them with a smile and said, "Hello. Good morning."

Eric was impressed. Probably not even thirty, she was slim, and on the tall side. She was dressed unpretentiously in black slacks, a white silk blouse, and a classy, gray tweed blazer jacket. Her brown hair was pulled back in a ponytail. Her face was slightly long with pleasantly sculpted features framing large, hazel-green eyes.

"I am Daria Kocánová," she said, as she reached the top of the stairs. Jessica and Eric introduced themselves. Daria shared a warm handshake with each of them, then handed each her business card.

Eric glanced at the card. It presented her as a lecturer in Cultural Anthropology at the Charles University in Prague.

"You're Czech?" he said.

"Yes."

Jessica led them to a space that doubled as a conference room and a lunchroom. "Please forgive the mess. We're not really set up to receive visitors."

"I understand," Daria said. "I am here because of what you do."

"You know about us?" Eric said.

"I know you are the founder of Equitable Health Alliance with Marc Wren."

"Marc was the driving force," Eric said. "We were still in medical school when we started talking about it."

"I hope I can also meet him today."

"He's in Haiti," Eric said.

The young woman appeared disappointed, but she kept her smile. "Your website said he spends June and July in Boston."

"Doesn't always work out that way," Eric said.

Jessica went into a well-honed sales pitch for the Equitable Health Alliance. The organization had been founded nine years earlier by Dr. Marc Wren and Dr. Eric Mun to support a medical clinic they'd launched in a remote mountain region, eighty miles distant from Port-Au-Prince, the capital of the earthquake-ravaged Caribbean nation of Haiti.

"You began there with nothing," Daria said.

"Started with a couple of tents," Eric responded. "Then, we built a hospital. Then, we had the earthquake."

"How is it now?"

"Our medical facility is mostly recovered," Eric said. "The hospital has forty beds, with an intensive care ward and a full-time staff."

"Including locals we've trained, we have more than a hundred on payroll," Jessica said.

"That's in Haiti," Daria said. "What about Ethiopia?"

"We have a program near the capital," Eric said. "It's been going for a little over two years."

"This is the place named Tesfa?" Daria said.

"Yes," Eric said. "It's a migrant settlement. The problems are similar to Haiti, but worse because of the population density."

"You and Marc Wren are infectious disease specialists?" Daria said.

Eric nodded. "That's not all we deal with, but it's a big problem among the poor."

"For this, your special focus is treatment-resistant tuberculosis," Daria said.

"You've done your homework," Eric said.

"I am wondering what you are doing to educate the people."

"You mean about TB?"

"Yes," Daria said.

"We do what we can," Jessica said. "We also teach sanitation, preventive health care, nutrition, family planning…"

"Your website mentions programs specifically for women," Daria said.

"We do a lot with the women, health wise," Jessica said. "Beyond that, not as much. Healthcare is our focus."

"Never enough money to do all that needs to be done," Eric said. "You have a particular interest in education?"

"Yes," Daria said. "I have developed a program that uses laptops and tablets for interactive learning. We focus on empowering women who are uneducated and limited by their cultures."

Eric's guard immediately went up. "Sounds like something that would expand our mission."

"Health issues are a part of our vision," Daria said, "but the emphasis is on educating women, helping them help themselves, and their family members, and their communities."

"There's certainly a need for that kind of initiative. Unfortunately, we don't have the resources to expand our mission beyond health care," Eric said.

"How do you see the costs being covered?" Jessica said.

"If I work with you, I will find the money," Daria said.

"Can you give us specifics?" Eric said.

"Not at this point," Daria said. "But, if it did work out, it would come with funding attached."

Eric glanced at Jessica. He could see she was excited.

"We're open to any possibility that comes with funding," Eric said.

"Marc needs to know about this," Jessica said.

"Of course," Daria said. "How soon can I meet him?"

"We could set up a phone meeting anytime," Eric said.

"For me, this is a big commitment," Daria said. "I would like to meet him face-to-face."

"We don't expect to see Marc here for at least another month," Eric said.

"He is in Haiti now?" Daria said.

"Yes," Jessica said.

"I will go to Haiti."

Eric assumed Daria was not aware of the difficulties and potential dangers that came from cultural differences when traveling to Haiti. "That may not be a good idea. At the moment, on top of everything else, Marc is dealing with a potentially serious cholera outbreak."

"Is there ever a good time to visit him in Haiti?" Daria asked.

Eric glanced at Jessica and raised his eyebrows.

"Our focus right now is on the epidemic," Jessica said to Daria. "We need funding for additional resources."

"What kind of resources?" Daria said with a smile.

Eric grinned and shook his head.

"Something is wrong?" Daria said.

"Are you always so cheerful?" Eric said.

Daria smiled brightly. "Why not?"

Eric chuckled and nodded his agreement.

Daria put her hand on his arm and continued, "I want Marc Wren to be happy to see me. How can I help him with this cholera?"

What an impressive young woman, Eric thought. Her English, though slightly accented, was flawless. She was attractive. She was charismatic. She was focused and very self-assured. Being referred to as the "complete package" was a lot to live up to, but this lady was no pretender.

Eric considered her question, then said, "You want to help Marc with this cholera outbreak, a pallet or two loaded with antibiotics and rehydration kits would be a good start."

CHAPTER 3

AMERICAN AIRLINES FLIGHT 308 TOUCHED down late after-noon in Port-au-Prince, Haiti. Daria Kocánová was one of the first passengers off the plane. Less than a week had passed since her initial meeting with EHA in Boston.

In the passenger terminal, Daria retrieved her luggage, had her passport stamped, then headed out into the public area, where she found herself amidst a chaotic mass of humanity. There were many Haitians, joyfully greeting family members just returned home. A handful of European aide volunteers were getting lots of attention from a coterie of ragtag opportunists, some seeking handouts, others selling tourist services and souvenirs. And there were lots of police and armed soldiers. Most appeared disinterested, while the rest were minimally engaged in maintaining order.

Daria was working her way through the jam of people when she spotted a tall, skinny white man standing near the exit doors, apart from the crowd. He was looking at her and waving.

From photos she'd seen, Daria knew the man was Marc Wren. His bio had indicated he was thirty-eight. Clean-shaven, with eyes a bit too close together, framing a nose that had a slight hump, Marc Wren was not handsome, but he wasn't unattractive either. From his photos, Daria knew he was bald. But his head was currently covered with a grubby, long-brimmed cap that had a short cloth back flap to protect his neck from the sun. He was wearing mud-caked sandals, wrinkled tan shorts, and a well-worn, blue dress shirt with sleeves rolled up. *A remarkably unassuming presence,* thought Daria, *considering the esteemed place he's already carved out for himself within the world's medical community.*

"Daria," he said with a smile.

"Dr. Wren," she said, while shaking his hand. "So nice to meet you, finally."

"Please. It's Marc."

He said something in Creole to a Haitian teenager who was with him.

The young man took control of the luggage cart from Daria and pushed it toward the exit.

"*Merci,*" Daria said to the teen.

"You speak French?" Marc said, as he led her out the door and through a noisy snarl of taxis and buses.

"Yes," she said, "but not good enough for a conversation in Creole."

"Wonderful language. Mostly French, with a lot of African influence. There's a joyful energy to it."

"The shipment," Daria said. "It has arrived?"

Marc gestured toward the cordoned-off area just ahead in the parking lot, where two Haitian men were standing by a dust-caked cargo truck whose best days were long past.

He said, "Loaded and ready to go."

"You got everything?"

Marc nodded. "Twenty cases of oral antibiotics, six pallets of rehydration kits, plus two surplus water purification units from the Bundeswehr. You must know somebody in the German government."

"I am fortunate to have a friend who could help."

"My deepest thanks to you and your friend," Marc said.

"We are so happy it worked out," Daria responded.

A few moments later, she was riding alongside Marc in a newer Toyota Landcruiser.

They were following the cargo truck as it slowly made its way along a potholed asphalt highway.

Amidst masses of earthquake rubble that had still not been cleared, nearly as far as the eye could see, were mostly tiny dwellings made of rusted corrugated metal, scrap wood, plastic tarps, and such.

"You see this in most every country in the world that is struggling," Marc said.

"How much is from the quake?"

Marc swerved the vehicle to avoid a scrawny chicken that appeared suddenly in the road.

Then, he said, "The quake was a curse. No question."

"You were here for that?"

"I was," Marc said.

"A lot of people died," Daria said.

"Horrible," Marc said. "But there was plenty of misery here before that happened. So many places around the world are failing the same way."

"What about the lawlessness?" Daria asked. Haiti had a reputation of being politically unstable and violent.

"The gangs don't bother us," Marc said. "They sometimes come to us for treatment. They respect what we're doing to help the people."

Daria's eyes fixed on two little girls standing barefoot by the road, staring blankly back at her. Flashes of her own childhood passed through her mind.

"It's not complicated," Marc said. "Too many people, too few re-sources."

"You have an answer for that?" Daria said.

Marc chuckled. "I wish I did. You know the legend of Sisyphus?"

"He was pushing the rock up the hill?"

Marc nodded. "The Greek gods cursed Sisyphus to push a rock up the hill, then watch it roll down again. Then, he had to push it up again, and again, and again, with no end."

"You are feeling this way?"

Marc responded with a look of resignation.

"It would be easy enough to have a different life," Daria said.

"There's a guy, a billionaire, more money than he could ever spend on himself," Marc said. "That guy just laid out five hundred million to build a yacht the size of a cruise ship. What kind of pathology drives a man like that when a billion-plus fellow humans are starving?"

"How would you change this man?"

Marc chuckled. "Force him to live like a Haitian."

"There are many ways to be rich," Daria said. "This man with the yacht is poor compared to you."

Marc smiled and nodded his agreement.

For the first time, Daria noticed the odor of raw sewage. Memories of her own childhood in Czechoslovakia again came to mind; memories of growing up alone with her mother, in a cold, one-room apartment, with little to eat through long winters. It was painful to think about. She refocused her mind on Haiti.

"Before the Europeans came, this land must have been very rich, biologically," Daria said.

"That's what they say," Marc said. "Haiti takes up about a third of the island of Hispaniola. The rest is the Dominican Republic."

"I've read, life is better there," Daria said.

"They still have forests," Marc said. "It's better, though maybe not as much as you might think."

Just ahead, the truck stopped suddenly. Marc braked hard to avoid running into it. Just as suddenly, the truck started moving again. Marc accelerated the Landcruiser ahead, steering around a skinny cow standing in the road.

"There was a time when this whole island was covered with trees," Marc said. "It went to hell when Columbus showed up. Prior to 1492, the Taino, the native people of Hispaniola, had been here for what, a thousand, ten thousand years? They'd never been exposed to European diseases. They had no chance."

"What diseases?"

"Smallpox, measles," Marc said. "The Taino had no immunity. Many were infected. Many died—hundreds of thousands, wiped out."

Daria sighed. "I can't imagine that kind of suffering."

"Spain gave the Western third of Hispaniola to France in 1697," Marc said. "This land, this French territory, became an important source of sugar, tobacco, and cotton. Hundreds of thousands of Africans were kidnapped and brought here as slaves. By the eighteenth century, there were many more slaves in Haiti than Europeans. The slaves rebelled. Haiti became the world's first independent black nation."

Up ahead, the traffic on the road was blocked.

"Check point," Marc said. He stopped the Landcruiser behind the cargo truck. "Nothing to worry about."

He pushed open the door, jumped out, and headed up the road toward the armed soldiers that were holding up traffic.

Daria thought about Marc. His warmth and kindness made him attractive to a degree she had not expected. She was glad she had come to Haiti to spend time with him. She turned her attention to the scarred and largely denuded rural landscape that flanked both sides of the road. There was a scattering of people walking along the road, which was cut precariously out of a cliff overlooking the Caribbean Sea. Small white caps marked the warm breeze pushing shallow waves gently into the rocky shoreline just two hundred feet below. The sea appeared idyllic compared to the land.

Through the Landcruiser's windshield, Daria could see Marc Wren engaged in friendly conversation with the uniformed men running the roadblock.

To Daria, Haiti was a place forsaken by the world's wealth. Outside of a few cities, there was minimal electricity. The land was mostly stripped of forest. Much was mountainous. Worst of all, Haiti was a place that could no longer produce enough food to feed itself. Hunger was something Daria could relate to. She understood, on that most basic level, what it was like to be Haitian.

A moment later, she heard the door open across from her.

"Looking for drug runners," Marc said, as he jumped in behind the wheel.

"What kind of drugs?"

"Mostly cocaine and fentanyl."

"People have money for that?"

"Doesn't stay here, just passing through on the way to the US."

Marc got the Landcruiser going again.

"Life is very hard for the people here," Daria said.

"On top of everything else, the place frequently becomes ground zero for hurricanes," Marc said. He carefully guided the Landcruiser around another deep furrow in the road, then continued. "For three centuries, a handful of elite families have fattened themselves at the expense of the uneducated masses, selling Haiti's resources and labor cheap to outsiders."

"Your own country must take some blame," Daria said.

"More than a little," Marc said. "The US government has a long history of intervention, nearly always on the side of the powerful families, and their mostly American business partners."

Marc reached for a two-liter bottle of water on the seat between them. He offered it to Daria. "Need to keep yourself hydrated."

Daria removed the cap from the bottle and took in a few swigs. Then, she handed it to Marc.

He gulped down some of the warm fluid, then continued, "Early in the twentieth century, the US actually occupied and controlled this country for sixteen years. In 1986, there was a rebellion by the poor. They called themselves the Lavalas. They threw out the dictator, a guy named Duvalier. The CIA wasn't happy. In 1990, a popular government won the election. The new president was an ex-priest."

Daria couldn't help but notice the way Marc's cheek dimpled as he talked.

He turned to look at her.

"Aristide," Daria said, as she returned the flash of his green eyes with her own, keeping eye contact a bit longer than she would normally.

"Yes," Marc said. "He got seventy percent of the vote. A year later, he was forced out by American hired guns. Here's how fickle the US government is: With our help, Aristide was returned to power. Then, Bush took over in Washington. Aristide was removed again at gunpoint by the US military."

"Not a pretty picture," Daria said.

"Seven out of ten Haitians live a rural, subsistence lifestyle," Marc said. "Eight of ten survive on a few dollars a day or less. Haitians are the poorest people in the Western Hemisphere. They don't have enough to eat. They don't have adequate, safe water supplies. Education is very limited. Average life span is fifty-nine, the lowest in the hemisphere."

Daria empathized completely with the outrage Marc was expressing. The real Haiti she was now seeing firsthand was a mess. She thought a bit more, then said, "There's a strong link between poverty and lack of education, particularly for girls."

"That's certainly true here," Marc said.

"The average Haitian woman gives birth to five children," Daria said. "Despite everything—the earthquake, the extreme weather, all the suffering and misery—the population grows. More than eleven million in this small country, fifty percent more than just ten years ago."

"Touchy subject," Marc said.

"The problems only get worse when you keep growing the population," Daria said.

"No question."

"You don't blame the church?"

"It's a mixed bag," Marc said. "More than the church, the problem goes to a lack of family planning services. When Haitians have money, they buy food, not contraceptives."

"Other than the daily difficulties, what are they like as people?"

"You have the good, and the bad, like most places," Marc said. "I wouldn't be working here if I didn't admire Haitians as people."

"You like them."

Marc smiled. "As bad as it gets, they find ways to endure. They suffer, but they still know how to laugh and find joy in their lives."

Daria felt sure at that moment that coming to Haiti to spend time with Marc Wren had been a very worthwhile decision.

Rolling along Highway 100 that followed the coastline, they passed through Gonaives before turning eastward and up into the mountains. By 7:00 p.m., they were off the paved highway, bumping along an uneven, crushed rock roadway into the central highlands.

Daria was appalled by the widespread damage to the landscape. Mud slides and deep erosion were common, particularly on the denuded vertical terrain.

Daylight gave way to darkness as the cargo truck and the Landcruiser switched back and forth, back and forth, time after time as they crawled gingerly up the narrow, often treacherous roadway. A sudden thundershower struck. Rain poured down. The roadway became a muddy swamp.

"Is this normal?" Daria asked.

"Pretty much," Marc said.

"How often do you make this trip?"

"Maybe twice a month," Marc said. "Our people do it nearly every day."

Just after the thundershower passed, the two vehicles came to a stream swollen with storm runoff. They had to stop. For more than an hour, they waited. Then, the runoff subsided, allowing safe passage across the stream bed.

Six hours after Daria arrived in Haiti, the vehicles came onto a plateau more than two thousand feet above sea level. The village-sized settlement there was called Mòn Anizan.

The Landcruiser passed a scattering of wood plank huts, interspersed with even more dwellings made of mud and straw. Then Daria saw a cluster of single-story concrete cinderblock buildings. The largest one was perhaps a hundred feet long and had many windows. A sign in front announced it as Solè Medikal Kote. A diesel-powered generator droned in the background.

"How many on your team?" Daria said.

"Five doctors, seventeen full-time nurses and medical technicians," Marc said. "Two doctors are Cuban, and everyone else is Haitian."

Marc led Daria into a two-story prefab building that was home for the hospital's staff. Some were gathered in the dining hall. Marc provided introductions. He and Daria shared a quick meal, then, he said, "I need to check on some patients."

Daria stood to join him.

"You should get some rest," Marc said. "One of the staff will show you."

"I would like to follow you," Daria said. "Is that a problem?"

"May take a while."

"That's okay," she said.

"Let's go," he said.

Daria trailed just behind Marc and one of his doctor colleagues, listening to them talk about patients and treatment while walking across the compound to the hospital.

In the well-equipped emergency room, the doctor on duty was busy setting the broken arm of a teenage boy. Marc and the two doctors who had accompanied him paused to assist. Then they headed into an open ward. The lights were dimmed. All forty beds in the hospital were full.

Daria studied Marc as he reviewed one patient chart after another. His face was lined with fatigue, but he was a picture of concentration and concern. *How does he do it?* she wondered. *How does he stay committed?* There had only been a traditional midwife in Mon Anizan when Marc Wren first visited more than twelve years ago, before even graduating from Harvard Medical School. He'd been here at least half the time since.

Tirelessly, and almost singlehandedly, Marc Wren had sold the idea of Solė Medikal Kote and raised the money to build it. Even now, when he wasn't treating patients here, or in Ethiopia, the other place with a hospital operated by his Equitable Health Alliance, he put most of his remaining time into fundraising to keep the whole thing going. His compassion and his stamina seemed boundless.

Athletes, rock musicians, and movie stars were often treated as larger-than-life heroes. Rarely were people like Marc Wren given such recognition. In the world Daria wished for, the greatest rewards would go to those whose stature was built on acts of kindness, decency, and courageous self-sacrifice. On those terms, Marc Wren was a hero of the highest order.

They left the hospital just before midnight. Marc switched on a flashlight and gestured for Daria to follow. "Past your bedtime."

"I'm thinking your day's been longer than mine," Daria said.

"I'm used to it," he said.

They headed through the darkness toward the far edge of the settlement.

"You sleep how many hours a night?" Daria asked.

"Four, I'm good as new," Marc said.

"The other twenty hours, you're working."

"Never enough time in a day."

They came to a slope covered with the only fully mature trees left in the area. Marc took Daria's hand and helped her down a gravel path to a secluded area on the hillside. Amidst the trees and a flourishing carpet of wild vegetation, there was a one-room, wood plank cabin. It was surrounded by beds of growing vegetables and a cluster of fruit trees. The cabin had a small porch with a roof overhang and a commanding view of the valley below.

"I like this," Daria said.

"My own private oasis," Marc said, as he opened the cabin door.

"This is your house?"

"My friends here built it for me," Marc said.

The cabin was all one room. There was a small bed shrouded in mosquito netting on one side. On the wall opposite the bed was a table made of unpainted plywood. On it was a laptop computer that had seen better days. Next to that was a closed-off space with a door. Marc opened the door. "Here we have the composting toilet. All the way from Sweden. Very good technology."

They went out onto the porch. Marc directed Daria's attention to a shower head hanging down from the porch roof. Two lengths of rope hung down by the showerhead.

Marc grabbed the end of one of the ropes. "Pull this one to turn the water on and the other to turn it off."

Daria was delighted. "Where does the water come from?"

"It's rainwater. There's a holding tank on the roof."

Daria slipped off her sneakers. "Can I use it now? You mind?"

"Of course not," he said. He turned to leave. "I'm bunking with the staff."

"I would not like that," Daria said, as she unbuttoned her blouse.

"It's okay. I've done it many times."

"Please. I would like you to stay," she said, while tossing her blouse aside.

There was an awkward silence. Daria's decision to behave provocatively with Marc was spontaneous. She'd learned to admire him even before arriving in Haiti. Now that she'd met him, she found that she was physically attracted to him to a degree she had not anticipated.

"You were not expecting to sleep with me," Daria teased.

Marc seemed unsure how to respond.

"I was not thinking about this either, until I came here," Daria said. Though he said nothing, Daria could see she had his full attention. "You give so much of yourself," she said. "This is so impressive."

"I do what I can," he said.

"You inspire me," she said. "You inspire so many people."

"Kind words are always appreciated," he said.

"Words are not enough," said Daria. She caressed his arm. "I know there is no woman in your life."

"Really," Marc said. "How do you know that?"

She had extracted a lot of information about Marc from Jessica Leonetti, while in Boston. She wasn't about to reveal her source to him. "I did my research."

Marc said, "I don't get a lot of opportunity."

"I'm here only two days," Daria said. "I want to be with you."

"I'm asking myself, why."

She said, "In your life, how many truly great people have you known?"

Marc thought about it, then said, "Two."

"Greatness is not common," Daria said. "We agree on this?"

"Yes."

"Dr. Marc Wren is an extraordinary human being," Daria said. "I know this. I have seen it with my own eyes."

"That's it?"

That really was it. Daria had no ulterior motive. She didn't need to sleep with him to get what she wanted. It really wasn't complicated. She admired him tremendously. She wanted to be with him and give him the kind of intimate pleasure she sensed he didn't get nearly often enough. She also saw real value in creating the kind of trusted bond that often comes with shared intimacy.

Daria leaned close and kissed him, then said, "If I am lucky, I will live a long life. When I am old, I will be so happy, so happy when I think back, so happy when I remember my special time together with a truly extraordinary man, whose name is Marc Wren."

Marc smiled but still seemed hesitant.

"You will have trouble if you stay with me?" she said.

"Not an issue," he said.

"I am free of any sexually transmitted diseases."

He chuckled. "So am I."

She was happy to hear that. "There is some other issue?"

Marc thought about it then let out a little laugh. "I don't know what to say."

She kissed him again, then stepped back and stripped off the rest of her clothes.

"You are a naughty girl," he said with good cheer.

"Sometimes," she said as she moved close until her body was touching him. She sniffed him playfully. "A shower would also be good for you."

She took his hand. "Let's go."

A moment later, they were naked together under the shower in the moonlight.

"I can't believe this is happening," Marc said. "I know almost nothing about you."

"There will be time for that," Daria said. The warm water pouring down on her felt so good. It relaxed her and made her feel sleepy. She shared a lingering kiss with Marc, then she slid behind him until her breasts were pressed into his back. She reached around and began to stroke his erection. He was very excited. In less than a minute, he went off powerfully.

She held him close, until he returned from orgasmic neverland.

"That was good?" she said.

"Are you kidding?" he said, obviously still caught up in the moment.

Daria tugged the rope that turned off the flow of water. Then she grabbed a towel and began to dry him.

He took her head in his hands, turned her face up to his, and kissed her. Then, he said, "Your turn."

She embraced him happily. "Tomorrow, after your work is done."

Marc couldn't hide his disappointment.

"It's okay," Daria said, with a yawn. "It's been a long day. I prefer to share my joy with you when I am wide awake."

Minutes later, she fell into a sound sleep, with Marc Wren stretched out on the bed beside her.

The next morning, she awakened when she felt a gentle push on her shoulder. She looked up and saw it was Marc. He was already dressed.

"What time is it?" she asked.

"Just after seven," Marc said. "Today, you will witness a minor miracle."

Less than half an hour later, after a quick breakfast of locally grown fruit and bread baked fresh in the staff kitchen's brick oven, Marc led Daria off on foot down a steep trail at the edge of the village. The narrow, twisting path took them through a long gulley, up the other side, then down and up another, and another.

Along the way, Daria and Marc talked about his life and his career. He was best known in the world medical community as an expert on treatment-resistant tuberculosis.

"TB had been largely eradicated in the developed world," he said. "At one time, it was highly treatable with a broad range of antibiotics."

"What happened?"

"Treatment-resistant strains have found a home among the world's poor."

"It's getting worse again," Daria said.

"Yes," Marc said. "The authorities believed there was no way to stop it in the most vulnerable places. We came up with a new protocol. We showed it can work."

Daria already knew about Marc's TB work, but she liked hearing him talk about it. "Your treatment is now the standard."

"In this area, yes," Marc said. "The challenge is to find money for the drugs."

They arrived at a settlement made up of several dozen scrappy-looking hovels. Few people were moving about.

"This is one of the local hotspots for cholera," Marc said. "Try not to touch anything. It's very contagious."

Daria knew that cholera was an extremely serious intestinal disorder caused mostly by exposure to water contaminated with sewage.

"The biggest threat is dehydration," Marc said. "Two million die from it every year. Ninety percent are children."

They came to a hut made of sticks, thatched straw, and a single blue plastic tarp held in place by some kind of homemade twine. Inside, they found a young mother tending to three children, the oldest of which could not have been more than eight years old. Laid out on a straw mat on the floor, the three children were quiet. They appeared very sick, very close to being comatose.

"One of our people put them on antibiotics yesterday evening," Marc said. "Still severely dehydrated."

Marc took three plastic bags filled with sterile fluid from his backpack. "These are hydration kits, from the German government shipment you got for us." Marc held up one of the bags and said, "Magic bullet."

"What is it?" Daria asked.

"A mix of saline, glucose, and essential electrolytes."

Each of the kits included a feeding tube and a sterile IV needle. Going from the youngest to the oldest, Marc gently inserted a needle in the arm of each child. "Now, for the miracle."

Within ten minutes of starting to receive the fluids, the children began to emerge from their lethargy. They started to cry. The young mother sobbed gratefully. She spoke to Marc in Creole like he was a messenger from heaven.

Tears filled Daria's eyes.

"Pretty amazing," Marc said with a smile.

Daria snapped photos as Marc gave the children's mother several plastic bottles of oral rehydration fluid, and a week's supply of cereal grain. Then, he handed the young woman three vials containing antibiotics, while telling her how to care for the children without getting herself sick.

An hour later, Marc and Daria arrived back in Món Anizan. At the walk-in outpatient clinic, more than a hundred people needing medical attention, most accompanied by family members, were lined up, waiting to be seen. Marc exchanged warm greetings with the people, then he went inside and began seeing patients. Daria watched him for a while. Then, she walked on into the hospital. She photographed the doctors, nurses, and aides at work and admired their dedication to patient care. Most of the staff were local people, trained by Marc and his small team of professionals.

Daria soon found herself helping a teenage girl staffer who was putting clean sheets on a bed. When that was done, Daria focused on an old woman patient, who appeared too weak to feed herself. She sat down next to the bedridden woman and began to spoon broth into her mouth.

Just after 4:00 p.m., Marc showed up in the hospital ward. After reviewing patient charts and conferring with the staff on duty, he came over to Daria. She saw the gleam in his eye.

Less than ten minutes later, they were in his cabin in his bed, intensely into each other. Daria and Marc both found great joy in their extended intimate encounter. When the sexual heat had subsided, Daria sat up and stroked Marc's chest.

"You've got something on your mind," he said.

"I am wondering what you would do if somebody gave you a million euros?"

Marc considered the question only a moment before responding, "You could knock down a lot of infectious disease with that kind of money."

It was the response Daria had expected.

"Right answer?" Marc said.

She laughed. "Yes, of course."

"Can you get us a million euros?"

"I cannot promise."

"You've done it before."

Daria had come to Mòn Anizan to find out if Marc Wren and his Equitable Health Alliance would be the right partner for her own, admittedly bold, ambition. She'd seen enough to convince her. She looked at Marc, and said, "What do you know about empowerment-based intervention?"

"By that, you mean, teaching people to help themselves?"

Daria nodded.

"We do that here," Marc said. "We train Haitians to go out and teach others on health issues."

"My program will use tablet computers to educate and empower women. We start by training maybe five women, then we pay those women to use our teaching modules to spread the learning to other women in the community."

"We'd do that a lot more of that if we had the money."

"You know my area of study is Cultural Anthropology."

"Yes."

"I'm working on my PhD."

"That's great," Marc said.

"For my research, I have developed this program for empowerment-based intervention. It's for women who have no education. Empowering women who have nothing is a good thing, you agree?"

"Absolutely."

"An example," Daria said, "here you have many women without education. We create modules that teach about health care, family planning, many subjects. We want uneducated women to learn and feel empowered."

"Big challenge," Marc said. "Women have been getting a raw deal for thousands of years."

Daria smiled. She kissed him several times, then said, "Every man should think like you."

"Why limit your program to women?" Marc said.

"It must start where the neglect is greatest."

"Have to be adapted to Creole."

"Of course," Daria said. "Interactive learning is not new. There are already many such programs for children. The new thing is to make it language specific, and for the women. This is why I am here. You are helping so many people. My idea could be tested here, and also in Ethiopia in the community where you have your hospital."

"Tesfa," Marc said.

Daria nodded.

"Where's the money coming from?"

"This is not for you to worry about."

Marc cupped her right breast in his hand and kissed it sweetly. Then he said, "Assuming you find the money, does that mean you'll be spending a lot of time here?"

"Some time. I would not say a lot of time. It must be Haitian women who are using the tools we provide to elevate other Haitian women."

Daria saw the disappointment in his face. She was not surprised that he'd fallen for her. She knew he'd never been married, and it seemed clear, from what she'd learned since her arrival in Haiti, that he was more than a bit shy, and that he found his personal life purpose by serving the needs of others. Marc Wren was, without question, the most selfless person she'd ever known. Very likely, his penchant for always putting others first had led him to deny his own needs.

Marc caressed her shoulders. "I'm thinking how wonderful it would be to come home to you every night."

Daria smiled and kissed him warmly. "You are thinking I could be someone I am not. If I said to you, come, let us live together in Prague, would that work for you?"

"Maybe not now."

"Please. Your place is here. You inspire so many people with your work. I must make my own contribution. I must do it in my own way. In this respect, I am a little like you."

"More than a little."

Daria kissed him and said, "Thank you. I am so pleased to hear this from you."

She relished the bond she felt she now shared with him. "How much time before we join your colleagues?"

Marc glanced at an alarm clock by the bed, then said, "Not quite an hour."

An instant later, they were locked together, touching and exploring. After several minutes of intense foreplay and a lot of laughing, hugging, and playful tongue wrestling, Daria rolled onto her back and opened herself to him.

Marc Wren was hardly the first person Daria had been intimate with, and he would not be the last. She felt a deep affection for him. At this moment in time, she had no thought of being anywhere else or wanting to be with anyone else. As his playful thrusting turned to passionate pounding, Daria was caught up in her own pleasure and was soon lost in the eager, intense rhythm of the moment.

CHAPTER 4

Two days later, Daria arrived back in Miami. She hurried through the airport terminal to catch a Lufthansa flight and headed across the Atlantic to Germany. She was happy and excited about the partnership she'd forged with Marc Wren and his Equitable Health Alliance.

Daria was convinced she could make a big difference in the lives of many, many women who remain uneducated and dismissed because of gender. Women struggling to survive in places left marginalized by the more advanced nations of the world.

The alliance with Marc Wren gave Daria's project a nonprofit home, which could receive and disperse the money needed to prove her idea could work. She thought about what was ahead of her. There was the internet. There was AI, Artificial Intelligence. There were new, cutting-edge learning technologies she wanted to employ. She would need expert collaborators, who could contribute their specialized knowledge to her vision. Hiring the right people, building the best digital learning tools, shaping an organizational structure that could be easily expanded, all those things were built into her project's million-euro budget. Now that Marc Wren and the Equitable Health Alliance were aboard, locking in the money was her priority.

Daria's flight landed in Munich late the next morning. A taxi took her into the city and delivered her to a three-story stadthaus on Kaulbach-Strasse, not far from Munich's Englischer Garten Park. The ivy-covered, nineteenth-century, cut stone facade of the mansion reflected the wealth behind it.

Daria used her key to let herself in through the Stadt Haus's front door. After dropping her luggage in the expansive, tastefully decorated vestibule, she headed down the wide corridor into a large, high-ceilinged ballroom that a century earlier had been the center of the social life of the house. Sunlight poured in through classic, nineteenth-century, three-meter-tall windows, trimmed with the same beautifully grained white oak that had been used to create the room's finely inlaid floor. The room now served as the workspace for an artist, whose creations were made of cloth. Several dozen three-dimensional fabric artworks, large and small, were scattered around the room. Hundreds of folded pieces of fabric of different colors, textures, and patterns were stacked on the floor and on tables, waiting to be stitched into some project or another.

At the far end of the room, Angelika Grünberg was seated at an industrial sewing machine, stitching folds of ragged, dark-brown fabric together.

Daria was approaching when Angelika glanced up and saw her.

"*Schatzi*," Angelika said, with a big smile.

The two women came together in an embrace that evolved into a heartfelt kiss, followed by a lingering hug that reflected the deep bond they shared. "I'm so happy to have you back."

At 5'8", Angelika was an inch taller than Daria. Though she was nearly twice Daria's age, Angelika was still beautiful in a classy, European way. At the moment, she was wearing a simple sundress over her slim, athletic figure. The dress's cheery design was complemented by a colorful band of yellow cloth wrapped around her neatly cropped and coiffured blond hair.

"So, you have found what you wanted in Haiti?" Angelika said.

"Marc Wren's hospital is amazing," Daria said. "He's doing so much good."

Daria smiled as she gazed up at the mostly completed, twenty-foot-tall fabric sculpture looming over them.

"You like it?" Angelika asked.

"Wonderful," Daria said. "So real."

The sculpture, built on a three-dimensional wire frame, was a sweetly rendered and remarkably realistic face of a young ape.

"The eyes, they are alive," Daria said. "The intelligence. You can see it in the eyes."

"I always know I will hear something sweet from my Schatzi," said Angelika, who then shared another hug and kiss with Daria.

"I'd just like to finish this piece," Angelika said, "You mind?"

"Of course not," Daria said.

Angelika returned to her place at the sewing machine. Daria picked up the end of the long piece of fabric and held it up as Angelika fed it through the machine. Daria glanced up again at the large fabric rendering of the ape that towered above her. "When I made my study," she said, "I was not thinking it could come to this."

It really is amazing, Daria thought. As part of her university studies, two years earlier, she'd been reviewing comparative literature on the behavioral traits of humans and their closest ape relatives. The bonobo, a little-known primate species that could only be found in the steamy equatorial forests of the Congo River region in Central Africa, became her focus. Bonobos looked a lot like chimpanzees but were somewhat smaller, and significantly less prone to violent and aggressive behavior. Genetically, they were ninety-eight percent the same as humans and might be second only to humans in brain power.

"In a previous life, I'm thinking you were a bonobo," Daria said.

"Would not be so bad." Angelika added another strip of fabric to the piece of sculpture she was sewing. Two things about bonobos particularly appealed to Angelika. First, their social groups were led by females. Second, sex was almost always on their minds. Daria recalled that one researcher had said that chimpanzees resolved sexual issues with power. Bonobos were the opposite. They resolved power issues with sex.

"Humans should be like this," Angelika had said, "always having sex, staying out of trouble."

A number of photos of bonobos were taped to the wall near where Angelika was working at the sewing machine. Daria recognized some of the faces. She and Angelika had come to know these individual animals when they'd traveled to the Democratic Republic of the Congo in Africa to see bonobos in the wild. For a week, they'd camped in a remote jungle region of the war-torn nation with a group of researchers, who, for nearly two decades, had been studying the social structure of three different bonobo family groups.

Daria focused on one of the photos on the wall, and said, "This is Fuzzy?"

"Yes," Angelika said. "She is my model."

Fuzzy was the name the researchers had given to a particularly sweet female bonobo with a goofy crop of red hair that stood straight up on the top of her head.

Daria smiled as she gazed at Angelika, who was busy at the sewing machine, carefully adding fine stitches to the pieces of fabric.

Angelika had always been a good and honorable person, but her unexpected passion for bonobos had inspired her to become so much more.

Before the trip to the Congo, Angelika's life had been mostly insubstantial, geared around living in luxury, traveling in high style, socializing frivolously with the rich and powerful. She was the widow of one of Europe's most successful entrepreneurs. As a young woman, she'd studied art at the Design Institute in Stuttgart. Then, when the textile tycoon Helmut Grünberg had come into her life, Angelika lost interest in being a working artist. Grünberg, who was thirty-one years older than Angelika, had begun to court her intensely when she was only twenty-one years old. For twelve years, she'd lived with Helmut Grünberg outside of marriage. She traveled with him to every corner of the world, enjoying the good life. Finally, they did get married. Then, when she was only thirty-seven years old, Angelika's husband had crashed his small, aerobatic biplane and killed himself. They'd had no children. Angelika was left alone with nearly all of her deceased husband's fortune, currently valued at more than two hundred million euros.

Following his death, Angelika had continued to honor her husband's example of generous philanthropy with annual gifts going to universities, museums, to health-related causes, and to the arts. Her busy social life had been built around the insular world of her highbrow friends, with the focus mostly on fashion and stylish sophistication.

Meeting the bonobos had changed Angelika.

On that first return flight home from their adventure in the Congo, all Angelika wanted to talk about was the bonobos—how sweet and innocent they were, how smart they were, how human-like they were, how perilous life had become for them.

Bonobos were highly endangered, with possibly as few as five thousand still in existence, including a small number in zoos around the world. The future of the bonobo was becoming more and more uncertain because of the loss of their habitat to human encroachment, and because they were being killed and eaten as 'bushmeat' by a steadily growing human population. The Democratic Republic of the Congo already had more than ninety million people. That number was expected to more than double in just the next three decades.

Hopelessly in love with bonobos, Angelika was now their stalwart champion. She was on the board of the African Primate Protection Foundation, through which she launched a fund to protect bonobo habitats in the Congo. She had donated more than four million euros of her own money to that fund. She also had become one of a number of influential people who had lobbied the Government of the Democratic Republic of the Congo to permanently protect more of the remote areas of the country where wild bonobos could still be found.

Angelika's life-changing bonobo experience had also rekindled her enthusiasm for creating art, which had been mostly dormant for the past three decades since the time Helmut Grünberg had come into her life.

"I love how the bonobos have changed you," Daria said.

"For this, you get the blame," Angelika said, as she added another stitch to the carefully shaped and sculpted hunk of fabric.

The sculpture of the face of Fuzzy the bonobo that Angelika was creating was destined to hang at the Tierpark Hellabrunn, the zoo in Munich, where a sprawling new, indoor/outdoor bonobo habitat was nearing completion. Angelika was chair of the committee in charge of raising funds to build the exhibit.

There was also a substantial link between the bonobos and Daria's project. The bonobos had been the focus of her first success as a big-time fundraiser. It had started while traveling on holiday with Angelika, when Daria had casually mentioned that she wished she had money to help the bonobos.

"There are plenty of wealthy men who could be charmed out of a million euros," Angelika had said.

At first, Daria had thought her friend was joking.

Angelika had been entirely serious. More or less, she'd said, "How many rich men know anything about bonobos?"

"I'm thinking not even one," Daria had answered.

"So, asking for anything like a million euros would be taken as a joke," said Angelika. "Unless, maybe, it is you who is asking for this money, and it is you who is explaining how the bonobos benefit from it, and it is you who maybe is the dessert in this package."

Daria had responded with decidedly mixed feelings. "I should have sex with a rich man for a million euros?"

"You want to help the bonobos?" Angelika said.

"Absolutely," Daria said.

"A million euros buys a lot of help," Angelika said.

"That is prostitution."

"Some will define it that way."

"Not you?"

"For me," Angelika said. "I see it a little differently. I can give a little of myself for a million euros."

"You would do this?"

"Why not?" Angelika said. "Think how satisfying it could be if a rich man would give so much to have you in his bed."

Daria thought about it. Such an arrangement could pose a risk to her academic standing.

"It would have to remain private," Daria said.

"We are talking about consensual intimacy between two people, neither of whom would benefit from public disclosure."

Daria knew how difficult it could be to raise money. Governments, corporations, and charitable foundations could be a source of funding, but the qualifying parameters were generally restrictive, with lots of competition for the funds available. The process from application to announcement of awards generally took several months to a year, or even longer in some cases. Raising money in this traditional way was fraught with obstacles and very often resulted in disappointment.

As far as morality was concerned, Daria was on the same page as Angelika. For a woman, sexual power is real power. It should not be subject to moral policing, especially when it could be channeled for a good purpose, such as assuring the future of bonobos in the wild.

"The job is finding this man," Daria said.

"Would you sleep with Wali for a million euros?" Angelika said.

Waldimir 'Wali' Goetz was a multi-millionaire Dutch financier friend of Angelika's, who had just retired and had too much time on his hands. Though he was married, Wali hadn't been shy about his interest in Daria on the two occasions they'd met.

"You think he would do that?" Daria said.

"If I were a man," Angelika said, "and I was bored, and I had much more money than I could ever spend, and I also knew the money would go to a very good purpose, I would pay a million euros to have you."

"I have never slept with a married man."

"I have. In fact, together with his wife, I have slept with Wali."

Daria chuckled. "Really?"

"It was fun," Angelika said. "Sigrid is my friend. I'm telling you, she knows Wali can be a dog. She doesn't care."

"You're sure of that?"

"She gets around herself."

Daria chuckled. She found the whole picture amusing.

"I'm telling you, Sigrid would be very pleased to see Wali give money for the bonobos."

"I cannot be somebody's mistress," Daria said.

"Wali would not expect that," Angelika said. "A long weekend would be enough."

Daria considered again the rewards and consequences that went with Angelika's proposal. She understood, given the world's highly charged brew of cultural mores, that many would condemn such behavior. For those people, particularly the women who would see things that way, Daria saw only one question to ask: "Assuming it remains a private matter between two consenting adults, would you give up your body for a weekend in return for a million euros to help a worthy cause?"

If this were the circumstance, Daria could not see how any woman with a caring heart could say no when so much good could come from it. Daria was certain the turndowns would be few…very few. She would certainly not be one of them.

Shortly after Angelika had issued the challenge, Daria's improbable yet undeniable success as a big-money fundraiser began. She'd arranged to meet Wali Goetz for lunch in Amsterdam. She'd started out telling him about the bonobos and what she and Angelika were doing to help them. Then, she turned up the seductive heat and made an unmistakable offer. If Wali would donate one million euros to the cause, she would spend a long weekend with him in a place of his choice. Daria had been stunned by Wali's instant response. It was, "Where do I wire the money?"

The rendezvous took place on a beautiful private island in the Seychelles off the southeast coast of Africa. Wali had been nearly sixty years old but was still in good health and reasonably attractive. Satisfying his substantial libido had kept Daria busy much of the time. When it was over, it was very clear that Wali Goetz was a happy man. It had been good for Daria as well. Her benefactor had been a very satisfying lover and the location had been wonderful.

The affair had been fun. It had also elevated Daria's confidence and put her fully in touch with her own considerable sexual power.

Just the same, there had been no intent to repeat the successful experiment. That is, until Daria found herself caught up in another urgent situation. Seven months after her tryst with Wali, she found a new cause. The Dyak indigenous forest dwellers of Borneo's traditional land was being shredded and stripped away by government-sanctioned clearcut logging. Daria traveled to Borneo. She hired a guide and saw vast stretches of landscape reduced to splintered stumps and streams choked with silty runoff. She joined a trek to a Dyak settlement and listened to the people tell their stories firsthand. Money was badly needed by Indigenous Action, a nonprofit set up to help the Dyak mount legal challenges against the government and the logging companies, and also to publicize and build public awareness of their culturally devastating plight.

Angelika had given Daria some of her own money for the Dyak and had offered to help find other possible donors. Gently but firmly, Daria made clear she wanted no further help from Angelika. This time, she wanted to see if she could raise the money on her own. She studied an online list of the five hundred richest people in the world. Out of that list, she reduced the number to four that she thought were real possibilities.

They were all men, all older, and all more or less retired from active life—single, one way or another.

Daria settled on Ian MacPherson, a Scot from Edinburgh, whose whiskey distilling net worth on paper exceeded a billion euros. She researched him thoroughly and learned he had an eye for attractive, young women. He also had a history of donating large sums of money to medical research. Over the ten previous years, his gifting had exceeded three hundred million euros.

Getting to MacPherson had turned out to be the biggest challenge. Like many wealthy people, he was well insulated against easy access. Then, Daria had learned that MacPherson visited London twice a month. When he did, he always stayed at the Dorchester, across from Hyde Park, and when in residence he habitually took his morning meal alone, in the hotel's promenade. Daria checked into the Dorchester and was present in the promenade one morning when MacPherson turned up.

Daria made no attempt to be coy. She went up to his table with a big smile and confidently introduced herself. He invited her to join him. She laid on the charm. The rest had been pretty straightforward. She told MacPherson the compelling story of the Dyak people and the terrible, ruinous logging that was laying waste to the forests they had called home for thousands of years. She told him what she was after, a million euros for Indigenous Action. Then, she had stared into his eyes seductively and, in subtle but unmistakable terms, offered herself as a final incentive to encourage his generosity. At that point, his cell phone had gone off, and he answered. Daria took that as a signal. She placed her business card on the table in front of him, then got up and made a graceful exit.

Daria heard nothing from MacPherson for more than a week. She'd thought she'd failed.

Then, he called. The money had been deposited in the Indigenous Action group's bank account. The assignation took place over a weekend at a palatial château in Gstaad, Switzerland. Ian MacPherson had been younger and better looking than Wali Goetz, but less fun in bed. Still, it had been pleasant enough, and the Dyak cause had benefited from a million euros that would not have been there otherwise.

Daria's attention went back to Angelika, who'd finished her work at the sewing machine.

"So," Angelika said, "you have your plan?"

"Yes, in Haiti and in Ethiopia, we can test the idea."

"You are sure the women will want to learn something new?" Angelika said.

"You cannot imagine the poverty," Daria said. "To survive another day for her family and for herself is a woman's first job. If there is time after that, I think they are eager for anything that can make life better."

Angelika hugged Daria and kissed her on the forehead. "How good you are to choose this direction for your life."

PART TWO

CHAPTER 5

THEY WERE LATE. GREG HATED being late for anything. The frustration he felt was the very thing his doctors had warned him to avoid. It was nearly 6:30 p.m. local time. Greg and his assistant, Michael, were in Brussels, caught in a traffic jam on the E40 headed toward city center. They'd arrived in Belgium on the company jet only forty minutes earlier.

The occasion was a reception for the Commerce Ministers of all the nations of the European Union given by The European Commissioner's Group on Fundamental Rights. The EU was proposing new parameters on media pluralism and consolidation, parameters that were not friendly to Starling's ambitious growth agenda. Greg was there to schmooze with top-level EU regulators. He had one goal: keep the European atmosphere on media consolidation as favorable as possible.

Five months had passed since the health scare of his life. This trip to Brussels was his first journey overseas since returning to a full work schedule. Physically, he was feeling okay, maybe even better than okay. But the road back had been difficult, emotionally and physically. He'd been stuck in his Park Avenue apartment overlooking Central Park for much of the time, feeling restless, with little to look forward to beyond sweating his way through a daily regimen of prescribed exercises. The only people he'd had around him were his paid staff, and, from time to time, friends who'd come in for brief visits.

By far, the hardest thing was not being able to talk to his father. Poppy hadn't made much progress recovering from his stroke and remained unable to speak. Greg's only sibling, his half-sister, Lydia, had moved to the family estate in Christchurch to look after their father. Lydia's son, Andre, was Greg's only other blood relative. Greg had never known Lydia when he was growing up. She clearly resented him, and he had found little reason to think much of her. In fact, it would be fair to say they despised each other. There was no ambiguity about why. Lydia had never been coy about her ambition for Andre to one day run the family media empire. No way was that acceptable to Greg.

Andre was hopelessly self-absorbed. He also had a substantial history of partying and frivolous womanizing. He'd made little effort to earn his place at the top of the Starling food chain. Both he and his mother saw it as an entitlement. The more they pushed the idea, the less Greg thought of them. On top of his personal animosity, Greg had no confidence that Andre could ever be trusted to maintain focus and effectively lead the company.

In the aftermath of his surgery, Greg had refused to relinquish control of Starling Worldwide to anyone, even temporarily. From the moment he'd left the hospital, he'd worked an hour or two a day, reading reports, retaining the high-level decision-making prerogative while recuperating at home.

There'd been a lot of time to think, and much of it went to self-examination. Greg had arrived at a painful realization. He didn't like the person he'd become. For his entire adult life, he'd been consumed with work, and it had almost killed him. It was painful to consider how little real happiness he'd found in the world he'd made for himself.

In a lot of ways, this quickie trip to Europe was emblematic of what had been and still was wrong in his life. There were surely better ways to spend one's time than flying six-plus hours from New York to Brussels for a cocktail reception, then flying back to the States the very same night so one could be at one's desk the next day.

Greg scanned the roadway ahead and saw the traffic was still a mess. He took a deep breath and relaxed. He had no control over the situation. He wasn't going to fret about it. If the big-shot reception at the European Union's Headquarters was over by the time he got there, so be it. In the final analysis, it wouldn't matter much. It wasn't as if anything earth-shaking was about to happen.

Daria smiled and listened politely. The young diplomat from Iceland who had her cornered was chattering away about his work on the geo-thermal energy assets of his country. He was not the man she'd come to meet. She glanced around the elegant, second-floor reception hall of the European Parliament. Nearly four hundred people were gathered in small clusters, sipping cocktails or wine, talking mostly about the business of the European Union. On an elevated platform in one corner, a chamber music group was performing a muted version of Haydn's *Third Quartet for Strings*.

The Icelandic fellow was actually quite attractive, and his work with clean energy was interesting, but Daria had her own agenda, and time was running short. She listened a moment longer, then excused herself by asking the location of the ladies' room.

In the restroom, Daria went to a sink and reapplied her lipstick. She was frustrated. Her mission wasn't going well. This was the second time she'd had to retreat to the ladies' room to escape unwanted attention. It was flattering to be noticed in a crowd with so many distinguished people. But it was also seriously cramping her intent. She was there to connect with Italian mega-millionaire Bruno-Carlo Chellini, the semi-retired Chairman of Gunot Condotto, Europe's largest producer of in-dustrial and residential piping and plumbing fixtures.

Chellini had fit the profile that Daria and Angelika had come up with to identify men with the best potential in her high-stakes fundrais-ing strategy. In his late fifties, Chellini was no longer operating in the corporate fast lane. His business was mostly turned over to a younger executive team. The wealthy Italian had a history of gifting large sums of money to worthy causes. He was also known to have a substantial appetite for young women.

Daria had spent more than a month trying to figure out how to get close to Chellini. Angelika had even hired a detective agency to find the easiest point of access. It turned out there was no simple way. Chellini was not a creature of habit. He bounced all over the place, and he never seemed to plan much of anything ahead. In the end, the only thing certain on his calendar was his attendance at this high-level European Union

Reception. Daria had known it would be a long shot, and she didn't know how she would get into such an exclusive gathering. Again, Angelika's connections within the German government had come through. The invitation had been arranged by the German Ministry of Commerce.

When Daria first showed up at the reception, she had managed to get within a few feet of a small group that included Chellini. While standing alone, waiting for the moment to introduce herself, two men had approached and begun talking with her. Before she could extract herself, Chellini moved off to another part of the room. She hadn't been able to get near him since. In the time left before the event ended, she had one more chance. She took a deep breath, then headed out to rejoin the reception.

She moved about the elegant, high-ceilinged reception hall, searching for Chellini. Out of the corner of her eye, she spotted the Icelandic fellow who'd forced her retreat to the restroom. She pretended not to notice he was headed straight toward her while she eagerly put space between them. Once she saw she was no longer being pursued, she resumed her search for Chellini. An instant later, she found she was standing practically next to him.

Daria avoided eye contact with anyone other than the man in her sights. She was startled when a woman, probably in her late thirties, took her arm and turned her away from Chellini and the group he was in. Daria didn't know the woman but recalled her being part of Chellini's entourage the first time she'd gotten close to him.

"You have an interest in Signore Chellini?" the woman said in English, with a mild Italian accent.

Daria studied the woman.

"I have seen you standing near him earlier," said the sultry-looking brunette.

"You are…?" Daria said.

"Signore Chellini's personal assistant," the woman said. "If you have business with him, perhaps I can help."

"I was hoping to have a few moments with him," Daria said. She knew this woman was more to Chellini than just a personal assistant.

"That would not be possible this evening," the woman said.

Daria was annoyed with herself. She hadn't anticipated a confrontation with what appeared to be a rival, and she sensed the woman was prepared to make a scene. It was a no-win situation. Daria smiled politely, acknowledged the woman with a nod, then moved away.

Almost immediately, the Icelandic fellow found her. Though she was upset that her effort with Chellini had failed, Daria smiled and allowed the man to engage her in conversation again.

⸎

The Starling Company Mercedes arrived at the Paul-Henri Spaak, the working headquarters of the European Union. Greg and Michael quickly left the vehicle and hurried into the impressive marble-and-glass parliament building.

Less than thirty minutes remained of the scheduled reception. Greg refused to care. It wasn't worth the stress. He would put in an appearance, try to interact with some of the important EU ministers he knew, and that would be it. If he was going to live his life like a hamster trapped on a spinning wheel, at least he could slow the pace and reduce the fretting to a level that was manageable.

After entering the building and passing through security, Greg and Michael crossed the lobby and headed up an escalator. A moment later, they were on the second floor, walking into the elegant chamber where the reception was winding down. Greg stopped and scanned the scene. He immediately spotted two people he knew. He had no reason to talk to either of them. Then, his eyes locked on a young woman standing about thirty feet away under a very large, cut crystal chandelier. She was listening to a man who seemed eager to make an impression.

Greg couldn't take his eyes off her. Looking perfectly slim in a classy gray pantsuit, she had dark-brown hair that caressed her shoulders. When she turned his way, laughing at something the young man had said, Greg saw she was quite attractive, with a wonderfully expressive face that reflected intelligence and warmth.

This was what was missing from his life. This was the kind of woman he envisioned when he thought of a companion, a lover, someone with whom he could let down his guard, be open with, and confide in. He'd never met a woman who could fill that complete bill, but this one, at least in the fantasy he'd quite suddenly conjured, looked just the way he imagined his perfect woman might.

At that moment, Greg saw her shake the hand of her male companion. Then she left him, heading toward the doors to leave. Walking with easy confidence, she was alone, coming directly toward Greg.

His normal way of dealing with people he didn't know was to ignore them, or if he was forced to acknowledge them, to do it with an impersonal nod while avoiding any circumstance that would force him to engage any further. He couldn't remember the last time he'd reached out to a complete stranger. That was how it was with the old Greg Hammond. He told himself he was no longer that person. His life had changed. He no longer wanted to be the aloof media mogul who was too full of self-importance to risk a close connection with anyone. There had been no joy in that. Being a rich and powerful corporate warrior had not brought Greg any real happiness. Just the opposite, it had almost killed him.

He couldn't let this beautiful young woman pass. If he did, she'd be gone in an instant, never to be seen again. He moved toward her, made eye contact, and smiled. She smiled back, making him feel giddy, even a little nervous.

He held up his hand, signaling his wish to talk.

She stopped and gave him her attention.

"Have we met?" was all he could think to say.

She smiled and said, "Where are you from?"

"New York," he said, noticing the fragrance she was wearing. There was a wonderful, unmistakable lavender accent to it. She smelled at least as good as she looked.

"I know a few people from New York," she said. "I don't remember meeting you."

"I'm Greg Hammond," he said, as he extended his right hand.

The young woman smiled again. "Daria Kocánová."

She clasped his hand graciously.

He savored her touch. After holding her hand a little too long, he released it, then pulled out a business card and handed it to her. A surge of energy pulsed through his body as he watched her scan the card.

She looked up and said, "So, you have a very big job, Mr. Hammond."

"Keeps me busy."

She smiled but didn't look the least bit impressed. She was looking into his eyes, sizing him up. Even more than her classy looks, he was captivated by her calm self-assurance. This was not someone who could be taken lightly. He was glad there was no ring on her finger.

The silence between them grew awkward.

"Where are you from?" he asked.

"Prague," she said.

"Prague. You're Czech?"

"Yes," she said. "Have you been there?"

"Not yet. I've heard Prague is a beautiful city."

"Yes," she said. "You must come and visit."

Greg was not about to let her walk away without knowing how to find her again. "Do you have a business card?"

She found a card in her purse and handed it to him.

He scanned it, then said, "You teach at this university?"

Daria nodded. "I am also finishing my own studies."

Greg wanted to go on, but a number of dignitaries had gathered nearby. They were lining up, waiting to talk to him. His moment with this impressive young woman no longer felt private. "I have to talk to some people now," he said. He took her hand and held it again. "It was my pleasure to meet you, Daria."

"For me as well," she said. "Good night."

"Good night to you," Greg said.

With that, she turned and headed out the door.

Before giving his attention to the political and business dignitaries standing nearby, Greg handed Daria's card to Michael, and whispered, "Find out about her."

The next afternoon, back in New York in his top-floor office at Starling Worldwide's 1st Avenue headquarters, Greg was churning up a sweat on an expensive cross-training machine while reviewing the most recently completed, but not yet broadcast, episode of his network's top-ranked TV series. *Vectors* was a crazy quilt of high-tech, shoot-'em-up action. Greg was not a fan. The show was one-dimensional, designed only to drive a lot of over-the-top mayhem. Despite that—or more likely because of it—audiences couldn't get enough of *Vectors*. Even in reruns, the show consistently delivered the prime 18-54 male demographics coveted by sponsors.

Despite his distaste for *Vectors*, Greg had to value the consistent profit it delivered.

Michael came into the office. "Sir, you wanted to know about the woman at the reception."

"Tell me."

Michael scanned the printout he was holding, then began to paraphrase.

"Daria Kocánová. Twenty-seven years old. Born in Dvorska, near Brno in the Moravian region of the Czech Republic. Height, 5'7", weight 117 pounds, brown hair, hazel eyes, father deceased, mother still living in Dvorska, seventh-year student at the Charles University in Prague, soon to be awarded a doctoral degree in Cultural Anthropology."

"That's it?"

Michael nodded.

"What'd you think?" Greg said.

"Very impressive, sir."

"What about her personality?"

Michael chuckled. "Go for it, Mr. Hammond."

Greg was amused by Michael's encouragement. "That's your advice?"

"Why not?" Michael said.

Questions flooded Greg's mind. Why was she studying anthropology? What was her personal history? Was she involved with someone? Then, he thought of Derek Slayton, the European consultant who sometimes handled discreet investigations for Starling's Mergers and Acquisitions team. Slayton was retired SIS, British Intelligence.

"Get a complete profile," Greg said. "Put Derek on the job."

"How soon do you want it?"

Greg's schedule rolled over in his mind. He was going home to New Zealand for his father's birthday at the end of the week. He'd be back in the office a few days after that. "Give it a week. If he needs more time, he'll tell us."

Greg noticed the gleam in Michael's eye.

"You have something more to say?" Greg said, playfully.

"A lady like this would be good for you, sir," Michael said. "I hope it works out."

Greg shrugged matter-of-factly. He didn't want to let on how excited he was about the prospect of really getting to know Daria Kocánová. She might be a fantasy in his mind, but maybe, just maybe, the reality was as good as what his imagination had conjured. Since taking over control of the company, Greg's life had been almost entirely about work. Over the years, there was no woman he could remember that had caught his attention in anywhere near the same way. Perhaps it was because his mind was now open to something he'd avoided before. Daria Kocánová might be a fantasy. In all likelihood, that would be the way it would turn out. But for now, she excited the hell out of him. She was beautiful, well-educated, she smelled great, and she appeared to have what seemed to be a very appealing personality. Just knowing that would be enough to keep her in his mind, at least until an investigation could reveal if she was something less, or, if the stars were aligned, perhaps something more.

As an afterthought, Greg turned to Michael and said, "I want photos."

CHAPTER 6

GREG PEERED OUT THE COCKPIT windows from the jump seat, just behind and between the two pilots. He saw the northeast coast of the South Island of New Zealand faintly on the midday horizon. They'd been flying for more than six hours since refueling in Honolulu.

The jet was awesome. As corporate perks went, the twin turbine Gulfstream G650ER was top-of-the-line. Used almost exclusively for Greg's personal travel, it was the ultimate extravagance. The cabin's glove-soft, tan leather interior smelled new. Starling Worldwide had taken delivery just two months before Greg's close encounter with death. It was the plane's first trip across the Pacific, and also Greg's first time home to see his father since the stroke.

Greg picked up the satellite phone on the cockpit's center console and dialed. A moment later, the call was answered by his father's caretaker, Eddie Ponaruma.

"Eddie," he said into the phone. "I'm good. Thanks… Thank you. How's Poppy?"

It was hard to hear over the incessant hiss of near-supersonic air flowing past the jet's fuselage.

Greg listened closely for a moment, then continued, "He still wants to come out to the airport? Okay, we should be landing in an hour… See you then… Thanks."

Fifty minutes later, the sleek twin-engine jet touched down on runway twenty at Christchurch International. The G650 was painted all glossy black and had no markings except for a golden kiwi painted on the tail. It taxied to a stop on the corporate aviation ramp. The engines shut down, then the airstair deployed. Once the steps were fully extended, Greg rushed down and headed across the ramp to the car where his father, Jack, was waiting with his longtime personal driver, and now his caretaker, Eddie. Both were smiling.

Greg embraced his father and held him close. His voice cracked with emotion. "Poppy, I'm so sorry this happened."

The old man had tears in his eyes. He looked so frail. Greg had never seen him this way. His father's right arm and hand remained seriously paralyzed. To a lesser extent, his right leg and the right side of his face had also been affected. He walked with difficulty with the help of a cane. The saddest thing and the most frustrating for Poppy was that he couldn't speak. His hearing, augmented by hearing aids, was pretty much unchanged from before the stroke. His memory was fine. He could process information as well as ever, but it was a major challenge for him to communicate what he was thinking.

Poppy tried to speak, but only a guttural sound came out. Greg noticed the frustration in his father's face. It was painful to see Poppy so diminished.

Greg turned his attention to his father's closest companion.

"You're looking good, Eddie," Greg said, as they shared a hug.

"So do you, Mr. Greg."

"Little Boss" had been the name Eddie had called Greg all through his childhood. After he'd gone to work for Starling in his twenties, the big Māori had changed it to Mr. Greg. He'd been Greg's closest mentor when he was growing up. It was always good to see him.

Greg turned back to his father and pointed to the company jet. "Poppy, what do you think?"

Jack Hammond smiled, nodded his head, and put his left thumb up.

Half an hour later, after taking on more fuel, they were back in the air. The old man was sitting up front with the pilots. Greg was in the rear of the plane with Eddie.

"How's he doing?" Greg asked.

"Not so good," Eddie said. "He thinks he's lost his dignity."

Greg's own experience made that easy to understand.

"Still no talking?" Greg said.

Eddie's expression was glum. "The doctors say, maybe we'll see no change for a long time. They also say, when it does come back—"

"You mean if," Greg said.

"Yeah, if it comes back, it could happen fast."

Greg had consulted a specialist in New York about his father's condition. Apparently, people responded to strokes in lots of different ways. Some never recovered, others did a lot better over time, and there was no real way to know which category his father would fall in.

"How does he communicate?" Greg asked.

"Usually, he just nods yes or no," Eddie said.

"Is he getting the right kind of help?"

Eddie shrugged. "Since Ms. Lydia moved in, she makes the decisions."

"How's that working out?"

Eddie's expression as much as said, *"Don't ask."*

Greg suddenly felt very guilty for not taking a more active role in his father's care. It was a troubling situation. He'd had his own health issues that had prevented him from returning home to New Zealand to see his father until now. Moreover, if he had come home and challenged Lydia about their father's welfare, undoubtedly, it would have resulted in an ugly confrontation. For his father's sake, the smart course had been to bite his tongue, keep the peace, and go along with Lydia as Poppy's primary caregiver.

Greg glanced out the window and saw Shamrock, the family estate, in the distance below.

The jet was flying slowly with gear down and flaps extended, just over a thousand feet above Kakapo Bay. As the aircraft banked toward the estate, Greg was surprised to see a huge tent set up on an open stretch of lawn adjacent to the house.

"A tent?"

Eddie said, "Yeah."

"For Poppy's birthday?"

"Yeah."

Greg groaned. In years past, he'd made a point to come home for his father's birthday. But it had always been kept to family and close friends.

"How many people did she invite?"

"A lot," said Eddie. "You know she's building a stable at Addington."

Greg hadn't known that. Addington was one of the top harness-racing tracks in New Zealand. It was in Christchurch, not more than twenty minutes from Shamrock. Building a harness-racing stable meant that Lydia was not just making herself at home at the family estate temporarily.

At fifty-one, Lydia was nearly nine years older than Greg. She had been the offspring of a brief relationship his father had with a young woman from Wellington when Starling Media was strictly a New Zealand phenomenon. Poppy hadn't married Lydia's mother. Though he had provided financial support, the whole affair had been kept quiet. Poppy later married Katherine Sulsman, a beautiful and good-hearted woman from a prominent family in Christchurch. Greg had been the only child from that marriage.

Sitting in the back of his private jet, Greg was struck by a wave of sadness as he relived his mother's death. He'd been only twenty-three years old and in the US, working on his master's degree in business at Stanford, when he'd learned about the drunk driver who hit her car head-on. The loss had left his father devastated and feeling very much alone. Soon after, Poppy had acknowledged Lydia publicly as the mother of his grandson, Andre. She'd been a thirty-some-year-old single mother at the time and living in Wellington with eight-year-old Andre.

Greg had understood Poppy's grandson born outside of marriage was an embarrassment that had to be kept secret.

Despite all that Lydia had been denied when she was younger, once she was fully vested in the family, she'd worked hard to ingratiate herself with Poppy. He'd been so eager to atone for the past that he embraced her, warts and all.

Greg's sister had been making up for lost time ever since. Lydia Akers was now well established as a powerful and prominent member of the privileged class in New Zealand. She'd done it by taking the family into uncharted territory. With Poppy's blessing, Lydia had spent lavishly to set herself up in the world of harness horse racing.

Now it appeared, after well over a decade of living back in Wellington and basing her horses and her high-society social life up there, that Lydia had every intention of settling in at Shamrock on New Zealand's South Island for the long term.

"Mr. Greg," Eddie said, over the roar of air rushing by, "you let her, she take everything."

Greg knew as much.

It was midafternoon by the time Eddie turned the Jaguar sedan into the family estate's driveway. Greg was sitting with his father in the back-seat of the car as it rolled up to the well-maintained Tudor mansion that was Shamrock's centerpiece. A squad of parking attendants had already gathered. Guests would be arriving for the party in less than ninety minutes.

After helping Eddie get Poppy up to his second-floor bedroom suite, Greg headed down the corridor to the office he kept next to his old room. He turned to enter and stopped cold. The office was gone. It was now a hair dressing parlor. Sitting in the room's chair surrounded by mirrors was Lydia. A young male stylist was hovering over her, making adjustments to her finely cut, auburn hair.

Lydia noticed Greg's reflection in the mirror in front of her.

"So nice to see you, brother," she said, with an unmistakable hint of sarcasm.

"What happened here?"

Lydia acted as though nothing was out of order.

"This was my office," Greg said.

"We needed the space," Lydia said.

"You could've asked."

"You're here for a day or two a year," she said. "You understand."

Greg detested her smarmy attitude.

"Use Andre's office across the hall. He won't mind if you borrow it while you're here."

Greg didn't want to give Lydia the satisfaction of knowing she'd gotten under his skin. He said nothing more and left.

Beyond the sibling rivalry, there were any number of reasons why Lydia would want to antagonize Greg. The biggest by far was that he did not support her ambition for her son. Seven years earlier, Lydia had pushed and pushed, and even enlisted Poppy's support, until Greg had backed down and agreed to take Andre into the company in an executive position with the understanding that he would eventually become President of the Asia Division. Between Lydia, Andre, and Poppy, there were enough voting stock shares to wreak havoc with the company's governance. Greg had been forced to accept Andre into the business to keep the peace.

What Lydia wanted now was for Andre to be anointed as successor to Greg as head of Starling International. That idea was intolerable. No way would Greg go along with such a prospect, not now, not ever.

Greg heard a dog bark. He turned and saw Hap and Randy, his father's two German Shepherds, bounding toward him. He got down on one knee and shared a greeting with each of the dogs, who were clearly happy to see him.

By 6:00 p.m., Poppy's birthday celebration was in full swing. Greg looked out over the scene from a window on the second floor. He was stunned by the scale of the thing. There had to be at least three hundred guests milling about, and a huge number of catering people to serve them. A big band set up next to the tent was playing a lively swing tune.

Though he would have preferred to be just about any place else, Greg put on a pleasant face and joined the gathering. He made his way through the crowd, acknowledging many greetings, mostly from people he didn't know. It was clear, the biggest share of those in attendance were Lydia's society friends and members of the wealthy crowd for whom horse racing was the common denominator.

Wandering among these strangers, Greg felt, for the first time in his life, like a guest in the place where he'd grown up. Because the celebration was honoring his father, he focused on remaining cordial.

The dinner under the tent was impressively laid out. There was a dais set up in front of many rows of round tables, each of which had eight settings.

Greg found his place on one end of the dais next to the head of the New Zealand Trotting Horse Association.

"Uncle," Greg heard someone call out. He turned and saw Andre stepping up onto the dais behind him.

"You look good," Andre said.

Greg accepted his nephew's handshake. Andre squeezed his hand hard. Greg tried to pull away.

"Release my hand," Greg said, firmly, without changing expression.

"You had to bust my balls again," Andre muttered.

Greg looked Andre squarely in the eye. "I don't respond to juvenile intimidation."

Andre let go of Greg's hand. "I would've been in New York in a heartbeat if you'd asked."

Greg said nothing, barely managing to keep his anger in check.

"Nice to see you, Uncle," Andre said, with an empty smile. Then he turned away and began greeting other guests on the dais.

Greg watched his nephew as he worked his way through a gauntlet of well-wishers to his seat at the center next to his mother and Poppy.

At thirty-one, Andre was tall, athletic, reasonably intelligent, and full of phony charm. His blond hair was distinctive, just shaggy enough to reflect his wild side while topping off his lean good looks. He was impressive, on the surface. That much, Greg was willing to admit. He also knew the real Andre was nothing like the public persona he'd created for himself. He was, in fact, a jerk, an empty suit with a dark side few people recognized.

There had actually been a time when Greg had gotten along well with his nephew. While a student at Yale, Andre had spent time working as an intern at Starling Headquarters in New York. He had accompanied Greg occasionally on his business travels. At that point, Greg had seriously considered Andre as his logical successor. That was before his half-sister's son had gone off the deep end. Instead of coming on with Starling after college, Andre had become a fixture on the French Riviera, binging on young women.

After six years of full-time playing around in Europe, Andre had wanted back in the business.

Greg had been emphatic. Andre was bad news. No way did he want him working at Starling.

In the end, the shareholders, led by Lydia and Poppy, had prevailed. Greg had been forced to install Andre as head of Starling Asia. In the time that followed, the Asia division continued to prosper. Andre had taken credit. Greg knew the truth. Andre was far more interested in being the big-shot celebrity boss than in actually doing much work. In fact, he was still spending June through August every year away from the Starling Asia offices in Auckland, relying on subordinates to manage the Asia operation, while he partied hard in Europe.

Greg gazed out on the people seated at the tables. He felt isolated and uncomfortable at his own father's party. He had no friends in this crowd. He watched Lydia move from table to table, socializing, and playing the role of host to the hilt. Though it was Poppy's birthday, the occasion was quite obviously much more about her than about their father.

After dinner, as dessert was being served, Lydia introduced a short video that had been put together to honor Poppy. The first few minutes featured old still images and grainy black-and-white film that showed Poppy's early life and the post-World War II beginnings of Starling Media. After that, almost all of the rest of the video was about Poppy and his life after Lydia and Andre came to live at Shamrock. There was little mention of Greg and not a word, or even a single photo, of Greg's mother in the video.

Greg was angry, more over the blatant disrespect to his long-deceased mother than anything else. This was no unintentional slight. It was a purposeful act. For Poppy's sake, Greg stifled his disgust. But he was done smiling, and he was done pretending to enjoy Lydia's social grandstanding. He got up from his place on the dais and walked off toward the house. The time difference between New York and New Zealand was like reversing night and day. He was seriously jet-lagged. Sleep was what he wanted most, with getting away from his sister's presence a close second.

Later on, just after he got into bed, a fireworks display began. For nearly ten minutes, the night air over Kakapo Bay was alive with thunderous starbursts and explosions of scintillating color. To Greg, this final, shameless extravagance symbolized Lydia's takeover at Shamrock. He got on his cell phone and called his chief pilot. He was cutting his visit short.

The next morning, Greg walked the beach with Poppy and Eddie and the dogs, Hap and Randy. He could've said something about the willful exclusion of his mother in the video tribute the night before. There was no point. It would only upset his father. Though he didn't let on, there was a deep sadness in Greg's heart. There'd never been a time when he'd felt so isolated from his father. Poppy had clearly enjoyed the party.

He seemed caught in Lydia's spell. She'd taken charge at Shamrock, and Poppy appeared comfortable with that. Greg could offer no alternative. It was probably best to leave well enough alone.

An hour later, after saying his goodbyes to his father, Greg was in the courtyard about to join Eddie in the car when Lydia came out of the house.

"Leaving so soon?" she said as she approached him.

Greg said nothing.

"You weren't very sociable last night."

She was looking for a fight. He didn't take the bait.

Lydia flashed one of her patented arrogant smiles. "Everyone said it was a wonderful party."

Greg couldn't hold back the sarcasm. "A bit over the top for my taste."

Lydia acted offended. "Poppy certainly enjoyed himself."

"Good for him."

"You haven't even asked about his condition."

"I read everything his doctors send me."

"How good of you to make time for that."

"He should be making more progress."

"His therapists are the best," said Lydia.

"You know that for sure?"

"Yes," Lydia said. "I do."

Greg stared coldly at her. "You like him this way. You like having him dependent on you."

Lydia exploded. "You think you can do better? Come home and take care of him yourself."

Greg turned and headed toward the car.

"Mr. Big Shot," she said.

He ignored her.

Lydia kept after him. "You almost died. It could happen again. Somebody has to be ready to step in."

Greg did not respond.

"You know how I feel," Lydia said. "You know how Poppy feels."

Yes, Greg thought, *now that you've got Poppy eating out of your hand.*

"Starling is a family business," Lydia said. "We expect it to stay that way."

Greg opened the front passenger door of the Jaguar. Then, he turned and unloaded on her. "You honestly believe Andre is qualified to run the company?"

"Financial reports don't lie," Lydia said. "Starling Asia has never performed better."

"And we should thank your son for that?" Greg said.

"Why not?"

"You're in denial, sister. That operation delivers *in spite of* Andre, not because of him. He's the founder's grandson. That's the only reason he's in that job."

"That is so unfair."

"I don't think so," Greg said.

"You got your chance," Lydia said. "Why shouldn't he?"

"Work is his least favorite thing."

"He doesn't have to be just like you."

"Commitment isn't an option," said Greg. "Andre isn't committed to anything but playing king stud."

"The shareholders want clarity," Lydia said. "You need to send them a signal."

"What did you have in mind?"

"I don't have to tell you."

No, she didn't. This was about China. More than a year ago, Greg had wrapped up negotiations in Beijing with the Media Ministry of the People's Republic of China. At that time, Andre had badly wanted the new operations in China to be under his control at Starling Asia.

Greg stabbed his finger at Lydia. "You know damn well the Chinese want their market handled separately."

"And you made damn sure they got what they wanted."

Yes, Greg thought with some satisfaction, *I certainly did.* The Chinese insistence on not being lumped in with the rest of Asia had played right into his hand. Andre had been denied.

He remained head of Starling Asia, but he was no longer seen as a sure bet to succeed Greg.

"People need to know what to expect," Lydia said.

"They should expect me to be around for a while," Greg said. He got in the car and signaled Eddie to drive on.

As the car accelerated down the driveway, Greg felt deeply frustrated. The succession issue was a pain in the ass. He hated the idea of his nephew being next in line. But no good alternative candidate had emerged, at least no one strong enough to be approved by Starling's directors and shareholders. No matter. The search for a qualified alternative would continue. As far as Greg was concerned, the person who would one day replace him as chairman and chief executive officer of Starling Worldwide would have to win the job on merit. Andre was not even on Greg's list, let alone at the top. His family connection had already taken him as far as he was going to go.

CHAPTER 7

L ORD RAMBLE SHOULD'VE APPEARED BY now. Daria was watching and waiting in a park across from the retired oil executive's East London mansion. She'd been there for more than an hour. She was on a bench set on a gravel walkway just off the park's primary path, waiting for her chance. Eight days had passed since her failed encounter with Bruno-Carlo Chellini. She glanced at her watch, which read 9:45 a.m. Fortunately, the weather was cooperating. It was warm and sunny, hardly the norm for late October in the UK. At least two dozen people, some with dogs on leashes, were scattered about the park. A pair of pint-sized Shih Tzu puppies were wrestling and running about nearby.

Daria's thoughts went to her unexpected encounter with Greg Hammond at the EU reception. On her return to Prague, she had taken the time to review what the internet had to say about the media mogul. During their brief interaction in Brussels, he'd been pleasant enough, but the record revealed him to be a hard-charging corporate kingpin, known for his relentless drive to expand the scale and influence of his media empire. The Starling brand had been purposely shaped to put profit over the public interest. Greg Hammond's network of newspapers, magazines, television and radio stations, and social media sites around the world sold a self-serving version of reality preferred by bankers, big business, and billionaire conservatives. Daria saw nothing honorable about the way Greg Hammond lived his life. It was too bad. She imagined the good that might come from a person of his power and influence who actually cared about the truth and the public interest.

Daria turned her attention back to the rambunctious Shi Tzu puppies. A moment later, out of the corner of her eye, she saw Lord Ramble emerge from his mansion, accompanied by a bodyguard. Both men were clad in jogging suits. They crossed the street into the park and began a series of warm-up exercises.

Lord Clive Ramble had gained fame and fortune as one of Britain's most successful business leaders. The former chairman of Shepard Petroleum had led his company for nearly two decades, expanding its reach across the British empire, then into every major oil market in the world. Ramble had not been on Daria's initial short list. He'd come up during a second review of her list of the world's richest people. Ramble hadn't made the cut the first time because he was seventy-four years old.

This time, despite his age, Daria had decided Ramble was worth a shot. She had to find a benefactor. The sooner it happened, the better. Much of the first-stage preparation for her educational empowerment program had already come together. She now had scripts for two teaching modules. The first provided women with the tools and knowledge they needed to make informed family planning decisions. The second was on personal empowerment, which was simply encouraging uneducated women to recognize that they were worthy of being educated. The scripts applied Daria's background in Cultural Anthropology to assure they were culturally sensitive and easily presented by local women enlisted to be facilitators at the community level. Both scripts had been translated into Haitian Creole and Amharic, one of the most prominently spoken native languages in Ethiopia.

The plan was ambitious, very ambitious. Daria couldn't go much further without a big infusion of funding. Angelika had offered to give her the money. Daria had turned her best friend down, at least four times already. She was determined to make the plan work on her own terms. That was the best way to honor the love and generosity Angelika had shown her from the moment they'd met eight years earlier.

Lord Ramble began his racewalk through the park.

Daria jumped up from the bench and jogged off along a trail that took her around through some trees. She turned up another narrow pathway. It soon intersected the park's central artery. Lord Ramble was just ahead on the same wide path, moving along quickly. Daria unzipped her jogging jacket, exposing her breasts, thinly covered by a spandex top. She took a deep breath and urged herself on.

Lord Ramble was walking very fast, making sure he had one foot touching the ground at all times. It looked awkward, but Daria assumed it must be good exercise. The bodyguard was hanging close behind Ramble, alert for any sign of trouble.

Daria noticed the bodyguard leering at her as she jogged past him. She caught up to Ramble, matched pace with him, then spoke up. "Lord Ramble, I've heard you are a very kind man."

Ramble's eyes fixed on her bouncing chest. She switched into seduction mode. "I've also heard you have a taste for young women."

Ramble seemed not to have understood her.

The bodyguard was about to intervene, when Ramble waved him off.

"I've heard you like young women," Daria said again, loud enough to be heard.

"Is that so?" Ramble said, without slowing down or moving his eyes from Daria.

She turned her torso to give Ramble a better view of her jiggling cleavage.

The old man slowed his pace, making it easy for her to keep up with him.

The bodyguard was right behind them. Daria glanced back at him and smiled. The beefy, middle-aged bodyguard smiled back.

Daria bit her lip to suppress a laugh as she watched Ramble scan her from top to bottom while maintaining his deliberate walking stride.

"How do you know about me?" Ramble said.

"I did an investigation."

"You did an investigation?" Ramble said. Then he smiled, while looking back at his bodyguard trailing behind. "Fancy this one, Reggie. She's found me out."

Though Daria didn't feel threatened in any way, she was surprised by Ramble's slightly squeaky voice and his oddly accentuated manner of speaking.

"Why would you investigate me?" Ramble said.

"I have a proposal."

At the intersection of two trails, Ramble stopped. Daria moved very close to him.

Wiping his head with a towel while catching his breath, the old man scanned her up and down again.

She flashed her eyes at him suggestively, and said, "May I tell you my proposal?"

Ramble thought for a moment, then said, "This proposal involves you?"

"Of course," Daria said, with a smile.

Ramble pointed to his house across the nearby street, and said, "I live just over there."

Daria was unsure how to respond.

Ramble turned and started back down the path. He motioned for her to follow.

She hesitated.

"Come on, then," Ramble said.

"Now?" she said.

"Definitely now," Ramble said.

Daria sensed that if she turned down Ramble's invitation, there would be no chance of enlisting him to underwrite her project. She touched the pocket on the right side of her jogging pants and felt a small canister of self-defense pepper spray. She was sure she wouldn't need it, but, just the same, it was reassuring to know it was there.

As the bells of a nearby church struck 10:00 a.m., Daria followed Lord Clive Ramble through the gate in the wrought iron fence that surrounded his property. They entered the mansion through the tall, ornately crested front door.

Fifteen minutes later, the same door opened again, and Daria was shown out by the bodyguard. After the door closed behind her, she muffled a laugh. Her encounter with Lord Ramble had taken an unexpected turn. She couldn't wait to tell Angelika.

CHAPTER 8

T HE DOORBELL RANG. GREG WAS expecting a courier from the office. He threw on a bathrobe and hurried to the entry foyer of his Park Avenue high-rise residence. Three days had passed since his early return from New Zealand.

He accepted the sealed parcel from the courier and headed for the kitchen. He found scissors in a drawer and cut open the envelope. Inside was Derek Slayton's detailed report on Daria Kocánová. Greg carried it to the master suite's marble bathroom.

After tossing aside his robe, he sat down on a towel laid out on the flat section of marble that edged the tub. He put his legs into the Jacuzzi's bubbling water and opened the report. He went right to its executive summary.

The new information confirmed his first impression of Daria Kocánová. She was quite obviously sophisticated and highly intelligent.

What he hadn't expected was her success as a big-time fundraiser. Two instances were documented. On both occasions, she'd managed to raise a million euros to serve a cause she'd become involved in. She'd done it for the African Primate Protection Foundation on behalf of some endangered apes, and she'd done it again for the Dyak people of Indonesia. In each case, the money she'd raised had come from a single wealthy male individual. Credit card and travel records obtained by Derek further confirmed that shortly after each million-euro gift had been transferred to the charity, Daria Kocánová had gone off on holiday with her wealthy benefactor.

The thoroughly researched profile concluded that Daria had taken no money or compensation for herself for what she'd accomplished. Each of the two cases detailed did seem to imply a quid pro quo arrangement between the charismatic young woman and her benefactor.

Greg's imagination ran wild thinking about what that arrangement might have included in a ritzy place like Gstaad, or on an exotic island off the coast of Africa.

Another paragraph in the summary talked about a project Daria had going that used interactive video to empower women in developing countries. She was intending to demonstrate the concept in Haiti and in Ethiopia.

Here, Greg thought, *is a woman who is smart and very compassionate toward the people of the world most in need.* The pattern he saw in the report suggested she was also a self-starter, an innovator, and a leader who got things done. Everything about her was impressive.

The last part of the investigation's summary talked about Daria Kocánová's relationship with a woman named Angelika Grünberg. This was a curious twist. The report speculated that the two women had shared an ongoing, non-exclusive relationship for years. Angelika Grünberg was a wealthy widow. It seemed that almost since their reported first meeting when Daria had been only twenty years old, this older woman had been her benefactor, paying her living expenses and the cost of her education. She had also purchased a cooperative apartment for Daria's mother and gifted the title to her.

There was a large envelope taped to the inside back cover of the report. Greg unsealed the envelope and pulled out a half dozen photos. Five were of Daria Kocánová. Each had been shot professionally during a brief time when she was a print fashion model. The photos all projected a bright, energetic personality.

The sixth photo in the envelope was of Angelika Grünberg. Greg studied it. He was impressed. The woman was over fifty years old, but she was still slim and remarkably attractive. The report indicated she had enjoyed a long relationship with Daria. Did that mean they were lovers? No confirmation, but it sure looked that way. Daria Kocánová might be, probably was, bisexual. That made her even more intriguing.

Greg had never been very adventurous sexually. It was not that he didn't like sex—he absolutely did. He deeply regretted the simple reality that for the longest time, his work had killed his appetite for it. He'd been consumed by building the company, doing the deals, being a successful capitalist warrior. Mostly, he'd just denied his need for a personal life. It just hadn't been a priority. More often than not, when he felt the urge for sex, masturbation had been the quick and easy solution. His social reclusiveness went beyond sex. Greg had almost invariably avoided anyone who tried to get more than superficially close to him. Friendship, let alone intimacy, required a level of personal engagement that Greg had not been willing to commit to. At least, that was the way it had been before his perilously close brush with death.

Greg set aside all of the photos except one. It was a close-up of Daria with her hair in a ponytail. He gazed at the photo for a long time. His mind became aroused as he fantasized about her at that moment, standing before him, inviting him to explore her body. A few moments later, he went off powerfully, with waves of intense pleasure rolling up his spine into his brain. A smile spread across his face. It was the most satisfying bit of self-stimulation he'd had in a very long time.

Feeling very mellow, he slipped into the soapy bathwater and submerged himself up to his neck. He expected he would probably end up making a fool of himself. He didn't care. He was determined to know Daria Kocánová. He began to consider his first move.

CHAPTER 9

"So, we are in Lord Ramble's big house," Daria said, "and I'm thinking things are getting creepy."

Daria was with Angelika in her Munich stadthaus. They were in the spacious kitchen, preparing lunch together.

"We are in the house," Daria said. "Ramble asks, 'How much is this going to cost me?' So, I tell him. I say, 'One million euros.'"

Daria chuckled, then continued, "He looks at me for a moment with his funny face. Then he gets a big, playful grin. He leans close, and says, 'Cheeky little tart.'"

Angelika laughed. "He's thinking you're a street girl."

Daria nodded. "I was asking myself, where is this going? Should I leave now? What should I do? Before I can show him my business card, he raises his eyebrows—he's got these big, bushy eyebrows."

Daria couldn't hold back the laughter. Angelika was laughing right with her.

"I'm gripping the pepper spray in my pocket," Daria said.

"You are wearing just the jogging suit."

Daria responded, "His eyes were very busy, like I was already undressed."

"You weren't afraid?"

"At that moment, I was telling myself I must stop this."

"The end?" Angelika asked. "How did this end?'

"I showed him my business card. I introduced myself."

"What did he say?"

"He was embarrassed, and also very mad."

"With you?"

"Much more, I think, with himself," Daria said.

"What about your proposal?"

"I tried to tell him about it."

"What did he say?"

"He seemed not to understand. He was mostly worried I would be trouble. I'm sure he was thinking I would blackmail him."

"I might also think that," Angelika said.

"If he thinks that, then, if I take his money, even if it is not the intent, it becomes—"

"Blackmail," Angelika said, finishing the thought.

"So, that was the end. I told him not to worry, forget it happened. I said I would never talk about him. I promised he would never see or hear from me again."

Angelika embraced Daria affectionately and kissed her. "You are so good. You must not waste time with this. I will give you the money."

"Stop," Daria said.

"I want to give you the money."

Daria did not want to hear it.

"You know this is not a problem for me."

"It is for me," Daria said. She loved her wealthy paramour's generous spirit, but she'd given so much already.

"You are being foolish," Angelika said.

"There is still time," Daria said. "I said I would find a good man who will support my work. I must believe in myself."

Angelika shrugged and said nothing.

They sat down at a small table across from each other and began their lunch.

After a moment, Angelika spoke up, "So, I also have a surprise for you."

"What?" Daria said. "Tell me."

"Better to show you."

Forty-five minutes later, they left Angelika's stadthaus on Kaulbach-Strasse. After walking to nearby Leopoldstrasse, they took an escalator down to the U-Bahn platform and caught the next train. Less than fifteen minutes later, they got off at the Tiergarten Station.

They entered the zoo and walked across to the Africa section. They soon arrived at the park's newest exhibit. It was called Bonobo River.

Angelika had paid more than half the three-million-euro cost of the exhibit, which included a forested outdoor area with a flowing stream and a building where the bonobos could be viewed inside when the weather was bad.

Daria had visited the new facility with Angelika a couple of times during the construction phase.

"Just more than three weeks from now, it opens to the public," said Angelika.

They entered the new building through an unlocked side door. Inside, by the entrance, they found Angelika's twenty-foot-tall fabric bonobo sculpture.

"It's too perfect," Daria said. "It looks like it was created just for this place." Daria embraced Angelika and said joyfully, "You made this happen. You did it."

"You are also responsible," Angelika said, as she playfully mussed Daria's hair.

The two women found the facility's head keeper. He led them into the private area behind the exhibit.

After passing through another door marked 'no entry,' Angelika took Daria's hand. "Now, we have the surprise."

On the other side of the open door was the new outdoor exhibit. They were actually in the exhibit, separated from the animals only by a wall of stainless-steel mesh. On the far side of the expansive, naturally landscaped open space were the bonobos.

"There are five," Angelika said. "One adult male. Two adult females, and two female juveniles."

"When did they get here?"

"Over the last week, from three other zoos. This was done to avoid inbreeding. They are just now bonding as a group. We stay here, let them come to us."

Daria had mixed feelings about the moment they were in. She said, "I wish they could be in the place they would call home."

"The place they call home is going away fast," Angelika said.

Daria understood what humans were doing to the planet. Bonobos were seriously endangered and could go extinct in their natural habitat within the next few decades. She wished humans were more aware, more compassionate about the plants and animals with whom they shared the planet Earth. She felt sad for the bonobos. After a moment, she said, "They have no choice."

"Captivity is not pretty," Angelika said agreeably. "We make it as happy for them as we can."

"In a cage, they lose their dignity."

"They are also safe," Angelika said. "To save them, we must not think this is a bad thing."

A moment later, Daria was thrilled when the oldest female bonobo, who had quickly become the group leader, began to move closer to her and Angelika. The other animals followed right behind their leader. After just ten minutes, all five of the apes were only a few feet away. Then, the two juveniles came up to the fence and allowed Daria and Angelika to scratch them and tickle them. Soon after, the adult females came up and seated themselves against the fence so that Daria and Angelika could groom them. The two youngsters continued to play, rolling, jumping, bouncing off the mesh wall separating them from their human visitors.

Though the lone male bonobo came close, he remained aloof.

"He's shy with people," Angelika said.

"What's his name?" Daria said.

"Toby."

Daria looked at Toby, who was about ten feet away, grooming himself. She called his name and held out her hands to him. He watched her out of the corner of his eye but remained disinterested.

Daria continued to speak to the young ape, encouraging him to trust her. After a couple of minutes, Toby got up, came over, and squatted down by the fence next to her. Finally, he reached out and touched her fingers.

Angelika was delighted. "So, another male who cannot resist you."

Daria was thrilled. She was with her beloved friend Angelika, in a beautiful facility, surrounded by five wonderful, intelligent wild creatures. The feeling for her was sheer, unbridled joy.

They stayed with the bonobos for nearly forty minutes. Afterward, they walked to the zoo's biergarten. While sipping from foam-topped steins of Bavarian beer, they talked about the bonobos and laughed some more about Lord Ramble.

Daria knew the biergarten location had a good cell signal. She pulled out her phone and checked her text messages.

Several were from her students in Prague. There was one from Marc Wren saying he'd found a video crew based in South Africa that could shoot the material needed for the first two interactive learning scripts. They would shoot the video in Pretoria in one of the city's sprawling slums, then dub the voices over into different languages as necessary.

Then, Daria downloaded her emails. Too many were spam that was getting through despite the system's digital firewall. Daria was deleting the junk when she came across a message from an address she didn't recognize. She started to delete it, then changed her mind and clicked on it.

It was from Greg Hammond. Daria was surprised.

"Look," she said as she handed the phone to Angelika.

Angelika read the message, then handed the device back to Daria. "So, this is unexpected."

Unexpected is right, thought Daria. She gazed at the message again: *"Coming to Prague. Would like to meet."*

Daria felt deeply conflicted. After their coincidental crossing of paths at the European Parliament reception almost two weeks earlier, she'd done her research on Greg Hammond and had not liked what she found. She had thought about him from time to time since then. What she'd seen of him in their one brief encounter had not been unpleasant. He'd been just a few inches taller than her, with a clean-shaven, clean-cut appearance that reflected wealth and prestige in the business world. He might be good-looking, but Daria had never been attracted to the kind of man the public record suggested he was.

"He has much more money than Lord Ramble," Angelika said.

"All of his company is like the *Euro Standard*," Daria said, referring to Europe's most prominent, continent-wide English language newspaper. It was owned by Greg Hammond's company.

"The *Euro Standard* is not a serious newspaper," Daria said. "This man is only interested in making himself rich."

"You know that for sure?" Angelika said.

"Not so long ago, he spent more than fifty million dollars on a jet to fly himself, just himself, from one place to another."

"So?"

"How can he think so much of himself?"

"He is doing exactly what so many others in his position are doing."

"So, this is not something I can respect."

"I have a lot of money," Angelika said. "Does this make me a bad person?"

"You know I am not against having money. If everybody who had money was like you, the world would be a much better place."

"You do not walk in his shoes."

"His company makes billions in profits. Almost none goes—"

"To the things you care about," Angelika responded.

"I don't like him."

"You don't know him."

Daria glared at Angelika, then swatted her playfully on the shoulder. "You should be on my side."

"What can you lose?" Angelika said.

"I have no time to waste."

"So, you give him an hour, maybe two."

"I must find a good man who will—"

"Give a million euros to have you in his bed."

"Yes," Daria said. "This man does not fit this profile."

"He does not have to."

"Why not?"

"You did not approach him," Angelika said. "He came to you. He is asking for your attention."

That much was true, Daria thought to herself.

"Maybe you don't like him," Angelika said. "Offer him some advice that will make him a better person."

CHAPTER 10

ON THE APPOINTED DAY, EARLY in the afternoon, Greg arrived in Prague aboard the company jet. He'd left New York for Europe four days earlier and had been staying in his London flat while adjusting to the time change. No way was he going to let fatigue from jet lag affect his first real meeting with Daria Kocánová.

In the old part of Prague, Greg checked into a small, luxury hotel known for its discretion and high-end clientele. He was surprised by how consumed he was with thoughts of Daria. In fact, he'd thought of little else since she'd accepted his invitation with a six-word response to his email that said, "When would you like to meet?"

Greg's reply had proposed Friday, the first day of November, and had also asked if she would be available beforehand to show him around Prague.

The date was accepted. They would meet at a restaurant she had recommended.

With the hour approaching, Greg began to prepare. After shaving, he jumped into the shower and scrubbed himself squeaky clean. While brushing his teeth after toweling off, he checked out his body. The exercise regimen he'd stuck to since his cardiac event had left him eleven pounds lighter. He was now carrying 178 pounds on his 5'10" frame. He thought about the fifteen-year age difference between himself and Daria. Was he starting to look old? As a man, he didn't want his age to be a factor. He wanted her to take him seriously.

A barber had trimmed Greg's hair to near perfect neatness the day before. He brushed it, then he spread moisturizing cream over his face and his upper torso. He had an expensive men's cologne in his toilet kit but decided not to wear it. He was afraid it might clash somehow with the scent coming from Daria. He hoped she would be wearing the same intoxicating fragrance she'd worn the first time he'd seen her.

After putting on a pair of finely woven, perfectly creased gray wool slacks, he donned a light-blue custom-tailored shirt from Hong Kong, a smart-looking silk tie, then his best Savile Row navy-blue blazer.

As Greg checked himself out in a full-length mirror on the hotel room's wall, he thought about the political differences that separated him from Daria. He was conservative, but not an ideologue. She was a scholar, whose politics were shaped by compassion. In the days leading up to his impending rendezvous with her, Greg had taken time to reconsider the progressive world view that defined her. He had to admit that were it not for the need for his values to reflect those of the bankers, billionaires, and corporatists that delivered the revenue stream Starling depended on, his views might well be more like hers. His brush with death had changed him. It had forced him to reconsider the direction he'd taken with his own life. He vowed to keep his mind open for Daria Kocánová and for the ideals that drove her.

Giddy with anticipation, Greg left the hotel twenty minutes before 7:00 p.m. He walked along a street called Parižkǎ until he reached another called Bilkova. A light rain began to fall as he moved through a maze of narrow, cobblestone alleys. Then, he came to a small plaza enclosed by a cluster of five-story apartment buildings, all straight out of the nineteenth century. Taking up the corner between two intersecting alleys was a quiet little restaurant on the street level of one of the residential buildings. Greg recognized the unique, Czech alphabet words engraved on the small brass sign by the door. The restaurant was named *Doutnajici Plamen*. He didn't know what the words meant, but he knew he was in the right place. He checked his watch. It was just before 7:00 p.m. He pulled the restaurant's rough-hewn wooden door open and went inside. The place was dark and quiet, intimate and modest at the same time. What little light there was came from a scattering of wall lamps hanging over the dining booths.

The restaurant's host showed Greg to a booth, enclosed on three sides to provide privacy. A large window on the opposite wall provided a clear view of the small plaza. Greg expected to see Daria Kocánová approaching any moment. He closed his eyes and willed himself to relax. Some of the nervous energy coursing through his body began to melt away. When he opened his eyes again, he saw her. She was just passing under a streetlamp holding an open umbrella over her head. Though he couldn't see her face clearly, he felt sure it was her from the confident way that she walked.

He got up from the booth and went to the front of the restaurant. She came in a moment later.

"Mr. Hammond," she said, with a smile.

"Please, it's Greg."

"Nice to see you, Greg."

"Thank you for coming," Greg said.

Daria nodded agreeably.

Greg took in the complete picture, as the restaurant host helped her out of her wet overcoat. Daria's brown hair was pulled back, looped behind her head, and held in place with a classy carved wood barrette. Her simple gemstone earrings sparkled and beautifully framed the radiant symmetry of her face. She wore little makeup. She didn't need it. Most of all, Greg was taken with her hazel eyes. They reflected a lively intelligence that he found enormously appealing.

He also liked her taste in clothes. She was wearing a simple, belted, black crepe dress with a hem that stopped two inches above her knees. It was classy and very flattering to her figure. She had on matching black heels and a strand of finely painted glass beads around her neck. In a word, she looked stunning.

Greg noticed that she was wearing the same fragrance. He couldn't get enough of it.

She clasped his arm as the host led them to their table.

"I like this place," Greg said. "What does the name mean in English?"

"The restaurant's name?"

"Yes."

Daria considered the question for a moment then responded, "Doutnajici Plamen… This best translates to something like 'Smoldering Flame.'"

"Smoldering Flame," Greg said, with a smile. "Very appropriate."

"So, what has brought you to Prague?" Daria asked.

He decided to respond assertively. "I came to see you."

"Really?" she said. "That was the only reason?"

"I've been working in London over the past week. You are the excuse I was waiting for to put this city on my schedule."

She smiled politely but said nothing.

Greg was not about to be deterred. He was caught up in her wonderful smell.

"That fragrance," he said. "Am I smelling lavender?"

"Yes. You know about fragrances?"

"I know what I like."

"It's a product of Moravia, where I come from," Daria said.

"What is it called?"

"In English, it would be Great Incitement."

"Great Incitement," Greg said. He paused for a moment before he came up with the words he was looking for. "On you, Great Incitement could not be more perfect."

Daria blushed.

At that point, Greg became concerned about being too eager. He changed the subject.

"Are we close to your university?"

"A short walk," Daria said. "I can show you after dinner."

"That would be nice," he said.

So far, so good, he thought. Her warmth made her immensely likable. He was very glad he'd made the effort to come to Prague to be with her.

The waitress came. Daria recommended a favorite Moravian red wine. Greg ordered a bottle. The waitress left.

Greg gave Daria his full attention. "I have to tell you, I'm very curious about how you got to be the person you are."

"Not so interesting."

"It is to me."

Daria hesitated. Then, she said, "I grew up in a small village, not far from the city of Brno."

"A nice place?"

"Now, it is."

"How does your story align with the end of communism?"

"I was very young then. We were just trying to survive."

"Brothers or sisters?"

"Just me and my mother."

"Must've been a hard life," Greg said.

"You know cabbage?"

"Cabbage? The vegetable?"

Daria nodded. "The first five years of my life, this is what we had to eat."

"Every meal?" he said.

"In the cold months, yes," she said. "The best time was late summer. Then, we also had beets, potatoes, and some other vegetables, also, apples and berries in season. Mostly, though, we ate cabbage."

"Every day?"

"Every day," she said. Then, she let out a little laugh. "Now, I am divorced from cabbage."

Greg wondered if he'd ordered anything from the restaurant's menu that contained the offensive vegetable.

"In those times," Daria said, "so many Czechs, Slovaks, Poles—all the peoples under Soviet influence—so many were struggling. When I was seven years old, I found an old woman dead in the street, covered with snow. She was skin and bones. No one should die this way, without dignity."

A story so different from my own, thought Greg. "You weren't sorry to see the communists go."

"This was when life began again for the Czech people."

"Things are much better for you now," he said.

"Yes, well, I was also very lucky."

"How so?"

"Sometimes, to be successful, a little help is needed. I was fortunate that way."

"Really?"

"I have someone in my life who has been very good to me," Daria said. "I am the person I am today because of her."

Greg assumed she was talking about Angelika Grünberg.

He said, "If this person has been good to you, I'm sure you've done something to deserve it."

Daria smiled. "We are good for each other."

Greg encouraged her to continue talking about her life. He appreciated her honesty and candor. What she revealed matched almost exactly with what he'd already learned from the report he'd received on her.

The waitress came with dinner, a vegetarian pasta for Daria and locally caught trout for Greg. He was pleased to see there was no cabbage on his plate.

As they worked through the meal, Daria told Greg about her studies in Cultural Anthropology, and about her ambitious project to bring a new kind of empowerment-based learning to the world. He was genuinely interested in what she had to say. He listened thoughtfully and tried to ask good questions.

There was a lull in the conversation. Daria switched to a new subject. "You are the publisher of the *Euro Standard*?"

"Yes," he said. "Are you a reader?"

"I know about it," Daria said.

Her expression implied she didn't like it.

"You don't approve?" Greg said.

"So many stories about nothing," Daria said.

"Outside of the UK, it's the most successful English language paper in Europe."

"In what way?"

"Revenue. Ad sales."

"This is the most important thing?"

"It is, when you're dealing with stockholders."

"Yes, of course," she said, as she looked away and scooped up the last of the salad on her plate.

This was the first time he'd sensed her disapproval since the evening had begun.

"Have you ever been to Haiti?" she asked.

"Personally, no," he said. "Our people were there after the quake."

"But not now?" she said.

"Wherever there's a story, we're there."

"So many places in the world are struggling."

"Unfortunately," was all he could think to say.

"I have never seen stories about those places in the *Euro Standard*," Daria said.

For Greg, it was an awkward moment. What Daria said was true. Starling reported only minimally on places out of civilization's mainstream. He could tell she'd noticed he was not comfortable with where the conversation was going. He was grateful when she turned the talk in a more pleasant direction.

She told him about the three Haitian children with cholera she'd gone to see with Marc Wren. She spoke about how rewarding it had been to see the little ones restored by the hydration kits provided by the German government.

It was well after 9:00 p.m. when they got up to leave. Until that moment, Greg hadn't noticed the rain had changed to snow. When they walked out of the restaurant, they found everything covered in white. A steady flow of snowflakes continued to flutter gently from the night sky.

"I must change my shoes," Daria said as she pulled a pair of low-cut boots from the shoulder bag she was carrying and put them on in place of her high heels.

"So, now we take a little tour," she said.

They walked out to the street called Bilkova. Greg stopped and took a deep breath. The air was clean and crisp. He liked the falling snow. He liked the sound of it crunching under his feet. He liked the way it muffled and mellowed even the sharpest sounds.

Daria put her arm in his as they walked along the dimly lit street.

Quiet evenings like this were rare for Greg Hammond. The life he knew was a constant drumbeat, always about the next deal, about serving shareholder interests, about maximizing the company's quarterly performance. *How nice it would be,* he thought, *if I could give at least some of that up for more time spent enjoying evenings like this with someone special, like Daria.*

"Prague is a beautiful city, you agree?" she said, with a smile.

"Especially in the snow."

"This was one of the few large cities in Europe that was not bombed during the war with the Nazis."

"That's why it looks so old," he said.

"Old but well preserved."

Daria pointed to some official-looking buildings up ahead that looked like they could be hundreds of years old.

"We are coming now to the university," Daria said. "It is called Univerzita Karlova, which is Charles University in English. It has been here since the year 1348."

"More than six hundred years."

"A long time," she said.

"This is your university?"

"Yes," she said. Then she pointed to one of the buildings. "Over there is the School of Anthropology. On the second floor, fourth window on the right is my office."

"You teach as well?"

"Sometimes."

"Are you teaching right now?"

He saw the question was not clear to her.

"Are you teaching a course for students?" he said.

"Yes."

"What subject?"

"Ummm, in English, it would be, Gender, Culture, and Human Development. You could say it's the history of gender relations."

"Interesting subject."

She smiled and nodded.

"How do men and women relate to each other?"

"Could be better," she said, with a laugh.

He had to smile. Her confidence and intelligence were very appealing.

"How did you choose anthropology?" he asked.

"The world is in big trouble. Anthropology helps us to know who we are."

"We have made a mess of things, haven't we?"

"We have."

"Why is that?"

Daria thought for a moment, then responded, "I think maybe this question requires more time to answer than we have now."

They came to the hundred-yard-wide Vltava River that bisected the city. Set high on a hill on the other side of the swiftly moving river, the city's sprawling castle loomed, partially obscured by falling snow.

"That is Prague Castle," Daria said. "First construction was in the ninth century."

Greg listened to her talk with pride about her city and its rich history. He glanced at his watch, and saw it was close to 10:00 p.m. The evening was winding down. He didn't want it to end.

He wanted Daria Kocánová in his life. He was sure she knew at least as much about him as he knew about her. How could it not be that way? His life was very public. It troubled him to think of the perception she likely had of him. He was very successful in the arena of big corporate commerce. He was almost a billionaire. Many people were intimidated just being in the same room with him. He was largely isolated from critics who disliked him and his company. The people that worked for him were respectful to the extreme. It had been too easy to take for granted that whatever he wanted, he could have, whenever he wanted it.

Daria had been relaxed, pleasant, and unassuming the entire evening. Still, it wasn't clear that she even liked him. At the very least, she was probably unimpressed by his larger-than-life public persona. She seemed to assign little value to wealth, power, or privilege, the very things that defined and elevated him—the very things he'd always relied on for an advantage in every kind of relationship.

Greg had managed his life for so long from a position of great advantage, he didn't know how to function when such advantage was assigned so little value. Daria seemed almost too good to be true. There was an unambiguous decency about her, a decency that was clearly reflected in the things that mattered to her and the direction she'd taken in her life. Greg was ashamed he couldn't say the same about himself. He was eager, almost frantic, to have her in his life, but he didn't feel worthy of her.

They came to the dimly lit river quay and began to walk along in the snow. Greg's mind was churning, searching desperately for something he could do, some action he could take, that would give him a chance.

"Are you okay?" she asked.

"I'm fine. Sorry, I was just thinking how perfect this evening has been."

"Yes," she said. "Your hotel is not far from here. First, there is one other place you must see."

What to do? His time with this splendid young woman was counting down to its final moments. He wanted so much for it to be a beginning, not the end.

Daria pointed to an arched stone bridge that crossed the river up ahead. "You see just down there…That is Karlovy most, our most famous bridge."

Abruptly, he said, "Would you come to work for me?"

He saw the surprise on her face. He'd blurted the words out impulsively. It was an act of desperation, but it was all he could think of doing.

"You are offering me a job?"

"When do you complete your studies?"

"The end of next year."

"Would you consider coming to work for Starling?"

He could see she was studying him and processing his offer.

"What would you have me doing?" she said.

"I haven't thought it through. I just know you would be a great asset."

"Thank you. To be frank, that is not the future I have in mind for myself."

"The compensation and benefits would be hard to beat."

"I'm sure," she said.

The job offer was stupid, a clumsy blunder. It had startled her and disrupted the harmony between them. He should never have gone there. As if he could ever win over this woman with the offer of a job.

"What do you see yourself doing?" he asked, trying to smooth over the awkwardness of the moment.

"I hope to work with the United Nations," Daria said. "I want to create a nonprofit that helps people to help themselves."

"That's what you're intending to do in Haiti and in Africa?"

"Africa is actually a continent in transition. Some parts are already well integrated into the modern world. Our interest is in elevating women and girls in those places most in need. We expect to test our learning tools in Ethiopia, which is one of those amazing countries in transition."

"You're working there already?"

"We will be as soon as funding is in place."

Greg recalled the investigative profile on her that he'd requested. It said that twice before she'd managed to raise a million euros for charity from wealthy men. Greg was puzzled. She'd obviously made some kind of pitch to those men. Something like a sales pitch had to have happened as a prelude to money changing hands. Some kind of arrangement had led to the time she'd spent with each man afterward.

She had talked during their dinner about her project but had not seemed to be pitching it.

She had not even mentioned how much it would cost.

"You're still looking for funding for your project?" he asked as they arrived at the Karlovy most and stepped onto its snow-slickened walkway.

"Yes," Daria said. "I am working on that."

Only a handful of people were in the area.

"I love this bridge. It dates from the fourteenth century," Daria said. "Vehicles are not allowed, just people."

Barely visible through the falling snow, farther along the bridge under one of its tall, glowing lamps, was a young couple, entangled in a moment of passion.

Greg was envious. He gazed at Daria and wished he was engaged the same way with her.

Why, he wondered, had she not spoken to him about supporting her project? He surely had more money than either of the two men that had supported her earlier causes. There'd been plenty of opportunity during dinner. She'd never talked to him about money, never come close to raising the subject. Was he so repulsive to her? Was he so unappealing that she'd dismissed him as a potential benefactor? Did she assume because of what she knew about him from the public record, that he was an unlikely prospect for persuasion?

Their time together, this evening at least, was coming to an end. They were so different. They'd come from such different backgrounds and had such different priorities. Was he agonizing over something that was hopelessly out of reach? He had all the money and power in the world, and here, it seemed, was someone he was genuinely attracted to, yet he was perilously close to seeing her walk out of his life forever.

"I'm surprised you haven't asked me for help," he said, making every effort to mask his desperation.

Daria looked at him for several moments, then said, "I hope this does not come across as offensive, but you do not have a reputation for generosity."

It was like a dagger piercing his chest. What she had said was undeniable, and it was all the more painful hearing it from her. His mind was spinning. He had only one card left to play.

He let down his guard in a way he never did with anyone. "Do you know what happened to me a few months ago?"

"Please," Daria said. "Tell me."

"I had an aortic aneurysm. That's a rupture of the largest artery that emerges from the heart."

Daria appeared to be aware of that part of his story. She said, "It must have been difficult for you."

"One moment it's indigestion, the next…I was dying. This condition has only a ten percent survival rate."

Daria comforted Greg with a gentle touch to his arm. "You look healthy now."

"In some ways. In others, not so much," Greg said. "I saw my life in a way I'd never seen it before."

He'd taken the dialogue in an emotionally uncertain direction. He didn't know what to say next.

He saw Daria studying him. Then, she said, "Are you telling me this to say you could support my project?"

"I'm saying, the Greg Hammond standing here with you, at this moment, is different from the one who existed six months ago."

"In what way?"

"I was a dead man. I got a second chance."

"This changed you?"

"I'm feeling very mortal," Greg said.

"Time is everyone's enemy," Daria said.

"I need to feel good about my life," Greg said. It was a statement that came directly from his soul.

After a moment, she said, "This is a big step, admitting these feelings."

Greg was so grateful for her understanding. "How much funding are you looking for?"

Daria seemed very pleased by his question. He listened intently as she reviewed what she wanted to accomplish. Then, she got to how much it would cost.

"It goes beyond the learning initiative," she said. "I also have an obligation to Marc Wren. I gave my word I would find money to expand his program for treating drug-resistant tuberculosis."

"How much to cover everything?"

She responded thoughtfully and directly, "Two million euros."

Greg had expected her to say a million. That kind of money, one million, two million, under any circumstance that could leave him vulnerable as chief executive officer of the third largest media company in the world.

For several moments, Greg was quiet, immersed in thought about Daria, and about how much he wanted her. He thought about his own life, about how screwed up it was, about how anxious he was to find a new, healthier and more emotionally satisfying direction, and how much he wanted Daria Kocánová to appreciate and value him.

He lost himself in thoughts about this singular moment on this six-hundred-year-old, medieval bridge in this wonderful, snow-etched city of Prague. He was captivated by this marvelous woman standing before him, illuminated by the warm glow of a rusted bridge lamp, with snowflakes in her hair.

He came back to reality and saw that Daria was looking at him, trying to read his feelings. Then, he sensed she was ready to open up to him.

"You understand what I'm trying to accomplish?" she said.

"Yes."

"You could consider being the benefactor for this kind of effort?"

He responded with a look intended to reflect his openness to her proposal.

"I want nothing for myself," she said. "The money goes directly to the Equitable Health Alliance."

He was aware from his investigation that she was not out for personal gain. He looked into her eyes. He sensed she understood what he wanted from her.

She began to transform. She became a quiet temptress, staring at him with the most alluring, provocative expression. She moved close, until she was almost, but not quite, touching him.

He breathed in her wonderful, lavender Great Incitement scent.

She said, softly, "I see how you look at me."

An exciting chill ran up Greg's spine.

She took his earlobe in her mouth. He felt her teeth pulling it gently. He immediately went fully hard.

Daria stared at him with smoldering eyes. "I know what you want."

At that moment, no one else existed in Greg Hammond's universe, no one but Daria Kocánová.

He thought about what to say. Then, words came to him. "What does a man get for two million euros?"

She slowly shifted position until her face was inches from his. She opened her lips and pursed them sensuously. Then, she whispered three words, loaded with innuendo, in his ear. "My full attention."

CHAPTER 11

“Mr. Samuelson calling from New York, sir,” said the female voice through the intercom.

Greg was back in London, in his office overlooking Charing Cross and Embankment Place on the Thames.

He got up from behind his desk and picked up the phone. “Tell me something, Carl.”

The voice that came through was Carl Samuelson, Starling’s Chief Legal Counsel. “We checked on this Equitable Health Alliance. Budget just over eleven million last year. Very dedicated people. All but four percent goes to operating clinics in Haiti and in Ethiopia.”

Carl’s numbers verified what Daria had told Greg.

“There is a problem.”

“What?” Greg said.

“As part of the basic health care this group provides, they do family planning services, contraceptives, that sort of thing.”

“Why is that a problem?”

“On occasion, they also refer patients to an abortion provider.”

Greg let out a groan.

“You would have to get that past your sister,” Carl said.

Lydia was the president of the Starling Foundation, the nonprofit that handled charitable giving by the company.

“We know how that would fly,” Greg said.

“Is she personally opposed?” Carl said.

“To me? Yes.”

Greg heard Carl chuckle at the other end of the phone.

"Forget the foundation idea," Greg said.

"Is there a particular reason you're thinking about this group?"

"I just got a briefing on them."

"I'm not saying they aren't worthy," Carl said. "But the word 'abortion' is like a dirty bomb waiting to go off. You don't want it in your house."

"Other than that, there's no problem?"

"Are you thinking you might do something for this group personally?"

Greg did not respond.

"You know what's going on with Lydia and Andre," Carl said.

Greg was acutely aware of what they were up to.

"I wouldn't give them any leverage," Carl said. "They'll slice you and dice you."

"Anything else I should know?"

"If you want to give away money, there are plenty of places you can go that don't have this kind of baggage. I can send you a list of gifting possibilities."

Greg thought about it, then said, "Send me the list. Thanks, Carl."

He hung up the phone, then he sat down at his desk and picked up a one-page summary of his personal assets that had come through from his personal financial advisor, Marg Glick. Total assets exceeded eight hundred million dollars. Despite the shaky economy, he was up nearly twenty-seven million since he'd last checked months ago, prior to his close encounter with the Reaper.

Much of what he had was tied up in the value of his Starling stock. He was the biggest single shareholder with a fraction under twenty percent of the total outstanding, voting equity shares. Marg had a lot of his personal money invested in companies that produced basic commodities, particularly energy commodities like uranium, gas, and oil. The power of supply and demand was at work big time in energy, and also with other non-elastic basic commodities. His portfolio also was in precious metals, like gold and platinum, as well as in real estate, stocks, bonds, mutual funds, and treasury paper. He had a little of everything, and it was spread around in asset management portfolios in places like the Cayman Islands and Vanuatu, where the tax implications were still favorable.

His liquid assets, the ones readily convertible to cash, amounted to nearly eighty million. A lot of that was stashed in a special account managed by a broker, who spent all day every day exploiting margins in the global currency exchange arena. It was highly speculative, but a lot of wealth was flowing into Greg's coffers from riding the tiny, day-to-day, incremental shifts in foreign currency floats. It was basically churning money, but it was legal and very profitable for people who had money and the right financial gamers in charge.

Marg had some of his money sitting in accounts in the Bank of Corsica. That was the logical place to pull out two million euros.

There was a knock at the door.

One of the local staffers poked her head in. "Got what you asked for, sir."

Greg got up from his desk. "Let's see."

She pushed the door all the way open and entered, carrying a glass vase filled with two dozen long stems loaded with tiny, purple lavender flowers. She placed the vase on the small conference table adjacent to the desk.

Greg leaned close and took in a deep breath. "They smell as good as they look."

"Yes, they are lovely," the staffer said. "Anything else I can get you, sir?"

"No. Thank you," Greg said.

The staffer retreated out the door and closed it behind her.

Greg gazed at the flowers and thought about Daria. She'd been right about him. Beyond going through the motions, he had virtually no history of being generous. The exception was the five million dollars he'd given the American Vascular Disease Foundation following his close encounter with the Reaper. That had been done anonymously to keep other donation seekers away.

It certainly wasn't because he couldn't afford to be generous. He wasn't that much of a spender. He'd always been too busy growing the Starling brand. The only major asset he owned was his Park Avenue Co-op in New York. He'd paid a shade over fourteen million for it six years earlier. Other than that, just about everything he needed in life was expensed to the company.

The gifting of two million euros from his personal assets could be written off and would be made up by returns on other investments in a short time, maybe in as little as a few weeks.

Greg recalled again the singular moment of the previous evening. Daria had said the boldest, most sexually provocative thing he'd ever heard uttered by a woman. Right after she said it, she'd looked into his eyes and smiled and raised her eyebrows in the most wonderfully suggestive way. Then, it was over. The whole thing lasted maybe a minute. It was an indelible moment, one he expected never to forget as long as he lived.

After that brief, extremely close encounter, the entire evening had come to an end less than fifteen minutes later. She'd walked him back to his hotel. They'd exchanged pleasantries.

Little more was said about her proposal or the extraordinarily potent offer she'd put on the table.

Though the sexual tension had remained high, their time together ended with a warm handshake, like two business executives who'd just come to an understanding.

She had left him at the hotel, disappearing into the snowy darkness after assuring him she lived nearby and was in no danger from walking alone at night.

Greg would have agreed to her proposal without a second thought, had it just been about the money. It wasn't that simple. Despite the strong emotion he'd been feeling, he could not afford to be reckless about it. He had to exercise at least some caution.

He'd stayed on in Europe instead of going back to New York. He'd asked Carl Samuelson to look into Daria's nonprofit just to be sure there were no red flags. Greg had assumed it would be a formality. He was wrong. The charity's association with abortion, however limited, was unsettling to say the least.

From its inception when his father was running the show, Starling Media had been about maximizing revenue. Jack Hammond was expert at keeping the company's advertising customers happy. Starling's media content was designed to pull in readers or viewers. More than that, advertisers coveted the demographic groups most likely to buy their particular products. Manufacturers of garments for young women wanted their ad dollars to reach 18–25-year-old females. Pro football and basketball broadcasts were dominated by slick ads for beer, cars, and the armed forces. They were designed to resonate with young, sports-crazed males, the kind that drank beer, bought hot cars, and were prime fodder for military recruitment.

Starling kept corporate advertisers happy by reflecting their values in the content of the news, print articles, and entertainment programming presented in publications and in radio and TV broadcasts. *Vectors*, Starling's one-hour weekly television drama, had been delivering large and loyal viewing audiences in broadcast markets worldwide for six years. Advertisers paid big bucks to buy commercial airtime on *Vectors*. Not only did it deliver the demographics—through action-thriller storylines that were a constant drumbeat of fear about terrorists of every size, shape, and form—*Vectors* was also sending a political message to viewers that corporate conservatives were eager to promote.

Starling did what all conservative media companies did to a greater or lesser extent. It maximized revenue by maintaining a rightist political bias. Corporate advertising money secured the loyalty of the conservative media, whose content was aligned with the political right-wing.

This was the world in which Greg Hammond had achieved stardom. His vast business enterprise had been shaped by assiduously serving the bottom line. The trouble was, Starling's rich and powerful customers maintained a loyal relationship with religious fundamentalist voters, the same extreme moralists who consider abortion a crime of the highest order.

Greg glanced out his office window and saw an InterCity Express departing Charing Cross railway station below. He watched the train clatter over the Thames on the Hungerford Bridge.

Donating millions to a medical nonprofit that delivered family planning, contraception, and only indirectly, abortion, shouldn't be controversial... but it was. The only sure way to avoid trouble was to forget the Equitable Health Alliance. Doing that would also surely kill any possibility with Daria.

Greg studied the vase brimming with tiny purple lavender. He leaned down and savored their wonderful scent. No way was he turning away from Daria Kocánová. He was ready and willing to donate two million euros of his personal fortune to the Equitable Health Alliance, but it would have to be done discreetly, and very much under the public radar.

CHAPTER 12

As Daria exercised on the only bit of open floor space in her tiny university office, her mind focused on the night before.

She had assumed she wouldn't like Greg Hammond. Her plan had been to cut the evening short if he'd proved to be insufferable as she had been expecting. As it turned out, she was surprised at how much he wasn't like that. Instead of being self-assured and arrogant, he'd been nervous and awkward at times. She'd expected he would talk a lot about himself. Instead, he'd done more listening than talking.

When Daria had first arrived at the restaurant, she was uncertain why he'd come to Prague. His words, together with his body language, had revealed his motive. It was not complicated. He was simply attracted to her. He was in Prague because he wanted to know her. That was nice. Having an outrageously wealthy man show more than a passing interest was always good for the ego, especially when he was the one who appeared to be intimidated.

As the evening had worn on, it became clear that Greg Hammond was more than just a little attracted to her. He'd been no good at hiding his infatuation. Still, if he'd been the hard case she'd originally expected, she never would have told him about her vision for empowerment-based learning. As it was, he seemed genuinely interested. So, she'd laid it out in detail. Even then, there was no thought that he might be a serious possibility for gifting the big-money support she was so eager to find.

While they were walking together in the snow, he'd brought up the health problem that had nearly killed him. Quite obviously, he was struggling with his newfound sense of mortality. His motives, where

Daria was concerned, were all too transparent. He wanted her. Why else would he offer her a job? Why else would he encourage her to lay out her project's cost? Why else was he still receptive after she'd revealed the two-million-euro price tag? He'd seemed emotionally unsettled, so eager for validation, and yes, it seemed, so eager to win her over, that she'd decided then and there to cast aside all restraint.

In university, her anthropology studies focused on human interpersonal relationships. She knew well the way men and women had related to each other, sexually and otherwise, all through history.

The night before, in the heat of the moment, Daria had switched into seduction mode and aroused Greg Hammond with a shameless sexual provocation. She knew it had excited him. Just saying the words had been a turn-on for her.

When they'd parted ways the previous night, Greg hadn't committed to anything. But Daria knew she had his attention. She was hoping he would come through. Even if he didn't, the evening had been worthwhile. She'd found him more attractive, more vulnerable, and far more likable than she'd ever thought possible.

Daria got up from the floor, went back to her laptop, and resumed work on the script for a new interactive learning module that would soon be added to her thesis initiative in its second phase.

Twenty minutes later, Daria saw an icon flashing on her computer screen, alerting her to an incoming email. It was from Greg Hammond. It said, quite simply, "Please send account information for transfer of two million euros."

Daria shrieked with delight, then jumped up and threw her hands in the air triumphantly.

Barely able to contain herself, she paced the tiny office, excitedly pumping a fist. Greg Hammond's brush with death had put him in touch with the better side of his nature. Daria was thrilled that her initial skepticism about him had not derailed a successful outcome, thrilled that empowerment-based learning in Haiti and Ethiopia now had a patron and was about to fly.

Unlike the earlier two instances where she'd traded personal favor for money, Daria recognized that lust was not the only factor that had driven Greg Hammond to pay so handsomely to be with her. His heart seemed to be as much of a factor as his libido. Despite the added complication, she was excited about getting to know him better, personally and intimately. Though she had no expectations, a part of her was very curious about where their time together might lead.

She returned to her desk and shuffled through the clutter until she found the bank information needed to complete a wire transfer to the Equitable Health Alliance. She emailed the information to Greg.

He responded less than two minutes later. His new email read: "When and where? Is tomorrow too soon?"

CHAPTER 13

GREG ACCELERATED THE BLACK VOLKSWAGEN sedan onto the number eight autobahn. The vehicle belonged to the Starling News Bureau in Munich. Greg was alone. Driving himself was the best way to avoid attention and maintain privacy.

His imagination was in overdrive. Daria had said he was going to experience her full attention. Wild fantasies rippled through his mind.

She'd agreed to spend three days with him, a long weekend, just the two of them. A flurry of texts comparing alternative dates and meeting sites had been exchanged. They settled on Schalchen, a village on the Chiemsee, a lake south of Munich. It was the best compromise given Greg's eagerness to get on with it as soon as possible. She'd asked in one text message if he had any sexually transmitted diseases or health problems she should know about. He had none, and she'd told him she also had none. He thought she was smart to get this issue out of the way ahead of time.

Nearly an hour of driving brought Greg to a sign announcing the exit to the Chiemsee. He turned off the autobahn onto a two-lane rural highway. As he drove along, he had depressing thoughts that he was setting himself up for a big disappointment, that Daria Kocánová, on close inspection, would not measure up to the idealized standard he had imagined. He shook off his misgivings. He told himself to have fun, to relax and enjoy the weekend for what it was, a rendezvous with an incredibly sexy and beautiful young woman. Afterward, if it felt right, who knew where it might lead.

After passing through two traditional German farm villages, Greg arrived in Schalchen at the tail end of an afternoon shower. He drove along a narrow, tree-lined road by the lake until he came to a private estate surrounded by a vine-covered, eight-foot-tall masonry wall. He turned the car in through an open gate and traveled half a kilometer up the forested driveway to the estate's large, Georgian-style, white brick house. It appeared to date back at least to the eighteenth century but had been beautifully maintained.

Greg left the car, grabbed his small suitcase, and headed to the front door. It was ajar. He pushed it open.

"Hello?" he called out.

No answer.

He stepped inside, nearly bursting with anticipation. The house's spacious interior was decorated with tastefully muted warm colors, comfortable, contemporary era furniture, and many original paintings, some classical, some modern. There were also at least a dozen beautifully crafted fabric sculptures on display. Greg ambled through the foyer to a large, high-ceilinged living room that was dominated by a massive hearth. One wall was almost entirely windows that looked out on the Chiemsee, which looked seasonally dreary at the moment.

Greg imagined the view was splendid when sunlit and warm.

"So, you have arrived."

Greg turned and saw Daria coming up to him. She was barefoot, wearing a kitchen apron over a red pullover sweater and black slacks. She helped him out of his overcoat. Then she put her arms around him and embraced him.

"What you have done makes me so happy," she said, with real emotion. "So many people who are suffering will have a better life because of this."

"You bring out the best in me," he said.

She laughed. "I hope this is so."

She brushed her lips against his, kissing him softly.

Greg seized the moment and took her in his arms. They shared a lingering kiss that was laced potently with genuine passion.

Then, he caught her lavender scent. "You smell so good."

She smiled and took his hand. A moment later, they were in the house's cozy, decorator-updated kitchen. She directed him to sit at a small table next to a window with a fabulous view of the lake and the Bavarian peaks looming over the opposite shore.

She placed a basket of sliced bread on the table. "Fresh from the village bakery."

Next, she brought a steaming bowl of soup. "Lentil, made by me."

Greg dipped a piece of the bread in the soup and tasted it. "Wonderful," he said. "On top of everything else, you can cook."

"Good food is always welcome," Daria said, as she sat down at the table across from him and stared at him cheerfully.

"You're not eating?"

"I'll have something after," she said.

"After?" he said.

Daria smiled, leaned close, looked into his eyes, and raised her eyebrows suggestively.

A grin spread across Greg's face. "Should I finish my soup?"

"Please," Daria said, while failing to suppress a laugh.

What a delight she was. Her playfulness relaxed him. He couldn't remember ever being so eager for anything.

They shared a bit of small talk while Greg polished off the soup. Then he remembered her aversion to a certain vegetable. "I find myself thinking about…cabbage."

Daria eyed him skeptically.

"That one vegetable deserves credit for you being here today."

Daria's expression twisted into a playful pout.

"Some garden greens get no respect," Greg continued, with a silly poker face.

Daria laughed.

Greg eyed her playfully.

"Cabbage, broccoli, brussel sprouts, all unappreciated and misunderstood."

"Keep going," Daria said, in a tone that was sensuous and fun. "I will think you want me to punish you."

Greg leaned in close and looked into her eyes. "I would love for you to punish me."

Daria tilted her head playfully and smiled. Her attention was fully on him. She stood up, pulled off her apron, and tossed it aside. She leered at him playfully for a moment, then dashed off toward the living room.

After gulping down one last spoonful of soup, Greg leaped from the chair and chased after her. He turned into the living room. She wasn't there. Then, he heard laughter behind him. He whirled around and saw her in the foyer, racing up the house's grand staircase. He was totally into this game. He hurried to the foyer and headed up the winding steps after her.

When he reached the second floor, he found he was in the middle of a corridor that stretched forty feet in each direction. He took a moment to consider his next move. Then he heard more laughing. He turned and watched Daria slowly emerge from a doorway near one end of the corridor. She had pulled off all her clothes except for a silky black thong. She faced him, shamelessly displaying herself.

A lusty smile spread across Greg's face. He began to disrobe. He took his time. He couldn't believe how sexy she was. He loved the way she teased. He loved giving it right back. This was fun, pure and simple. When he was down to his boxer shorts, he smiled at her for a long moment.

She turned her back to him, then slid her thong down until it dropped to the floor.

He let his shorts drop away, exposing his fully engorged manhood.

Daria turned to face him. She touched the neatly shaved triangle between her legs.

Greg leered at her, then teased with a two-syllable provocation. "Cab-bage."

She pouted playfully and scolded him with her finger, then she rose up on the balls of her feet and touched her breasts. Her ankles stretched gracefully, and she lingered for a moment, teasing and displaying herself, then she sauntered out of sight through the nearest doorway.

Greg followed her and found himself in a large bedroom with a high-vaulted ceiling and large windows overlooking the lake just beyond.

Daria was on her knees on a very large, ornately carved, nineteenth-century four-poster bed. She faced him and began running her hands over her naked torso.

He saw her eyeing his crotch.

"Such a big boy," she teased, with a grin.

She arched backward onto her left elbow, spread her legs, and stroked her inner thigh with her right hand.

He moved toward her.

Just before he reached the bed, she raised her hand in a halting gesture.

She got off the bed, then pointed for him to lie down on it.

Greg eagerly complied.

Daria switched on some mellow, new-age jazz music. Then, she began to dance, moving gracefully, displaying herself, touching herself in the most confidently sexual way.

"Are you suffering?" she said.

Greg smiled. "Not enough."

Daria moved close to him and intensified the provocation.

Greg loved her tight, beautifully proportioned body. He loved how comfortable she was with herself, how playful she was with her sexuality.

She turned her back to him and bent to display herself.

He smiled, then beckoned her to come to him.

She moved to the bed and stretched out next to him. She stroked his stiff erection playfully, then took it in her mouth. He closed his eyes. It was the most wonderful kind of suffering.

Over and over, Daria brought him almost to climax. Then she backed off and began again. It was so good, so satisfying.

Greg thought about her, about how beautiful she was, how good she was, how much fun she was, what a wild, sensual animal she was. He wanted to touch her in the most intimate ways. He wanted to see her respond to him. He touched her head and nudged her away from his groin. Then, he urged her over onto her back.

She opened her legs and spread her knees wide, revealing a vulva fully engorged and lubricated with arousal. He gently plunged two fingers inside her wetness. She moaned, and her body tightened. Her back arched as he applied more pleasure with his fingers.

Greg loved her passion, loved the moans and groans, loved the feel of her body writhing as she became more and more excited.

Finally, he knew his own need couldn't wait much longer. He worked to arouse her once more. This time, he kept going, kept applying stimulation. She was so open, so responsive to his touch. Finally, her torso arched and shuddered. Orgasmic pleasure flooded through her body. She shuddered and groaned until she was completely spent.

For Greg, it was an indelible moment, an absolute, exquisite joy. He loved experiencing this incredible woman, loved seeing her respond to him, loved seeing her climax in such an amazing, beautiful way.

Daria's afterglow was equally awesome. For the longest time, she remained still, lost in her own pleasure. Then, she returned to the moment.

Energized and alert, she shifted into sexual overdrive.

She sat up, shoved Greg onto his back, straddled him, and began to grind her hips into his groin. She lifted her arms high and ran her fingers sensuously through her disheveled hair. Then, she arched her back, playfully displaying her breasts.

Greg elevated himself on one elbow. He pulled her face to his. She thrust her tongue into his mouth and locked her lips to his.

She pulled away and shoved him back onto the bed. She leaned close and went eye to eye with him. She wrapped a hand around his engorged penis. She squeezed it and said, "I want this one."

At that moment, Greg could barely contain his excitement. At that moment, Daria Kocánová again became his whole universe.

She pursed her lips sensuously, then said, "Are you ready for my worst punishment?"

Greg was totally ready.

She lifted her hips and guided his manhood inside her.

For Greg, it was a singular joy.

She cooed and moaned as she rocked up and down, working her hips to maximize their shared pleasure.

For Greg, by far, she was the most exciting woman he'd ever known. His need became ever more urgent, then it became overwhelming. He concentrated all his attention on his own satisfaction. Very soon, he felt himself coming. It began in his loins and swept upward along his spine into his brain. His pleasure became ever more intense, spreading through the rest of his body.

Suddenly, a groan erupted from his core. An explosion of bliss shuddered through him as he lost himself in the orgasmic moment.

Later, when Greg awoke, she was not there. He checked his watch. It was late afternoon. Several hours had passed since Daria had most assuredly given him her full attention and the most satisfying intimate experience of his life. He noticed a white terrycloth bathrobe lying neatly at the bottom of the bed. After a quick stop in the bathroom, he threw on the robe and went looking for Daria.

He found her in the kitchen in a white robe identical to the one he was wearing. She was standing over the sink, cutting up vegetables.

She blew him a kiss.

He came up behind her, wrapped his arms around her, and pressed his face into the creamy skin of her neck. "That was awesome."

She smiled.

"Best ever," he said. "Off the scale."

Greg turned her to face him. She touched his nose playfully. They shared a deep, drawn-out kiss, then a warm and heartfelt embrace.

"It's good to see you happy," Daria said. "I think this has been missing from your life."

"You make me happy."

"We are both happy," she said, with a smile. She kissed him once more, then returned to preparing vegetables.

Greg noticed steam coming from a covered pot on the stove.

"What's this?"

"Pasta. We add some vegetables, some mushrooms, some olive oil, some spices."

"No meat?"

"No meat."

"Are you vegetarian?"

"Yes," Daria said, with a chuckle. "Except for cabbage."

After straining the hot water from the cooking pot, she added a pile of chopped carrots and onions to the pasta. Then, she turned to Greg. "It takes ten kilos of grain to make one kilo of meat. Did you know that?"

"Never thought about it."

"You want to be healthy?"

"Doesn't everybody?"

"To be healthy, eat no meat or at least much less meat," she said, with a smile.

Greg shrugged. "That would be difficult."

"Wouldn't it be nice if no animal had to die so you could eat?"

"When you put it that way."

"You can do it," she said. "Every morning when you get up, say to yourself, 'Today, I will eat no meat. Today, I am vegetarian.'"

Greg shrugged and smiled agreeably.

"Say it," Daria said. "Today, I'm vegetarian."

"Today, I'm vegetarian," Greg said amiably.

"Today, I'm vegetarian," she repeated.

"Today, I'm vegetarian."

"You see?" Daria said. "Doesn't it feel good to say this?"

Greg grinned and nodded agreeably.

They were soon seated across from each other, enjoying Daria's pasta.

"Very tasty," he said.

"Good for your heart."

"I believe it."

"So, you are now vegetarian."

Greg laughed. "I guess we'll see."

After the meal, while Daria cleaned up in the kitchen, Greg went to the living room hearth. He placed three splits of wood atop the glowing embers and rekindled the fire. He and Daria were soon cuddled up together on a big sofa in front of the roaring warmth of the hearth.

She began to tell him more about her life. Angelika's name came up.

"This is your friend's home?" he said.

"Yes. She is here mostly in the summer."

"What about you?"

"When Angelika is here, I am often here."

"Great place," Greg said. "Wonderful location."

He was intensely curious about Daria's relationship with the house's wealthy owner.

"How did you meet this lady?"

"I was modeling for fashion magazines to pay for university. There was more work in Berlin. I went there. I met Angelika at an event. We had some lunch."

The picture was pretty clear to Greg. He said, "You started spending time with her?"

"She lives in Munich. I would take the train from Prague. That was the beginning. For eight years, we have been very close."

"She's good to you?"

"She would do anything for me, as I would for her."

"Can I ask a personal question?"

"Of course."

"Are you bisexual?"

Daria smiled. "Would this bother you?"

"Actually, I find the idea of two beautiful women having sex… It's a turn-on, a man's fantasy. What can I say?"

He was surprised to see a hint of disappointment in her expression.

"Did I say something wrong?"

"No, we are all sexual animals," she said.

"Please. Tell me what you're thinking."

Daria faced him more directly. She took a moment to consider her words, then said, "Most often, if a man sees two women holding hands, his mind is reducing them to sexual beings. He is not seeing them as human beings. He is not seeing anything beyond the sexual."

"It seems like that comes from instinct."

"Of course, for all humans, it's normal to think about sex, but I can tell you, most women do not like to be seen only in this way, as sexual objects."

Greg looked into her eyes and smiled. "For me, you are very much more than that."

Daria caressed his cheek, then she said, "This also goes to the issue of equality. My message to all men is, respect us. We are all human. Accept us as equals, all humans as equals. That is how we make a better world together."

Greg appreciated her wisdom. They shared a lingering kiss, then he laid back and nestled his head in Daria's lap. As she stroked his head, he closed his eyes and said, "I could get used to this."

Daria began to question him about the details of his own life. In the past, he'd talked to no one intimately about himself, not even with his father. That was the past. Though it was totally out of character, he was ready, in fact eager, to open up. He had a need to reveal himself to her. He was convinced she could be trusted. He imagined her to be what he didn't have in his life, a confidante, a person to whom he could vent, a person with whom he could unburden at least some of the frustrations he'd been carrying inside himself for too long.

"My father had a stroke the same day I had my cardiac scare," he said. "It was a reaction to what happened to me."

"Must've been difficult for you," Daria said.

"He's the one person I talked to, and now he can't talk."

"How do you communicate with him?"

"I write him emails," Greg said. "He lives in New Zealand. I'm in New York. In the past, we talked every day on the phone… Not now."

"He responds to your emails?"

"With difficulty. He can't use his right hand. That pretty much limits what he can do on a computer. Speech is something we all take for granted. When it's taken away—"

Greg choked back a sudden flare of emotion. Then he sat up next to her, and continued, "My father feels lost."

Daria touched Greg's arm sympathetically.

He told her about the petty jealousies that defined his relationship with his half-sister, Lydia. He described his self-absorbed nephew, Andre, and the pressure he was getting to accept Andre as his eventual successor as head of Starling Worldwide.

"You have too much stress," she said.

Greg had to agree with her.

"Sometimes, the best way is to ignore these problems."

"Wish it were that easy," Greg said.

"It's difficult only if you allow it to be so."

Greg could see she didn't understand. He said, "It's about control of the company."

"In what way?"

"I'm the largest shareholder. I have just under twenty percent of the voting stock. My father started the company. He had forty-four percent up until my mother died. At that point, he publicly acknowledged Lydia and Andre for the first time. Lydia pressured him into giving her and Andre a part of his holdings. My father now has eighteen percent of the voting stock, Lydia has eighteen percent, and Andre has eight percent. Most of the rest is held by investment banks and other institutional investors."

"So, these bad relatives are in control?"

"They have a lot of leverage."

"This is the source of your stress?"

"A lot of it."

Greg sensed Daria's concern was genuine. It pleased him very much.

Daria stood, then pulled Greg to his feet. "There is a wine rack in the kitchen. Pick a bottle you like."

Daria started off toward the foyer in her robe and bare feet.

"Where you going?"

"I will show you my best cure for the stress," Daria said as she started up the spiral staircase.

Whatever the cure was, Greg felt certain it was going to be fun. His mind filled with delicious fantasy.

He headed to the kitchen. Five minutes later, he returned with the wine and found Daria placing a large air mattress on the open floor in front of the fireplace.

Greg showed her the bottle. "Oppenheimer Riesling, 1974."

"I know that one. Very good."

Greg removed the cork and poured a goblet for each of them.

"So, off with this, please," she said, as she tugged on the knot holding the front of his robe together.

Greg eagerly pulled off his robe.

"Down on the mattress, please," she said as she let her own robe drop away.

Greg loved the warm firelight licking her naked body as he stretched out on the inflated mattress.

"Face down, please."

He did as she asked. Daria got down on her knees next to him. A moment later, he felt a warm liquid being poured onto his back, then his butt cheeks, then his legs. It had a familiar odor.

"What is that?"

"A wonderful kind of lavender oil."

"Feels good."

"It gets better."

He couldn't wait.

She was pouring a lot of oil on him. Then, a moment later, he felt her naked body pressing into his back until all her weight was on him.

"Oooh, nice," he said.

He savored the tactile pleasure of her lubricated body slithering around on top of him.

Daria sat up, straddled him, and began to slowly grind her oil-soaked thighs back and forth over his butt cheeks and back.

Greg loved it. "What do you call this?"

"In Czech?"

"Yes."

"Ummmmm. How about *Přislovce hnist*," she said.

Greg liked the sound of it.

She laughed, then offered a translation. "Sexy fun."

An instant later, she intensified her delicious, slippery grinding against his body.

Greg felt her tongue penetrate his right ear. There was a tingling in his spine that radiated outward from his head and neck. It was so, so good.

Relaxed to his core, Greg closed his eyes. He savored the feel of her oil-slicked skin sliding over his body.

After a while, he was ready for a variation on this theme. He said, "Can we switch?"

Daria eagerly exchanged places with him. He kneeled over her and poured oil on her legs and back. He massaged the slippery wetness into her skin. He loved hearing her moan blissfully as his hands slid over her body. Giving her pleasure was as joyful for him as being on the receiving end.

Sexy fun with Daria Kocánová was just too exciting, too much fun. He felt a wonderful, deeply satisfying happiness wash over him. He did not want it to end.

CHAPTER 14

Three hundred ten pounds were pressed against Andre's thigh and calf muscles. Knees pulled up almost to his chest, he sucked in several breaths, then gritted his teeth and pushed, extending his legs smoothly against the weight. Eleven more reps followed. Then he locked the leg press machine in the closed position and rolled out onto his feet. His home gym was the size of a basketball court. Mirrors lined every wall. Top-of-the-line exercise machines were set in four rows, six machines in each row. The gym took up most of a large building separate from the house on Andre's sprawling hilltop estate outside Auckland, New Zealand.

Andre turned to the closest mirror and studied his reflection. Dripping with sweat, wearing only gym trunks, socks, and training shoes, he flexed his upper torso. Every muscle on his body was splendidly defined. He loved looking at himself, loved the one hundred eighty-six pounds of lean strength draped on his 6'3" frame. At thirty-one, he still was in the gym five times a week. That much was required to maintain his exceptional physique. Maintenance was all he was interested in. He didn't need the commitment of a bodybuilder to attract the ladies. They liked him very much just the way he was.

He turned sideways to the mirror and flexed again. He examined himself from top to bottom. He was happy with everything he saw until the stubble on his head caught his attention. He leaned close to the mirror to study it. He was annoyed. The brown natural color was beginning to show at the roots. He made a mental note to have his regular appointment with his hairstylist moved up. Then, he grabbed a towel off a nearby chair and swabbed the sweat from his head and shoulders.

He glanced at his two mates, Morty and Bernard. They were across the room, racing each other on a pair of treadmills. Working out was one of many things Andre shared with them.

Morty had been his close friend since high school. Bernard had been with him since his first summer in France, twelve years earlier. Like Andre, they were good-looking, they were buff, and they shared his unquenchable appetite for young women.

Andre turned his attention to a nearby refrigerator. He went and opened it, expecting to find bottled water. There was none.

"Something's wrong here," Andre roared to no one in particular.

Morty and Bernard both gave him their attention.

"Is it too much to ask to keep this thing stocked?"

"Sorry, mate," Morty shouted back to him. "I'm on it."

Morty headed for the door.

Andre paid his two friends well to be loyal companions. He expected them to be available when needed, running errands, coddling his ego, laughing at his jokes. Andre was the alpha. Morty and Bernard were his entourage. They were okay with that. It was his house they shared, his boatload of money that paid for their extravagances and vices.

Andre turned his attention to the torso rotation machine. He went to it and began doing repetitions of the heavily weighted twisting motion that was so good for defining the washboard ripple of his transverse abdominals. He thought about the world he'd made for himself. Most men could only dream about living Andre's life.

When he'd first returned to work for Starling, he'd thought he'd have to give up his lifestyle. His appointment as president of Starling's Asia region could easily have become all-consuming. Fortunately, being in charge in Auckland had allowed him to shape his job description to fit his own agenda. He'd never been interested in hanging about in the office. He knew well that having good help was much more than half the battle. He'd told his people what he expected, and they'd come through. Andre had become the poster boy for hands-off management. Starling Asia's financial performance consistently equaled or exceeded projections. Big profits translated to plenty of cover against critics like his uncle. Andre was still able to devote a substantial amount of his time to working out, goofing off, and staying ahead of his two mates on the number of made women.

Andre didn't care what his uncle thought. They'd never lived under the same roof. There was an eleven-year difference between them. Greg had been off in college, and Andre had been a young boy when he and his mother had gone to live with Poppy at Shamrock. Andre and Greg had hardly known each other until long after Greg had taken over the company. Maybe Greg was jealous of the relationship Andre had built with Poppy when he was growing up. Whatever it was, Andre was fed up with Greg's disrespect. Poppy had gone toe-to-toe with Greg before he'd backed down and agreed to give Andre a chance to prove himself at Starling Asia. Despite the very respectable profits posted there since Andre's appointment, things hadn't gotten better with Greg.

As he flexed through another set on the torso rotation machine, Andre reviewed his grievances. He was most aggravated about Greg's attitude toward company sponsorship of an offshore powerboat racing team. Greg knew about Andre's passion for fast boats. Had Starling taken on the sponsorship, Andre would've been the boat's lead driver. Instead of supporting Andre, Greg had blown the idea off completely. Then, there was the thing with China. Greg had passed Andre over completely. He wasn't even at the table when the deal was made in Beijing. The final straw was Greg's heart scare. He had been out of commission for months. He could've brought Andre to New York to serve as acting CEO. Doing so would've sent a clear signal that Andre would one day succeed his uncle. The call never came.

Sure, there were differences in style. Andre knew how to have a good time. No one could say that about his uncle. Moreover, Andre had proved that a large media business could be successful, even if the boss wasn't micro-managing and manipulating the levers every hour of the day.

Morty pushed open a nearby door and came into the gym. He was carrying a case of bottled water. He pulled out one of the liter containers and handed it to Andre.

Andre said nothing. His mind was still fixed on the insults he'd absorbed from his uncle. He took a swig of water then went on to another exercise machine. Starling might be a global enterprise, but it was still a family-run business. If Greg was going to deny Andre the same opportunity Poppy had given him, so be it. The time had come to push back, and now, unexpectedly, he had the means.

The first sign of Greg Hammond's misstep had come two days earlier. Andre, with his mother's encouragement, had been using an independent security service in France to keep track of his uncle. The service used the same bank transaction surveillance system that had been put in place originally to identify criminal money laundering and bank transactions by terrorist groups. It had picked up a wire transfer of two million euros from one of Greg Hammond's personal accounts to the Equitable Health Alliance. A lot more had been revealed since then.

The money had been gifted by his uncle anonymously. A woman named Daria Kocánová had been designated to administer the funds. Andre's people already knew a lot about her, and about the Equitable Health Alliance. Credit card transactions had placed the woman in a small Bavarian village named Schalchen as recently as twenty-four hours ago. The Starling Media executive jet, the same jet Greg had never once allowed Andre to use, had been parked on the airport tarmac in Munich for nearly twenty-four hours. Coincidence? Andre didn't think so. The exact whereabouts of his uncle were still unknown. But Andre's people were on the job, working diligently to get that information.

For Andre, the die had been cast. Greg Hammond had screwed up. He'd done something reckless for somebody in his position. He'd put Starling Worldwide's standing with its most loyal and important corporate customers at risk. Andre had no intention of letting his uncle off the hook. If this episode played out as Andre hoped, it would weaken Greg's control enough to bring him down entirely. At the very least, his leadership of the company would be seriously discredited. Either way, for Andre, it was a win, the kind of win that could assure his future as leader of the Starling empire.

CHAPTER 15

DARIA TALKED GREG INTO A bike ride to the village. They had breakfast at the bakery. It tasted so good, and he was feeling so good. The exercise routine he'd followed since his surgery had made his legs and endurance strong. He'd forgotten what a relaxing, pleasant experience a bike ride could be. They were headed back to the estate, pedaling easily along the road that followed the lake's tranquil contours. The weather was clear and unseasonably warm.

During the night, Greg had sat up in bed for a time and gazed at Daria sleeping beside him. She was so beautiful, so comfortable in her own skin. Being with her made him so happy.

Shortly after sunrise, she'd awakened him with freshly brewed coffee. Then, almost immediately, there'd been another wonderful round of wrestling under the sheets. Sex had never been so joyful. Daria told him this was a celebration, this was how sex should be. He agreed wholeheartedly.

Marriage had not worked for Greg the first time. He'd loved his ex-wife, at least at the beginning. But he could not and did not blame anyone but himself and his overheated work commitment for killing that relationship.

Spending time with Daria had made Greg acutely aware of his personal shortcomings, and his need to change his ways.

He'd been alone in self-imposed isolation for a long time. He was tired of it. Daria Kocánová was the change he desperately longed for. Given his reserved nature and instinct for caution, he never expected that he would fall so hard. He'd never met anyone who'd touched his heart so deeply. How awesome it would be to celebrate his successes and his good fortune with her. How great it would be to stand beside her as she achieved her own great destiny. This was more than infatuation. But was it love? Was this wonderful woman the love he longed for? It sure felt like it. What to do about it? That was the question.

He wasn't at all sure of her feelings. Was the intimacy he'd shared with her just her way of meeting an obligation? He didn't think so. She did seem to care for him. But it was so hard to gauge how serious that was. She was much younger. Her priorities were so much different. She had a great need to make life better for others who were less fortunate. He, on the other hand, had no real history of benevolence. The gulf between them was substantial in that regard. He knew he would have to close that gap. He would have to open his heart and become much more like her. He was surprised by how much that idea appealed to him. He wanted to be a better person. He'd had enough of being self-absorbed, aloof, and alone. He didn't much like the old Greg Hammond anymore. He was eager to reveal a new and improved version. Winning the heart of an extraordinary woman like Daria Kocánová would undoubtedly require him to be a better man than he'd ever been before.

The estate was just a bit farther down the road. When they got back, he was expecting they would enjoy another intense romp in bed. In the afterglow, with her cuddled under the covers with him, he would open a dialogue and begin to explore the possibility of a more substantial future with her. For now, he thought—

"Greg," she called out. "Something's wrong."

She was pointing up the road.

Greg saw the entrance to the walled estate half a kilometer ahead. Four cars were parked in front of it. At least a dozen men were also there.

"Must be an accident," he heard Daria say as she sped off on her bike. He accelerated after her.

Then Greg saw that he and Daria had been spotted by the men clustered around the parked vehicles. He saw them bring out cameras and news video equipment.

"Daria, stop!" he called out, while jamming on his bike's brakes.

The two of them skidded to a halt about two hundred yards from the estate's entrance.

The men began running toward them with cameras and video.

"Paparazzi," he said. "They're paparazzi."

He saw the alarm on her face. He looked around for a quick escape route.

Daria took that as a cue. She turned her bike and started back up the road in the opposite direction.

"Follow me," she shouted.

He turned his bike and accelerated after her.

The paparazzi ran back to their cars. Almost immediately, they were in pursuit and closing the gap.

Daria and Greg raced up the road. The edge of the wall that bordered the estate wasn't far ahead. Just where the wall parallel to the road ended, Daria veered off the asphalt onto the road's gravel apron. She turned down a narrow path that ran away from the road along the long section of wall that stretched toward the lake. Greg was right behind her. He glanced back over his shoulder. The paparazzi were leaving their cars and chasing after them on foot.

There was an entry door built into the high wall up ahead. It was overgrown with vegetation. Daria skidded to a stop next to it. She jumped off her bike and pulled a ring of keys out of the right front pocket of her blue jeans. There were four large keys on the ring that might work in the door's old iron lock. She tried the first. It got jammed in the lock. It wouldn't come out. Greg stepped in and helped her. They got the key out. The paparazzi were getting closer.

The second key didn't work. They tried the third. It fit, but the lock was rusty. It didn't want to move. Greg struggled to turn it. Finally, it broke loose. He hit the door hard with his shoulder and pushed it open. He and Daria rushed inside with their bikes. Greg shoved the door closed just as the paparazzi were rushing up to them.

Greg locked the door, then took a moment to catch his breath.

Daria was looking very distressed. She shouted, "Who are those people?"

"Paparazzi," said Greg. He started walking his bike toward the house.

Daria was a few steps behind.

"Why?" she said.

Greg's mind was racing. How did they find him? How could this have happened?

"Somebody must have tipped them off," he said. "Somebody told them I was here."

He saw no other way to explain it. Something similar had happened to him once before, years earlier. A well-known Broadway actress had made herself available to him. He was intercepted coming out of her apartment building by a squad of paparazzi one morning. There'd never really been a relationship. No matter to the paparazzi. They had one goal. Get pictures to go with their salacious, made-up tabloid story.

"Are you okay?" Daria said.

Greg didn't respond. He was upset with himself. He'd taken precautions. He'd been careful to cover his tracks, but he knew he shouldn't be surprised. He'd deluded himself, plain and simple.

They dropped the bikes next to the house and hurried inside.

"What do they want?" Daria asked.

"Pictures. Pictures of the two of us together."

"Why?'

"I have enemies," he said, as he started up the stairs to the second floor.

Daria stayed right with him. "You know who has done this?"

He had a pretty good idea but said nothing.

When they got to the bedroom, Greg stopped to assess the moment. He understood the depth of the trouble that was coming. He felt deeply ashamed at having exposed Daria. He went to her and took her into his arms. He looked into her eyes, then kissed her forehead and said, "I told myself this wouldn't happen. I knew there was a risk. I am so sorry."

Daria was definitely mad, but her anger was directed at the intruders, not Greg. She broke away from him. "I will call the *polizei*."

Greg caught her arm and held her back. "Not a good idea."

"These people should not be here," she said angrily, as she tried to break away from him. "The polizei can make them go away."

"The way to handle this is to stay out of sight," he said.

He could see she wasn't convinced.

"Please," he said. "I know about these things."

After a moment, she calmed herself and nodded.

He searched through his travel bag lying open on the floor and found his cell phone. He'd turned the handheld device off before leaving Munich. He switched it back on. There were a slew of text messages, most of them from his assistant, Michael.

Greg looked at his watch. It was early afternoon in Germany. He thought that translated to around 8:00 a.m. in New York. He hit the speed dial for Michael's cell number. After a moment, Michael answered. Greg spent the next ten minutes on the phone conferring and plotting an exit strategy with Michael.

When Greg finished, he pocketed the phone, turned his attention back to Daria, and said, "I have to get away from here."

"No," she protested. "We have another day."

"This could get ugly. The best way I can protect you is to draw the attention away from you."

"I have to say something to somebody."

"Bad idea," he said. Then, he backed away from her and headed for the bathroom. He picked up his things from the sink and threw them in his toilet kit. He glanced up at the mirror and saw Daria standing in the doorway, staring at him sadly.

"How did these people find us?" she said.

Michael had provided the answer to that question.

"The car I drove here belongs to the company. Apparently, it has a theft transponder that can be activated by satellite."

"How did they know to look for this car?"

Greg chose to ignore the question. He looked at his watch again. "My assistant is arranging for a helicopter to pick me up."

Daria followed him back into the bedroom. He stuffed his toilet kit in a corner of his travel bag.

"You should not let them drive you away," Daria said.

"When I fly out, they'll leave," Greg said. "Getting away from here is the best thing I can do for you at this point."

He was beginning to feel sick to his stomach. He knew the cause was extreme stress. Rage, and, in a few cases, high anxiety had caused the same symptoms before. He didn't want Daria to know. He didn't want to appear weak in front of her. He knew only one way to hide it from her.

"I need to make some calls," Greg said. "Can I meet you down-stairs?"

He watched her expression change. She looked very disappointed.

"You are blaming yourself for this."

He had to be honest with her. He had to make her understand her new reality.

"Have you ever been in the public eye?"

"No," she said,

"This could get ugly," he responded.

"Because we are together?"

"They'll make it what they want to make it," he said.

"What will they say?"

"Something salacious, probably very salacious."

"Whatever comes, I will get over it."

She was trying to be cheery. It frustrated him.

"You don't know what it's like to be chased by the media."

"I am an adult."

"You're not getting it," he said.

"I have done nothing wrong," said Daria. "You have done nothing wrong."

"Doesn't matter," Greg said. "These people make their own reality. They cut, paste, and shape to fit the message."

"What message?"

"Whatever their client wants."

"What client?"

Greg lied. "Too early to know."

He struggled to contain his emotions. Though he'd forced himself to stay cool and totally in control on the outside, he was nearly consumed with rage. He knew damned well who was behind the betrayal.

Daria came to him and looked into his eyes. "Whatever they say, I don't care. I will never regret that I have been here with you."

He couldn't remember ever feeling guilty like he did at that moment. The magic he'd shared with Daria had been shattered. He'd been so happy. There had been such joy in his heart. Until the intrusion of the paparazzi, he'd been eager and excited about the possibility of a seri-ous commitment with Daria. The pendulum had now shifted hard the other direction. He understood too well the trouble that was coming. His stomach began to cramp.

He hugged her, then backed away. He picked up his cell phone, then looked at Daria.

"I need to do damage control. It may take a while."

She studied him for a moment, then said. "Would you like some tea?"

"That would be good," Greg said. "Thank you."

She gave his arm a reassuring touch, then turned and left the room.

Greg knew her life was going to be turned upside down. He'd blown it. He couldn't imagine the possibility of another chance with her. It was painful beyond words.

CHAPTER 16

GREG CHECKED HIS WATCH AS his helicopter ride approached the airport in Innsbruck, Austria. Less than four hours had passed since the paparazzi had killed his weekend with Daria. As soon as the rotorcraft touched the ground, Greg jumped out and sprinted across the tarmac to the company jet. Ten minutes later, the G650 roared down the runway into the sky.

Almost immediately, the sleek jet banked eastward, away from the low afternoon sun.

Greg felt the increased pressure from the aircraft's hard turn pushing against him. He looked out the window at the rapidly receding ground below. Daria had tried to get him to eat before the helicopter arrived. He hadn't felt like it. Now that his gut had settled down, he was ravenous. He unbuckled his seatbelt and went to the small galley just behind the jet's cockpit. In the fridge, he found his favorite snack, sliced turkey with provolone on a kaiser bun. He grabbed for it, then stopped. He thought about Daria, playfully teasing him about his meat habit. He pushed the sandwich back into the fridge and took out a pre-packaged salad instead. He began to devour it.

The satellite phone by the cabin's small, fold-out desk began to buzz. Greg settled into the leather chair by the phone and pulled it from its bulkhead cradle. Caller ID showed it was Michael phoning from the Starling office in New York.

Greg put the phone to his ear. "What do we know?"

"Breaking out all over, sir."

"What's the line?"

"Two lines," Michael said. "You know Pastor Red Mickens?"

"Remind me."

"Mega-church preacher in Houston."

"What about him?"

"He's demanding a boycott," Michael said. "All Starling publications and broadcasts."

"Let me guess," Greg said. "My money is now in the hands of radical abortionists."

"They hurt the company, they hurt you, sir," Michael said.

That's the whole point, Greg thought. A hack preacher couldn't have launched that kind of attack on his own, no way. Couldn't have happened so quickly, unless someone was deliberately stirring the pot, purposely trying to link Greg's generosity to abortion, despite there being only the flimsiest, indirect connection.

"What's the other line?" Greg said.

"Sex for money," Michael said. "Radio talkers are all over it."

Greg had expected that as well. He'd stipulated that his entire donation should be directed to Daria's program to empower women, and to provide medicine to fight treatment-resistant tuberculosis among the poor. None of the media appeared to be covering that part of the erupting media story.

"Anything out of the Asia group?"

"Nothing, sir."

Greg wasn't surprised. Andre was too smart to allow his own newspapers, magazines, and TV networks to report on the scandal. Though he had no proof, Greg was certain Andre was behind it all. He had to be the one who tipped off the tabloids. How else could the paparazzi have found him in Schalchen? Who else had reason to betray him? Who else had the motivation to launch a media assault, perfectly pitched to undermine Greg's standing with the company's directors and shareholders?

Andre's vanity and arrogance were beyond description. His only real distinction was his all-star status as a sexual predator. Until now, Greg had viewed Andre primarily with scorn. He'd never taken his nephew seriously as an adversary. In retrospect, that was a major league error.

The concept of anonymity had become increasingly vaporous in recent decades because of the proliferation of advanced AI spying and surveillance technology, and the power of social media. Greg had been fully aware of the risk in the arrangement he'd made with Daria. He'd allowed his personal need to overrule his professional judgment. He was disgusted with himself for giving Andre an opening.

"All company outlets have been alerted," Michael said. "None of them will cover the story. We're also asking our competitors for professional courtesy."

"Fat chance," Greg said. His industry rivals were not his friends. Asking them to back off the story was a formality. Even in the case of those few rivals with whom Greg maintained cordial relationships, the best that could be hoped for was maybe a little less edge and sensationalism in their reporting.

The media jackals were circling. Greg knew he couldn't afford to let blind emotion impair his judgment, at least no more than he had already. He had to knock the story down quickly before it became a firestorm.

"Where are you, sir?"

"Just out of Innsbruck for Mumbai, then direct to Auckland," Greg said. "Anything else?"

"The M&A team wants to help."

Greg was pleased but not surprised. The eleven young men and women that were on his Mergers and Acquisitions Team were all outstanding, all entirely committed and eager for success. Like Michael, they shared a special loyalty to Greg. Over the years, graduates from his M&A team had gone on to fill top executive positions throughout the company. A lot of the company's success came down to these people. Greg had hired them all personally. Technically, team members were consultants to Starling, not employees. Their employment contracts were with Greg. He paid their salaries. They reported to him only, directly or through Michael. No one else in the company was privy to their work. No one saw any of it without his approval.

"A little out of the box for them."

"Might be an advantage," Michael said.

Greg liked it. In the past, he'd given team members special assignments from time to time, but never anything of this consequence. His 'To-Do' list included the hiring of an outside PR firm to restore his reputation and push back against those trying to tear down Daria. That was not a role for Starling's in-house PR people. They had to be focused strictly on damage control for the company.

From Greg's perspective, trust was the critical factor. The M&A group were his close support. He preferred not to assign his personal welfare or, more important, Daria's future directly to outsiders. "What's the team thinking?"

"The public needs to recognize your gift for what it was," Michael said. "An act of kindness and generosity."

"How?"

"Reframe the story," Michael said. "Saturate the media with honest information about this Equitable Health Alliance. We've checked them out. Trust me, sir, there's no shame in being associated with them. They're good people."

"Whatever we do, it's got to be rooted in truth," Greg said. "No phony bull."

"We understand the need for discretion, sir," Michael said. "M&A will handle everything down to the copywriting. We use outside help only to get the message out."

"Only as distributors," Greg said.

"Yes, sir."

Greg quickly responded, "Words and pictures come from us."

"Yes, sir."

"The team should also consider Ms. Kocánová their client," Greg said. "Whatever they can do to dampen the crap being thrown at her, they should do."

Just over five hours later, the Starling jet touched down in Mumbai, India, to refuel. Greg was feeling better. He'd had time to rest and shed some of the toxic emotion in his body. He'd had time to think.

Direct confrontation with Andre didn't look good anymore. Nothing positive could come from a titanic, face-to-face showdown. Greg decided to put all his energy into pushing back against his nephew's betrayal.

Greg told his pilots to alter the flight plan. They would now fly directly from Mumbai to Christchurch.

As the Starling jet sped eastward, Greg got regular satellite phone reports from Michael. The emerging stories presented Greg as a foolish and irresponsible philanderer who'd insanely paid two million euros for sex. The story stuck because it had elements of truth. Shading things in the media through obfuscation, misdirection, bluster, and outright fabrication was easy. You could sell almost any idea if the media's focus could be shaped and maintained long enough.

Daria was being portrayed mercilessly, particularly by European tabloids, as a big-money whore. Greg felt both angry and guilty about it. But he had to keep his head. The best way he could help Daria was to push back aggressively against the assault. The M&A team had gotten back to him with a plan. They were now operating in crisis mode, trying to reframe the story, limit its spread, and dampen its impact. They were doing all they could for Daria.

Given that fact, Greg focused his attention on defending his leadership of the company. Michael had an unconfirmed report that Andre was talking with Starling's major shareholders. No doubt, he wanted the ugly gossip story to expand into a major controversy that required the board to intercede. If Andre were successful, he'd have a legitimate shot at bringing Greg down as CEO.

Andre and Lydia needed thumbs-down from two-thirds of all shareholders to remove Greg as CEO. Poppy had eighteen percent of the voting shares in the company. Greg had twenty percent. Poppy's votes were all that was keeping Greg in place. It was a tenuous circumstance, but it hadn't ever mattered because Greg's performance as CEO had always been so impressive and so profitable. Nobody was going to kick a guy out when he was making them big money.

Starling's fat profits were now at risk. Greg couldn't afford to assume Poppy would stand behind him. Job one was mending that fence. He had to keep Poppy on his side. If he could secure old Jack Hammond's blessing, the media fire might be quenched before it got out of hand.

The relationship between father and son had always been strong. But Greg had lived halfway around the world from Poppy for much more than a decade. Face-to-face meetings rarely happened more than once a year. Before the stroke, they'd talked daily by phone. Since then, it had been sporadic at best. Greg blamed himself for not being more diligent in maintaining his relationship with his father. He knew well that Lydia and Andre had filled the void in the old man's life. They'd made themselves at home and built a strong relationship with Poppy. Proof of that had come when they convinced Poppy to use his influence against Greg, forcing him to install Andre as CEO of Starling Asia.

The Starling Company jet arrived midafternoon in Christchurch, twenty-one hours after leaving Innsbruck. Greg was exhausted. He was also pumped on adrenaline. He jumped in a taxi. Less than an hour later, he pushed open the front door at Shamrock. He hadn't called ahead. No one was expecting him. At least, that's what he'd thought.

Lydia suddenly emerged from a nearby room.

"Brother," she said.

Greg kept his anger in check. "Where's Poppy?"

"You think walking in here unannounced will get you somewhere?"

"Where is he?"

"He knows what you did," Lydia said. "He knows the damage you've done."

She wanted a fight. Greg had more important business. He turned away from her. A few moments later, he found his father napping outside on the veranda. Eddie was nearby, as were Hap and Randy. The dogs barked and came to Greg, tails wagging excitedly. Greg spent a few moments with them, then he shared a hug with Eddie.

Greg glanced at his father, who was just coming out of his nap.

"How's he doing?" Greg said to Eddie.

"Not happy with you," Eddie said.

Greg went over and bent down and shared a hug with Poppy. Then, the old man swatted him with his left hand.

"Poppy, you haven't heard my side of the story."

The old man shook his fist at Greg and made a noise like a snarl.

Greg pulled up a chair and began to lay out events as he saw them. He told his father about Daria Kocánová, and about her impressive work. None of that made any kind of good impression. The old man was angry.

Greg understood. For his father, the issue was simple. Greg had been a damned fool. His reckless behavior had damaged Starling's standing with its all-important ad buyers and undermined the company's shareholder value.

A one-time, two-million-euro donation to a group whose mission was about alleviating suffering and providing health care to people who had no place else to go should be above reproach. Providing family planning, contraception, and abortion was a very small part of what they did. Under any other circumstance, no one would even have noticed. The thing had become ugly because it was purposely exposed to the world with the abortion tag placed front and center. Lydia was obviously in cahoots with Andre, fanning the flames, poisoning Poppy's perception.

Frustrated and weary from his long journey, Greg said, "Poppy, yes or no, do I have your support?"

Poppy stared at him with an aggravated expression but offered no signal that defined his thinking.

"Yes or no, Poppy," Greg said. "I need to know."

The old man appeared to be purposely withholding his answer.

"You started the company. I made it what it is now, right?"

No response.

"Isn't that right?" Greg said. "I made the company what it is, yes or no?"

Reluctantly, Poppy agreed.

"I need your support," Greg said. "I need your support so I can make things right."

The old man grumbled unintelligibly.

"Poppy, I need an answer," Greg said. "We can't leave this hanging. Do I have your support, yes or no?"

After a moment, the old man nodded affirmatively.

Greg wanted in the worst way to point the finger at Lydia and Andre. He wanted to make the case against them, to expose their betrayal, to vent the rage he felt. At the same time, he understood how much more it would stress his father to be backed into a corner and forced to choose between his only son or his only daughter and only grandchild. At some point, there would be a reckoning. But, given Poppy's fragile condition, now was not the time.

"Poppy, we both know I'm under attack," Greg said. "It's not going to go away. Not for a while."

Jack was looking directly at Greg. He might not be able to speak, but his mind appeared to be functioning well enough.

"I'm counting on you," Greg said. "I need to know you're watching my back."

Jack raised his good arm and shook a warning finger at Greg.

"No worries," Greg said. "We've got our best people on this. We'll make it right."

Jack calmed himself and nodded affirmatively.

Greg leaned back in his chair and took a deep breath. He felt completely drained, emotionally and physically. He couldn't leave for New York right away. He had to remain in New Zealand at least a day while his air crew got the legally required rest time after the long flight from Europe. He thought about checking into a hotel, then dismissed the idea. He'd be damned if he was going to let Lydia drive him away from the house where he grew up. He went down to the kitchen, had a quick meal, then went up to his old bedroom and crashed.

Early the next morning, he called his pilots and told them to get ready for departure. Then, he dressed and joined his father for breakfast. It was more pleasant, more like old times, than the night before.

Jack Hammond affirmed his support once more.

Greg wondered what had happened to Lydia. When he arrived, she'd appeared suddenly as if she'd been expecting him. In the time since, he hadn't seen her. He was eager to get to the airport, but he also felt a great need to confront his sister.

"Have you seen Lydia?" Greg asked Eddie.

"Outside," Eddie said. He pointed out one of the large windows that overlooked the gardens that stretched to the bay.

Greg went to the window. Lydia was lounging in the gazebo some distance from the house. Greg wasn't surprised. She'd put herself in a place that was conducive to argument without being overheard by Poppy in the house.

"See you at the car," Greg said to Eddie. Then, after saying his good-byes to his father, he went outside and headed straight for the gazebo.

Lydia was stretched out on a cushioned lounge, smoking a cigarette and reading some kind of romance novel. She saw Greg approaching. She ignored him.

Greg came up and stood over her. He was determined to keep his head.

"How do I deal with you?" Greg said coldly to Lydia.

She glared at him with a smug expression.

Greg continued, "It feels like I'm caught up in some kind of lame Shakespearean tragedy."

"You made your own mess," Lydia said dismissively.

"Can we dispense with the bullshit?" Greg said. "We both know why I'm under attack."

"Look in the mirror," she said. "Your wounds are self-inflicted."

Greg was disgusted with Lydia's attitude.

"We share the same father," Greg said. "How do you think this kind of backstabbing affects him?"

Lydia jumped up from the lounge chair and got in Greg's face. "Don't lecture me about Poppy. If you cared about him, you'd show up here more than once a year. What's the motivation for this visit, family reminiscing or saving your ass?"

Greg was stung by the ring of truth in what Lydia had just said. There were choices he had to atone for, but he wasn't about to hash them out with his self-absorbed sister.

"Show Andre some respect," said Lydia. "That's the way to get along."

"I see," Greg said. "I kiss his ass, all is well."

"He wants the world to know he's next in line."

Greg stepped in close until his face was inches from hers. "You tell my dear nephew, he fucks with me again, we'll see who's left standing."

Lydia didn't flinch. "You're done. It's just a matter of time."

"Consider yourself warned," he said. Then he turned and walked away.

Lydia called out, "Congratulations on your new world record, most ever paid for a one-night shag."

Greg kept his rage in check and continued walking.

CHAPTER 17

DARIA WIPED AWAY THE CONDENSATION fogging her office window. She peered out. The media thugs were still there. All day they'd been there, seven paparazzi armed with video gear hanging out under a tree near the Anthropology Building's entrance. Two campus security people were also there, keeping the scandal mongers separated from several dozen angry students, who were shouting insults and demanding their removal.

In the eleven days since Daria's connection to Greg Hammond had been exposed, she'd kept to her schedule at the university. The ragged squad of media scandal mongers had hounded her every public moment. It was embarrassing and deeply intrusive. She despised the paparazzi, but she refused to hide. She was not going to compromise her dignity. She was not going to cower in the shadows.

She glanced into a mirror hanging on a nearby wall. She felt good about the person she saw. The moral corruption the scandal mongers were claiming was a sham. Since the trouble began, she'd held her head high and refused to respond to ugly stories in the media. When in public, she was followed by reporters and cameras. She ignored them and the questions, crude and otherwise, that they hurled at her. She was not going to apologize for using her personal sexual power to achieve outcomes that were positive and decent. It did make her angry that the media showed little interest in reporting the compassionate context of her work. She was determined to rise above their slander. What she could not accept was the intrusion on her time. She had a project she was committed to. The media attention was seriously hampering her ability to advance her agenda. It was hard to get useful things accomplished while she was being hounded every waking moment by a camera-toting goon squad.

There was also some concern about the impact the media attacks might have on her academic standing. Her thesis advisor, Professor Mittermeier, and other members of the Department of Anthropology faculty, were firmly behind her, but the university administration was not happy about the negative attention.

Far from feeling shame, Daria was proud of what she stood for, but no question, the attacks on her personal integrity were putting her project and her future at risk.

Daria's cell phone signaled an incoming text. The car she'd been expecting was waiting. She grabbed her trench coat and pulled it on. The time had come to confront the controversy.

When the paparazzi saw Daria come out of the Anthropology Building, they came running. The two campus security people ignored the paparazzi and held off the protesting students.

A boorish, overweight guy barely in his twenties thrust a microphone in Daria's face.

"Tom Tarver, *Atlanta Beat*. What's a two-million-dollar fuck feel like?"

Daria ignored the crude provocation. She had experienced two other guys just like this, sent by sleazy social media outlets to provoke an angry reaction from her. She kept a neutral expression, her eyes straight ahead, looking at the street fifty meters distant.

"Give us a look, bitch," a voice behind her said.

She ignored the remark.

The guy with the microphone hurled another question. "Tom Tarver, *Atlanta Beat*. How much for a big-money blowjob?"

Daria didn't care how offensive it got. She was not going to react.

Then, she felt somebody grab her sleeve from behind. She was spun around and pulled off balance. A storm of camera flashes fired off.

Enraged, the students standing by broke away from the security officials and rushed toward Daria and her assailants.

Daria faced the students and held up her hands.

"Stop," she shouted. "Stop, please. No fighting, please."

The students pulled up short of attacking the paparazzi. The two security officials quickly placed themselves between the students and the media thugs.

Daria smiled at the students and said, "Thank you for this gesture."

The air crackled with tension. The paparazzi held their ground and kept taking photos. The students continued to hurl insults. They would not back off. The entire university community knew what was happening to Daria. She was acquainted with many of the students who were there to support her.

Daria looked at the security officials and pointed at the students. "You have an objection if my friends walk with me?"

The two officials looked at each other, then they turned their attention to holding back the paparazzi.

Daria gestured for the students to join her. They formed a protective screen around her as she walked toward the street. One student came up and hugged her, then another, and another. By the time they reached the street, she'd exchanged warm greetings with all the students escorting her.

She spotted the silver BMW sedan waiting nearby. So did the paparazzi. They went running for their cars.

Daria thanked the students one more time, then she jumped in the BMW and pulled the door shut.

The vehicle accelerated on its way.

A petite brunette woman in her early forties was sitting across from Daria in the back seat. Anke Vögel, was CEO of Fangen Gruppe, one of Germany's largest and most influential public relations firms. Anke was also a friend of Angelika.

"You okay?" Anke said.

"Yes," Daria said. She was furious. "That was almost a fight."

"I saw what happened," Anke said. "You handled it very well."

"Somebody could've been hurt."

"Didn't happen," Anke said. "You stopped it."

"So crude," Daria said. "I ignore them, they get more aggressive."

"They provoke to get a reaction," Anke said.

Angelika had hired Anke without Daria's knowledge three days earlier. At first, Daria had resisted. Angelika had insisted she at least listen to what Anke had to say. There was a conference call. Daria liked Anke's contention that her misfortune with the media could be turned to advantage. She also liked Anke's proposed strategy.

"One of them grabbed me," Daria said. "This is harassment."

"They are hired for their aggression," Anke said.

"It is not welcome," Daria said angrily. She thought about Angelika. She was keeping her distance. So far, the relationship they shared had not become part of the salacious gossip. Daria had kept frustration in check because she knew Angelika was still a mere phone call away. They had talked by phone countless times in recent days. She wished Angelika could be with her now.

As the BMW turned a corner onto another street, Anke said, "I have good news."

Daria was eager to hear something positive.

"We have a service that tracks stories for us," Anke said. "We had them pull everything they could find on you. They found a lot."

"How is that good?"

"In the first days, the reporting was all negative," Anke said. "Now, not so much. Somebody is working very hard behind the scenes to push positive stories about your work with EHA."

Daria assumed it was Greg. Four days had passed since she'd heard from him. The call had been awkward. His anger had barely been in check. He'd apologized over and over and had given her assurances he was using his considerable resources to dampen the media frenzy that had taken over her life. Since then, she had not heard from him.

Before the conversation had ended, Daria had asked Greg if he would object if she chose at some point to talk to the media about her program for the women of Haiti and Ethiopia. He'd been totally supportive. Whatever she wanted to do in that regard was fine with him. If he hadn't said that she would not be on her way to her first public interview.

Anke had done another very good thing. She'd said Daria's media project should have a name, a handle that was relatable and easily assimilated. The title Anke came up with was *Bright Eve.*

The title for her project had not been high on Daria's list of priorities, but *Bright Eve* felt like such a good fit that she'd embraced it immediately.

Daria glanced back and saw the paparazzi were in their cars, following right behind the BMW. She disliked them intensely. She wanted her life back. She convinced herself again that Anke's strategy was going to work. At the very least, she hoped it would be enough to get rid of her unwanted entourage.

There was nothing complicated about the plan. It had two parts. The first was specifically designed to diminish Daria's value to the paparazzi. Hours earlier, Anke's people had flooded the internet with photos of Daria. They were royalty-free. News outlets didn't have to pay for them. Why pay for intrusive, high-priced freelance paparazzi photos, when a ton of free images were readily available? That was the idea. Kill the demand for what the paparazzi were pedaling.

Feeding the television news monster was the other part of the strategy. Anke had worked back channels to create the right opportunity. The moment was at hand. Daria wanted to be at her best. She sat back in the car seat, closed her eyes, focused inward, and allowed the tension in her body to flow away.

Less than ten minutes later, the BMW arrived at the Metropole, a new hotel off the six motorway, west of Prague, near the airport. Daria and Anke took the elevator to the twelfth floor. They found the BBC News broadcast crew set up in a suite with a view of old Prague's skyline six miles distant.

At 5:10 p.m., Daria was seated in front of the video crew, ready to go. The link opened to London via satellite. The interview was live on the hour-long *Daily News Review* that was broadcast weekdays on BBC2. The interviewer, Sue Nevin, was in-studio at BBC Television Centre.

After introducing the segment, Sue Nevin turned her attention to Daria. "Good evening, Ms. Kocánová."

Daria smiled and nodded agreeably.

"We've just been informed that you were at the center of a testy exchange today at your university," said Sue Nevin. "Could you talk about that?"

Amazing, Daria thought. *The incident happened much less than an hour ago, and the BBC already knows about it.* After carefully considering her answer, she said, "I was walking at my university, and a man grabbed me from behind."

"A paparazzi?"

"Yes," Daria said. Then she chuckled. "I am very popular with them these days."

"What happened?"

"I was almost pulled down. Some students saw this. They came to my aid. That is the end of the story."

"Nothing happened?"

"Nothing," Daria said.

"Some outlets are reporting things got quite ugly," Sue Nevin said.

Daria smiled, shook her head, and said, "Nothing happened."

Sue Nevin accepted Daria's confident response, then she glanced at her interview notes, and went on, "The Equitable Health Alliance has confirmed it recently received an anonymous gift of two million euros to which you are attached as administrator. What can you tell us about that?"

Daria had been advised by Anke to keep her answers short, a few sentences at most. She responded to the question with a brief review of her *Bright Eve* empowerment program for women and an endorsement of Marc Wren's ground-breaking work with treatment-resistant tuberculosis.

"How does abortion fit into this?" Sue Nevin said.

"There is no connection," Daria said. "The money for our program goes only to education, nothing more."

"If that is so—"

"I assure you, it is so."

"Then you oppose abortion?"

"Not at all. I support choice. Abortion is a personal decision for each woman. It should not be a public issue."

"What do you say to people who criticize your abortion stance?"

"They are misguided," Daria said. "The work we do is focused entirely on education for women."

"You must know that, especially in the US, you are being heavily criticized."

"I have heard that."

"How do you answer your critics?"

"They are wrong to impose their ideology on others, especially people whose stories they don't—can't possibly—understand."

"You've seen this firsthand?"

"I have. The point is this: we have one place to live. This is the only planet we have. There are too many of us, too many people. More than eight billion humans on Earth, much more than double the population just fifty years ago. We know more than a billion of those people, maybe two billion, don't have enough to eat. They do not have enough clean water, no sanitation, not even the most basic medical care, little or no education… So many of those people are in constant fear of violence. We all should imagine ourselves living this way."

"That would make a difference?"

"Compassion begins with awareness and understanding."

"The work you do with the Equitable Health Alliance is a step in the right direction?"

"Yes, of course. We focus on educating women in developing countries. We want to help them help themselves."

"Why women?"

"Half of us are female. That half of humanity is not getting the attention they deserve. In many traditional societies, women receive little or no education and are still treated as if they are property."

"Modern-day slavery," Sue Nevin said.

"We know, providing women with access to even the most basic education gives them the tools they need to feel empowered to accomplish their goals. We encourage women so they can help themselves and their communities. This is a very positive step."

Sue Nevin glanced at her notes, then took the dialogue in a new direction. "You know Starling Media CEO, Greg Hammond?"

"Yes."

"He has a reputation for being tough and very assertive in business."

"I have not seen that."

"You like him?"

"Yes," Daria said. "What I see is a good man."

"There's been a lot of speculation about the time you recently spent with him."

"Yes."

"Would you like to clarify the record on that?"

"No," Daria said, with a smile. "This is not somebody else's business."

"Do you worry that remaining quiet on this leaves the media open to fill in the blanks themselves?"

"They have already been doing that."

"It doesn't bother you?"

"I don't care. I know the truth."

"Is Greg Hammond the anonymous donor of the two million euros?"

Daria thought a moment, then answered, "The definition of anonymous is clear enough. The focus should be on the good that will come from this gift."

"The tabloids have been over the top on the money-for-sex angle of this story. What do you say to that?"

"People can think what they like. I focus on the positive that will come from what we are doing."

"What do you stand to gain personally from your efforts?"

"I feel good about myself."

"No financial reward?"

"The money that was gifted goes to people who are most in need."

"You got none of it?"

"None," Daria said. "The accounting is clear. EHA has made it public. I am fortunate. I have a busy life. For me, the greatest satisfaction comes from helping women have a voice."

"That's what motivates you?"

"You can be part of the problem or you can be part of the solution," Daria said.

"You see yourself as part of the solution," Sue Nevin said.

Daria nodded. "Half of all people on this planet are women. In too many places, they have no voice. This must change."

"Why is it that men and women find it so hard to get on the same page?"

"We are together in many ways," Daria said. "In the human society we know, to be a man carries with it the expectation of being dominant. This is a curse. For thousands of years, this has been a burden for all people. Men believe their job is to conquer and control. This affects every aspect of life. We must find a better direction. We must choose cooperation. For women, this comes more naturally than for men. More cooperation, making women full partners to men, equal in all ways, this is the way the world must go."

"Women have been working toward equality for a long time," Sue Nevin said.

"Many men have also come far."

Sue Nevin responded, "We still have a way to go."

"Of course," Daria said. "The world has many problems. Some are very big. We cannot—we will not—have a good future without a cultural commitment to human cooperation on all levels."

"Wonderful sentiment," Sue Nevin said. "What do you make of all the attention you've been getting?"

"This is not something I have wished for."

"You seem to be handling it well."

"You must understand," Daria said, "I have work to do. Useful things rarely get done when the spotlight shines so brightly."

"Fame doesn't suit you."

"Not even a little."

With that, Sue Nevin thanked Daria and ended the interview.

------◆------

Greg was in his New York office, viewing a taped replay of Daria's BBC interview on one of the video monitors adjacent to his desk. He'd already watched it twice. In a word, Daria had been stunning. The interview had completely overshadowed the other emerging story on Daria, that just prior to the interview, she had assaulted a photographer and had nearly caused a riot on her university campus.

That story was particularly infuriating for Greg. It was a fabrication, a brazen, audacious lie. That fact had been confirmed, when he watched raw video of the entire incident shot by a student and posted on YouTube. In that footage, the truth was unambiguous. It was Daria who'd been attacked. She had instigated nothing, and had, in fact, been a conciliator, calming students coming to her aid, preventing a potentially violent incident with the paparazzi.

It was after 7:00 p.m. in New York. The lights were turned off in Greg's office. He was alone, thinking how much he hated the ugliness that had come Daria's way. Even more, he was mad at himself, angry and pained by the fact that he was the cause of it. He'd recognized the threat but had failed to prepare for it in a serious way. Sure, his relationship with Lydia and Andre was toxic. But he hadn't expected it could become as malignant as this.

Greg reached down and opened the big drawer on the bottom left side of his desk. Then, he leaned back in his chair, put his feet up on the open drawer, and closed his eyes.

Despite the seed being aggressively planted, the baseless fabrication that Greg Hammond hated babies and had recklessly given money to abortionists had not taken root. The company's public relations group had done its job. The price of Starling common stock was nearly back to the pre-incident level. Advertising revenue had dipped but had rebounded to where it had been.

In an unexpected way, Greg's image had also evolved. He'd never tried to discourage the public perception that he was a power-hungry, corporate predator. He knew there was truth in that observation. At times, it had been useful to be feared. He'd operated that way for years, pretty much indifferent to the consequences.

It seemed that, as a result of the gifting of two million euros to the Equitable Health Alliance, the public view of Greg Hammond had begun to shift. News polls conducted over the past few days had been pretty consistent. His anonymous gift was no longer anonymous. The public in general still wasn't crazy about him, but they did approve of his generosity. Moreover, his extreme 'unfavorables' had shrunk by nearly twenty percent.

Though significant credit was due to the company's PR people, Greg knew his M&A team was most responsible. Operating entirely under the table, they'd focused on promoting the Equitable Health Alliance, elevating it from a mostly obscure existence to a relevant place on the public stage. People now knew the EHA as an organization with entirely noble and decent intentions. The reporting also showed Daria to be an activist with deep and abiding conviction. It was a potent counterweight against the pernicious assault by moral extremists.

Since the incident began, along with the polling, Greg's office had received daily surveys of the stories on the issue appearing in the media. Around the world, the number of places still reporting on the incident had dropped off substantially. Where interest remained, media outlets were providing at least as many favorable stories as unfavorable. He appreciated very much what the M&A team had done for Daria's image and for his own.

Greg got up from his desk and walked over in front of the big video monitor on which a loop of Daria's interview was playing. She was just saying, "You can be part of the problem, or you can be part of the solution."

Powerful words. Everything Daria had said reflected her intelligence, integrity, and decency. Without a doubt, she was her own greatest advocate.

Greg felt certain she was going to be okay, maybe even better than okay. Everything was now trending in the right direction.

On the video screen, Daria was saying, "Useful things rarely get done when the spotlight shines so brightly."

Her wisdom is elegant, Greg thought. He punched a button, freezing Daria's image on the screen. He wanted to call her. He wanted to tell her how brilliant she'd been in her interview. He started to pull out his cell phone. Then, he thought about it some more.

He had to be honest with himself. Yes, his heart was filled with passion for Daria. When they'd been together, she made him feel like he was the only man in the world. It had been wonderful. He'd felt completely connected to her.

But the ugliness that followed had altered the landscape dramatically. How could Daria have any real feelings for him given the anguish he'd brought her? He shoved the phone back into his pocket.

Because of Greg's incaution, Daria had been caught up in a sex scandal that had become an ugly sensation worldwide. Her interview made clear she was not happy about it. She wanted it to go away. It just seemed there was so much working against them. On top of everything else, there were other men in her life, and there was her long-standing relationship with Angelika Grünberg.

What would calling her accomplish? It would be awkward at best, painfully distressing at worst. Moreover, it would be directly contrary to the advice of his lawyers. They had strongly urged Greg to avoid any further contact with her.

There was so little common ground. They were so different. He'd flourished as an enabler of power and privilege. She was blossoming as a champion of indigent women. Was a lasting relationship possible under such circumstances? Perhaps, but only if he became more like her. He doubted she could ever be comfortable in the high-end world of commerce where he lived.

There was also Greg's responsibility to Starling shareholders, and to the nearly twenty-three thousand Starling employees around the world. He couldn't allow the company to fall into the hands of his nephew. Such a prospect was intolerable.

No question, there was plenty to be pleased about. Andre's treachery had fallen flat. The firestorm over the two-million-euro gift to the Equitable Health Alliance was near to being extinguished. All the large institutional shareholders in the company had affirmed their support.

Greg's leadership was secure, but he saw himself trapped in a Faustian compromise. To prevent the intolerable, he had no choice. Remaining in place as Starling CEO, keeping the company operating business as usual, was the only way for him to block Andre's eventual coronation. It was the only way to buy time while a more acceptable strategy for succession could emerge.

Sitting in front of the computer at his desk, Greg punched in a search request for images of Daria. Hundreds of images came up. A substantial share were royalty-free. There were even video clips from the moment he and Daria were first spotted by the paparazzi on the road by the lake in Germany. Greg began to cycle through the photos. Some reflected the paparazzi assault Daria had been forced to endure. Others were from her time as a fashion model. More than a few images showcased her in remote locations—the Congo with bonobos, in Southeast Asia, supporting the Dyak Indigenous peoples, in Haiti, at the EHA-funded medical clinic.

Daria clearly had a deep well of caring and decency in her heart. Some was manifested as romantic passion but even more seemed directed into her genuine and uncommon empathy for nature and for the literally hundreds of millions of people in the world who endured life at its most basic and unvarnished.

Greg focused his mind again. He was desperate for inspiration, eager for some idea or pathway that offered a chance of a future with Daria. The picture he saw was depressing. It seemed the best way to support her at this point was to leave her alone and allow her to get on with her life.

Christmas was coming. There would be parties to attend, much schmoozing with the rich and famous. But there would be no joy in it. Despite socializing, for Greg, it boiled down to another holiday season alone. Daria was the gift he wanted most of all. In his life, there'd never been anything or anyone he wished for more. But, as wealthy as he was, as influential as he was, there seemed no strategy, no card that could be turned over, that offered a realistic chance for a future with her. As holidays went, this one was going to be especially painful to endure.

CHAPTER 18

DARIA SIPPED FROM A CUP of hot, cinnamon apple cider. She loved the Christmas Market in Munich's Marienplatz. The place was jammed with shoppers visiting colorfully lit booths selling all kinds of homemade crafts and holiday treats.

Beneath the Neues Rathaus-Glockenspiel Tower, Daria and Angelika took a moment from their shopping to listen to a horn quartet playing a festive version of *O' Tannenbaum.*

The happiest thing about the holiday this year was the absence of the paparazzi. Anke's clever strategy had worked brilliantly. It was such a relief to stroll the market with Angelika in the early-evening chill without being hounded by a clutch of ill-mannered thugs clicking cameras in her face.

Following the interview on the BBC just over a week earlier, a big-time cover story had appeared in the German weekly, *Der Spiegel.* The article, written by the magazine's rising star investigative journalist, Elsie Liesl Krauss, focused not on the scandal but on Daria's relationship with the Equitable Health Alliance and Marc Wren. The article included many photographs of Marc and his team working with patients in Haiti and Ethiopia. The chronic poverty in those places was starkly presented in pictures. The story was brought close to home by Daria's retelling of the miracle of the three deathly sick Haitian children who were reanimated before her eyes by hydration fluids contributed by the German government. There was only one picture of Daria. It showed her feeding a sick patient in Marc's hospital in Haiti.

For Daria, the biggest thrill was the way her empowerment program was showcased.

Daria loved the positive press *Bright Eve* was receiving but was annoyed by the continuing media focus on her. She had thought the print coverage would diminish the public's interest. Instead, the opposite happened. After the *Der Spiegel* article came out, there were even more requests for print and television interviews. It seemed the whole world knew about her.

Earlier in the day, before coming to the Marienplatz, she and Angelika had stopped at the Tiergarten with treats for the bonobos. The exhibit was now open to the public. While there, Daria had been approached by several people who recognized her from the *Der Speigel* article. One of them had insisted on giving her a hug. Becoming a public figure had come without warning, but if it helped to bring more focus to the ongoing human struggle in places like Haiti, she could learn to live with it, and heartfelt hugs were always welcome.

A few minutes later, in the Marienplatz, while Daria was purchasing gingerbread from a Christmas vendor, an elderly shopper approached her. Yes, she told the woman, she was the one who'd been in *Der Spiegel*. The old frau took Daria's hand and thanked her for being strong, and for trying to make the world better for those living on the margins.

It was very gratifying to be appreciated this way. Daria hoped her elevated public profile would help her *Bright Eve* program. So far, the signs were encouraging. The video material for the first learning module was to be shot in South Africa in January by a freelance video crew that regularly worked with UNESCO, the United Nations Education, Science, and Health Organization. One of the education specialists from the university was going down with an assistant professor who had directed many educational videos. They would manage the production, to ensure the scripts were followed and the highest production value was achieved.

For Daria, it was thrilling to think that within months, she would be in the field, launching *Bright Eve's* demonstration phase.

An hour later, just after dark, a taxi dropped Daria and Angelika back at the Kaulbach-Strasse stadthaus. They carried their bags of holiday gifts and goodies purchased in the Marienplatz to the front door and entered the house. On a chair by the door, there were two FedEx boxes. They'd been signed for by Angelika's part-time housekeeper. The return address on both was Starling Worldwide, New York.

"So," Angelika said, "he finally makes contact."

Daria was surprised and pleased to hear from Greg. She said, "One for each of us."

They opened the boxes as they walked into the house's elegant, high-ceilinged parlor. Inside each box was a small Christmas package along with a sealed card. They opened their cards and read them.

"Tell me," Daria said.

"Handwritten, from Greg," Angelika said. She read Greg's note aloud. "Thank you for sharing your wonderful friend with me. She is a treasure beyond description."

Daria blushed.

"I would love for a man to say this about me," Angelika said. "Especially one who is rich and powerful like this one."

Daria turned her attention to her card from Greg. She opened it and read it aloud. "Words cannot describe how much I will always cherish our time together. You are extraordinary. Merry Christmas."

She was deeply touched. She knew the words were heartfelt.

"The packages now?" Angelika said.

Daria nodded. "You first."

Angelika carefully removed the Christmas wrap on her package. Inside was a very classy, velvet jewelry case. Angelika opened the case to reveal a necklace inside. She took it in her hand and lifted it from the case. Then she broke out in a happy smile. "It's a bonobo."

Attached to the fine gold chain was a solid gold pendant, custom cast to perfectly replicate Angelika's fabric bonobo sculpture now on prominent display in the Munich Tiergarten.

Daria loved the pendant. "So beautiful."

Greg had never met or even talked to Angelika. *What a wonderful gesture,* thought Daria. She'd told Greg about the bonobos and Angelika's sculpture. He must have taken that as his inspiration.

"And yours?" Angelika said. "We must see what he gives you."

Daria opened her jewelry case. She lit up with a beaming smile as she lifted out a gold chain and pendant.

Angelika's eyes grew wide with delight. "It's a cabbage!"

They fell over each other, laughing. Daria had told Angelika about the fun she'd had with Greg over her distaste for cabbage.

"Can you believe this?" Daria said.

"Wonderful," Angelika said. "He has made certain you can never forget him."

Daria held the little gold cabbage up and examined it closely.

"This man is in love with you," Angelika pronounced.

Daria felt that herself. It pleased her, but it was also more than a little troubling. Yes, they'd enjoyed a wonderful time together in Schalchen, up until the moment it was disrupted by the paparazzi. What had surprised Daria was the extent to which she'd been emotionally drawn to him. She could only wonder where their connection might have led had their time together not been so rudely cut short. Daria had certainly not gone into their weekend together thinking it might result in a genuine emotional bond. Greg, on the other hand, had been completely guileless about his feelings. She had not been prepared for that. She'd found his vulnerability enormously appealing. Still, they were so different in so many ways. His world view was almost diametrically opposed to hers. She was striving with her heart and soul to make the world more inclusive, more equal and fairer. Greg ran a giant media corporation that was focused on keeping the world's wealth and power in the hands of the privileged few. There was so little common ground.

"Could you be happy with someone like him?" Daria said.

"You told me you like him," Angelika said.

"I do like him." Then, she added, "He lives on the dark side."

"You said he is not happy with himself," Angelika said. "Think what might happen if you were with him?"

"He is wedded to his empire," Daria said. "He is not strong enough to change."

"So," Angelika said, "you should help him to be free."

"Easy to say," Daria said. She made a dismissive gesture with her right hand. "His work is his life."

"This is your perception," Angelika said, as she helped Daria fasten the gold chain and pendant around her neck. "I'm telling you, don't let this one get away."

Daria thought about it another moment, then said, "When he calls, if he calls, we see what happens."

She had no illusions. Greg hadn't called since a few days after they'd last seen each other in Schalchen. Though she really did care for him, she thought it a waste to invest any more of herself emotionally in him. Besides, it wasn't as if she didn't already have a lot on her plate.

PART THREE

CHAPTER 19

As was his habit, Andre arrived in the South of France with Morty the second week in June. Bernard picked them up at the airport in Nice. He'd already been there two weeks, getting the villa ready for the season.

Though he was weary from the twenty-seven-hour journey from New Zealand, Andre loved that he was back in France. He smiled as he took in the rugged beauty of the Mediterranean coast. He thought about the girls, the nubile ones who flooded the Riviera in the summer months. So many hot women, perfectly ripe and eager.

This was the twelfth summer in a row for Andre on the Côte d'Azur. He'd purchased the ocean-view villa when he'd been only nineteen years old. The one-story, bleached stucco house just off the Boulevard de Bacon had walls that opened to the ocean breeze. There was a swimming pool, a Jacuzzi, a tennis court, and a shaded, open-air workout space, equipped with the same top-of-the-line exercise machines that were in his gym in Auckland.

Tonight, despite some serious jet lag, Andre expected to make the circuit, trolling favored hotels, restaurants, and bars for young women easily seduced by the prospect of hanging out with the rich and powerful.

Two days after arriving, Andre heard a rumor he had to investigate. He and his two mates piled into his red Mercedes convertible and drove, top down, to Port de Nuit yacht basin. They parked beside a building with a sign identifying it as home to *La Mer Seigneur Racing*. Andre knew the owner, Luc Pelletier. The rumor was that Luc was looking to sell. Other than seriously hot women, there was nothing that excited Andre more than ridiculously fast boats.

Andre and his two mates entered the building. There, taking up nearly all the space, was the new boat, *La Mer Cinq*. An absolute brute, it was fifty-two feet long, with twin stiletto hulls, and an enclosed racing cockpit.

Two mechanics were on top, working in the big boat's engine compartment. They called out a greeting. Luc wasn't there but was expected back any moment.

Andre ran his hand over the glassy smooth hull. If boats were cocks, this one had been designed to be king stud of them all. It was sitting in a custom-designed transport cradle. It appeared almost ready to go into the water for the first time.

"What's the power plant?" Andre called out in French to the two mechanics.

"Gas turbine," one of them responded. "Twelve hundred shaft horse-power."

Andre walked around to the back and inspected the propeller. It was a marvel, custom fabricated, brass alloy, with five blades pitched to deliver maximum speed. The theoretical performance had to be well over a hundred forty kilometers per hour in light swells. Andre was excited just thinking about it.

Two years earlier, Luc Pelletier had approached him about sponsorship. It was an expensive proposition. An unlimited class, offshore racing boat required a huge amount of maintenance, starting with five highly skilled mechanics and technicians for the various sub-systems. There was also the very high cost of building and maintaining the one-of-a-kind, custom-designed carbon fiber hulls. There were customized racing engines costing half a million or more each. There was the cost of the fuel to run those very thirsty engines. Moving the team from one race venue to another during the short season was also expensive. Sponsorship of Luc's team had a price tag of fifteen million euros a year, with a required five years guaranteed. Andre was very wealthy from his shares in Starling, but it was mostly on paper.

Andre had leveraged Luc's interest in pulling him into a sponsorship to get an occasional gig as a co-driver on *La Mer Seigneur Racing*'s previous boat. Andre had driven the boat multiple times on the practice course offshore from Port de Nuit. It was a rush like none he had ever experienced. He wanted more.

When the sponsorship had been offered, Andre had made a concerted pitch to his uncle to get Starling to sponsor *La Mer Seigneur Racing*. The proposal was dismissed out of hand.

"It's the kind of thing you do when your business is beer or tobacco," his uncle had said, when he blew off the idea.

Andre believed then, and he still believed that such a sponsorship, though expensive, was justified when weighed by the positive publicity it would generate. As a business enterprise, Starling was colorless. It had no public persona, except as an outlet for anti-tax, anti-regulation types. That was one of the first things Andre would fix once he took over.

Andre was about to climb up on the scaffolding that provided access to *La Mer Cinq's* cockpit when Luc Pelletier entered the building. A stocky, balding man in his forties, Luc smiled when he saw his visitors.

"So, the prince returns," Luc said, as he came up and exchanged greetings with Andre, Bernard, and Morty.

"I hear you're open to a buyout," Andre said.

"For the right price."

Luc motioned for Andre to follow him. They retreated to the boathouse's disheveled office.

"How much?" Andre said, as he settled into a chair by the office's lone desk.

"Twelve million, not including the debt."

"Including the debt."

"Nineteen million."

A lot of money, Andre thought. He also knew well that wealthy people rarely got into offshore powerboat racing. The small group that kept the thing going were obscenely rich speed freaks chasing the ultimate, indulgent adrenaline rush. Andre wanted in on the game. He wanted to own *La Mer Seigneur Racing*. If it were his boat, he would be the driver. He wanted to be the one applying full throttle. He saw himself gripping the steering wheel, holding his beast on course as it ripped and pounded its way through the salty swells. What a teeth-rattling, high-adrenaline brand of exhilaration.

Luc was getting antsy.

"You look desperate," Andre said.

"You think so?"

"I think so."

Luc became emotional. He unleashed a long-winded explanation of his motives. One of his kids was in trouble. His wife might leave him. It was all bullshit sales talk. Andre tuned it out and thought about the operating cost for the team. That was the rub. Gaming at this level was a bottomless pit for spending. The winners had the best hull designs, the most powerful engines, *and* the biggest and best support teams. Everybody in powerboat racing had big money. The winners outspent the competition. Almost always, it came down to that. Andre knew if he got into it, it wouldn't be enough to just compete.

To buy or not to buy *La Mer Seigneur Racing* would not even be a question if Andre had the weight of Starling Worldwide behind him. Six months had passed since he'd set the media against his uncle. The controversy had long since subsided. Greg had escaped pretty much unscathed, but Andre was still being treated like a pariah by Starling's senior people in New York. They obviously reflected his uncle's attitude. Not a word had passed between Andre and Greg since the incident.

Poppy's support had saved Greg's ass this time, but his reputation had been damaged, especially with Poppy. That made Greg vulnerable.

Andre had not come out of the conflict unscathed. His reputation, his competence, even his personal lifestyle, were under much more scrutiny now by media competitors thanks to his uncle's manipulation.

Screw the critics, Andre thought. He couldn't care less. He was the patriarch's grandson. Poppy had a soft spot for him. His standing with the old man had to be near equal with that of his uncle. Poppy knew about his grandson's appetite for young women. He'd never said he approved. He'd also never discouraged it. Poppy had been a hound himself once. It seemed to please him that his grandson was cut from the same cloth.

Uncle Greg hadn't been busted as Andre had hoped. Starling Worldwide's financial statement for the most recent quarter had been very strong. The company's publicly traded stock was near an all-time high. Greg's position was secure, for the moment at least. But he still hadn't come up with any kind of succession plan.

As long as Starling Asia continued to perform, and as long as Poppy was behind him, Andre was still the odds-on favorite to take over at Starling. Greg's standing as the company's leader was no longer secure. His health could fail him again, or more likely, he would screw up again. When that happened, Andre would be damned sure to set the hook deep enough that Greg would be unable to redeem himself a second time.

"Are you listening to me?" Luc asked.

"Sorry," Andre said. He signaled Morty and Bernard that he was ready to go.

"Wait," Luc said.

"I don't need this."

"You do," Luc said. "You know you do."

Andre didn't like Luc's attitude, but he wanted what Luc had. *La Mer Cinq* was the rooster tail all could see. With icy focus, Andre went eye to eye with Luc. "Some people will come here. Show them everything. Answer all their questions. After that, we'll see."

"Seventeen million," Luc said.

Andre smiled but said nothing. He left the office, with Morty and Bernard just behind.

They jumped into the open-top Mercedes and headed out of the yacht basin.

Andre loved cruising the oceanfront along Avenue de Verdun and Promenade de Grasse. The season had arrived. There were women everywhere. Andre loved it. From now through the end of August, it would be two, sometimes three different hotties every week. At the end of the season, he, Morty, and Bernard would compare scores. It wasn't really a competition. Andre always got the ones he wanted, always came out on top. His mates were smart enough not to overshadow him. His personal record was thirty-two babes in one season. He'd been younger then. More recently, the conquests had been fewer. Being president of Starling Asia required at least some discretion, some precaution. Now, he almost always used a condom, and the girls had to sign a legal form that affirmed they had no STDs. The form also legally required them to agree never to talk to anyone about Andre or their time with him.

Occasionally, a girl refused to sign. When that happened, she was sent away. They almost always went along. French girls, Spanish girls, Italians, Brits, Dutch, Danes, all good-looking, all hot to trot. They came to enjoy the sun and have fun on the Côte d'Azur. Any female over eighteen was fair game. Andre liked the young ones best. They were so eager to please.

Andre thought about his uncle. Two million for a piece of ass. Unbelievable. If getting laid was a problem for Greg, he should have come to Antibes. A week in the summer with Andre, that's what should've happened. That would've solved everything. Greg could've had all the women he could handle. If Greg had just been cool and shown a little respect, they would be friends, and there would be no question about who would be the next CEO at Starling.

Too bad for Greg it hadn't turned out that way.

As they passed the beaches along Boulevard James Wyllie, Andre's thoughts went back to *La Mer Seigneur Racing*. It was a temptation he couldn't resist. He had the money. He was ridiculously rich. What he did want was to lay off as much of the cost as possible. The team had some sponsors. All were small. A principal underwriter was still needed. Andre knew exactly where he was going for that. He was visualizing *La Mer Cinq* painted like the Starling jet, glossy black with gold trim, when his attention shifted to four very attractive young women enjoying lunch at an outdoor table in one of his favorite beachfront restaurants.

Andre turned to his mates. "Anybody hungry?"

CHAPTER 20

THE CLOCK ON THE NIGHTSTAND read 2:47 a.m. Greg turned his attention to the woman asleep next to him. Hanna Beecher was tall, blond, and beautiful. She was the co-anchor of the 6:00 and 11:00 p.m. news for Starling's Chicago affiliate.

Hanna shifted position under the covers. Her head was now inches from his. The faint scent of her perfume hung in the air. It was their first night together. The sex had been good, just as it had been with the other two women he'd slept with in the past few months. There was just one problem. In his heart and mind, he couldn't stop comparing them with Daria.

He gave in to his restlessness and got out of bed. He headed into the kitchen. In the refrigerator, he found a bowl of steamed broccoli florets. In the past, a late-night snack would have been cookies, ice cream, or some kind of sliced meat slapped on a bun. Now, it was raw veggies or a container of low-fat, blueberry yogurt. Where diet was concerned, there was the pre-Schalchen Greg who'd liked a good steak, and there was the post-Schalchen Greg, who wanted no part of it. He'd stayed with the veggies partly as a gesture to Daria, but more importantly, because he felt healthier, and he thought he looked better. Combined with the exercise program he'd stuck with, the new diet had caused him to drop another seven pounds since the first of the year. He would soon need new suits tailored to fit his increasingly lean, vegetarian body.

It wasn't just his diet that Daria had affected. He'd also directed his investment advisors to begin to shift his substantial holdings in oil, gas, and uranium to stocks and securities related to renewable energy and the newest cellular agriculture techs. He saw it as a positive gesture. He'd felt good about it from the first moment. Not only had it been the morally correct thing to do, it was also proving to be a smart investment decision.

Hanna was Greg's most recent attempt at finding a suitable paramour to fill the empty spot in his life. He liked her. Not only was she gorgeous to look at, she also had an engaging, vivacious personality, and she was certainly all any man could handle in bed. But she wasn't somebody he could love. Though Hanna was a ratings winner delivering the news to Chicago and the surrounding region every night, when off camera, she was largely disinterested in the affairs of the world. Her life was more about mindless globetrotting and vacuous social trendiness than things of substance.

Greg was tired, very tired of being alone. But Daria had made the task of finding a life partner very difficult. She'd become the bar set so high other women paled in comparison. As much as he wanted to move on with his life, his thoughts always went back to Daria. It was a dilemma he seemed unable to escape.

He'd had no contact with Daria for more than six months. He'd tried to blot her from his memory. He'd made a point of not keeping up with what she was doing, though it had been impossible not to notice that her noble ambition was still attracting attention from the media.

He'd tried so hard to dim her imprint on his psyche. It was making him crazy.

Very little of his personal stress came from his work. Probably, that was because he'd lost a lot of his appetite for the M&A game. That fact had not hurt Starling. The company was still clicking on all cylinders.

Greg knew well that his restlessness was driven by his inability to shake off his passion for Daria. She was the one he wanted. His distress was rooted in the denial of his need.

The curtains for his living room's large windows were open. Beyond that was a mega-million-dollar view of Central Park and the west side of Manhattan. As Greg gazed at the city's well-lit skyline, he sensed his mind shifting. He was fed up. Though half a year had passed, he wanted Daria back in his life. He saw his reflection in a nearby mirror. He stared at himself and vowed to reconnect with Daria. He would reconnect with her and win her heart by being a better person. He knew the way to do that. He had to be making the kind of business and life choices that Daria would appreciate.

At that moment, Greg found the personal resolve that had been missing these past few months. He felt elated. It was like a fresh breeze washing over his psyche. Why should he sacrifice his own happiness? Why should he worry about what others might think? Screw the personally imposed constraints. He'd made Starling what it was. He'd made it a global force. He'd made the shareholders a ton of money. Daria Kocánová was the one he wanted. His nephew and anybody else who didn't like it could go to hell.

Greg crossed the living room to his study.

He got in front of his computer. He thought about calling Daria. He decided to Google her name first to see if there was anything new since he'd last checked. There were a lot of Daria Kocánová references. Most were from last December, when the intensity of the controversy was peaking. The most recent magazine profile of her was less than a month old.

Next, he pulled up the website for Equitable Health Alliance. Prominently displayed was a link to a page for *Bright Eve,* a Czech nonprofit Daria had recently launched. Greg went to the *Bright Eve* website. It was very impressive—outstanding graphics, excellent photos, well-designed interface. Buried in the "Who We Are" page was the only reference to Daria. She was listed as the organization's Creative Director. Other people had been put into *Bright Eve's* more senior positions. Greg had given Daria complete control of the money he provided. She had to be the one behind this organizational structure. Very smart move. She appeared to be pulling the primary levers out of the spotlight, while delegating the mostly mundane day-to-day details to people with serious administrative skills.

Bright Eve was spun off from the Equity Health Alliance specifically to take on the implementation of Daria's program. The top people at EHA were on *Bright Eve's* Board, as were Daria and her friend Angelika Grünberg.

A slick streaming video screen was embedded in the *Bright Eve* site's opening page. It allowed the site's visitors to experience a sample of one of its interactive learning modules. It was professionally done, very engaging, very impressive.

Hours later, after a farewell morning romp, Hanna Beecher left to catch a flight back to Chicago. Greg never let on that their final heated round of adult fun had been enjoyed with someone else in mind.

Back in his study, he confirmed the time difference. Prague was six hours ahead of New York. He took a deep breath. He believed his place with the company was secure. But, if it turned out otherwise, if he was going to be forced into a fight for control, Greg told himself it was time he bet on himself.

Though it was late in the day in Prague, Greg took a chance and dialed the number for *Bright Eve*. A moment later, a woman answered the phone. Greg wasn't surprised in the least to find somebody working late into the evening.

"Is Daria Kocánová available?" Greg asked.

"She is not here at this time," the woman answered, in warmly accented English.

"When do you expect her?"

"She is on travel at the moment."

"Where is she?"

"By now, she has arrived in Ethiopia."

CHAPTER 21

"WHY ETHIOPIA?"

"This is where the Equitable Health Alliance has established its first presence in Africa," Daria answered.

She was being interviewed on the phone by Elsie Liesl Krauss, the distinguished journalist who'd first written about her in the German magazine *Der Spiegel* more than half a year ago. Elsie's thoughtful and eloquent reporting had helped restore Daria's damaged reputation. Now, Elsie was eager to write about Daria's work with *Bright Eve*.

Daria was in her guest room at the Hotel Excelsior in Addis Ababa, Capital of the Federal Democratic Republic of Ethiopia. It was the second Tuesday of June.

Elsie was calling from *Der Spiegel's* office in Hamburg, Germany.

"Can you tell me about the place where you are working?" said Elsie.

"I haven't been there yet. My first two days in-country have been focused on getting needed approvals from the government."

"This place you will be working is called Tesfa?"

"Yes," Daria said.

"When will you go there?"

"Marc Wren arrives in-country tonight. We travel to Tesfa for the first time tomorrow."

"Ethiopia is considered to be on the rise in many ways. Why did Dr. Wren go there to build his first hospital in Africa?"

"He would start by telling you there's definitely a need. It's a big country. Nearly four Germanys could fit in Ethiopia. It has much more than 100 million people, the second biggest population in Africa. Too many have never seen a doctor. There is little or no access to birth control. The population continues to expand by nearly three percent annually."

"Aren't there other countries in Africa with more need?"

"If you had never been to Africa, and your ambition was to prove you could build a hospital from scratch, for people who have no place to turn when they are sick or injured, would you not choose to do it in a country that has a need, but is progressing in other ways?"

"So, Tesfa is a good place to start with *Bright Eve*?"

"I think so. I hope so," Daria said.

"What else should I know about Ethiopia?"

"Most of the people are pastoralists or farmers, living off the land as their ancestors have for thousands of years. Nearly ninety different tribal languages are spoken in Ethiopia. It was never colonialized by Europeans, like most of Africa was in the nineteenth century. It's now a parliamentary democracy. You can say Ethiopia is a bit authoritarian, but it seems to be stable and thriving in many ways."

"How many people in Addis Ababa?"

"They say three million. Addis is more than just the capital of Ethiopia, it's also effectively the capital city of the entire continent. The African Union, which represents the common political interests of all of the continent's nations, is based here."

"I am visualizing a lot of desert," Elsie said.

"In the southeast part of Ethiopia, yes. Up near Eritrea, yes. Much of the country is high plateau and mountains, a lot of it deforested. In the capital, Addis Ababa, where I am staying, it's cold at night, warm in the day. One thing I was not expecting is the elevation. Here, it is almost 2,400 meters."

"Very high. Must be hard to breathe."

"Marc told me I would get used to it."

"Are the people friendly?"

"So far, those I have met have been very much that way. Marc gives three reasons for choosing Ethiopia for his first hospital in Africa. Number one, there is a need. Number two, it's a safe place to work— very low risk for violence or terrorism. Number three, the government here has welcomed him and is covering part of the cost."

"You say there is a need. Tell me about this place where you will work with Dr. Wren."

"Tesfa is a settlement that did not exist ten years ago. In the Amhara language, the name means *hope*."

"Troubled humans seeking something better."

"You could absolutely say that."

"Where is Tesfa located?"

"About forty kilometers Northeast of Addis Ababa."

"Who are the people there?"

"Nearly all of them are Amhara. They are migrants with little or no education, who have traditionally lived as farmers and herders of cattle and goats."

"What has brought them to this place?"

"Those who arrived initially migrated there because of drought that left them unable to survive on their traditional lands. More recently, younger Amhara people are arriving there, hoping to get work in Addis as construction laborers."

"How many people living in Tesfa?"

"There is no accurate count. Best guess is about 14,000. No electricity. No improved sanitation. Primary schools only and for boys only. No health care, until just two years ago, when Marc opened his hospital."

"What about food?"

"Many are undernourished. A whole family survives on one or two euros a day. In the worst times, the UN World Food Programme coordinates with some aide groups to provide grain and clean drinking water."

"Too many places in the world are now like that."

"Yes," Daria said.

"You will test your *Bright Eve* program for women in this place?"

"We hope. We must win the cooperation of the people first. You must understand, Tesfa operates by traditional patriarchal rules. The men are dominant."

"But your program focuses on lifting the women."

"Only about one of twenty people in Tesfa has even a primary education. Virtually all of those are men."

"*Bright Eve* will teach the women to read and write?"

"Our computer-based interactive learning is designed to reach illiterate women. It's not about teaching them reading and writing. Our first video is called *Facing the Future*. It's twelve minutes."

"What can you tell me about it?"

"There's an opening tease that showcases people from the world's developing nations actively shaping their future. We show people, particularly women, in these places struggling with the unprecedented forces in their lives. This would include droughts, floods, and other challenges caused by climate change. We are adding to this an overview of fertility and population, the simple, relentless arithmetic of more and more people competing for fewer and fewer resources like water and food. First, we show the terrible reality these people are experiencing in their own lives. Then we show good people, who have suffered these same challenges, actively overcoming these very real challenges. We show women working alongside men. We show communities of people successfully building schools, water supplies, solar panels, even small wind turbines, and health care facilities. We are showing the way forward, and we are saying: to achieve this, women must have an equal place with men. All people, male and female, in a community must work together to educate themselves and their children. Girl children should be educated equally with boys."

"You say all that in twelve minutes of video?"

"We hope the women and the men will respond to this message."

"You need the men to go along."

"Yes. The message has been carefully constructed to be acceptable to the men. We show them what the community can achieve if they rethink tradition and find ways to relate to their women."

"You believe it can work?"

"This is why we are here, to test how the people of Tesfa respond to our messaging. After that, we find out what works, what doesn't work, until we get it right. Then, we use what we learn to make more videos, offering more solutions for getting along in the world they know."

"You are saying to give women an equal place is the big first step."

"It's about empowering women and girls with self-esteem, to show them they have rights, that they are worthy of being educated. They are equal to men. And, we must have the men accept this."

"Would you say that is your biggest challenge?"

"In these traditional cultures, men make the rules. Since forever, females have been treated as property, not persons with rights. Too often, they are subjected to abuse. They are denied education, denied any choice about their own fertility, denied even the right to choose when and to whom they marry. In many traditional cultures, young girls are sold into marriage. It is not uncommon for girls to be raped, then forced to marry their rapist. In other cases, young girls are simply kidnapped in the night. The point is this: Half of all the people in the world are women. No matter the culture, you cannot achieve an inclusive society that is life-affirming and sustainable without gender equality."

"Who will be delivering this message?"

"This is a good question. The narrator in our videos will communicate in the same language of the people we are trying to reach. In the case of Tesfa, here in Ethiopia, our message will be delivered in the Amhara language."

"You want your message to be relatable."

"And also, culturally sensitive."

"You are doing *Bright Eve* in cooperation with the Equitable Health Alliance."

"Yes. Marc Wren and his colleagues are amazing. The compassion and decency they bring to their work inspires me. Marc Wren inspires me. You should do a story about him."

"I will be telling his story when I write about you and *Bright Eve*."

"Thank you. He and his colleagues don't get nearly enough appreciation for their dedication and sacrifice."

"We can also say that about you."

"Attention is not something I wish for. I am just happy to do something useful with my life."

"What about you and Dr. Wren? Are you in a relationship with him?"

Daria's guard went up. She paused for a moment, then said, "This is a part of my life I wish to keep private."

"Okay," Elsie said. "Can I ask about Mr. Greg Hammond? What can we write about him?"

That was also a sore subject. Greg had weathered the storm and retained his place as head of his Starling Media empire. Daria was glad for that, but she had not heard from Greg since Christmas. After receiving his gift, she had texted him with words that had expressed a heartfelt 'Thank You' for the 'Cabbage' pendant, and also warm wishes for the holiday season.

Greg had not responded further. A part of Daria was more than a little disappointed. She had hoped to retain at least cordial contact with him. The prospects appeared unlikely for even that at this point. She accepted his decision not to stay in touch with her. She wanted nothing but the best for him, and it seemed the less she said about him, the better for him.

Daria considered her answer for another moment, then said to Elsie, "Whatever good we can achieve with *Bright Eve*, it would not be happening if not for Greg Hammond."

"There is much about your story with him that you have never confirmed."

"I will say this, he is not the dark soul some people believe him to be."

"Would he talk to me for this story?"

"He prefers to downplay his connection with my work."

"When you talk to him, can you ask if he would be willing to be interviewed?"

"Of course," Daria said. "I will let you know."

In fact, Daria did not expect to be talking to Greg Hammond. Not now, not in the future. It had been his choice to stop communicating. She accepted that decision. She intended to do what she could to discourage Elsie Krauss, and anyone else for that matter, from any further intrusion in his life.

"When can we talk again?" Elsie asked.

"I am back in Europe next week. I will be in touch when I have more to tell you."

"Thank you for trusting me to tell this story."

"As it unfolds, I think you will find much to write about," Daria said. She appreciated Elsie's interest. Knowing that the emergence of *Bright Eve* would be reported on by *Der Spiegel,* and likely by other parts of the media, was added incentive for her.

A moment later, the call with Elsie ended.

Alone with her thoughts, Daria's mind went to the millions of women and girls in Africa and other parts of the world who lived with oppression because of their gender. She felt a deep sense of kinship and compassion for them. A rush of emotion spread through her body. Her chance to make a difference was almost at hand. She was determined to make the most of it.

CHAPTER 22

T HE NEXT MORNING WAS SUNNY and pleasantly cool. Daria and Marc were riding in the back seat of a white United Nations Food Programme minivan that was part of a caravan that included a second minivan and two large, unmarked cargo trucks loaded to capacity with sacks of grain. Daria was focused on the sprawling, open-air market they were slowly passing through. The scene was dominated by row after row of merchant tables with abundant supplies of a wide variety of fresh vegetables, eggs, and other locally grown edibles for sale. Spread about the market, many Ethiopians were there buying the food they needed.

Daria said, "I'm not seeing a lot of undernourished people here."

"The city's economy actually works pretty well for a lot of people, but there's also plenty of poverty here," Marc said.

The urban core of Addis Ababa was a mix of government ministries, open-air markets, hotels, apartment buildings, storefronts, and schools. None of the structures were more than about ten stories in height. There were also a lot of new buildings in various stages of construction.

The city's roads were busy with buses, trucks, and other vehicles of every size and shape, occasionally mixed in with small carts, some towed by animals in harness, others being dragged along by indigent Ethiopians.

The UN caravan soon passed beyond the urban boundary, on to a two-lane stretch of highway that was flanked by open land covered almost entirely with scrub brush.

Daria was focused introspectively. She was thinking about the woman she was going to meet with shortly in Tesfa. Her name was Aberash. She was the community's chief female elder.

In fact, she was called Emama by all the people: Emama Aberash. She was the widow of a revered chief. Her status had emerged from her long-standing reputation for wise counsel to her late husband, and to Tesfa's community of women.

Daria had read a three-page profile of Emama Aberash, prepared by the UN.

Emama was thought to be sixty-one years old. She was known for not suffering fools, and for her well-considered resolve. Though she had little formal education, Emama Aberash was not one to be underestimated.

"I am wondering if Aberash understands English," Daria thought out loud.

"She understands some English," Marc said. "She communicates only in Amharic."

"She's the alpha female?" Daria asked.

She saw Marc nod. She also noticed his troubled body language. It seemed clear he wanted to say more. Daria knew what it was about. The argument had started the previous evening, following Marc's arrival after nearly twenty-one hours of traveling from Haiti.

"Why can't we get past this?" Daria said.

Marc said nothing.

Daria understood that Marc was still concerned that she might go off script in her meeting with the Emama.

"How many times have you met this lady?" Daria said.

"That's irrelevant," Marc said. "When the issue involves women or children, Emama Aberash calls the shots."

"We've had this conversation, at least three times. She cannot be so scary."

"I guess we'll see, won't we?" Marc said.

Daria was surprised by his sarcasm.

The resurgent argument was over a cultural tradition still practiced widely in Africa. Up until two decades ago, it was referred to in English as female genital mutilation, or FGM. In recent times, it was called the more politically correct, Female Genital Cutting, or FGC, in cultural deference to Indigenous peoples that still maintained the tradition.

For at least a thousand years, FGC had been a rite of passage for girls across Africa and parts of the Middle East. More than two hundred million females currently living had been subjected to culturally enforced genital cutting. It amounted to the removal of parts of a girl child's labia and the clitoral hood at the vaginal opening. It was carried out in most cultures by female elders, using a razor blade, a knife, or a sharp piece of glass. In some places, health workers were hired by families to perform the ritual cutting. In nearly all cases, there was no anesthetic, nothing to moderate the pain, and no modern medicine to treat the wound.

The cultural belief behind the ritual was that cutting the genitals of a girl will assure she will remain chaste and not be subject to the sexual urges and temptations that come naturally. A female uncut was thought to be unclean, a disgrace to her family and unworthy of marriage. In many communities where FGC was still practiced, the people would shun women who were not cut. No one would eat food cooked by an uncut woman, and they would not take water from her. They would not even sit with her.

Daria was adamant that female genital cutting was an act of violence, a desecration applied to females only. She understood that circumcision was still practiced widely on boys. It was not the same thing. Circumcision was an expression of dominance. That's what the broadly accepted anthropological evidence strongly suggested.

For females, genital cutting was a brutal way of enforcing gender obedience, a reflection of male dominance over females. For Daria, it was a gender-specific human right violation and a cultural disconnect of the highest order. FGM, or the more politically correct FGC, was a ritual that effectively reinforced the subjugation of females. There was absolutely no medical benefit to FGC. In fact, it left the young girls who endured it physically and emotionally traumatized and often scarred for life. In many instances, it led to infection. In some cases, infection resulted in death.

Daria understood that taking on FGC as part of her *Bright Eve* mandate could put the entire project at risk. Still, she was eager, even desperate, for an opportunity to address this brutal tradition with the women of Tesfa.

"FGC is already on the way out," Marc said. "Across this continent, there are good people working to change things."

"For every place that has changed, a hundred are getting no attention."

"The path to ending FGC is about enlisting locals. You do that by showing restraint and sensitivity. You win over a few people, then you encourage them to carry the message to their peers. That's how you change minds."

"I'm thinking about all the young girls who are facing this tradition right now. They have no time for patience. Once they are cut, they live with it for life."

"What you find in Tesfa are mostly good people, struggling to survive. They're grateful when good people come to help them. They can get very defensive when they think outsiders like us are undermining their traditions."

Daria said, "I am not resisting your perspective on this issue. but cutting girls is antithetical to empowering girls."

"I am not suggesting you avoid the subject completely. I'm saying, tread lightly. First, gain some trust."

Daria recognized that Marc's caution was prudent. She had no plan to talk about FGC today, but she was prepared, whenever the right moment came.

Though all of the people in the Tesfa settlement were Ethiopian Orthodox Christian, they still held on to many of their core indigenous beliefs.

"In this country, more than half of the women have been cut," Marc said.

"The percentage is much higher for people living in traditional communities, like Tesfa," Daria added.

Marc put his arm around her shoulders. He hugged her warmly and said, "You're not going to just walk in and stop something that's been part of the culture for thousands of years. You must be careful with what you say."

Daria took a deep breath and let the tension flow out of her body, then she said, "I get that."

After a moment, Daria glanced up at Abeba Danichew, the young Ethiopian woman dressed in traditional Amhara skirt and woven wool jacket and head cover, sitting in the vehicle's front seat.

"Are you ready for this?" Daria asked.

Abeba smiled, nodded confidently, then said in imperfect English, "I am so proud to stand with you."

Daria reached forward from the back seat. She clasped Abeba's hand warmly, then said, "You give me strength."

If every decision Daria made was as good as the one that resulted in the hiring of Abeba Danichew, the *Bright Eve* program would be a success for sure. Abeba was a 25-year-old Ethiopian native who'd just earned a PhD in Education at the University of Bristol in the UK. She'd grown up traditionally, the daughter of Amhara tribal people. It was Abeba who'd translated the initial interactive learning scripts into her native spoken language. One of the biggest challenges of this kind of outreach was Africa's legacy of languages. Nearly two thousand were ethnologically distinct, a hundred of those were considered major. This was one of the reasons interactive learning for adult women was not already being widely used. It was time-consuming and costly to modify the software for a specific language. Who was going to do it? Not the computer software giants. There was no profit to be made. The United Nations didn't have the resources. It was too busy meeting more basic needs. The UN and most all of the other world relief agencies operating in Ethiopia had encouraged Daria's initiative because it focused on a need that was not being adequately addressed.

Daria turned her focus to Tesfa, which was now in sight, ahead on both sides of the road. A decade earlier, it had been unoccupied scrubland. Now, it was a community of desperate rural people, migrated to this place in an attempt to survive.

Though Daria had never been to Ethiopia until now, she knew Tesfa well. She'd reviewed every report and research paper she could find that had been published on the community since it had materialized as a settlement.

The UN caravan slowed to a crawl, assertively making its way, avoiding people and animals ahead on the road.

Daria took in the full picture of Tesfa. The living was primitive to be sure: no electricity, no potable water. Pit latrines, offering little privacy and much health risk, were spaced among the small dwellings whole families called home. Some were traditional huts made of sticks and hardened clay, reinforced with plant fiber, many others were domes made of a scaffolding of woven sticks, covered with a thatch of plant material. In many cases, blue plastic tarps were stretched over the top to keep out the weather.

Scattered about were some goats, a few cows, and more than a few dogs, most roaming freely.

Groups of children of differing ages were chasing each other about, playing traditional games.

A stream flowing through the community was the primary source of water. Tesfa also had two primitive wells, both of which had been contaminated by sewage leaching from unimproved latrines. Except during the rainy season, potable water was always an issue.

On top of everything else, Tesfa was growing by sometimes as many as a hundred new migrants a month.

Daria had seen poverty before, in many different forms, and she'd known intellectually what to expect. This moment, like the other encounters she'd had with inadequate human conditions, was a substantial reminder of her own difficult childhood.

The UN caravan slowly made its way along the road until it reached the far side of the Tesfa settlement. On the left side of the tarmac was EHA's hospital and clinic.

The two large trucks loaded with grain turned onto a narrow, rutted dirt lane that ran parallel with the edge of the settlement and headed for a food dispersal point. The two minivans peeled off and parked next to the hospital building, which was a very basic, single-story concrete box of about 5,000 square feet. The roof was a solar electric PV prefab design imported from India.

Several hundred people, separated into four different lines, were waiting for treatment.

New arrivals were met by Amhara-speaking health evaluators trained in-country as nurse assistants. The evaluators separated the patients according to need. The most acutely sick or injured were the first priority.

Daria's all-important meeting with Emama Aberash, the gatekeeper to the women in Tesfa, would come later. This moment was for Marc to show her his clinic.

Daria and Abeba climbed out of the minivan, just behind Marc. They were joined by a photographer from the UN and two uniformed security officers, who'd been in the other minivan.

Waiting by the hospital's entrance was a young Hispanic man, who was wearing a white doctor's coat. He had a big smile as he shared a hug with Marc Wren. Then Marc turned and introduced him to Daria and Abeba. "This is our medical director, Arnoldo Diaz Parma."

Daria knew a bit about Dr. Parma. He was Cuban, recruited directly out of the top medical school in Havana. Daria liked him immediately. She shared a warm handshake with him and said, "It seems being Cuban is a big advantage with Marc in a job interview."

"First-rate medical training," Marc said.

"Yes," Arnoldo said, with a pleasant grin. "He also likes me because I work cheap."

"Arnoldo is brilliant at diagnosing and treating patients under pressure," Marc said.

He'd already told Daria he was determined to maintain a high standard at the Tesfa Clinic, making sure it was always staffed by competent, caring professionals and always stocked adequately with medicines and medical expendables.

Marc was also intent on keeping his personal profile low. The clinic's staff knew better than to make a fuss over his return. When Daria followed Marc into the clinic's treatment room, she watched him share a warm but brief greeting with the staff on duty. Then, almost immediately, he fell into treating patients, just another attending physician working with human beings in need.

Arnoldo led Daria on a quick tour. There was a hospital ward with thirty beds. All were occupied by sick patients, some of whom were surrounded by concerned family members. Six more patients, all moribund, were lying on sheets spread on the floor. The place was unheated, and a noticeable antiseptic odor hung in the air.

Back in the treatment room, two Ethiopian doctors were there along with Marc, working with an endless succession of sick or injured men, women, and children taken from the lines that stretched outside and down the road. Arnoldo quickly went back to treating patients.

The plan was that Marc would attend Daria's meeting with Emama Aberash, the leader of Tesfa's women.

When the time came to leave, Daria knew Marc really wanted to treat patients.

"Stay," she told him.

"I need another minute," Marc said, as he swabbed an open wound on a teary-eyed preadolescent girl who was trying to be brave.

"I'm leaving," Daria said. "Stay and do your work."

"You sure?"

"Abeba will take care of me," Daria said, as she gave the young Ethiopian woman a reassuring touch on her shoulder. "And, we have the security guys."

That was good enough for Marc. He said, "Remember what I said about the Emama. You'll earn points if you treat her with respect."

Then, Marc turned back to giving his full attention to his young patient.

It was probably best that he remained at the clinic, thought Daria. If he was right about Emama Aberash, winning her over was unlikely to be easy. Marc had the welfare of the clinic to consider. Better for him to stay separate from Daria's work, at least for now.

Moments later, Daria, Abeba, and the two uniformed officers returned to one of the minivans, which then headed back down the adjacent highway. The vehicle soon turned onto a narrow, dusty lane that penetrated into the heart of Tesfa. People and animals moved aside as the minivan rolled slowly ahead on the heavily rutted roadway.

Daria was still agonizing over the female cutting issue and its possible impact on the launch of *Bright Eve*. She knew she had no good choice. Change had to come incrementally. Women first had to win control of their lives. The cutting of girls had already ended in virtually every African community where women had been empowered. Daria believed *Bright Eve* could have a big impact. It was designed to behave virally in the way it delivered knowledge—first to a few, then those few quickly carried the message to others, who connected with others, until empowerment was dispersing like fire in a hot wind. At least, that was the vision.

Daria's studies in anthropology had convinced her that the world would never heal until all its women were elevated to an equal place in society. Much progress had already been made on gender rights within the larger human culture, but there were still too many subsets of humanity mired in traditional male dominance. Tesfa was a perfect example. The people needed to find a place in the twenty-first century interlace of human society that celebrated equality.

The white UN minivan came to an open area about the size of a tennis court. Daria sensed it was a space often used for ceremonies and public meetings. A dozen children were there running about, chasing after a ball. They stopped and gave their attention to the UN vehicle.

Beyond the children, there was a hut with pounded dirt walls about twenty feet on each side. A thatch of sticks formed a roof that was covered with blue plastic tarps. By the home's open entry, four older women were sitting together on a large sheet of plastic. Above them was another blue tarp held up by poles, like an awning, providing shade from the intense sunlight. The four women got to their feet as the UN minivan stopped close to them. All were clad in ankle-length skirts, pieces of well-worn Western clothing, and rubber flip-flops on their feet.

Abeba directed Daria's attention to the tallest of the women, and said, "That is Emama Aberash."

Daria steeled herself. She knew her program couldn't start in Tesfa without Aberash's blessing. If Daria failed, she was prepared to move on to two other refugee settlements not far from Addis that had been identified as alternate possibilities. She could do that, but she really wanted her program to launch in Tesfa. Beyond the obvious tie-in with Marc Wren's hospital, this place was more culturally homogeneous, and much more accessible than the other two options. She didn't want to have to go to plan B or C. She felt certain Tesfa was the best place to launch *Bright Eve.*

Daria gave her full attention to Emama Aberash. Her stare was penetrating, her expression impassive—not hostile, but not friendly either.

"This is a tough lady," Daria said.

"I think not so much as you," Abeba said.

Daria appreciated Abeba's expression of confidence. She squeezed Abeba's hand in a gesture of hope, then the two of them got out of their vehicle. They moved toward Aberash, who was flanked by the three somewhat younger women. Daria judged them to be elders who fell just behind Aberash in the community's female social hierarchy.

Daria waited as Abeba went up to the formidable-looking woman and greeted her deferentially. Then, Abeba signaled Daria to come forward.

Mustering every ounce of her innate confidence, Daria walked up to the Emama. She smiled as she spoke. "It is my honor and pleasure to meet Emama Aberash Zewdu, leader of the good women of Tesfa."

Aberash stared at Daria. Her expression was unreadable. Then she said something in her native language.

Abeba immediately translated for Daria. "The Emama thanks us for our visit. She invites us to sit with her."

Daria and Abeba sat down on the piece of plastic next to Aberash, whose expression remained impassive.

After studying Daria for another moment, Aberash spoke directly to her.

Abeba translated. "Why have you come to us?"

Daria wanted the Emama to know her personal story. She spoke about growing up destitute in the European nation that was once known as Czechoslovakia. She talked emotionally about her widowed mother and herself shivering through frigid winters, often with very little food.

"My experience was difficult, but it was nothing compared to what the people of Tesfa endure every day," Daria said.

"You have known how it is to suffer," Aberash said. "Now, you wish to help us?"

Daria smiled and nodded agreeably.

"Other people have come here," Aberash said. "They have said they want to help us. They stay for a time, then they go away. For our people, life has not become better."

"There are no easy answers," Daria said. "We are here to help you to find ways to help yourselves."

Again, Aberash studied Daria, then she said, "We know about you."

Daria was thrown off guard by the comment.

"We have heard that no man has ever paid more to have a woman than was paid for you," Aberash continued.

Daria's heart sank.

"Is this true?" Aberash said.

Daria had not expected to have to talk about this. It troubled her that she had to defend herself this way. She carefully considered her words, then responded honestly.

"If you ask, did I sleep with a powerful man, I do not deny this. If you ask did this man give a lot of money to my organization, I say yes. If you ask, did I take any of this money for myself, I say no. We all must make choices. I made a personal choice that has given me the money I need to help people in places like Tesfa."

Daria paused and kept her eyes firmly on Aberash. Then, she continued, "We are here today. We are able to stand with you and your people because of some choices I have made."

Again, Aberash studied Daria for a long moment, then she said, "How would you help us?"

"By giving your women access to education," Daria said as she opened the laptop she brought with her. It was already powered up. She cued up the *Facing the Future* video, then nodded to Abeba.

The young Ethiopian woman looked at Emama Aberash and said in Amharic, "Tesfa can be a place where women find a new direction and a better life."

Daria then launched the video and handed the laptop to Aberash.

Over the next twelve minutes, Daria closely studied the reactions of Emama Aberash and her three elder women colleagues as the video rolled from beginning to conclusion. The message of *Facing the Future* was abundantly clear: For humans, Earth is the only home we have. Every human has a stake in protecting our planet's biosphere. The best future is possible only if women are treated as equals to men, and all people work together as equals to protect the Earth we all depend on.

The video presented examples of people from all the still-emerging parts of the world, people who were at the poor end of the spectrum. The video was skewed particularly to showcase women who had overcome the obstacles lined up against them. In every instance, whole communities of women had improved self-esteem and greater optimism about the future when they gained access to education for their girl children and for themselves. The same held true when woman had genuine reproductive choice, including access to family planning and contraception.

The reality was that more than a few regions of the continent of Africa were in trouble. A primary cause was expanding numbers of people, and not enough food, water, shelter, medical care, and education. Too many of the things woven into the fabric of a successful society were in seriously short supply. These conditions could be found in countries outside of Africa, like Haiti, for instance. But the number of the world's nations that were struggling had declined in recent decades. A substantial share of those human societies that were continuing to slide further into trouble were in Africa. The reasons for this included the long-standing impact of colonialism, the prevalence of corrupt, post-colonial dictatorship politics, and the continued, mostly unregulated, exploitation of the continent's bounty of natural resources by foreign interests.

The *Facing the Future* video showed that a primary factor holding back emerging nations was the continued oppression and disenfranchisement of their female humans. The case was effectively made that the way forward for troubled nations was to educate girl children, and to embrace gender equality and reproductive choice for women.

When the video was over, Aberash conferred quietly with her three female lieutenants, then she turned to Daria and said, "Show us again."

Daria punched a command into the computer. The same video began playing a second time. Daria was thrilled by the rapt attention Aberash and her colleagues were giving the video. Though she couldn't be sure, Daria thought it might be the first interactive learning video ever done specifically for women in the Amharic language.

Trying to effect profound change in so many culturally and language diverse places was daunting, to say the least. Ethiopia was making great strides, but there was still plenty of need in places like Tesfa. Daria felt deeply privileged to be in a position to make even a small contribution.

It was in individual communities, places like Tesfa, where change had to come first. And it had to come from within. Informed women could be the driving force. It wasn't about coercing lower fertility, or about coercion of any form, for that matter. It was simply about providing honest information, showing women that together, and empowered, they could have their voices heard on the issues they cared about.

Facing the Future had been created as proof of concept. The idea was to gain a foothold of trust and enthusiasm that could be built on.

After the second viewing, Daria immediately went into demonstrating the computer's interactive educational software for Aberash and her three colleagues. Their eyes were glued to the laptop's screen as the narrator, speaking in their own native language, explained video images of women like themselves learning about education, about basic health care, about self-esteem, about the great things women had achieved in other cultures, and about all the untapped potential that existed within themselves.

When it was over, Aberash looked at Daria and said, "You have created this?"

"Many people have contributed."

"Your message is very strong," Aberash said thoughtfully. "These are real people in this video?"

"Real situations, real people, helping themselves," Daria said.

"How can we use this to help our people?" Aberash said.

"Abeba will train three of your young women to be teachers," Daria said. "They will learn how to use the computer and how to teach others with it. We start with three teachers. They go out and teach other women. Then some of those other women will also become teachers."

"Every teacher will have this machine?"

Daria nodded. "Each computer will start with the same interactive teaching modules. More interactive programs will be added as time goes on."

"The teachers can be paid?"

"Yes, and as long as the program is working successfully, we will also provide you and your three colleagues with some income."

Abeba translated in Amhara.

Aberash and her three colleagues broke out in big smiles and chattered happily with each other. Then, after a moment, Aberash spoke seriously.

Abeba turned to Daria and translated Aberash's comments into English. "The Emama has said, it is good you have used our language for this video. She says it would also be good to see Amhara people in your videos."

Daria considered the suggestion. She had thought it would be enough to use the Amhara language to communicate the video's intent effectively. She said, "Please thank the Emama for her suggestion. Tell her she will see Amhara people in our next video."

Abeba hesitated. Then, instead of translating Daria's answer, she said quietly in English, "We do have a video with Amhara people."

Daria knew well what Abeba was talking about. It was a three-minute video Abeba herself had made when she was still a university student in England. It was what had initially brought Abeba to Daria's attention, and a big reason she had hired Abeba for her *Bright Eve* project. The video, Abeba's video, did feature several Amhara students who had been at the University of Bristol along with her. The subject of the video was FGC. Abeba had her own dark history with the cutting.

"With your approval, I would like to show my video to the Emama," Abeba said.

Daria shared Abeba's passion for confronting FGC. There could be no real gender parity in Tesfa as long as the practice of cutting girls continued. At the same time, Daria worried that raising the issue now could put the introduction of *Bright Eve* in Tesfa at serious risk.

"Is this the right time for that?" Daria said.

"The Emama is wise. I think she will be open to our message on FGC."

Daria thought about it a moment longer, then, despite her misgivings, she decided to trust her young protégée. She nodded her approval.

Abeba turned to Aberash and said in Amharic, "May we show you another short video? This one shows our people talking about the cutting."

The matriarch studied Daria and Abeba for a moment, then said, "Show us."

Abeba launched the FGC video on the laptop. It featured Abeba as narrator, and young Amhara women on screen. It reported that continent wide, something like 200 million females were living with the consequences of having their vaginal openings cut and scarred. It was a cultural tradition that each generation endured and perpetuated. Even now, every single day, six thousand girls in Africa and other parts of the world were ritualistically scarred by FGC. The video went to an African hospital treating young patients with complications from ritual cutting. An Ethiopian nurse talked about the patients, their suffering, and the kind of lasting complications from cutting that were typical. The nurse made a clear case that female genital cutting was medically unnecessary and frustrated progress for everyone in the communities that still practiced it.

Abeba had recruited a group of young Amhara women to appear in the video. They spoke courageously about the pain and indignity of FGC. They said women were repudiating FGC all across the African continent. They said that ending the cutting was necessary and inevitable for achieving progress.

Finally, the video featured a young married Amhara couple, Meron and Dawit. When they were married, Meron had defiantly worn a sign over her wedding dress that said, "I am not cut." And Dawit had supported her, with a sign he wore that said, "I am proud that my new wife is not cut." Together, they made a powerful statement for abandoning the practice of female genital cutting.

Daria and Abeba both wanted desperately to make a difference for the girl children being born now that deserved to be spared from this practice. What female would want to be the last one 'cut' in a cultural ritual that had been discredited and disenfranchised by the emergence of a genuine, equal partnership between males and females?

When the video was over, Daria and Abeba remained quiet as Aberash and her three elder colleagues discussed it in their own language.

Then Aberash said, "This is our way."

Daria remained quiet. She looked to Abeba to respond.

In the most non-confrontational way possible, Abeba said, "In a world where men and women are equals, there is no cutting."

Aberash appeared to be unmoved.

At that moment, Daria could no longer remain silent. She said, "We understand how hard this is for you. There is no good time to change."

Calmly but emphatically, Aberash said, "A friend would not talk of this."

Daria looked Aberash squarely in the eyes, and said, "You have no better friends than Abeba and me. Only true friends will respect you and speak the truth you do not want to hear."

Aberash thought for a moment, then said, "Our honor, our dignity, the joy we once knew, all these things have been taken from us."

Daria knew they could only go forward. They could not back down. She said, "We urge you to consider your future. We implore you to redefine yourselves in a way that offers hope for your girl children."

For the longest time, Aberash thought about how to respond.

Daria glanced at Abeba. The young Ethiopian women took it as a cue. She began to talk in a quiet, comforting way. Though she was speaking Amharic, Daria knew what Abeba was saying. She was telling the Emama her own story. That she was not cut, that she had run away and chosen to be educated, rather than be subjected to the pain and humiliation of being cut.

Abeba grew emotional as she explained that her defiance stemmed from seeing her own mother suffer terribly through a day-long childbirth when she herself was just seven years old. The problem was scar tissue left from when her mother had been subjected to genital cutting. Her vaginal opening no longer had enough elasticity for the baby to come out. Finally, a knife had been used, but by then it was too late.

Abeba was crying as she said in Amharic, "My sister was born dead. My mother lost all her blood. My mother died. They both died because she was cut."

Daria comforted Abeba, then she turned to Aberash, who appeared to have been deeply moved by Abeba's story.

"If cutting is how it should be," Daria said, "why are females born as they are?"

Aberash looked at Daria for several tense moments, then said, "We see that the world is changing."

For now, Daria knew the discussion of FGC was over. For now, all that should be said about it had been said. The NGOs that had worked successfully to end FGC in other places in Africa had all approached the process with patience and sensitivity. She would do the same and leave it to Abeba to carry the *Bright Eve* message about FGC in Ethiopia from this point on.

The Emama was still staring. Daria was determined not to be intimidated.

After another few moments of uncomfortable silence, Aberash spoke again. "Our people wish to learn things that will make them stronger. Is this your intention?"

Daria listened as Abeba translated the Emama's words. Then, after a taking moment to consider her answer, she responded, "Yes, we would like to know what you would like to see in our videos. We are thinking of introducing everything from how to open and manage a bank account to family planning and contraception. We want to use our teaching tools to help your people understand the forces at work in your lives."

"Like what?" the Emama asked.

"Climate change," Daria said, "and the drought that comes with it, all the various kinds of weather extremes."

"We do not often hear about these things, but we know they have not been good for us," the Emama said.

"What you will see in our teaching videos are people like yourselves talking about the most important issues of our time. You will hear them talk about how their lives are affected, and about what can be done. You will see them actively engaged in adapting to their new reality. In all of our videos, you will see women sharing the decision-making with men. The biggest lesson of all that comes from our *Bright Eve* program is that the only good future will come with women and their men working together as equals."

"We want to know the truth about what is happening in the world. We want to understand why life has become so much more difficult for us. We want to know what we can do about it ourselves," Aberash said.

She thought a bit more, then continued, "The first video you showed us gives us hope. Will the videos you show us later be presented the same way, in our language, so our people can understand?"

Daria smiled and nodded. "All of the learning modules we will show you will be presented in your own Amhara language."

"Will you stay with us while we show the video you have brought us to our other women elders?"

"If that is your wish," Daria said.

Aberash turned to her three elder companions and told them what she wanted. The three women got up and went to the adolescent children playing nearby. After getting instructions from the elders, the children quickly scattered into the Tesfa community.

Abeba was giddy with excitement. She said to Daria, "They are calling all the elder women together."

Within minutes, elder women began to show up from every direction.

Abeba told Daria, "These are the women leaders of the various clans represented in Tesfa."

After another ten minutes, more than a hundred elder women were gathered in the open space outside of Emama Aberash's home.

Daria was very encouraged by what she was seeing.

Aberash smiled. She put her hands on Daria's shoulders and said something that was obviously heartfelt.

Abeba translated, "She says we are her strong sisters. She says we give her hope."

Daria was deeply touched. "Tell the Emama she honors us with her kind words."

Abeba translated for Aberash, who smiled and nodded appreciatively. She took Daria's hand and Abeba's hand and led them to a place in front of the gathered women.

Daria made eye contact with the two UN security officers. They appeared to be alert but not overly concerned.

Emama Aberash gazed out over the gathering with a smile.

"We bring our elder sisters great news," Aberash said loudly enough to be heard by everyone.

She took Daria's hand and Abeba's hand and lifted them high. "Here is our sister from the land of the Czech, and here is our daughter, now educated and returned home. They have brought to our people a powerful gift."

The gathering of women raised their hands and joined in a warm and colorful round of clapping and appreciative chanting.

Aberash lifted the palm of her hand. The women went silent. Then, Aberash opened the laptop computer for all to see and said, "Here is the gift they bring to us, a tool for teaching our people, and particularly our sisters and daughters, many things. A tool that can help us make a better life for ourselves and for our children."

After leading the gathering in another loud and enthusiastic expression of appreciation, Aberash turned to Daria, and said, "You will please show the first video to our women." Aberash pointed to the place in front of her home that was shaded by a tarp strung between poles. She said, "Go there. We will send them in small groups."

Daria moved with Abeba to the place under the plastic tarp awning. Less than five minutes later, the first group of about twenty women was huddled close around Abeba, their attention riveted to the laptop she was holding. The women were watching the *Facing the Future* video.

Daria observed the women closely as they watched. Their enthusiasm for the message was undeniable.

When the first group moved off, the second group came in to view the video. Daria was very encouraged. The spark had been lit. The women were responding enthusiastically to her teaching tool and its message. She was sorry Marc Wren was not present to witness this moment.

The photographer had also stayed back at the clinic to acquire images of the work there.

Fortunately, Daria had her cell phone. She used it to take lots of pictures.

Just after 5:00 p.m., as the seventh group of women was viewing the video on the laptop, a commotion broke out at one end of the crowded open area.

Daria could see women shrinking back from a squad of men who were pushing their way through, heading directly toward her. Daria glanced at the two UN security men. One was frantically trying to get through to someone on his cell phone. The other one was moving through the jam of women, trying to reach Daria and Abeba.

Daria was concerned. She leaned close to Abeba and asked, "Who are they?"

"Enforcers, sent by the leaders," Abeba said.

"They don't look friendly," Daria said.

"I know the one in front," Abeba said. "His name is Hakim. He is a hot head."

Daria noticed that Emama Aberash was scowling at the approaching men. If she wasn't intimidated, Daria wasn't going to be either.

Flanked by his cadre of young, menacing males, Hakim came right up to Daria. Lean, muscular, and wearing tattered Western clothing, Hakim glared coldly at Daria and the other women. Though no weapons were visible, this was definitely a show of force.

Hakim's face was drawn into a tight scowl. He eyed Daria closely. Then he pointed his finger at her like a dagger, and shouted in Amharic, "What are you doing? What is going on here?"

Aberash stepped in front of Daria and began to shout Hakim down. She made a dismissive gesture and demanded he go away.

Hakim bared his teeth in a threatening way, then he turned his Amharic rage back on Daria. "You think you can come here with your magic? You think you can cast your spell on our women? We are not fools! We are not fools!"

Hakim suddenly snatched up the laptop.

"Go away!" he shouted at Daria. "Go away now!"

Before Daria could say anything, Hakim whirled and headed off with the computer, his warrior phalanx pushing women aside to clear the way.

Aberash offered Daria a comforting hand. "They want to see what you have shown us. This is a necessary step. We cannot go to a new place without our men."

Daria agreed. She wasn't worried about the computer. They were replaceable. What had just happened was a good thing. As dismaying as it was, as aggressive and full of bloated bluster as the confrontation had been, it might just be the first step to getting her program past Tesfa's dominant male hierarchy. They were the ultimate gatekeepers. Daria had no doubt the computer would be taken directly to Tesfa's male leaders. The first thing they would do is turn it on and look at *Facing the Future*. The message in the video had been fine-tuned to resonate with these people, women and men. It was not coercive. It was honest and culturally sensitive, and intuitively obvious. It amounted to a stark but encouraging confrontation with reality for the leaders of Tesfa.

Daria grabbed her backpack. She pulled out two additional batteries and handed them to Aberash, "Emama, I ask you to have someone take these to the men."

Aberash quickly summoned three teenage boys lingering nearby. She handed over the batteries and directed the boys to deliver them.

Daria watched the rail-thin squad of teens race away with the batteries. Though she kept her expression neutral, she was thrilled. *Bright Eve's* life-affirming message was spreading, faster, it seemed, than she could ever have hoped for. She was living her dream, connecting with the community through its women. She wanted the people of Tesfa to find value in the knowledge and ideas she was bringing to them. She wanted them to embrace the message and be inspired to find their own solutions to their own problems. *Bright Eve*, at its core, was a wellspring—at least, that was the intent.

Daria shared a heartfelt hug with the Emama, then with Abeba. Other women elders came up and thanked her and Abeba for the hope they had brought to the people of Tesfa. It was a heady feeling. *Bright Eve* appeared to be on its way.

CHAPTER 23

"WELCOME TO ETHIOPIA, MR. HAMMOND," said the Minister of Trade, a lean and elegant black man in his fifties, who was clad in a business suit.

Four other high-level bureaucrats, also wearing business attire, shook hands with Greg as they were introduced by the trade minister.

Greg had just stepped off his corporate jet at Bole Airport in Addis Ababa. He was wearing lightweight brown slacks and an open-collared, white dress shirt with the sleeves rolled up.

"President Sitota sends his greetings," the minister said. "He is pleased that you have accepted his invitation to meet with him at the palace."

"Thank you," Greg said. "Have you located the person I asked about?"

"Yes. We know where she is working. We will take you there tomorrow."

Greg looked at his watch. It was only midafternoon. "Could we go there now?"

"It would be best to go in the morning," the minister said. "Our president has invited you to join him for a private dinner this evening. We were thinking you would want to rest and freshen up after your trip. Of course, if—"

"No. No, that's fine," Greg said. "Was Dr. Kocánová invited?"

"You must forgive us," said the minister. "We were told you did not wish her to be notified you were coming."

"That's fine. I'll see her tomorrow."

The minister pulled out his cell phone. "I will ask the president."

"No, don't trouble him," Greg said. He was tired from the trip as it was. He preferred to see Daria when he'd had some rest and was looking and feeling his best. Besides, it seemed President Sitota intended for the dinner to be one-on-one. That was okay with Greg. Even he didn't get that kind of face time with a head of state very often. It would also be a good opportunity to score some points for Daria by lobbying for her program.

"I'll see her tomorrow," Greg said. "Thank you."

Greg climbed into the back of a government SUV with the trade minister. A moment later, they were on the way led by one security vehicle in front and another behind.

The trade minister went into a pre-rehearsed sales pitch about the opportunities Ethiopia offered to foreign investors as their vehicle rolled along. Greg kept just enough of his attention on the minister to appear interested. With the rest of his mind, he thought about the chain of events that had culminated with his arrival in Addis.

After learning two days earlier that Daria was in Ethiopia, Greg had cleared his schedule and headed to London. While there, arrangements were made for him to travel on to Addis Ababa. Starling had no one working in Ethiopia, so everything was set up through the Ethiopian Embassy in London. The ambassador had recommended Greg conduct his visit as a formal guest of the government. It was the best way to assure his security while in-country. Though Ethiopia was generally safe for foreign visitors, kidnapping was a risk that could not be entirely ruled out. Greg Hammond, like it or not, would be a big prize for people who were in that business. Better to be safe than sorry.

Greg hadn't had any contact with Daria in more than six months. He was excited about the prospect of being part of her life again. He was also eager to see how she was using the money he'd given to the Equitable Health Alliance to make life better for the Ethiopian people.

As the motorcade carrying Greg rolled away from the airport, thoughts of his nephew, Andre, passed through his mind. He hadn't gone public with this trip to Ethiopia, but he assumed Andre would know. Greg didn't care. He felt he was on solid ground with his stewardship of Starling Worldwide. There would be no more apologies for doing something decent with his own money, and no more denying his passion for Daria Kocánová. If they ended up in the tabloids again, so be it. Greg was prepared to defend her and himself vigorously from Andre's baseless and malicious attacks with every tool at his disposal.

CHAPTER 24

WHEN DARIA AND MARC WREN got to the Tesfa Clinic at 7:45 the next morning, they were met by Arnoldo Diaz Parma. Looking quite somber, he told them about a six-year-old child who had come in the night before.

They hurried into the hospital ward to the little girl's bedside. She was unconscious, under mosquito netting.

"Her name is Nani," Arnoldo said.

"What happened to her?" Daria said.

Arnoldo said nothing. He pulled back the mosquito netting. The sedated child had a bandage covering the space between her legs, with a catheter emerging from it that was connected to a urine catch bag.

Daria looked at Arnoldo and said, "FGC?"

Arnoldo nodded.

Daria put a hand over her mouth. She was horrified and became tearful.

Marc immediately wrapped her in his arms and said, "It's not your fault. It would have happened anyway."

That didn't make it any easier. For Daria, until this moment, FGC had always been an abstract—a cultural construct, unseen but abhorred. Now, the ugly, cruel reality was right in front of her. Daria could barely contain her emotions.

Even in her unconscious state, Nani was gripping a blue plastic duck in her hand.

Daria sensed the scuffed-up and partly crumpled bathtub toy might be the child's only possession in the world.

Daria wanted to go someplace private, someplace she could confront the anger she felt toward herself and toward the adults who had desecrated this child. She fought back her frayed emotions, then said, "How bad is it?"

"She has a serious blood infection," Arnoldo said. "We're hoping it will respond to treatment."

"What if it doesn't?"

Arnoldo's grave expression was answer enough.

Daria's sorrow turned into calm rage. She could not understand how any human being could do such a brutal thing to another, especially to a child.

Arnoldo touched Daria's arm and directed her attention to a young woman, little more than skin and bones, who was curled up against the wall by the child's bed. "This is Nani's mother."

"What's her name?" Daria asked.

"Selam," Arnoldo said.

"Can Selam tell us how this happened?" Daria said.

Arnoldo spoke to the young woman in Amharic.

Selam explained that her husband was dead. Her brother-in-law, the child's uncle, was now the guardian of her and her children. Two days earlier, in the evening, without warning, the uncle, the child's grandparents, and other adult relatives had separated Nani from her mother. They had taken the terrified child to an elder woman who performs ritual cuttings on girls. They had done it to uphold the family's honor, and apparently, according to Selam, it was also done to protect the child's future place in the community.

Selam was beside herself with anguish. She said her little daughter had suffered terrible pain. Her in-laws had confined her in their one-room hut for more than a day before allowing her to bring her daughter to the hospital.

For Daria, it was too horrible. She'd come to Tesfa with the idea of using her *Bright Eve* empowerment program to improve the lives of girls and women in particular. In the moment of securing approval for her program from the community's women leaders, she had allowed the FGC issue to become part of the discussion. There was no question in her mind that the timing of Nani's cutting was not coincidental. It had come hours after the cutting issue had been raised with Emama Aberash, hours after Hakim and his squad of young males had confronted her and taken the computer.

Daria gazed at the tiny child, lying unconscious in the hospital bed. She was devastated by what had been done to Nani.

"It would have happened anyway at some point," Marc said.

That didn't make Daria feel any less distressed about it. This little girl was now fighting for her life. She was a direct casualty in a cultural awakening that had to come to Tesfa. Daria vowed not to let this tragedy dim her resolve.

Marc wanted to get on with hospital rounds before moving to the clinic and the patients lined up outside.

"I'll stay here with Selam," Daria said.

"You okay?" Marc said.

Daria put a reassuring hand on his shoulder. "I'll be fine."

Marc and Arnoldo went off to their work.

It appeared to Daria that Nani's mother hadn't had any nourishment in a long time.

Daria slid down the wall and sat on the floor next to Selam. Daria had carried only a small bag of steamed vegetables prepared for her by the hotel to eat during the day. She fished through her backpack until she found the bag of vegetables and the bottle of water she'd brought with her. She held them out to Selam.

Though she was obviously starving, Nani's young mother declined the offer.

Daria smiled at her and was insistent. Finally, Selam accepted Daria's kind gesture gratefully. She quickly devoured a peeled carrot. Daria gently urged her to slow down. Selam nodded appreciatively and began to eat more slowly.

Daria put her arm around the frail young woman and held her close. Then, she thought about the frustration of the last few days. More than thirty-six hours had passed since the *Bright Eve* computer had been taken by the enforcers. There'd been no word about its fate, no word from Tesfa's male leaders.

When Marc had found out about the confrontation over the com-puter, he was angry. He had insisted what she'd done was reckless. She did not agree. They hadn't slept together since. Yes, Daria had allowed the FGC issue to be raised with Emama Aberash, but she had not pressed it. Tesfa's male leaders had been informed ahead of time by UN authorities that she would be talking to Emama Aberash. They had reacted with indifference. There had been no reason to anticipate the kind of gender-based confrontation that took place when Hakim and his band of young toughs had taken the laptop.

Things had gotten worse yesterday morning. When Daria walked out of the hotel with Marc to go with their UN escort to Tesfa, she'd been told she could not go. The local UN commander had decided the incident on Tuesday created concerns for her personal safety. Daria thought that was nonsense. She argued vehemently but got nowhere.

Marc had gone off and spent the day working at his hospital. Daria was left fuming at the hotel. The commander who'd restricted her movement refused to talk to her. She went over his head to the United Nations Food Programme Directorate for North Africa.

Word had finally come back the previous night. She'd received permission to travel with Marc to the hospital this morning, on the condition she agree not to go anywhere else in Tesfa. Reluctantly, Daria had accepted the restriction, thinking she could at least make herself useful helping with patients.

Despite the setbacks, Daria was determined to finish what she started. She had to see it through, for the sake of all the little girls who would most certainly be subjected to the same ugly fate as Nani if she failed. She had to stay strong. She vowed to work with Abeba to find a way to move Tesfa in the right direction. She was thinking hard about that when she noticed one of the Ethiopian caregivers approaching her. The young woman said to her in broken English, "Excuse me, sister. A man has come to see you."

Daria wondered who that might be. She said, "Where is he?"

The caregiver pointed outside.

Daria got up and headed for the door. She hoped it was somebody who was part of Tesfa's male leadership. She reminded herself, don't play the blame game.

When Daria stepped outside, what she found was a young Ethiopian man with a big grin and two missing front teeth. He was just slightly taller than her, and very lean and muscular. He was wearing a ragged, orange-and-black T-shirt that said, "Oregon State Beavers."

"Mrs. Kocánová?" he said, in thickly accented English. "You are Mrs. Kocánová?"

"Yes."

"My name is Cervantes," said the young man.

He was dirty, and he smelled heavily of sweat, but he had a beaming smile and a cheeriness that Daria found instantly appealing. He held up several batteries that Daria recognized as having come from the laptop Hakim had taken two days ago.

"You must forgive me," Cervantes said. "I was sent to get these recharged."

"Where is the laptop?"

"It is in safe hands."

"Whose hands?"

"Our leaders," Cervantes said.

"What are they doing with it?"

"Before batteries died, they were watching your video."

Finally, a positive sign, thought Daria. "What did they think?"

"Some good, some not. They watched, and watched again, and again, then the batteries went dead."

"Did you see the video?"

"Yes," Cervantes said.

"What did you think?"

"Very good. You want people to learn, this is very smart way."

"You know about computers?"

Cervantes nodded. "I was student at the Oregon State University in America."

He pulled on his T-shirt to display the university logo.

"What are you doing here?"

"You want to know my story?"

"Yes," Daria said. "I would like that."

They moved away from the lines of people waiting to be seen at the outpatient clinic to a quiet place on the shady side of the concrete hospital building.

Cervantes began talking about growing up with his family of cattle herders in the distant countryside.

"When I was eight years old, some anthropologists were near my home," Cervantes said. "They were digging in a hillside for the bones."

"They were anthropologists?"

"Yes. Yes," Cervantes said. "You know anthropologists?"

Daria chuckled. "I am an anthropologist."

Cervantes's eyes grew wide, and his face lit up with absolute delight.

"You?" he said. "You are anthropologist?"

"Yes."

"First human people on Earth come from Ethiopia," Cervantes spouted out, proudly.

"Could be," Daria responded, with an enthusiastic grin. She really liked Cervantes.

"I showed the anthropologists a place with many old bones. They were happy, very, very happy. They gave me a book. This book was *Don Quixote*. This was first book I ever see. I was watching cattle all day, reading this book."

"*Don Quixote* was written by Cervantes," Daria said.

"Yes. You know this book?"

Daria nodded.

"All the time, I was reading this book, I was telling everybody, my name is Cervantes."

"That's not your real name?"

"Real name, Zalalem Birhanie. To everybody here, I am Cervantes."

"You taught yourself English by reading *Don Quixote*?"

"Yes. Then, later, I got a small radio. After that, I was sent to a school, where I learned more English."

Daria pointed to the logo on his orange T-shirt. "How did you get to this place?"

"I was good student. My government sent me to America to study agriculture."

"How did you end up here?"

"After two years, government cut scholarship program. I had no money. I returned to Ethiopia. I found my family in Tesfa."

"Do you know why I'm here?"

"You want to help the women?"

"The women, yes," Daria said. "Not just the women."

Cervantes's eyes grew wide. "You are saying all people?"

"Yes."

"This true? You will also help the men?"

Daria smiled. "Women, children, men—everybody."

An enthusiastic grin spread across Cervantes's face.

"I do have a problem," Daria said.

Cervantes's expression instantly became distressed.

"Are you married?" Daria asked.

"No."

"Do you want to get married in the future?"

"Yes, of course."

Daria could see that Cervantes was uncomfortable with the personal nature of her questions. Still, she pressed on. "Would you marry a woman who is not cut?"

Cervantes shrank with embarrassment. After a moment, he collected himself and said, "We have heard this is issue for you."

"What can we do about it?" Daria asked.

"Is difficult for our people to stop these old ways," Cervantes said.

"Would you marry a woman who is not cut?"

"My opinion," Cervantes said, "this tradition is not good. For you, I will say, I want wife who is not cut."

Daria didn't want him to do it for her.

Cervantes seemed to pick up on her concern. "I have seen this thing with my own eyes. Alyia is my sister. When I was boy, I heard her screams when she was cut. This was very bad. I was feeling very bad about this. For a long time, my sister suffered. Still, she suffers. It is wrong to do this."

Daria appreciated his reassurance. "How would you end this practice?"

"You are asking me?"

"Yes."

"Really? You want my opinion?"

"Yes."

Cervantes was delighted. He thought very hard for a moment, then said, "I think you must show the way to have a better life. Everybody wants to have good life and make a good life for the children."

"How would you do that?"

"First is education," Cervantes said.

"That's why I'm here," Daria said. "What else?"

"You know Dr. Muhammad Yunus?"

Daria nodded and said, "How do you know about him?"

"I read his book," said Cervantes. "He is hero for the people."

Daria knew a lot about Yunus. He was the Bengali economist who started the Grameen Bank, which was noted for its innovative policy of giving small, unsecured loans, mostly to poor women, allowing them to start their own businesses. Yunus's empowering idea had been an inspiration for Daria. It had spread from Bangladesh so successfully, variations of the Grameen micro-loan program were now helping millions of people in dozens of countries around the world. Muhammad Yunus had been awarded a Nobel Prize for his effort.

"What would you say to Yunus if he came to Tesfa?" Daria asked.

"I would tell him to bring his money here," Cervantes said. "Make the loan. Give people a way to have some income."

"That's what you would do if you were Tesfa's leader?"

"More than that," Cervantes said. "You know, we need good toilets. Very bad we need this, for the health, for the dignity. For me, if I have money, I would teach the men to build good toilets. Your computer can do this. A video can show them how to do it. They can do it."

Daria loved the idea. "If you had money, that's what you would do?"

Cervantes was barely able to contain his enthusiasm. "I buy concrete, and some tools. Cost very small, very small. Then I would pay our men to build toilets. Also, I would pay to make system to catch water from rainy season. We buy land. We pay people to grow food. We build schools. We pay people to teach the children. We pay people to do what is needed. We give people work, then they have money to buy things from other people. For me, this is making economy."

Daria was delighted. She loved Cervantes's animated personality, and she loved the way he thought. What he'd just laid out was very close to the same prescription she believed offered the best chance of elevating literally a billion people out of poverty around the world. Funding relief agencies to support expensive programs to give indigent people food, water, and other basics was only one part of the equation. The other big part was to help them help themselves. Give them the education, the tools, and the resources to create a better future for themselves.

Cervantes had a remarkable understanding of how to help his own people.

"Could you sell this idea to your leaders?"

"Me? You are asking me?"

"Why not you?"

"The leaders are old. They will not listen."

"They trusted you to come here to see me."

"Only because I speak English."

"Is anyone else in Tesfa educated like you?"

"No," Cervantes said. "Educated people would not live in this place."

"You do," Daria said.

"My family is here. Only for this reason."

Suddenly, their attention was drawn to the sound of approaching vehicles. They looked up and saw several trucks loaded with armed soldiers leading a caravan of vehicles.

A loud vocal call began to echo among the people of Tesfa, alerting everyone that something unexpected was happening.

The Ethiopian Army trucks pulled up and stopped at the hospital. The soldiers jumped down and quickly spread out to form a protective perimeter. Then two large, white SUVs rolled up and stopped very close to Daria and Cervantes. A group of men wearing dark business suits jumped out of the first SUV. They appeared to be some sort of high-level security team.

Men, women, and children came pouring out of the recesses of Tesfa and began congregating around the hospital. Marc Wren, Arnoldo Diaz Parma, and other staffers rushed out of the clinic to check on the commotion.

One of the dark-suited men went to the second SUV and opened the back door. Two men were inside.

Cervantes grabbed Daria's arm and shook it excitedly when he saw the first man step out of the SUV. "President Sitota! That is President of Ethiopia."

Daria was astonished and overjoyed when she saw the second man. It was Greg Hammond.

CHAPTER 25

*D*ARIA LOOKS SO SURPRISED, THOUGHT Greg. That was certainly understandable. She hadn't seen or heard from him in half a year, and he didn't have a history of showing interest in countries like Ethiopia, let alone in visiting them. What mattered was she looked happy, even excited to see him.

In the worst way, he wanted to go to her, to touch her, to take her in his arms. But he was with the president of the country. Decorum was required. Moreover, sudden movements were probably not a good idea when surrounded by bodyguards and armed soldiers trained to react to anything unexpected.

In fact, the moments following their arrival turned out to be comically awkward.

President Sitota was the visiting dignitary, waiting for someone to step forward and greet him. No one did.

Finally, the Ethiopian president chuckled, and said, "It seems we should take the lead."

Greg followed along as the president waved a greeting and started toward the doctors and staff standing by the hospital. As he walked alongside the president, Greg glanced at Daria. He gestured for her to come forward.

She smiled and moved to join him.

Greg was surprised by her muted appearance. This was not the Daria he'd come to know. She seemed to have gone out of her way to suppress her natural beauty, to look more ordinary and accessible. She was dressed modestly in baggy field pants, a simple, long-sleeved print blouse, and a white hat with floppy brim to keep the sun off her face.

When they came together a few moments later, he took her hand and squeezed it affectionately, but no intimate word passed between them. The focus was on introductions.

"Mr. President," Greg said. "This is my friend, Dr. Daria Kocánová, the anthropologist."

Daria blushed. She was not a PhD, not yet, but she appreciated Greg's effort to elevate her. She shared a warm handshake with the Ethiopian president. "I hope you will also be my friend, Dr. Kocánová."

"Thank you, Mr. President," Daria said. "Thank you for honoring the people of Tesfa with your presence."

The president acknowledged her words with a friendly bow, then he said, "Perhaps you can provide further introductions."

Daria quickly introduced Marc Wren and Arnoldo Diaz Parma to the president and to Greg. Then, she backed away graciously as the two doctors introduced other members of the medical staff.

So, thought Greg, *this is Marc Wren.*

He wasn't terribly impressive in person. Daria had talked about him like he was some kind of living saint.

Immediately, Greg scolded himself. He knew he was being peevish. Marc Wren clearly was a remarkable man. Daria had presented abundant evidence, and further proof was right here at this hospital in this place of wretched poverty. Even so, Greg's feelings about Marc Wren were ambivalent, undeniably because the good doctor appeared to be a serious rival where Daria was concerned.

As the introductions continued, Greg noticed Marc glancing at him. He sensed a hint of jealousy in the look. Why would Marc Wren appear jealous unless he saw Greg as a competitor?

Greg found himself wondering if Daria had been sleeping with the good doctor. She certainly admired him. They were here in Ethiopia together.

For Greg, it didn't change anything. He wasn't angry or upset about it. She had a right to keep company with another man. Greg had no claim on her. He had effectively walled himself off from her for many months. Now, he wanted her back in his life. Knowing that another man was competing for her attention only reinforced his determination.

The opportunity to steal a moment with Daria came when Marc Wren and the other doctors led President Sitota off on a tour of the hospital. Greg and Daria dropped back a few steps. Then he took her hand in his and squeezed it affectionately.

Daria leaned close and said quietly, "What are you doing here?"

"I came to see you."

"You have given me a very big shock."

"I hope you don't mind."

"This is not something I would expect from you," she said, with a look that reflected real appreciation.

"I hope I'm not intruding," Greg said. "I didn't know the president would decide to join me this morning."

"This is wonderful," Daria said. "It's good that he comes to see this place. And you…all this way."

Greg felt relieved. He hadn't been sure how she would react to him suddenly showing up after being out of her life for so long.

"Now you can see what happens with this money you have given," Daria said.

"I definitely see the need," he said.

Greg saw that Daria's attention was now on Arnoldo Diaz Parma leading President Sitota past the hospital ward without taking him inside.

"Mr. President," Daria called out, as she left Greg and hurried to catch up with the Ethiopian leader. "Before we go farther, there is a patient you and Mr. Hammond should see."

She took the president's arm and turned him back toward the entrance to the hospital ward.

Greg caught the look in Marc Wren's eyes. He appeared less than happy with what she was doing.

Daria led President Sitota and Greg to the bed of Nani. The little girl was still unconscious.

"When I came here this morning, I was told about this child," said Daria, who appeared barely able to contain her emotions. "Her name is Nani. Two days ago, her relatives cut her genitals. She has lost a lot of blood. She is in danger of dying from infection. She is sedated to spare her the terrible pain of what was done to her."

Daria paused to choke back a sudden rush of emotion. Then, she continued, "This child is six years old."

Greg was deeply shaken by the scene, and he could see that President Sitota was feeling very uncomfortable.

"Please forgive me if this is distressing for you, Mr. President," Daria said. "I assure you, it is nothing compared to what Nani will feel when she wakes up and will live with for the rest of her life, assuming she survives."

The president took in the scene for another moment, then said, "I am very sorry to see this. We have laws against this practice."

President Sitota looked at the doctors. "Can this child be moved? I can take her to our best hospital. Would that improve her chances?"

Marc Wren spoke up. "Definitely, it would, Mr. President."

The medical staff immediately began preparing Nani to travel. While this was happening, Daria talked more about female genital cutting. Greg had known almost nothing about it until this moment. He was shocked that such a practice could still be happening on such a wide scale.

Daria turned to him. "You are the leader of a very large media company. Is it possible, you could use this great resource to tell Nani's story?"

"We don't have any people in this country."

"You are seeing this yourself," Daria said. "You can write about your experience."

Greg thought about it. She'd put him on the spot. But there was nothing wrong with her logic, and there was nothing stopping him. He reached into his pocket and pulled out his cell phone. It wasn't like he didn't know how to write a story. The first real job he'd had was staff reporter for the company's original newspaper in Christchurch.

Greg touched her on the arm and said, "Thank you for the inspiration."

He started snapping pictures. He got shots of Nani being prepared for travel by Arnoldo and the hospital staff, shots of one of the president's security guards picking up Nani in his arms and carrying her outside. He got a splendid image of President Sitota, Daria, and Marc Wren following behind as the child was carried out of the hospital.

Greg looked around and was surprised to see even more people had gathered. He took pictures of the crowd. He saw that Daria's attention was on a group of adult men standing together. He snapped pictures as she went and spoke to them. Then she huddled with the young man named Cervantes. Greg moved closer and listened in as Daria conferred with Cervantes.

"That is Hakim," Daria said. "Are those men with him the leaders of Tesfa?"

"Yes," Cervantes said.

"You must go and tell them what has happened," Daria said. "You must tell them what we talked about earlier, about the possibilities for Tesfa."

"What if they don't listen?"

"Cervantes, I just met you. I have seen that you are a leader," Daria said. "You can convince them. I know you will say just the right thing. Now is the time. Now is the time to choose a better future for their children and themselves. Go and talk to them."

Cervantes appeared energized, He took another moment to get himself mentally focused, then, with a look of determination, he headed toward the cluster of elders.

Daria turned her attention back to Greg. She pointed to the unconscious child being taken to one of President Sitota's SUVs. "Don't look at me. Get more photos."

Greg snapped more images of Nani and her mother as they were moved into the SUV, which then sped away.

Then, Greg focused his cell phone camera on Cervantes, who was communicating animatedly with the male leaders of the community. Greg didn't know what was being said, but it was clear Cervantes had their full attention, and he was working hard to sell Daria's proposal.

Greg noticed Daria urging two women to come forward out of the crowd. When they came up, Daria motioned for them to follow as she approached President Sitota.

"Mr. President," Daria said, "May I introduce you to Emama Aberash Zewdu, our mother from Tesfa, and this is my sister, Abeba Danichew, the director of our effort here in Ethiopia."

The president nodded graciously to each woman.

Emama Aberash, who was holding on tightly to Daria's arm, could barely contain her excitement at meeting her nation's president.

Less than ten minutes later, as President Sitota was preparing to depart, Cervantes came running up to Daria.

"Great lady, I have news."

Everybody's attention, including President Sitota's, went to Cervantes.

"The elders want to make deal."

"The things we talked about?" Daria said.

"Yes. Everybody like to do this."

Daria summarized for Greg and President Sitota. "I have said to Cervantes, if they allow their women and girl children to participate in our *Bright Eve* program, I will find money for them to have jobs building toilets, making the schools, doing work that makes life better."

Daria was about to bring up the issue of FGC. The raw emotion she was feeling for Nani was still close to the surface. Then, she decided Marc Wren was right. Better to be smart and not overreach. She would take the patient, culturally respectful approach that had already ended the cutting in many traditional communities. With that settled in her mind, she turned to Cervantes and said, "So, they accept the terms."

"They are asking also for other things," Cervantes said.

"What other things?" Daria asked.

"They want to have the television. They want to watch BBC."

Greg pretended to be annoyed. "BBC? What about Starling?"

"Your network has no signal here," President Sitota said.

"We'll fix that," Greg said.

President Sitota appeared to be uneasy with the discussion. "I'm afraid there are other issues."

"Can you say what they are?" Daria said.

"For one, the land this place occupies is not theirs," the president said.

"Who owns the land?" Daria said.

"The government. Official policy discourages this kind of thing from happening. It is better if the people stay on their traditional lands."

Daria responded, "Mr. President, they're here because their traditional lands can no longer support them."

"Yes. There is no good answer for this problem."

"You are the government," Daria said. "If you can't fix this, there is no hope."

"I understand," the president said.

"Tesfa can become a great example to the world," Daria said, with conviction. "Mr. Hammond can use his media company to tell the world about Tesfa and about your visionary leadership."

The president thought about it, then said, "Let me see what I can do."

Daria turned back to Cervantes. "Tell your leaders we have a deal."

"There is something else," Cervantes said.

Daria waited for Cervantes to explain.

"The leaders are asking for something else."

"Please. Tell us," Daria said.

Cervantes hesitated, then said, "Electricity for all of Tesfa."

Daria thought about it, then said, "That would be quite costly. It may have to wait."

Greg chimed in. "What are we talking about?"

Cervantes spoke up, "Solar panels for every home."

Daria looked at Cervantes with a knowing smile and said, "Electricity. Who gave them that idea?"

Cervantes shrugged and grinned sheepishly.

Greg leaned close to Daria and quietly said, "Make the deal. I'll give you the money."

Daria stared at him with grateful eyes and said quietly, "Thank you."

Then, she gave her attention back to Cervantes and said, "Toilets, television, plus electricity, they agree for the women to do *Bright Eve*?"

Cervantes nodded.

Daria turned to President Sitota and said, "Mr. President, if we brought electricity to Tesfa, could we count on your government for the necessary permits?"

The Ethiopian leader said, "If Mr. Hammond will support this plan, so will we."

Daria turned to Greg. "What do you think?"

"Sounds like a deal to me," said Greg.

Daria said to Cervantes, "Tell the elders, we have a deal. Tell them if they honor their part of it, Mr. Hammond will make certain all the world knows about the good that happens here in Tesfa."

Cervantes turned to leave.

"Cervantes," Daria called to him.

He gave his attention back to Daria.

"I have a condition," she said. "You must agree to be our coordinator for the men."

Cervantes lit up with excitement. "You are offering me a job?"

Daria called Abeba over. "This is Abeba Danichew. She is the director for *Bright Eve* in Ethiopia. You will report to Abeba as coordinator of the men's programs in Tesfa."

"I have a job?"

"You have a job," Daria said.

Bursting with joy, Cervantes did a little dance. Then, he composed himself, and said, "I tell the leaders, we have deal."

Daria smiled as Cervantes left to rejoin the elder men.

"You are a force, Dr. Kocánová," President Sitota said. "I pity the person who gets in your way."

"Mr. President, I think this would not have happened if you had not come here today."

"You can thank Mr. Hammond for that. You are fortunate to have such an enthusiastic and powerful admirer."

Daria smiled and touched Greg's arm warmly. "He knows I appreciate him."

Greg was elated and in awe of Daria's ability to use her initiative and charm to seize the moment and facilitate such a remarkable outcome.

When President Sitota departed with his entourage a few minutes later, Greg stayed behind with Daria. Just as Marc and the other doctors were heading back into the clinic to resume treating patients, Cervantes returned with the computer that had been taken two days earlier.

"The agreement is done," Cervantes said proudly.

Daria accepted the computer from Cervantes, shook his hand enthusiastically, and said, "You are *Bright Eve's* man in Ethiopia."

Cervantes threw his arms up triumphantly and let out a joyous howl.

Daria turned her attention to Aberash. "My Emama, you, and the women of Tesfa, must stand behind this agreement."

Abeba translated Daria's words, then Aberash's reply.

"You have my word, sister," said Aberash, who was quite obviously very pleased.

Daria handed the laptop to Aberash and said, "I ask you to work with our sister, Abeba, and with Cervantes, to make *Bright Eve* a success. It will be a success if you make it so."

Cervantes said, "We need more batteries and some device for charging."

"Abeba has batteries, solar charging units, and when the time comes, she'll have more computers," Daria said.

Then she turned to Greg. "I'm sorry. I must give this my attention."

"That's okay. Do what you have to do."

She urged him toward the clinic. "Go inside. See how Marc and his team help these people."

Then, she gave her attention back to Abeba, Aberash, and Cervantes.

Despite the heat, Greg felt a chill go down his spine. Swarms of people were milling about, all living on survival's edge. Here was Daria, totally focused, humbly, respectfully, assertively, leveraging the moment to launch her *Bright Eve* program.

Greg began snapping photos of the remarkable scene.

Forty-five minutes later, he was just coming out of the clinic when Daria rejoined him.

"So, you've seen the clinic at work?" she said.

"Yes," Greg said. "Good people, doing good work."

Daria pulled off her hat and swabbed the gritty sweat from her brow.

"You okay?" he said.

"Yes, sure," she said, with a weary smile.

Greg sensed she was seriously dehydrated. He pulled a liter bottle of water from his shoulder bag and offered it to her.

She pushed it back in his bag, then urged him to follow her. They went to a narrow space between a parked mini-bus and the clinic building.

Daria looked around. She saw they couldn't be seen. Then she reached into his bag, pulled out the water bottle, and drank down several long gulps.

"Thank you for this," Daria said, as she handed the bottle back to him. "You understand clean water is not something that comes easy here. I cannot drink in front of these people."

Greg's heart stirred. He loved the sensitivity and compassion that defined her character.

"The president called you a force. That was an understatement," Greg said.

Daria grinned and touched his cheek. "I am so happy to see you."

Greg was about to kiss her when she began to cough.

She cleared her throat, then took more water from him.

"You know this fellow Cervantes?" she said, as she pulled out a handkerchief.

"Yes. He is impressive," Greg said.

"Today, just before you arrived, I met him for the first time," she said, wiping sweat and dust from her face. "You believe that? Just before you arrived, he came to me. You could not invent such a person."

"Sometimes it helps to get lucky," Greg said. "You might want to get him some new clothes."

"We need him to influence the men here. For now, the best thing is for him to stay just as he is," Daria said. "If he does this job well, we'll send him back to finish his studies at university."

Greg's thoughts turned to Nani. "I'm so sorry about the little girl."

"At least now, she has a chance to survive," Daria said. "You want to do something for her?"

"I would like that."

"Her mother is twenty-two years old, already a widow. She also has a son, three years old."

"Can you come up with a plan for them?" Greg said.

"You want this responsibility?"

"Yes," Greg said. "I would like that."

"Abeba can set something up," Daria said. "You want to help, don't stop there. Tell the world what happened to Nani. Tell them what you saw."

"I will."

"Thank you," Daria said. "It means so much that you have come here."

"I had to come. I had to see you."

Daria smiled.

He touched his forehead to hers. "I need to be alone with you."

"Not here."

Greg wondered if he'd already lost her. "Marc Wren?"

"No person on Earth is more decent," Daria said.

Greg felt his heart skip a beat. Then, before he could think, he said, "Are you in love with him?"

Daria looked at Greg thoughtfully, then said, "He is my friend."

"How much of a friend?"

"I've heard nothing from you in many months," Daria said, in a tone that seemed purposely to be friendly and encouraging.

Greg wanted to stay, but he also felt he should offer her an easy out. "I don't want to be a disruption. I'll be leaving tomorrow."

Daria quickly responded, "You must not think that way. There is nothing serious between Marc and me."

"Are you staying together?"

"In the same hotel, yes," Daria said. Then, she added, "I can say he would be upset if I was with you while we are all here together."

Greg understood but couldn't hide his disappointment.

Daria took his hand in hers. "Two days from now, I am back in Europe. We have some time then if you like."

No way did he want to wait that long.

CHAPTER 26

DESPITE GREG'S EAGERNESS, OVER THE next thirty-six hours, Daria remained true to her word. Except a few moments of playful teasing, and a couple of stolen kisses, there was no intimate contact.

She'd been right about Marc. Greg had watched him at work, tirelessly treating the sick and injured in his Tesfa hospital. On the night before departure, the three of them spent several pleasant hours at dinner at the Hotel Excelsior talking about Daria's *Bright Eve* project and Marc's work.

Greg was determined that if nothing was going to happen while he and Daria remained in Ethiopia, they could at least fly back to Europe together on the Starling corporate jet. At first, she'd politely refused. Greg wouldn't be put off. He enticed her with the prospect of doing something neither had done before, joining the mile high club. That was too much for Daria to pass up. She made it clear, though, it would be the first and only time she would travel on a private jet.

Her rationale was that the aircraft would have to make the trip whether she was aboard or not.

The afternoon of departure, Greg stopped to express his appreciation to his host, President Sitota, then he was driven in one of the government's white SUVs to the Hotel Excelsior. Daria was there, waiting. She joined him in the back seat of the vehicle.

Next, they stopped at the Ethio-Swedish Pediatric Hospital to visit Nani. The little girl was conscious, and thankfully, not in any pain.

"Look at you," Daria said to Nani. "You're doing so well."

Her young mother, Selam, was there. She cried and was so grateful to Daria and Greg for all they'd done for her daughter. Nani was no longer in danger, but it was too early to tell how severely she'd been maimed or how badly she would be scarred.

"Abeba will watch over them," Daria said to Greg. "How fortunate for this little girl that you came into her life."

"You saved her," Greg said. "I didn't do anything."

"But you will," Daria said. "You will give her a life worth living."

They said their goodbyes to the child and her mother, then headed out of the hospital. Just as they were getting back into the white SUV, Greg noticed the gold chain and pendant he'd given Daria, hanging around her neck. "I see you are wearing the cabbage."

"I love this one," she said, touching the gold pendant.

"But you're still opposed to the actual vegetable?" he said.

She chuckled.

"I've made myself an expert on cabbage," Greg said.

Daria's mouth twisted to a playful smirk.

"The world record for eating cabbage is more than six pounds in just nine minutes."

Daria laughed playfully, then said, "You are digging yourself a big hole."

He leaned close and muttered, "Punish me, please."

Daria clenched a fist and socked him softly on the chin.

Greg sniffed her neck, then said, "I'm missing that special fragrance."

Daria opened her backpack.

"You have it with you?" Greg said.

Daria searched through the pouch and found a small vial of cologne. She pulled it out and displayed it for him.

He smiled and let two words roll off his tongue, "Great Incitement."

She sprayed it on her neck and her wrists. Then she put her wrist under his nose. He savored the wonderful scent.

"It's your signature," he said, as his mind filled with thoughts of her wearing Great Incitement and nothing else.

The pilots were waiting when they arrived at the airport. The flight would be nonstop to London, 3,652 air miles, with just under eight hours from takeoff to touchdown. The front third of the aircraft was for the crew, the back two-thirds made up the passenger cabin. A privacy door sealed off the back from the front.

After the black jet was safely airborne, Greg went to the cockpit. The two pilots were the only crew on board. He told them he didn't want to be disturbed. They seemed to know well enough what was up. The captain told him to have a good time. Greg tapped him playfully on the shoulder then headed back to the passenger cabin. When he opened the door, he found Daria standing all the way in the back. She must have read his mind. She was wearing only her gold chain and cabbage pendant.

He closed the cabin door and locked it. Then he turned to her. "Do you have any idea how much I love seeing you naked?"

"This is my plan," Daria said. "This is how I make you suffer."

He went to her. They shared a long, passionate kiss, then he flipped a lever on the cabin's long sofa. It converted quickly to a bed that spanned from one side of the cabin to the other.

He stared at her playfully as he stripped out of his clothes.

Daria looked him over with approval. "You've lost weight."

"Since Schalchen, I'm ninety percent vegetarian."

"This is wonderful. I'm so proud of you."

They stretched out together on the bed. There was no urgency. Greg was quite happy to curl up quietly and intimately with her under a blanket. She soon fell asleep, snuggled with him. He stroked her hair and thought how lucky he was to have another chance with her. For him, real happiness had long been an elusive commodity. He'd experienced it last during his brief encounter with Daria in Schalchen. Now, he'd found her again. He dozed off, determined not to let her get away from him a second time.

Later, somewhere over the eastern Mediterranean, they awakened and began to touch and tease each other playfully. Then, the executive jet began shaking and bouncing in moderate turbulence. Greg and Daria hung on and had great fun, laughing and teasing while being tossed about wildly.

After the jet was cruising along in smooth air again, there was a lot of kissing, caressing, and cuddling. Then, Daria turned until she was on elbows and knees, looking back at him with an inviting expression. For

Greg, it was too exciting. He couldn't hold back. He gasped and groaned as his body shuddered with explosive release. Daria continued to stimulate herself until she went off powerfully. They laughed and collapsed together in the serene afterglow. It was wonderful. They'd just done it at thirty-four thousand feet, speeding along at something like ten miles a minute. It might not make the Guinness Book, but Greg knew he would think about this delicious moment and delight in it for the rest of his life.

Just after 9:00 p.m. London time, they arrived at Greg's flat. The housekeeper had stocked the refrigerator. They had something to eat, then retreated to the bedroom. Though Greg was weary from the trip, he felt giddy with excitement. He hoped he could sleep. In the morning, he was going to ask her to marry him.

CHAPTER 27

"Have you ever tried tantric sex?" she asked.

"What exactly is that?" Greg said.

They were in the luxurious bath of his London flat. It was Sunday morning. Daria was already out of the shower and drying herself, when Greg turned the water off, came out, and grabbed a towel for himself.

She took his hand. "Come. We try."

A moment later, they passed through shafts of sunlight blasting through the windows as they returned to bed.

"Sit with your body upright."

Greg eagerly followed her direction.

"Put your hands back to the sides and behind you. Be sure you are comfortable… Pull your feet together and spread your knees wide."

He followed her direction.

Then she straddled him until she was face-to-face with him, legs wrapped around him tightly.

"This is called Yab Yum," said Daria. "You can make it more complicated. I like it simple."

She put her arms around his neck and whispered, "Close your eyes… Relax… Connect yourself with the universe."

After a moment, he said, "That's all there is to it?"

"You are not relaxing," she said. "Start in your head, focus on the tension in your body. Let it flow freely… Allow it to escape through your fingers, your feet, and the top of your head."

Now, she could tell he was releasing the tension in his body.

"What should I be feeling?" he asked.

"For me, the best word for this is… bliss," she said. "I close my eyes. I allow my body to connect with yours. Together, we go to a beautiful place far from Earth."

"What place?"

She touched a finger to his lips and whispered, "Quiet. You must be quiet. Think of what is blissful."

A moment later, she felt him kissing her.

"I love you," he said, his voice hushed and raw with passion. "I love you so much, Daria Kocánová."

She had expected she would be hearing something like that from him. It excited her and troubled her at the same time.

"I want you in my life."

For now, she preferred to remain in the uncomplicated, tantric moment.

"Quiet," she whispered.

"We need to talk."

"Later," she said, as she kissed him and ran her fingers through his hair. "For now, you must relax."

He said nothing. She sensed his body relaxing again. She could feel his respiration slow.

He was finally getting it.

Daria loved connecting with the universe. She loved being this way with Greg. He was the first man with whom she'd shared herself this way. She had experienced this kind of spiritual intimacy with only one other person, her best friend in the world. It was a technique they'd enjoyed learning together.

Where Greg was concerned, Daria hated the confusion she felt. The attraction to him was real and stronger than she wanted to admit. While she didn't like the selfish world he occupied, she admired him for being enormously successful in that world. It was exciting to be wanted by a man of such wealth and stature. At the same time, she despised many of the things he'd done to get to the top of his mountain. She knew he was troubled by this himself. He wanted new direction. She'd thought about how to respond when she heard him express his love. She still wasn't sure what she wanted. If the decision could be based solely on physical attraction, she could easily see herself sharing her life with him. Too bad it wasn't that simple.

At that moment, she was happy just being cupped in a warm embrace with him. She soon lost herself in a higher consciousness, in search of her own bliss.

Sometime later, she returned from her far reaches when she felt his sweet, loving kisses on her eyes, face, and neck.

"I want to die this way," he said, almost too faintly to hear.

"You are happy."

"Too happy," he said. After a moment, he continued, "I need this. I need this so much. My life is insane. I hate what I'm doing."

"You must change what you are doing."

"I wish it were that simple."

"You know how you have lived. You are not so proud of this."

He was quiet for a moment. Then, in a tone that reflected sadness rather than irritation, he said, "There's not another person in my life that would dare say something like that to me."

"You have a voice inside that is telling you just the same thing," she said.

He kissed her again, then said, "I need you to be the last one I talk to every day. I need you to be my partner and closest advisor."

Daria nuzzled him affectionately, then said, "If you ask me, is there love in my heart for you, I have to say yes. If you ask, can I spend my life with you, I have to say, I am thinking this would not work."

"Why not?" he said, obviously wounded.

"An example is yesterday we traveled from Ethiopia to here in your big airplane, just the two of us."

"There were also two pilots."

"We don't count them. They were there only because you needed them to be. How much time did we fly?"

"About eight hours."

"How far?"

"Maybe four thousand miles."

"How much fuel?"

He took a moment to think, then said, "Probably five thousand gallons."

"So, one gallon of fuel burned makes twenty pounds of carbon. Just from this one trip, that's 100,000 pounds of dirty carbon air pollution into the sky. Compare this to Tesfa, for all the people, many thousands of people, it takes several days, maybe even a week, or two weeks, to do such damage."

"You flew there on a jet."

"Yes, but there were 250 passengers. The carbon footprint for each passenger was much less than was yours alone when you flew to Addis."

"That's splitting hairs."

"I do not suggest returning to live in caves. It is possible to balance quality of life with limiting the damage we do."

"You think I'm on the wrong side of that?"

"How would you answer this question?"

He had no response.

She sensed how conflicted he was feeling. "This is why we would not be good together. You don't think about these things. You've always taken for granted that you should live this way."

She could feel the tension taking over his body.

She kissed his forehead and held him tight. "Please. We are just talking."

His emotions appeared totally exposed. "I need you in my life. I love everything about you."

She caressed his arm and comforted him. He might be a billionaire or close to it, he might be an alpha male in the dark world he occupied, but deep down, he was sensitive and emotionally fragile.

She kissed him again, then extracted herself from his tantric embrace and got up off the bed.

"Come on," she said. "Some tea would be good."

He took the hand she offered. They headed out to the kitchen together.

She saw him gazing at her as she put two cups of water into the microwave. There was no mistaking the adoration in his eyes.

"I do care for you," she said.

"But you couldn't love me?"

"Trust me when I say this," she said, "I would make you crazy."

"You want to help people," he said. "I have money. We could create a foundation. I could put at least five hundred million into it. A lot gets done with that kind of money."

"You make it sound very tempting," she said.

"Outside of Gates and a few others, not many have been willing to give up that much of their wealth."

"It's a lot of money," she said. "You know me by now. I am not happy to do something only halfway."

"What more would you want?"

She took the cups of hot water out of the microwave, dropped in tea bags, then sat across from him at a small table.

"One-third of all the people in the world are surviving, just barely," said Daria. "For me, I'm happy I can do something to help at least some of those people. If I were you, if I had the ability to reach billions of people around the world, I would do things differently."

"In what way?"

"You have newspapers, television, the net media. You deliver so much information. Your job is to tell people about the world they live in. You don't do that. Instead, you shape the news to fit how the rich and powerful see the world."

"You think I have a choice about that?"

"The *Euro Standard*," Daria said, "would you say the information in this paper is the same as on your television and your other kinds of media?"

"Pretty much."

"Did you know the American military budget is much more than eight hundred billion dollars every year? All the other developed countries in the world put together do not spend that much money on weapons and war. How often did you report this in the *Euro Standard*? I have never seen it. How often have you done stories on the people living in places like Tesfa? That's much more than a billion people. Just think, so many people with barely enough to eat, with little or no clean water, living with endless suffering, often no access to education… Almost all the world's population growth—much more than seventy million additional people every year—almost all are in the poorest countries. I have never seen any of this reported in the *Euro Standard*."

"Our shareholders get antsy if the stock drops two points," Greg said. "They expect me to deliver a profit."

"Only this?"

"Fact of life," he said.

"*Vectors* is your television show."

"Yes.

"In many parts of the world, people see *Vectors*?"

"Yes," Greg said.

"Always, it has terrorists from poor countries attacking the rich nations with every kind of mass murder device your writers can imagine."

"I'm not crazy about *Vectors* either," Greg said.

"Can we agree it encourages people's worst fears? It makes them see threats around every corner. It labels all poor people as terrorists. You really think the world is like that? On *Vectors*, the heroes, your good guys, are sometimes doing what amounts to torture. This is a proper message?"

Greg was obviously distressed by what she was saying, but he made no effort to defend his company's track record.

"I am who I am," Daria said. "I have to be this kind of honest to be happy. I have to say what I'm thinking."

Greg offered no response.

Daria continued, "If I had a resource like yours, I would use it to inspire people. I would use it to educate the world about climate change, on gender equality, on education. I would be reporting on all the millions of suffering people who are growing up terribly in the world's most troubled places, especially the young people. They have nothing. They are the ones we should be reading about in the *Euro Standard*. It used to be, people living on the margins didn't know what was going on in Europe and the US. Now they know everything. They see it on the internet. Every day, they see it. Even the poorest people often have access to this information. If you were one of those young people living without hope, how would you feel seeing what people have and seeing how the worst kind of people behave in the rich countries? The word that describes this is resentment. There is so much resentment. So many people are feeling this. Have you ever written about that reality in the *Euro Standard*? Has this ever been part of a story on your show called *Vectors*?"

Greg was clearly not feeling good about himself. He had no answer for Daria's criticism.

She felt bad for him. She reached over and put a comforting hand over his.

"I'm sorry," she said. "I get started, and I cannot stop myself. This is the point. If I was with you, I would make your life worse, not better."

"It doesn't have to be that way."

"I know myself. If I was sleeping with you every night, you would know what I was thinking. I could not stay quiet."

"I wouldn't expect you to."

"I have a big mouth. You would hate me."

"I can't imagine that."

"I could."

"There's only so much I can do," he pleaded. "If I change the company game plan, the machine starts to sputter."

"You understand what I am saying?" she said. "As long as the Starling Company is the way it is, for us, it would not work—too much frustration, too much friction."

"If I disrupt the company's profitability, I lose control."

"I understand."

"You know about Lydia and Andre. I can make small changes. I can pledge my personal wealth. I can do that. I will do that. What I can't do is put the company's bottom line at risk."

"You've already done so much," she said. "You must not think I am ungrateful."

He was looking so unhappy. She went around the table and settled into his lap. She cuddled him close and kissed his forehead affectionately.

"You must believe me," she said. "I'm doing you a favor."

"Can't we negotiate something that would work for you and for me?"

Before she could answer, his cell phone rang. He grabbed it from the kitchen counter. He recognized the number on the phone's screen. "It's my assistant. I need to take this. You mind?"

"Not at all," Daria said. She left him behind in the kitchen and went back to the master bathroom.

She began to apply a creamy lotion to her skin. She thought about the possibilities that could come from being with Greg. He'd said he would create a foundation endowed with half a billion dollars. That kind of money could do a lot of good for the world. It certainly wasn't easy to walk away from something like that. Still, she knew herself. How could she be happy being that close to the center of power of a media empire that distorted, marginalized, or completely ignored the real problems in the world? Starling was not the most conservative of the half dozen corporate media giants that delivered information to the people of the world's wealthiest nations. But, where journalistic integrity was concerned, the company's history was anything but stellar. So much could be accomplished if that kind of power was used honestly and truthfully to serve the greater good. She believed Greg when he'd said he wanted to transform the company. She also understood the forces that made it so difficult for him to affect change without putting his own future at risk. Could she learn to live with that? He said he was willing to push things as far as he could. Should that be enough? The prospect of a life with him was not unappealing. She really did care for him.

Greg came into the bathroom. "I have to get back to New York. Andre's at it again."

Daria scowled. "I do not like this nephew of yours."

"He bought a boat racing team."

"You have already stopped him from this."

"I said no when he asked for sponsorship money," Greg said. "That was before he became the boat's owner. This time he's going directly to the board members."

"He can do that?"

"Yes," Greg said. "My father is supporting him. It may be smart to let Andre win this one."

"When will you leave?"

"This afternoon," Greg said. He took her in his arms and kissed her. "You and I have unfinished business."

"Yes," she said, as she playfully slapped his butt. "You have made me your target for acquisition."

"What about that?"

Daria considered the question, then looked into his eyes and said, "My heart is saying one thing, but my head is telling me another."

"You're not saying no?"

"Honestly, I'm thinking this would be a mistake," Daria said, while smoothing his mussed hair. "I also know there could be many worse things than spending my life with you."

"So, we're making progress?" Greg said.

"The more you know me, the less you will like me."

"The more I know you, the more I admire you," Greg said. He thought a bit more, then added, "In my heart, there will never be anything but love for Daria Kocánová."

She stared into his eyes, with what felt like love in her heart. She shared a long, passionate kiss with him, then asked, "How much time before you leave?"

"Four hours, maybe five."

Daria broke out of his embrace. She took his hand and led him back into the bedroom.

"You haven't answered my question," he said.

"Which question?" she said as she flopped onto the bed, rolled onto her back, and displayed herself provocatively.

"What about us?"

"I have told you my concerns," she said. "For now, I hope we can see each other from time to time."

He chuckled and said, "You mean the next time you need two million euros?"

She laughed. "For certain, it will happen then."

He got down on the bed and stretched out on his back beside her.

She ran her fingers over the line of fine hairs that went up the center of his abdomen, then said, "If you call me, I will answer. If you want to see me, I will try to make time for you."

"No more million-euro weekends with rich guys?"

"We can never say never to that."

"Promise you'll come to me first?" Greg said.

"This will make you happy?"

"For now," he said, as he shifted onto his right hip and took in her intoxicating aura.

A moment later, he leaned close, nuzzled her neck sensuously, and said, "We have a deal?"

"Mmmm," she muttered as she cuddled close to him.

CHAPTER 28

L*A MER CINQ* WAS DEAD in the water five miles off the coast of Antibes in gentle swells. Andre was pissed. It was hot as hell, and he was sweating profusely in his fireproof racing suit.

His boat was like a sleeping whale. Barely more than the top if its broad, glassy smooth hull was visible above the waterline. On top, the cockpit hatch was open, as was the engine access hatch. Andre was sitting on the hull, watching his team of technicians and mechanics replace a fuel line.

It had taken more than an hour to tow the boat out to the offshore practice course. When *La Mer Cinq* separated from its tender, Andre was in the driver's seat. During the checklist to engine start, a sensor had gone off, indicating a possible fuel leak. It shouldn't have happened.

The crew was getting paid big money to have the boat ready.

Andre wanted it fixed now. They damn well better get it done. If the day's practice runs ended up being scrubbed without even an engine start, he was going to put his fireproof boot firmly up the crew chief's ass.

The letter of intent to purchase *La Mer Seigneur Racing* had been signed by both parties only three days earlier. Andre's lawyers were preparing the contracts to finalize the sale. The deal had been sealed after Andre made a quick trip back to New Zealand the previous week to sell his mother and his grandfather on his plan. His mother hadn't been crazy about it but was supportive nonetheless. Poppy was the surprise. He'd been totally enthusiastic.

Andre had shown Poppy pictures and video of *La Mer Quatre,* the predecessor of *Cinq* in action. Poppy loved it. He was always eager to hear about Andre's exploits. At some level, the old man was reliving his vibrant, young adult years through his grandson. Not only had Poppy fronted the money to buy the racing team, he'd also agreed to use his influence to get Starling Worldwide to take on principal sponsorship. Andre wished he'd thought of going to Poppy when he first floated the idea of sponsoring the team several years earlier. Maybe Greg wouldn't have been able to quash the idea. No matter. That was old news. Now Andre's ownership and Starling's sponsorship was a done deal.

The team's tender, a 110-foot custom-built motor yacht, was nearby. Along with Morty and Bernard, there were four very attractive young ladies from Norway on board, vacationers whom Bernard had recruited on the promenade the day before. They were acting like most of the young hotties who visited Antibes in the summertime. They couldn't believe their dumb luck to have fallen in with three guys with money that could show them a good time. Andre didn't want to disappoint them. He had a need to show them some speed. They'd been brought along to get them primed and ready for the night ahead. Andre had already picked the two he wanted. He was eager for them to see him slicing through the water like a screaming fiend in *La Mer Cinq*. He was ready to show off.

Andre smiled and waved to the girls. Despite the momentary aggravation, he was feeling good. He felt sure he was going to end up as Starling's CEO. Poppy was the only person standing in the way. The old man was still supporting Greg, but in principle, he also supported Andre. For the moment, Poppy wasn't willing to force Greg to accept Andre as his successor, but it was only a matter of time. Greg's act was wearing thin. Andre knew exactly what he was up to. He knew Greg had just returned from Ethiopia with his Czech girlfriend. He knew Greg had shacked up with her at his place in London. She was a very hot babe. She was also working overtime to establish herself as some kind of hero for all the sad cases of the world. Andre had met plenty like her. She was the kind of bitch that knew everything and couldn't keep her mouth shut, the type that liked to mess with a man's head. Greg had kept his distance for a while. Now he was back after her again. The longer Greg hung with her, the more inevitable that he would end up in deep shit again.

Starling Worldwide's latest quarterly statement showed the company was still performing adequately. But Greg had lost his edge. His appetite for growing the company through mergers and acquisitions had virtually disappeared. Andre's inside man at Starling's New York headquarters had told him there was no significant activity in that arena at all. Greg had also done virtually nothing about finding an alternative to Andre as successor.

Things might be at an impasse at the moment, but no way was Andre sitting on his hands. He was damned sure engaged in a big-league pissing contest with his uncle. Somebody was going to end up on the floor. It was not going to be Andre.

The best people at doing professional dirty work were right down the street from the White House in Washington, DC. Of all the public relations firms in DC, Erskine and Hyndes was the most aggressive and the most transactional. Andre had hired them to facilitate his succession to CEO of Starling. Their fees were insane, but they had a well-earned reputation for getting results. If they couldn't get something done legally, they had access to freelancers who specialized in operating effectively outside of such constraints. Without a doubt, Erskine and Hyndes were bad dudes, pricks of the first order. Already, they were engaged in an aggressive, below-the-radar, campaign to undermine Greg's leadership at Starling. Every misstep would be distorted, every false move was going to be turned against Greg in the media and magnified in the worst possible way. Erskine and Hyndes were also quietly promoting Andre. First, with the public, by planting stories in the media that inflated perceptions and made Andre appear to be prime CEO material. Second, by very subtly manipulating Starling's board members and shareholders, to encourage a positive perception of Andre among them.

Greg Hammond might be a seasoned competitor with a winning record in the corporate arena, where there were at least some rules. But Andre fancied himself to be a cage fighter. Rules were almost non-existent. The winner was nearly always the combatant willing to do whatever was necessary. The fight was on. No more sit-downs between rounds. This time, it was to the finish. Andre was on the offense. He was playing dirty. He liked his chances. Too bad for Uncle Greg. It didn't have to be this way.

Andre saw his boat's crew chief give the thumbs-up. The mechanics were closing the hatch to the engine compartment.

Twenty minutes later, Andre, former owner/designer Luc Pelletier, and the boat's chief mechanic were strapped tightly in *La Mer Cinq's* surprisingly spacious cockpit. It had to be that way. The boat was designed to operate continuously in offshore racing competitions that sometimes went for hours of all-out, pounding, teeth-rattling speed on the open ocean.

After going through the checklist, they started the big turbine engine. The boat moved forward and began to lift out of the water onto its stiletto-thin sponsons. Andre turned the muscular racing machine onto the buoy-marked course. The team's helicopter flew by. A moment later, word came through from the chopper that the course was clear. Andre pushed the throttle forward less than halfway. The engine whine grew louder and higher in pitch as the turbine spooled up. *La Mer Cinq* surged forward. The massive vessel rose on its twin sponsons. It accelerated rapidly and was quickly blasting through the light ocean swells at 115 kilometers per hour, barely out of idle.

In four minutes, the boat was around the course and ripping through the swells past his two mates and the girls on the tender. If showing off was part of the game, this was an awesome and very unique way to do it. For Andre, in the driver's seat, it was like steering a wild horse.

Just hanging on was a chore. The speed was unbelievable—135 kilometers per hour with plenty of power to spare. It was one thing ripping along at this speed in a car on a smooth roadway. Here and now, in a sea monster, pounding and slicing through waves of seawater, this kind of speed was a strapped-in rush like no other.

Andre spotted a pair of jet skis scooting along together several hundred yards ahead. The small watercraft were just outside the buoys marking the racecourse. Andre turned his powerful racing boat until it was headed straight for the much smaller and slower intruders. The guys on the jet skis quickly veered out of the way.

Andre loved *La Mer Cinq*. He intended for it to become the symbol of Starling Worldwide. He wanted the shareholders and the public to see Starling as aggressive, devastatingly powerful, and relentless about rolling over anything unfortunate enough to get in the way. *La Mer Cinq* was the perfect reflection of what Andre intended to make the company when he became CEO. Arrangements had already been made. As soon as the sale closed and the team was his, *La Mer Cinq* would go to the shop to be repainted in black and gold, the colors of Starling Worldwide.

CHAPTER 29

G REG ARRIVED AT THE STARLING Building in New York just before 9:00 a.m. Instead of going directly to his office, he got off the elevator two floors below and went to the suite occupied by Bob McErney, Starling's executive vice president for marketing and communications. The talk went immediately to Andre.

"What's he up to?" Greg asked.

"Same as before," said McErney, who looked like a middle-aged male model with perfectly groomed blond hair and crisp executive attire. "He wants Starling to back his boat racing."

McErney picked up a folder from his desk and handed it to Greg. It was full of slickly prepared photos, graphics, and promotional mock-ups that showed off Andre's racing boat with its new name in black and gold.

"Starling One," Greg said. "What about this? Does it have any merit?"

"Could do worse with the money," McErney said.

"How do we stop it?"

"Your father is backing him."

Greg quickly scanned Andre's proposal. It included a strong endorsement from Poppy, who was still Starling's number two shareholder, after Greg.

"What do you want to do?" McErney said.

"If anybody asks, it's under review," Greg said, as he tossed the folder of material back onto McErney's desk.

"Andre's not going to sit still," McErney said.

"We don't operate on his schedule," said Greg. He turned and headed out of the office. It was clear where this fight was going. Poppy's support made the difference. That was the confrontation, what Andre wanted. Greg would resist his nephew's game just enough to piss him off. Then he would relent and allow Starling to be drawn into the elite world of offshore powerboat racing at a sponsorship cost of ten million dollars annually. Fortunately, there was an upside.

Andre's obsession with his boat racing would draw even more of his attention away from Starling. Maybe he would be less intent on trying to force Greg out before he was ready to go.

Greg went down two more floors to the legal department. He found Starling's chief legal counsel, Carl Samuelson, conferring with some of his staff. The two of them retreated into Carl's office and closed the door behind them.

"What's Andre up to?" Greg said.

"Nothing good," Carl said.

Greg knew Carl was watching his back. He trusted him implicitly.

"Tell me."

"He's got Erskine and Hyndes working overtime."

Greg already knew that.

"They know you're seeing your Czech lady friend again. They know you were with her in Africa. Did you see the piece that just ran on the Financial Reporter blog?"

"No."

"It's about you."

"Okay."

"It says you've become a dull knife in a world of hard cheese."

Clever metaphor, Greg thought. He couldn't dispute its contention. Focusing laser-like on maximizing profit to the exclusion of all else no longer appealed to him.

"Can I get a copy of that blog?" Greg asked.

Carl printed out the blog on his computer and handed it to Greg.

"Off the record?" Carl said.

"Off the record," Greg said.

"I worry you're underestimating Andre."

Greg appreciated Carl's candor.

"You haven't been yourself since you came back from the surgery."

"It's that obvious?" said Greg.

"To everybody. The buzz in-house is the same as outside."

Greg had already assumed as much.

"Erskine and Hyndes is no chicken-shit outfit," Carl said. "They're black-hearted assassins."

Greg understood what he was up against.

"Your reputation is getting hammered," Carl said. "I'm serious. Those guys take no prisoners. You are under siege."

Greg was late for a scheduled meeting with his M&A Team. He gave Carl a reassuring pat on the shoulder, then he walked out. He tried to mask the somber mood he was in by warmly acknowledging the many greetings that came his way from employees as he headed up to the fifty-third floor.

The M&A crew was already gathered and waiting when Greg arrived in the executive suite's conference room. He sat down at the head of the long table. Greg hadn't met formally with them for nearly a month, an eternity by his old standards. Prior to his health scare, these guys had been working an intense schedule. There had always been at least three deals in play, and a lot more under serious scrutiny. Many of the more recent takeover targets had been internet related. That was the future of mass media distribution. Greg had been determined that Starling would not be left behind. The company was now firmly established in that arena in Europe, North America, and Asia.

The lights in the room dimmed. The team began its presentation. It was impressive, as always, but Greg was in no mood for it. He kept a portion of his mind tuned in. The rest went to thoughts of his life at Starling. He'd worked for the company for nearly a quarter century, the last seventeen years as CEO. The company had come far in that time, and so had he. But his world view was changing. He didn't have the appetite for business as usual anymore. In the final analysis, it was just a game, a very sophisticated and unforgiving game. The reward was profit, power, and prestige. It was heady stuff, and he'd played the game aggressively, and won consistently, for many years.

No question, he could preserve his leadership if he went back to being aggressive and unrelenting. He saw no other path that would stave off Andre's ambition. Even at that, given Poppy's support, there was probably no stopping the sponsorship of Andre's speedboat on steroids. The imposition of that sponsorship would widely be seen as a personal defeat for Greg as well as a signal that Andre was de facto heir to the leadership of the company. Greg found it hard to imagine himself being happy knowing Andre was a virtual certainty, looming in the wings.

There was nothing left to prove. Greg had been at the top of the mountain for a long time. Staying at the summit a bit longer, business as usual, had no appeal. On the other hand, Greg was damned if he was going to be the floor mat for Andre's ambition.

The other reason to retain control of the company was Daria. She was right about the power he had at his disposal. His reach through Starling extended to sixty-four countries through the internet, television, radio, as well as books, magazines, and other kinds of print media. Up till now, the company had been focused almost entirely on attracting prime audience demographics in order to maximize ad revenue and profitability. Too often, that translated into programming compromises that were more about pleasing Starling's corporate customers than anything else.

If Greg stayed at the company helm, he could begin to move the beast in a more positive, life-affirming direction. He could deliver on at least some of Starling's potential to reach billions of people with informative, forward-thinking, and inspiring stories and programming that might rally public opinion toward the kind of fundamental change that was sorely needed. At least he could try. Not just for Daria, he needed to do it for himself as well. He felt a great compulsion to atone for the indifference he'd shown to life's ugly realities in the past.

The M&A team finished their presentation. It was mostly focused on a proposal to launch a new internet provider for Indonesia and Malaysia. Greg asked a few questions, then he thanked everyone and told them he would get back to them after reviewing the written material they'd provided.

Trevor Bingham was the M&A team member responsible for the photos and the graphics.

Greg got his attention. "I need a favor."

Trevor, at age twenty-six, was a wizard with graphics programs like Photoshop and InDesign.

They went into Greg's office. He found his small SD memory card in his briefcase. He handed it to Trevor, and said, "I took photos in Africa. Can you clean them up and email me the best ones?"

"Any preference on format?" Trevor said.

"Something our print and online people can work with."

"Tomorrow morning okay?"

"Perfect," Greg said.

Trevor left.

Greg settled in behind his desk. He hadn't written anything for publication in more than fifteen years. He could've assigned someone on staff to write about Nani. He had experienced the story himself. He was determined to own it. He spent the rest of the workday developing his piece on Tesfa. He took it home and worked on it until 1:00 a.m. When he needed a relevant fact, he researched it himself on the net. Before he went to bed, he had forged and honed an 1,800-word feature article that carried his own byline. He emailed the piece to Michael and requested a review and comments.

When he returned to the office the next morning, Michael was waiting.

"Nice work, Mr. Hammond," Michael said. "You should do this more often."

Greg trusted Michael's judgment. He didn't say things just to stroke the boss's ego. Aside from a few suggestions on grammar, and the shifting of two sentences from one paragraph to a more appropriate place further into the piece, Michael had no other comments.

Greg went to his emails and found the photos Trevor had sent back to him after they had been cleaned up in Photoshop. Three were particularly affecting.

"Attach these images to the article," said Greg to Michael. "Email the package to all of our newspaper and net editors. Have them publish it in Friday's edition. Feature section lead with a tease on the cover page."

"This is great, sir," Michael said. "You surprised me with this one."

Greg acknowledged his assistant's approval with a playful salute. "Get after it. We don't want to miss the cut off."

CHAPTER 30

WALKING BRISKLY, DARIA PASSED THE old cemetery by her university. A text message from Greg strongly urged her to go out and get a copy of the day's *Euro Standard*. At the newsstand near one corner of Wenceslas Square, she bought the latest edition of the paper. Almost immediately, she spotted a front-page tease on the lower left side. The slug line read: "Nani's Story."

Daria quickly turned to the article in the paper's feature section. There, four column inches wide, from top to bottom on the outside border of the page, was "Nani's Story." The opening page featured a powerful photo that showed the Ethiopian president's bodyguard carrying Nani in the foreground. Following along, in the photo's background, were Ethiopian President Sitota, Marc, Arnoldo, and herself, all looking very concerned.

Daria was thrilled. She went to a low brick wall nearby, sat down, and began to read. The story spilled over onto a second, then to a third page. It included three photos and a map graphic that showed where Ethiopia and Tesfa were located. She became emotional as she finished reading the article. She wiped away a tear, then checked her watch. It was already after 5:00 p.m. She had to get back to her office. Greg had said he would call her there at 5:30 p.m.

Daria scanned parts of the article again, as she headed back to the university campus. The written text was wonderful. Greg had used "Nani's Story" as a wraparound to present an engaging, richly nuanced profile of Tesfa, its people, and the environmental, social, and political conditions that had driven so many into a life of poverty. The article was effusive in its admiration of Marc Wren and the doctors and staff that worked with him. It praised President Sitota for working diligently to help his people. Greg also wrote about her, and *Bright Eve,* and about FGC, using Nani's personal story of genital cutting as the context. It was heart-wrenching. Daria couldn't imagine anyone reading it without being emotionally touched by it.

She entered the university building where her office was located just before 5:30 p.m. and hurried up the worn granite steps. When she reached the second floor, she turned down the corridor toward her office. Standing there, in front of her door, was Greg. He had not been expected.

She ran to him and embraced him.

"This story you have written—beautiful. Completely beautiful."

She pecked him all over his face with kisses. Then they shared a long, passionate kiss, and the warmest of embraces.

"You like to surprise me," Daria said. She paused a moment to catch her breath. Then she held up her copy of the *Euro Standard* for him.

"Such a wonderful thing," she said. "So many people will learn something good from this."

His beaming smile told her how pleased he was to have her approval.

She showed him her small, cluttered office. Then they left the building. Greg had a black carry-on suitcase on wheels with him. He towed it behind him as they walked the streets, side by side.

"You cannot believe all that has happened just since we are back from Ethiopia," said Daria. "In only a week, just this one week, all of the adult women and men in Tesfa have seen our video. They now have six laptops and ten tablets with the videos and the teaching modules on them. Already, they are demanding to see more, to learn more. What am I going to do?"

"Good problem to have," Greg said.

"It's happening too quickly."

"What are you doing about getting more material?"

"We have two additional interactive programs in post-production. Soon, three more will go into production, and another two are now being translated."

"How will you determine if you're achieving a good result?"

"The local women working with us will provide feedback that we can use to improve our program. So far, it's going better than I could have hoped. We are hiring more people. It's too fast, too soon. We must try to get ahead of it."

"May I offer some advice?" Greg said.

"Please," said Daria.

"Get a video crew into Tesfa. Do it now."

"Abeba is working on that. She's already found a for-hire news crew based in Addis."

"Even better, find some exceptional young people living in Tesfa. Pay the Addis guys to train them. Set them up with a video package. Put them to work acquiring material. Teach them to tell stories, real human stories."

"What will we do with this material?"

"You have a lot of ambition for Tesfa," Greg said. "The struggle to get where you want to go is a real-life drama."

"A documentary?"

"Maybe more. I've got people who can advise you."

Daria was excited to see Greg becoming personally engaged in *Bright Eve.*

"I'd get that going right away," Greg said. "We need to get a lot of B-roll footage of the way the place is now, before any kind of transforming takes place."

"It's already late in Addis," Daria said.

"Does Abeba have a phone?"

"Yes."

"I'd call her now."

Daria pulled out her cell phone. She dialed in a long series of numbers. After a few moments, she had Abeba on the line. She quickly briefed Abeba about Greg's newspaper article, and about his sense of urgency in getting young people trained to acquire raw video footage of Tesfa. She suggested Abeba work with Cervantes to recruit the people needed. Then, she urged Greg to take the phone. "Can you tell her what you have in mind?"

Greg took the phone.

"Abeba… How are you? … Can you get Cervantes a cell phone? He's going to need it. Yes, we need to start acquiring video material right away. No delay. We have to be able to show people what Tesfa was like before it changed… Yes, it will change. For the better, I'm sure. You and Daria will settle for nothing less."

Daria took the phone back and quickly closed off the call.

Then, she said to Greg, "Are you sure you want to get involved this deeply?"

"I'm just advising," he said. "You're the center of this."

"That, I do not wish for. Abeba and Cervantes should be at the center in Ethiopia. In Haiti, Marc will find the right people."

"Someday, what you're doing could be a very big deal," Greg said. "The spotlight will find you whether you like it or not."

Daria wasn't averse to the idea of being recognized as long as it was acknowledged that the really hard part was being done by local people who were living the story.

Greg took her hand and held it as they walked along. "Ask me how I got here."

"How did you get here?"

"I flew commercial."

"Really?" Daria said. "No more private jet?"

"No more mile high club."

Daria kissed him enthusiastically, then pulled out her phone. "I must tell Angelika."

She called her friend and told her about Greg's article in the *Euro Standard*, and that he'd given up his private jet.

After a moment, Daria turned to Greg. "She's asking to speak with you."

He took the phone. "Hello, Angelika… I wanted to surprise her."

Daria could hear Angelika telling Greg how much she appreciated the gold bonobo pendant.

"I'm so happy you liked it," he said.

Angelika invited him to visit Munich.

Daria chuckled. "You want a threesome, this would be your chance."

Greg bopped her playfully on top of her head, then spoke into the phone. "She's just being naughty. I'm guessing she learned that from you."

Daria heard Angelika's laugh come through the phone.

"I have to thank you for what you've done to make this one so wonderful. She's too good," said Greg. Then he turned the phone back to Daria.

She and Angelika talked for another minute, then the call ended.

Greg and Daria turned onto a narrow street in the Staré Město District called Ve Smečkách. It was flanked by tall, nineteenth-century residential buildings. Daria pulled out her key as they reached the third building on the right. It was four stories and appeared to have had its facade recently restored with a white limestone plaster.

They entered the building and started up the stairs that zigzagged steeply upward along the back wall. Finally, they reached the fifth floor. Daria opened the door to her apartment. It was a neat, but somewhat cramped, studio, with a cooking space in one corner by the entry door, and a closet-sized bath in the other.

"Nice," Greg said. "Very nice. Could be a little bigger."

"I have been here since I started university."

There were two skylights. One was directly over a single bed.

"I hope you are in the mood," Daria said with a devilish grin as she began to pull off her clothes. "I'm feeling very excited at this moment."

Greg needed no more prompt than that. He set aside his suitcase.

For more than an hour, amidst a lot of laughing, teasing, and heavy breathing, they set about joyfully and energetically satisfying each other.

Afterward, they cuddled blissfully.

Daria still wasn't sure how her blossoming relationship with Greg was going to turn out, but being with him felt so comfortable, and he'd done such a wonderful thing with "Nani's Story." On top of all that, he'd done another thing that had very much pleased her. He'd talked like a friend to Angelika. She would always be a big part of Daria's life. A lot of men might be threatened by this, but not Greg. He acted as though he would even welcome it. For Daria, this was a big deal. It made the idea of commitment much less scary.

"You took a big risk today," Daria said. "Nani's story will make your enemies angry."

"The idea is to hang on and do the right thing at the same time," Greg said.

"Your nephew cares nothing about that," Daria said. "He will attack again."

"No doubt."

"Why do you take this chance?"

"I'm done with the person I was," Greg said. "Can't go back to that."

"Are you ready to give up all you've accomplished?"

"Didn't say that," Greg said, with a smile. "The goal is to keep the shareholders happy while quietly redefining Starling's DNA."

"This is not something that can be done quietly."

"Probably not."

"It seems you want to have this confrontation with Andre."

"If it comes to that, so be it," Greg said.

CHAPTER 31

A NDRE WAS PISSED. HE HADN'T expected to be back in Christchurch so soon. Flying commercial to New Zealand from the South of France was grueling—thirty-two hours en route, through London, Los Angeles, and Auckland.

It wasn't just jet lag and the long trip that had Andre steamed. There was another big source of aggravation. He wasn't sure if it was true. He hoped their inside man would provide the answer. His flight from Auckland had landed.

A moment later, Andre saw Bob McErney emerge from the terminal. McErney was supposed to be taking a few days' vacation.

No one from Starling New York knew he was in New Zealand.

Andre was waiting behind the wheel of a rented Porsche parked at the pick-up curb. He hit the horn. McErney saw him and came over and got in beside him.

"What do you know about the jet?" Andre said, as he accelerated the car away from the curb.

"Nothing official," McErney said. "Word is he told legal to dump the lease."

Andrew swore under his breath. If there was one thing he coveted more than anything about being Starling's CEO, it was the G650. It would allow him to cut the time between Europe and home by at least half a day, and he would be able to sleep much of the way, or party with his mates. Scoring at altitude might even become part of the regular routine.

Greg's tree-hugging bitch was behind his latest move. Andre was sure of that. She'd turned his uncle from a hardcore corporate predator into some kind of limp dick, bleeding heart.

Andre turned the Porsche onto Memorial Avenue. He thought about what was coming with Bob McErney. One of the Erskine and Hyndes guys had recruited the company's chief marketing officer. Apparently, McErney was alarmed by the potentially damaging impact of Greg's recent lack of direction and leadership of the company. McErney didn't want to end up the fall guy for the consequences of Greg's shaky leadership. He'd come over to the opposition to avoid going down on Greg's watch. The hook had been an implied promise of advancement to the presidency of the company when Andre became CEO.

Of course, there was no way Andre would honor that commitment. No way did he want a shifty guy like McErney backing him up. He could never be trusted. When the transition came, McErney would be eased out with a fat severance package once he signed an air-tight non-disclosure agreement. Today, all he had to do was deliver a great dog and pony show. That was something Andre couldn't have gotten away with himself. The conflict of interest would have been too obvious to his grandfather.

McErney understood what was expected. He was clearly an arrogant prick. *It takes one to know one,* Andre thought. He recognized full well and was not the least bit ashamed of being a big-time member of the club of arrogant pricks. The world consisted of a lot of losers and a few winners. The biggest winners were all arrogant pricks. Andre was a winner, and winners got that way by being pricks. Screw his uncle. Andre was going to bring him down. That was his path to power. He had plenty of money. He had all the fine pussy he could handle. Real power was all that was missing. Power was the element that rounded it all out. Few men in history had ever had all three. And the ones that did got it by being arrogant fucking pricks.

Andre wore the badge with pride.

If McErney came through, they'd have what they needed to take Greg down. It would happen at the upcoming annual board meeting, which was on the calendar in New York in just over two weeks. The sooner it happened, the better. Andre didn't want the company jet to get away from him. He'd already come up with a way to stop that from happening. Greg wouldn't be able to unload the jet if it was out of commission. A highly skilled airframe mechanic could easily induce a serious mechanical problem on the G650, a problem that would keep the jet grounded for repairs for at least the next month. Erskine and Hyndes could take care of that. They would surely have someone on call that could do the deed.

Just over a mile southwest of downtown Christchurch, Andre steered the Porsche in through the gate to Addington Raceway Park. The park was currently hosting greyhound racing, but there was no racing scheduled for this day. Only a few people were around.

Andre drove around to the far side of the grandstand and down along the backstretch into the stable area for the harness horses. He parked in front of a new facility that appeared to have been built with no expense spared.

Inside, they found Lydia showing off her new stable to Poppy. No one else was there.

Lydia had ordered the trainers and staff to get lost until she and Poppy were gone.

Poppy knew Bob McErney. They'd met several times over the years. He seemed genuinely pleased to see him.

"Poppy," Andre said. "Bob is here to talk to us. No one in New York knows."

Poppy appeared to be confused.

"We need to hear what he has to say," Lydia said.

She knew damned well what he was going to say. *Women can be arrogant pricks too,* thought Andre. His mother was living proof.

After switching on his iPad and setting up his portable digital projector, McErney began his presentation. Andre had to hand it to him. It was impressive: excellent graphics, and some slick video clips. McErney was a salesman to the core. He made the case that Greg had lost his appetite for aggressive leadership.

"Not one new merger or acquisition since the medical emergency," McErney said. "The financial performance is still good enough, but the company has stopped growing."

Poppy knew damn well that growth was a primary driver of expanded shareholder value.

Andre could see the old man was getting more depressed with every bullet point.

"Starling shares have stagnated," McErney said. "Except, of course, when Greg gave money to that abortion charity. When that happened, there was a nine percent dip in share value."

McErney laid it on heavily. At one point, he pulled a two-inch-thick pile of magazines, newspaper clippings, and copies of internet blogs from his briefcase. All were critical of Greg in some way or another. Nearly all had been spawned in the K Street offices of Erskine and Hyndes, then planted by stringers in a whole range of high-profile print and electronic media outlets.

Greg's political direction was the next thing McErney challenged. Starling had been conservative since Poppy had first applied for a corporate charter. The company's revenue stream was driven largely by conservative corporations. Greg was gravitating away from the company's core values in a direction that was clearly antagonistic to Starling's customer base.

"The piece with his byline that appeared in all our newspapers is the most recent example."

"The one on his experience in Africa?" Andre said, as if he didn't already know.

"Yes," McErney said. "It's becoming a pattern."

"What do you mean by that?" Lydia said, as if she didn't already know.

"We don't know how far he's going to go with it," McErney said.

"The family has always been conservative," Lydia said.

"It feels like betrayal," Andre said. He could see that his grandfather was getting angry.

Poppy's politics were staunchly conservative. With him, it was a long-standing personal conviction, not just a politically expedient and profitable way to be.

"Greg's become unbalanced," Lydia said.

"It's that Czech woman he's been seeing," Andre said. He knew the right buttons to push with Poppy. He looked directly at the old man, to assure his next words would have maximum impact. "I had her investigated. She's a socialist. She was born in a Soviet-occupied country. Her father was a communist *apparatchik.*"

The last point was a complete fabrication. Andre couldn't care less. Arrogant pricks weren't above lying to get ahead.

"That woman has become very influential in Greg's thinking," McErney said.

"What makes you say that?" Lydia looked at Poppy to be sure he was listening to her question and wouldn't miss a word of McErney's carefully scripted answer.

"I can give you one example that I confirmed shortly before I left New York," McErney said. "You know *Vectors* is our number one series. It's been that way since it came out six years ago."

"It's a leader in ad revenue in most of our markets," Andre said.

"Greg has been talking to the producers," McErney said. "He wants to, in his words, 'lighten up on the fear mongering.' He wants to change the tone of the show."

"You heard this from the producer?" Andre said.

"I did," McErney said. "Greg seems to want the writing to be more positive."

"Great way to kill the show," Andre said.

"Ridiculous," Lydia said, shaking her head. "If he's not stopped, he'll destroy the business."

Way to go, Ma, Andre thought, struggling to cover his smirk. *What a performer.*

"I hope you can forgive me," McErney said. "I'm sorry to have to bring you this news. I can see where this is headed. I don't want to be dragged down when blame is assigned. I work for the shareholders, not any one person. Something needs to be done, before it's too late."

"We appreciate your loyalty," Andre said.

"How do we deal with this?" Lydia asked, as if she didn't know what was coming next.

"You're asking me?" McErney said.

"Yes," Andre said. "We can't allow this to continue."

"If there's going to be a transition, you want it to go as smoothly as possible, and as painlessly as possible for everyone involved," McErney said.

"How do we do that?" Lydia said.

"If it was me, I'd go to Greg, tell him the votes are stacked against him, and offer him a deal he can't refuse to retire quietly."

"Makes sense," Lydia said. "If he's not happy being the person he was, let's make it easy for him to become who he wants to be."

"He's been there nearly sixteen years," McErney said. "New leadership would be good for the company."

Andre could see Poppy was buying the line, seriously considering what they were saying.

"Somebody will need to be ready to step in," McErney said, looking right at Andre. "You haven't asked me, but, if you want my opinion, I'd have to say, you would be the logical choice to become the next CEO of the company."

Andre pretended to ponder the idea thoughtfully, then said, "I've never hidden my interest in the job. I just wish it could happen under better circumstances."

"Greg won't go quietly, unless he knows he has no chance to win," McErney said.

"We'd be doing him a favor," Lydia said. "He can go off and marry this lady he's involved with. If they want to save the world, they can do it together."

"He needs to know he has no chance to win," McErney said. "That's the only way to avoid a fight."

"Let me ask you something slightly off the subject," Andre said. "Have you heard anything about Greg trying to dump the company jet?"

"I can't confirm it, but I have heard that," McErney said.

"That's just crazy," Lydia said. "Why would he want to do that?"

McErney shrugged.

Lydia turned to her father and said, "Do you have any questions, Poppy?"

Poppy made a slurred sound that seemed to be a "no." He was quite obviously very upset.

"I think you've told us what we need to know," said Lydia to McErney. "Thank you for coming all the way out here to talk to us about this."

A half hour later, Andre delivered McErney to the downtown hotel where a room had been booked for him. He would remain in Christchurch until midday tomorrow in case he was needed further.

Back at the family estate on Kakapo Bay, after dinner, the staff, including Eddie, Poppy's caretaker, was dismissed for the evening.

In the parlor in Poppy's bedroom suite, Andre and his mother sat down with the ailing family patriarch.

Poppy was deeply troubled. Pulling his support from his only son was obviously a very painful thing for him to consider.

Andre had to give his mother credit. She had insisted, from the moment they'd come into Poppy's life full time, that they treat him with respectful deference. He loved and trusted them.

They had also been careful to keep Poppy from knowing they had any kind of animosity toward Greg. In fact, they'd effectively nurtured the notion that if anything, it was Greg who felt threatened. It was Greg who was consumed with animosity.

Andre and Lydia were with Poppy. They were the good guys, interested only in the welfare of the company and its shareholders. They were the voices of reason. In the face of this undeniable threat, the shareholders and the company board had to take action. They had to do something. Greg was totally complicit in his own undoing. He'd violated the trust of all the shareholders. He was on a course that would bring Starling down unless he was stopped. That was the ongoing story Lydia and Andre had very effectively been feeding Poppy.

Now, the moment had come to close the deal with the old man. Lydia and Andre began their staged conversation.

"We have to do something," Lydia said. "We have to save Greg from himself."

Andre could see his grandfather was listening intently.

"It would be negligent to let this go on," Lydia said.

"Big step," Andre said, careful to keep a tone of doubt for Poppy's benefit.

"Starling's future is at stake," Lydia said.

"Maybe we should talk to him."

"It's not like he hasn't been warned," Lydia said. "He knows what he's doing. It's almost as if he's daring us to put him out of his misery."

"He's lost sight of the shareholders' interests," Andre said.

"What do you think, Poppy?" Lydia said.

The old man angrily swept his good arm through the air.

"What if we do nothing?" Lydia said. "What if we sit on this, and Greg ends up taking the company over a cliff?"

"No way. That's not an option," Andre said.

"If the bottom falls out, we could end up getting sued," Lydia said.

"The shareholders won't sit by if the company goes down and we do nothing," Andre said.

"Greg's heart isn't in it anymore," Lydia said. "We do him a favor by helping him make the right decision."

"We have to do it," Andre said. "We have to tell him the shareholders are ready to drop him."

"If he resigns, there's no fight," Lydia said. "He can go out with dignity."

"Sweeten the deal," Andre said. "Give him a ton of money, honor his service, and let him go out quietly."

"He can focus on what he really wants to do," Lydia said.

Poppy was looking deeply disheartened.

"We have no choice," Lydia said. "He'll go quietly if he sees he has no chance."

"Resign, or else," Andre said. "That's the only way."

"We have to stand together on this," Lydia said. "For Greg's sake, and the company's sake."

"There's no guarantee he'll go along," Andre said.

"We have to stand firm," Lydia said.

"You'll vote to have him removed?" Andre said.

"If he won't step aside quietly," Lydia said.

"If it comes to a fight, so be it," Andre said.

"I hope we can get it done painlessly," Lydia said. "Our best chance to end this quietly comes if we make it clear we won't back down, no matter what."

Andre studied Poppy closely. He seemed to still be wavering.

"Are you ready to step in?" Lydia said to Andre. "Are you ready to take responsibility for the entire company?"

"I am," Andre said without hesitation. "I wish it wasn't happening under these circumstances, but yes, I'm ready."

"Poppy," Lydia said, "we can't make this work without you."

The old man nodded. He obviously understood but seemed deeply conflicted by what was at stake.

"We can't delay," Lydia said. "The board meeting is only two weeks away. The transition should be announced before that meeting."

"If I were Greg, I'd want some time to think about it," Andre said.

"We're doing him a favor," Lydia said.

Tears welled up in Poppy's eyes. He pounded the arm of his chair with his good hand.

"If we drop the ball on this, we fail our fellow shareholders, and we fail Greg," Lydia said. "We have to be responsible. We have to make the decision now."

Poppy began to sob.

"Poppy, we know how you feel," Lydia said. "You're not betraying Greg. You're setting him free."

"That's what he really wants," Andre said. "His actions have been telling us that all along."

"Poppy, we need an answer," Lydia said. "Are you with us?"

Still sobbing, Poppy nodded his head affirmatively.

"You vote your shares with us on this?" Lydia said.

Again, Poppy nodded affirmatively.

Andre turned away and smiled gleefully. Too bad for his uncle. This time, there would be no forgiveness, no second chance, and no escape.

CHAPTER 32

"**P**UT HER ON HOLD," GREG said to Mindy, his receptionist. "Tell Michael I need him."

Though he had no interest in talking to Lydia, Greg decided he'd better hear what she had to say.

Michael appeared.

"Come in. Close the door," Greg said as he pulled a small digital voice recorder from the middle drawer of his desk.

"My sister's on the line. Whatever she says, you're my witness."

Greg switched on the recorder. Then he activated the speaker on his phone. "You have something to discuss?"

"Yes, brother," Lydia said through the speakerphone. "Your retirement."

Greg glanced quickly at Michael, then said, "I'm listening."

"Your behavior speaks volumes," Lydia said. "We understand you're suffering."

"I'm suffering?"

"You haven't been yourself since your illness," Lydia said.

"Okay," Greg said. He was having a hard time keeping his disdain in check.

"You've lost your way," Lydia said. "You know it. Our shareholders know it."

"Perhaps we should dispense with the bullshit," Greg said. "If you've got something to say, say it."

"No need to be that way," Lydia said. "You can retire on top. You can get on with your life. You and your girlfriend can save the world together."

"This is an ultimatum?" Greg said.

"Only if you choose to take it that way," Lydia said. "Our wish is to make this easy for all involved."

"I'm sure," Greg said.

"You've already lost," Lydia said. "Why make this more difficult than it needs to be? We have the votes on the board and the shareholder support needed to have you removed. Of course, we prefer it not come to that."

"Am I correct in assuming Andre will take my place?" Greg said.

"That's a decision the shareholders will make," Lydia said.

"With a little help from you," Greg said. "Where's Poppy in all this?"

"He's upset," Lydia said. "Very upset. He prefers that you make a quiet and dignified exit."

"He wants that, or you want that?"

"He doesn't want to go against you," Lydia said. "You left him no choice."

Greg was deeply disappointed that Poppy had pulled his support, but he wasn't surprised.

Lydia and Andre had been working full time to turn his father against him.

"The sooner you announce your retirement, the better for all involved," Lydia said.

He wanted to call her every vile name in the book. Instead, he kept his cool and said, "You truly are a nasty piece of work."

"Make it easy on yourself and everybody else," Lydia said. "If you do that, I'm sure you'll get a very attractive retirement package."

"I'll take it up with my advisors," Greg said. Then he broke the phone connection. After a moment, he looked at Michael, and said, "You have a sister don't you, Michael?"

"Actually two, sir," Michael said.

"Either of them like that?"

"Not even a little."

"Lucky you," said Greg. He looked at his watch. It was just after 3:00 p.m.

Michael appeared stunned by what he'd just heard. He said, "Sounds like you're in trouble, Boss."

"Nothing we weren't expecting, right?"

"Whatever you need, just tell me," Michael said.

"Thanks. Give me some time to think," said Greg. "Stay close by."

"Whatever happens, I'm with you."

Greg was truly grateful for Michael's loyalty. He turned a thumb up, and said, "I appreciate that."

Michael left and closed the door. Greg trusted his closest assistant would not repeat what he'd heard.

Greg was not surprised by what had just happened. He'd assumed Lydia and Andre would come after him again once they thought they had enough to turn Poppy against him.

In truth, a part of Greg welcomed it. There was nothing left to prove at Starling. He could easily transition into running a mega-foundation in partnership with Daria. She still hadn't agreed to it, but there was no longer any doubt in his mind about her feelings. He knew she was seriously thinking about a future with him.

What a marvelous person she was. She'd taken him down a road he'd never traveled, a road that had forced him to emerge from his self-generated bubble of corporate conservatism. She'd shown him the ugly face of human indifference, an indifference born out of the selfish mentality of radical right politics. For Greg, being a major facilitator of the conservative us-versus-them agenda was a stain he'd never be able to completely erase.

For so many years, he'd worshipped at the temple of profit. What had come of it? A lot of money, and a fleeting infusion of power, the kind of power a cyclist experienced, that moved one forward but required a constant churning of the pedals. Greg had worked the pedals with the best of them. In the process of churning up the landscape while battling his competitors, he'd almost killed himself.

If anybody had told him he would one day meet somebody who would force him to question everything he'd stood for, he wouldn't have believed it, not for a second. But his core beliefs had been shaken, in the most profound way. Daria Kocánová had provided the stark dose of reality that had forced Greg to review and reconsider his whole life. If ever there was a time to turn the page and begin anew, it was now.

He could resign. That would be the easiest course to follow. But, if he did that, he'd have to accept defeat. He would have to lie down and allow Andre to roll over him without a fight.

Greg had to admit, Andre probably was capable of maintaining Starling as a profitable company.

He wasn't incompetent, not entirely. What the world would get with Andre Akers running Starling Worldwide would be business as usual, more media fine-tuned to spreading a muted and manipulated, conservative version of reality that ignored life in the real world.

The real world needed exactly the opposite. The real world desperately needed the truth served up in spades. Allowing Andre to take over Starling without a fight would be inexcusable.

Greg checked his watch. It was after 10:00 p.m. in Prague. He dialed her cell number and found she was just walking home from her office. They exchanged affectionate greetings, then he played back the audio tape of his conversation with Lydia.

"She likes that she's hurting you," Daria said, after hearing the recording.

"How would you respond?" Greg said.

"I would not go quietly," Daria said.

Greg laughed. "No doubt."

"What will you do?"

"Not going down without a fight."

"Yes," Daria said. "You must fight."

"Where are you with your new video material?"

"Going as fast as we can," Daria said. "We have so many new people."

"Starling has a major news operation in Hamburg," Greg said. "They have tons of stock video footage. They can move raw video through post to finished product very quickly. That's what they do. I'll have the bureau chief call you. Tell her what you need. Whatever you need, just ask. I may not be around much longer. While I'm here, let's do what we can."

"Thank you," Daria said. "I want to help you. Tell me what I can do."

The offer was so tempting, but Greg knew it wasn't a good idea. He said, "You've got enough to do already. I've got good people I can count on."

"You will be okay?"

"I'll be fine," Greg said. "I need to sign off. Not much time. A lot to do."

"Please stay in touch," Daria said. "I need to know you are okay."

Greg thought a moment, then said, "Whatever happens, when this is over, I intend to make you an offer you can't refuse."

"I am waiting," she said.

Greg hung up the phone and began to consider his next move. It was one thing to resolve to fight. Developing an effective counteroffensive with so little time was something else entirely.

An idea was formulating in his head. He went to his computer and began to write it down. After forty minutes, he had it honed to a paragraph. He printed it out. Then, he called Michael to his office.

"Get the M&A crew together in the conference room," Greg said. "Fifteen minutes. Tell them it's urgent. Ask them to cancel any plans they have."

Michael hurried out of Greg's office.

Greg took a deep breath, then got up from his desk and walked out of his office. He smiled at Mindy at the reception desk and continued down the corridor to the conference room. He took a chair at the center of the long table. While waiting for his team to arrive, his thoughts turned to his father. Lydia had turned Poppy against him. Greg could travel to New Zealand to see Poppy and try to get him to reconsider. Would it make a difference? Greg doubted it. Poppy was a hard head. Trying to sway him would just cause him to dig in his heels. Greg knew what he would be up against. He was cut from the same cloth as his father. He could go and meet with Poppy, or he could work with his team to come up with an aggressive response to Andre's treachery.

Greg knew damned well, the best way to influence Poppy and retain his respect would be to stand up and fight for what he believed in.

Five minutes later, the M&A crew showed up together with Michael, who took his place next to Greg. The other team members sat across from them.

Greg didn't say a word. He switched on his digital recorder and played his conversation with Lydia.

When it was over, Greg spoke up, "Two weeks from now, one of two things will happen: I will be gone and my nephew Andre will be CEO, or… or Starling will be reinvented into a media organization with a new mandate and a new vision of itself. I intend to do all I can between now and the board meeting to present the new Starling Media to the world. You are here because you've always delivered. You've never let me down. I need you to adapt your skills. I need you to find the motivation within yourselves. Things look bleak. I understand... Did any of you read my story about Nani?"

The entire team nodded affirmatively.

"We owe it to the Nanis of the world," Greg said. "We've got nothing to lose. We have to give it our best shot for their sake."

Greg passed out copies of his one paragraph mission statement. It read:

Our world is in trouble. We have not been telling the real story. That must change. Starling Worldwide must become a voice of reason that serves the common interest. We must be honest and open about our failures. We must be bold in presenting a new media vision for the twenty-first century. We must become a model for journalism that is sustainable, and also good for our investors and our employees. Most importantly, Starling must work for the public as a source of trustworthy, relevant, and unbiased information.

Greg watched as everyone present digested his statement. After a moment, Michael pushed back his chair, got to his feet, and began to clap enthusiastically. The M&A team members quickly joined him.

"You make us proud, sir," Michael said.

Greg was deeply touched. He smiled and gestured for them to sit down.

"Needless to say, if anybody wants to bail, no hard feelings," Greg said. As he expected, everybody pledged absolute loyalty and support.

"Any sane person would say there's simply not enough time," Greg said. "We can't worry about that. We may not be able to do much. But we can do something. We need a plan. We need an effective way to launch it. We need to make the case that our new direction is the best way for our world and also good for our business."

Greg glanced at his watch, then he said, "It's almost four. By eight, we need an overall vision on paper. By eleven, I want an action plan for launching the vision. After that, we'll work out individual assignments. Any questions?"

The questions came flying. The give-and-take was urgent and very animated. Greg was excited. Everybody was on the same page. Everyone grasped the remarkable opportunity that was at hand. Everyone wanted to be a part of changing the face of the modern media. There was no hand-wringing, no waste of energy on the odds stacked against them. It was game on.

Everybody had ideas.

The process went even faster than Greg had expected. By 8:00 p.m., they'd settled on a simple set of specific objectives that would build on Greg's original mission statement. By 10:30, they had an action plan with assignments and a timetable. The meeting broke up shortly thereafter. The team would reassemble at 11:00 a.m. the following day. By then, Greg would've already initiated the first bold step in their plan.

CHAPTER 33

ANDRE AWAKENED WHEN HE FELT a tap on his shoulder. He glanced over at the young, redheaded hottie lying asleep in the bed next to him. All he could remember about her was she was nineteen and from Scotland. He rolled over the other direction and saw Bernard standing over him.

"You have to call your mother," Bernard said.

Andre had a serious hangover. On top of that, he was still dealing with jet lag from having been to New Zealand and back in less than a week.

"She told me to drag your ass out of the bed," Bernard said. "She said it's important."

"What could be so fucking important?" Andre said as he put his feet on the floor and got up. He threw on a robe and headed down the corridor to the office he maintained in the house.

He grabbed his cell phone and dialed his mother in New Zealand. A moment later she was on the phone.

"I'm jet-lagged, and I'm beat to hell. Why—"

"Shut up and listen," Lydia barked through the phone. "You know what's happened?"

"What?"

"Greg canceled *Vectors* this morning," Lydia said.

Andre suddenly became alert.

"He canceled *Vectors*," Lydia repeated.

"The whole series?" Andre said.

"Talk to our guy," Lydia said. "Get back to me as soon as you know something."

The phone connection broke.

Fucking Greg. He couldn't go quietly—he just had to make a stink.

Andre dialed McErney's cell number.

"What the fuck is going on?" Andre said when he picked up.

"Five minutes," McErney said. "I'll call back."

The connection broke. Andre struggled to control his anger. What was Greg doing? Didn't he get that he was pissing in the wind?

It was the last Tuesday in June. It would be over in two fucking weeks. The board meeting was two weeks from today. At the meeting, the motion would be introduced. The Starling directors would dump Greg as company CEO. He was toast. No way could he win. The votes were there. The deal was done.

Following the board meeting, Andre intended to have his uncle barred from his office. Officially, he'd be out of a job as soon as the shareholders got together to validate the board's decision. In two weeks, the hammer would come down. But, between now and then, his hands were mostly tied.

Andre smiled. He got what was happening. For two more weeks, Greg would still be calling the shots at Starling. A lot of damage could be done. Greg had already canceled *Vectors*, the biggest of the company's primetime profit engines. What else could he be planning?

Andre called up another number on his cell. A moment later, he had his contact at Erskine and Hyndes on the line.

"Where are we with the jet?" Andre said.

The man assured Andre they'd found somebody for the job. It would be done by the end of the week.

"No," Andre said. "Tonight. It gets done tonight."

Andre listened to the man's response. He didn't like it.

"Don't tell me that. Find a way!"

The man offered another excuse.

"You know what, I don't give a shit how hard it is," Andre roared. "I pay you big money to do the hard things!"

Andre quelled his rage and listened again for a moment. Then, he shouted, "Get it done! Tonight!"

He broke the connection, then he quickly dialed another number on the phone. A few moments later, a receptionist put him through to the French lawyer handling his business for *La Mer Seigneur Racing*.

"The sponsorship with Starling," Andre said. "Where do we stand?"

The lawyer told Andre they hadn't heard back from Starling.

"Call them," Andre said. "Get an answer from them."

The lawyer said he would do it right away.

A call was coming in on Andre's phone. He broke the connection to the lawyer and took the new call. It was McErney.

"Sorry I couldn't talk earlier," McErney said.

"What the fuck is going on?" Andre said.

"He killed *Vectors* this morning," McErney said.

"Why?" Andre said.

"Nobody knows," McErney said. "Nobody knows what's going on."

"No press release. No explanation?"

"Nothing," McErney said. "I called the *Vectors* office. Everybody there is in shock."

"None of the production people know anything?" Andre asked.

"The producers got a call from Greg's assistant this morning," McErney said. "They were told to shut down production immediately."

Andre's head was spinning. He had to get himself together. He had to get in front of whatever trouble Greg was planning.

"That's all you know?" Andre said.

"My people are trying to get information," McErney said.

"What about my boat? What about the sponsorship?" Andre said.

"Nothing."

"It's supposed to be a done deal," said Andre.

"He's got it locked up in legal," McErney said. "Hold on a second."

As he waited, Andre wondered how far Greg would go. Was he intending to go out scorched Earth? Was he intending to destroy the company? Why would he do that? He was the biggest shareholder. Was he just digging a huge hole for spite? Was he just being a prick? Probably, it was just that simple. If things were reversed, it's what Andre would have done. It appeared losing had brought out the worst in his uncle.

Andre heard McErney come back on the phone.

"Press release out of Greg's office," McErney said. "Just came through. He's gonna be interviewed tonight on *Evening Journal*."

The *Evening Journal* was Starling Network's daily news magazine show. It was fed to all Starling broadcast outlets worldwide, with a potential audience of nearly half of the world's people.

"Tonight?"

"According to this release," McErney said.

Andre ended the call. He could see where things were headed. Dumping *Vectors* was an insurgency. It was ballsy. Make a big fucking scene, you create a huge audience for yourself. Just the kind of thing he should have expected from his arrogant prick of an uncle.

CHAPTER 34

A T 4:30 THAT AFTERNOON, GREG took the elevator to the broadcast center five floors down. Michael and two members of the M&A team were with him. While Greg was in makeup being readied for the broadcast, Michael went to meet with the show's producer and its two hosts, Lanie Fletcher and Alex Paul. The two M&A team members went up to the glassed-in booth where the show's technical director managed the broadcast. They had a media disk with them with video clips that were to be inserted during the broadcast to illustrate and support Greg's remarks.

The announcement about *Vectors* earlier in the day had stunned the entire world's broadcast community. Starling, and Greg in particular, had been inundated by requests for more information, interviews, etc.

Greg liked the way the strategy was unfolding. He'd purposely kept quiet through the day to maximize interest in the television interview that was just minutes away. As he waited for the *Evening Journal* broadcast to begin, he thought about how far he'd come politically. For nearly two decades, he'd led an empire that had grown dramatically while quietly manipulating its media output to fit a narrow, conservative world view. At the time, it had made complete sense. Unlike his father, Greg had never been an ideologue. He'd simply followed the path of least resistance to profit. The payoff had been huge over the years, but there'd always been a measure of immorality to it. No political narrative could justify treating the poorest half of humanity like it didn't exist. For too long, Greg had been unashamedly complicit. His time in Ethiopia had been the final dose of reality. Being indifferent was no longer acceptable.

Daria had played an important role in facilitating his personal evolution. But it wasn't just her. He'd taken the time in recent days to better inform himself on the social, political, and environmental dysfunction that was shaping life on Earth, now and into the future. He gave himself credit for finally recognizing the urgent need for a global-scale cultural vision that was sustainable over the long haul.

Greg stood by as Starling's *Evening Journal* went on the air. Lanie and Alex, the show's hosts, gave a quick recap of the day's news, then they sent the show to commercial break after promising to return with a live interview with Starling's chairman about his controversial decision to cancel the network's top-rated TV series.

During the break, with the lights dimmed, Greg exchanged greetings with the two hosts then sat down on the set with them. Two minutes later, the lights came up again. They were back on the air.

"We are joined this evening by Mr. Greg Hammond, chairman and chief executive officer of Starling Worldwide," said Lanie. "Mr. Hammond has successfully led this company, of which we are a part, for the past fifteen years. During that time, Starling has grown to be one of the world's largest media enterprises."

"Good evening, Mr. Hammond," Alex said.

"Nice to see you both."

"Why cancel *Vectors*?" Alex said.

"The short answer is the formula of the show had become increasingly troubling."

"In what way?" Alex said.

"It presented the world one-dimensionally," Greg said. "Every week, it was a new group of terrorists threatening mayhem in every imaginable way."

"What's wrong with that?" Lanie said. "Terrorism is a reality."

"Yes, but too often that threat is exaggerated. The message that comes from *Vectors* is danger lurks around every corner, that we should all live in constant fear. It emphasizes a need to be protected by massive military expenditures. Are you aware, the US defense budget is bigger than the defense budgets of all the other major nations in the world combined?"

"You don't see that as necessary?"

"Every dollar we spend on defense is a dollar we don't have to spend on health care, education, infrastructure, clean, renewable energy, social security. The things that serve the direct good of the people, we are falling short on. Instead, we spend massively on missile defense shields, more aircraft carriers, more fighter jets. *Vectors* encourages fear. It promotes ethnic stereotypes. We can do better."

"Is this some kind of bold step to signal a network-wide transformation?" Alex said.

Greg chuckled. "We are looking at doing some things."

"What kind of things?" Alex said.

"There are areas we think we can improve, at no cost at all."

"Like what?" Alex said.

"Re-emphasizing truth and honesty in the way we deliver information."

"Aren't we doing that already?" Lanie said.

"We can do better," Greg said. "We have to do better."

"Why now?" Alex said.

"We live in extraordinary times," Greg said. "Some of the biggest issues ever faced by humanity are largely ignored by the commercial media, us included."

"Can you give an example?" Lanie said.

"Well, for one, we still don't talk about population," said Greg. "A major share of the economic, social, and environmental problems we have are caused either directly or indirectly by the sheer number of humans competing with each other for the planet's rapidly shrinking resources."

"I thought that was under control," Lanie said.

"In the developed countries, we're doing better," Greg said. "It's still a huge issue in the world's emerging countries. We're adding twelve cities the size of Los Angeles every year to the human population, mostly in places that already don't have enough of even the basics like food, water, and shelter. I saw this firsthand recently on a trip to Africa."

"It changed you?" Lanie said.

"It did," Greg said. "We cannot keep doing things business as usual."

"We're talking with Starling Chairman, Greg Hammond," Alex said to the camera. "Our conversation continues when we return."

The show went to commercial. The hot studio lights faded.

"Mr. Hammond," Lanie said, "forgive me for saying this, but it seems like you're going very far out on a limb. Is that what you want?"

"We're fine," Greg said, with a smile. "Keep it going the way we're going."

Getting into the defense budget was probably a stretch. Since Daria had raised the issue, though, Greg hadn't been able to get over the simple, stark reality of it. A massive share of the federal budget was earmarked for the military, while the nation's people had pressing needs that were being neglected. Screw it. If he only had two weeks left in the company driver's seat, he was going to speak his mind. The reference to the government's war machine would likely generate a lot of backlash from conservatives and the weapons industry. So be it. It was the truth.

The studio lights came up again. They were back on the air.

"So, changes are afoot at Starling," Lanie said.

"Our world has some very serious problems," Greg said. "Climate change, oil dependency. Starling has an obligation to pay attention and be part of the solution."

"How do you see that happening?"

"We'll offer specifics after we share our plan with our employees," Greg said. "I can tell you what we've already done with our series *Remaking*."

Lanie interjected, "This is Starling's primetime series that features families in need having their lives remade."

"Usually, it involves building them a new home," Greg said.

"You're remaking *Remaking*?" Alex said.

"From now on, everything will be built to achieve LEED certification," Greg said.

Alex seemed not to understand.

"LEED is a design standard," Greg said. "It stands for Leadership in Energy and Environmental Design. We're talking energy efficiency, sustainable building materials. Easy to do, and it sends the right message to the show's audience."

"Should we expect that kind of thinking to spread to the rest of the network's programming?" Alex said.

"Absolutely. Over time, it'll affect every part of the company's operation," said Greg. "We'll look at solar PV and other kinds of renewable energy for the many facilities we operate around the world. We'll look at water use. Everything we can do within the framework of our business will be subject to reinvention with efficiency and sustainability in mind."

"It's probably safe to say this initiative you've launched comes as a stunning surprise to just about everyone," Lanie said. "Why roll it out this way?"

Greg chuckled. "You mean, without warning?"

"Yes."

"It was time," Greg said. "In the past, we've generally avoided actions that don't fit the quarterly context of profitability and shareholder value. A bold step was necessary. I think this is the way to go. I hope our employees, our directors, and our shareholders will rally behind our new vision for Starling."

"What if you don't get the support you're hoping for?" Lanie said.

"That remains to be seen. I believe we will get a lot of support," Greg said, sounding a lot more assured than he actually felt.

"How do you think viewing audiences will respond to your new vision for Starling?" Alex said.

"Ultimately, we live and die by the quality of the audiences we deliver for our advertisers," Greg said. "We can never turn away from that. We also know that, for the most part, the public is way ahead of the politicians and business leaders on these matters. The public wants something done about global warming. They want something done about the cost of energy and our dependence on oil. They want a clean and healthy environment. They don't want the government spending all its wealth on weapons and war. They don't want the media to marginalize billions of the world's people who are struggling to survive every day."

"You don't think there's enough urgency about those issues?" Lanie said.

"Not nearly enough," Greg said. "Too many stories are either ignored or underreported. We've been guilty of that ourselves."

"You believe turning Starling green will pay off with increased audiences?" Alex said.

"We hope so," Greg said. "We hope people will watch what we put on the air. We hope they'll go to our webpages and read our publications. That would be the best way for the public to validate the steps we're taking and will continue to take."

"No doubt this change will be controversial, but it seems to be very much needed and will be welcome in many circles. Thank you for your time, Mr. Hammond," Alex said.

The show faded to another commercial. After a bit of small talk with the hosts and the producer, Greg went to have his makeup removed, all the while wondering how long it would take for the shit to hit the fan.

At Shamrock, the family estate in New Zealand, Lydia and Poppy had just watched Greg's television interview. The time was nearly 9:30 a.m. New Zealand was sixteen hours ahead of New York.

"You see what he's doing, Poppy?" Lydia said. "He's gone completely off the track."

Poppy was confused and very upset. Several times, he struggled to speak. The garbled word that came out over and over was, "Why? Why?"

"I don't know why," Lydia said. "I told him we wanted the process to be dignified."

Lydia left Poppy and went to her office at the other end of the house. She picked up the phone and dialed. A few moments later, she had Andre on the line.

"You saw the interview?" Lydia said.

"I watched it," Andre said. "Have you seen what's happened in the market?"

"No," Lydia said.

"We opened at eighty-two. That was before the announcement about *Vectors*. At closing, Starling common was down to seventy-four. By close tomorrow, it'll be below seventy.

"He's creating a minefield for you," Lydia said. "He's got two weeks and nothing to lose."

"He thinks he's got two weeks," Andre said.

"He does have two weeks."

"Not if I can help it," said Andre.

CHAPTER 35

"SOMETHING YOU CANNOT IMAGINE HAS happened," Daria said.

Angelika had just picked her up at the München Hauptbahnhof. They'd spent little time together since Christmas. It was the first Thursday in July, two days since Greg Hammond had turned his world upside down with his announcement about remaking his company into a paragon of media responsibility. Daria would have liked to be in New York with him. She also knew her presence would be a distraction. So, she'd kept to her long-scheduled holiday with Angelika at Schalchen.

"This thing," Angelika said. "It is good?"

"Yes, it's good," Daria said.

"About Greg?"

"I wish," Daria said.

"Something you had not expected?" Angelika said, as she turned the new Audi EV sedan up an access ramp onto autobahn number eight, headed south, out of the city.

Daria nodded, happily. "No one would see this coming."

Daria teased Angelika by going playfully mute.

"Okay," Angelika said. "So, tell me."

"You remember Lord Ramble?"

Angelika laughed and said, "The English oilman?"

"Yes," Daria said. "He has done a wonderful thing."

"Really?" said Angelika.

"Yesterday, a letter was delivered to the *Bright Eve* offices. It was addressed to me. This letter was from Lord Ramble. He said he has read Greg's article about Nani in the *Euro Standard*. He writes that he appreciates what we are doing."

"That's it?"

"No," Daria said. Again, she fell silent.

"Come on," Angelika said.

"When I was on the train on the way here, my cell signaled a call from my colleague at Bright Eve."

Daria paused again to maximize the drama of the moment, then she broke out in a big smile. "Just this morning, one million euros were deposited in the foundation's bank account. It was an anonymous gift from Lord Ramble."

Angelika shrieked with delight.

"I am still feeling the shock," Daria said, with a big laugh. She loved sharing moments like this with Angelika. They were both looking forward to some fun and relaxation at the lake house in Schalchen.

Angelika liked to drive fast. As the Audi cruised along in the autobahn's high-speed lane, Daria delivered more good news.

"Cervantes has organized some men into a construction team," Daria said. "Already, they are building the first proper, sanitary toilets in Tesfa."

"How lucky that he turned up the way he did," Angelika said. "You must encourage him."

"He gets plenty of that from me and also from Abeba," Daria said.

As the autobahn took them into the foothills of Bavaria, the talk turned to Greg and Starling Worldwide.

"I spoke with him last evening," Daria said. "The story is getting a lot of attention."

"From his competitors?"

"So many are reporting on him as if he has lost his mind."

"No support?"

"From the media, no," Daria said. "He has enemies. They know he's in trouble. They are paying him back."

"I was not expecting him to take such a big risk," Angelika said.

"This is my fault," Daria said.

"You cannot blame yourself," Angelika said. "He's not naive. He knows what he is doing."

"He will lose the company," Daria said. "I have asked too much from him."

"What does he say about this?"

"He insists only he is responsible."

"This is right," Angelika said. "You should accept this."

"Not so easy to do."

"He's giving up his old life," Angelika said. "He's becoming the man you want him to be. It is his choice. If I am him, and I know you are thinking this way, I would be upset."

"I could have handled it better."

"This is not a good way to think. The best way is to focus on what happens from this point on."

Daria knew Angelika was right. If she was going to help Greg, she had to calm her mind, and keep it open to every possibility.

Early that afternoon, they arrived in Schalchen. After a quick stop to buy food, they drove to the lakeside estate. An hour later, they were on the dock preparing to head out on to the Chiemsee in Angelika's six-meter-long Lightning Class sailboat. Angelika had taught Daria to sail in this small boat. It was a simple craft, a mast, a boom that swung from one side of the small open boat to the other, depending on the direction of the wind that filled the sail. A tiller was attached to the rudder board for steering.

They raised the sail. There was a gentle breeze, just enough to fill the looming sheet of canvas. They were on their way. Angelika steered with the tiller bar at the back of the boat. Daria sat on the gunnel that ran along the port side of the small vessel and slathered suntan oil on her skin. Daria always looked forward to sailing on the lake. It was so relaxing and quiet, such a pleasant way to pass the time on a warm summer afternoon.

After a moment, the conversation went back to Greg and his future at Starling.

"There must be something I can do to help him," Daria said.

"Let's think about this together," Angelika said. "Tell me his story, again."

Daria hesitated. She'd already told Angelika everything she knew about Greg. Not just once, but many times.

"Again," Angelika said. "Everything."

Why not? Daria thought. There was nothing wrong with going over it again. Talking about him might even bring some kind of inspiration.

CHAPTER 36

The ovation was thunderous and sustained.

"Wow. What a nice welcome," Greg said.

The audience gallery of Studio 6A on the forty-third floor of the Starling Headquarters building, a space normally used for taping game shows, was jammed with applauding employees.

Greg was thrilled to receive such enthusiastic approval, especially when, less than a week earlier, he'd unleashed his insurgency out of the blue, steering the Starling Media empire and all its people down a treacherous and uncertain path. He knew his audacious vision would fail without the employees buying in. They needed to understand the reason behind the changes he was implementing, and they had to be convinced he was sincere and entirely committed to his bold new course.

Greg raised his hands, urging the Starling employees in the studio to end their clapping and cheering. "Thank you. Thank you all for being here this morning."

When the audience had settled into their seats, he began his presentation to them and to those watching via live stream.

"Today is for you, the twenty-three thousand employees of Starling Worldwide. You are the ones who make our business work on every level. Some of you are here in-studio, many more are participating via streaming video on the company's private link. I'm sure you all know by now, we've launched a new era at Starling. This morning, we have a guest who can help us to understand the existential challenges we now face as a global society. Dex Green is one of the world's foremost eco-

economists. He's the author of the graphic book, *Planetary Stewardship: Dignity and Responsibility in the 21st Century*."

Greg held up a well-worn copy of the book and displayed some of its pages marked up by yellow highlighter.

"As you can see, my copy has received a lot of attention," Greg said. "Dex Green is in touch with the pulse of the planet. He speaks with great authority."

Greg looked toward the stage left and urged a distinguished-looking, older gentleman with a thin mantle of curly gray hair to join him. As the man came forward, Greg looked back at the audience and said, "Please welcome, Dex Green."

The audience applauded enthusiastically.

Greg offered Dex Green a warm handshake.

"Thank you for having me," Dex said.

The two men settled into comfortable chairs set close to each other.

Greg saw his role this day as a facilitator, encouraging an effective dialogue with his guest. He looked at Dex and said, "The world seems to be in trouble on so many fronts. How did we get ourselves into this mess?"

"Where to start?" said Dex, with a little laugh. "Since the beginning of the twentieth century, not much more than a hundred years ago, the world economy has expanded twenty times, and the size of the human population is nearly five times larger. Today, more than eight billion humans are putting demands on our planet's natural systems, exceeding their sustainable capacity by at least double."

"How do we put that in layman's terms?" Greg said.

"There are now so many of us humans placing such heavy demands on the earth that we are overwhelming its natural capacities to meet our needs," Dex Green said. "The world's great forest carbon sinks are being stripped away. Each year, overgrazing converts vast areas of grassland to desert. The pumping of underground water substantially exceeds natural recharge in countries containing half the world's people. Farmers can't produce enough grain to meet market demand. Three-fourths of the world's ocean fisheries, a major source of protein in the human diet, are being exploited beyond their limits. Some fisheries are already exhausted. Within a few decades, there will be more human plastic waste in our oceans than living biomass."

"Is it really that bad?"

"I wish I could say otherwise. There are some good people—actually, many more than a few good people—who are planting new forests, switching to electric cars, being the changes our common home desperately needs. But, as a whole, we humans are not changing our ways fast enough."

"Who's responsible?" Greg said.

"The short answer is, we all are," Dex said. "I'll give you an example of how it works. True story. In 1941, the US Navy set up a navigation station on Saint Matthews, an uninhabited island between Alaska and Siberia. In order to ensure there would be adequate food for the station's crew, in case of emergency, the navy imported twenty-nine reindeer to the island. No reindeer had been there before. The entire island was covered by a lush, four-inch-thick layer of lichen. It was a paradise for reindeer. After a year or so, the navy abandoned Saint Matthews, leaving the reindeer behind. Biologists estimated the island could sustain a population of no more than 1,200 reindeer. By 1957 there were 1,350. In 1963, the number had grown to 6,000, and the island was severely degraded. Three years after that, in 1966, scientists returned and found the reindeer population had collapsed to just forty-two animals. By 1980, there were no reindeer left on Saint Matthews Island. This is a real-life analogy for what humans are doing to Earth as a whole. It's called resource overshoot. It can happen to humans as well. The best-known example is the Rapa Nui culture on Easter Island off the coast of Chile."

"What happened there?"

"It's a very isolated place. In a nutshell, the population grew, and they ended up cutting down all the trees. They used up their critical resources. The population collapsed. This kind of overreach has happened many times, in many places over the many millennia of human advancement—the Viking culture of Greenland, the Maya of Mexico, the Anasazi of the American Southwest."

"We're still guilty of the same kind of hubris," Greg said.

"We are," said Dex. "These days, when we make decisions—it doesn't matter if we're consumers, corporate planners, government policymakers, or investment bankers—when we make decisions, we depend on economic signals for information."

"You're saying we're not getting the right signals?" Greg said.

"The market in many ways is an incredible institution," Dex said. "It allocates resources with an efficiency that no central planning body can match, and it effectively balances supply with demand. But the market we know is fundamentally flawed. It doesn't incorporate into prices the indirect cost of producing goods. It doesn't properly allocate value to nature's services. And it doesn't respect the sustainability thresholds of natural systems. It also focuses on near-term profit, while ignoring the consequences left for future generations."

"So, the market needs to do a better job of sending the correct signals?" Greg said.

"Yes. We need public awareness and political will," Dex said. "If we have those things, we can fix the market so it will send good signals."

"It's not a lost cause?" Greg said.

"Not at all. South Korea provides a splendid example. Not so long ago, it was a barren, treeless country. Now, sixty-five percent of South Korea is covered by forest. That has prevented flooding and soil erosion and has also restored the health and resiliency of the countryside."

"At this moment in time, how do we put ourselves on a worthy path?" said Greg.

"Focus on four goals: stabilizing population, stabilizing the climate, eradicating poverty, and restoring Earth's ecosystems."

"How do we do that?" Greg said.

"The challenge for our current generation is to build a new economic order that is powered largely by renewable sources of energy. We need to create a highly diversified transport system, and we need to evolve the way we do things so that everything gets reused and recycled. It's called a circular economy."

Dex paused for a moment, then continued, "We also need to help the third of the world's people who are living on the margins."

"None of those things are easy."

"True, but they're all critically important if we're going to build a world that can be sustained for future generations," Dex said.

"For the longest time," Greg said, "Starling has failed to report effectively on many issues, including the gap that divides the privileged few from the masses. How do we fix that?"

"A good start would be to stop ignoring population as an issue."

"We have to talk about it."

"Yes," Dex Green said. "You've got something like forty countries that are caught in a steep downward spiral. These countries are developed enough to reduce mortality, but not yet enough to reduce fertility. They're caught in a trap where rapid population growth inflates poverty, and poverty exacerbates population growth. Failing states are an early sign of a failing civilization."

"How so?"

"Nations fail when their governments lose control. When they can't ensure the personal security of their people, when they can't provide basic services like education and health care and food security, they lose their legitimacy. Such places often regress into civil war. They become threats to neighboring countries and can become training grounds for international terrorism."

"A very large share of the world's population growth is now taking place in countries that could be characterized as failing," Greg said.

"Of the top twenty failing states, seventeen have rapid population growth," Dex said. "Many are expanding at rates close to three percent annually."

"What does that mean in practical terms?"

"If the population is ten million to start, in a hundred years, it becomes nearly two hundred million."

"Scary."

"In the majority of these failing states, forty percent or even more of the population is under the age of fifteen," Dex said. "This is a sure sign of political instability. Young men especially, can become very troublesome when they lack basic needs and feel left out. More than three billion people are trapped in poverty in these failed states. These places are incubators of anger and terrorism."

Dex looked out over the audience of Starling employees and said, "In a very substantial way, your industry has contributed to this rising resentment."

An unsettled murmur spread through the studio audience.

"Television and the internet social media have extended their impact to every corner of the globe," Dex said. "Your network and others broadcast twenty-four hours a day to every country in the world."

"Isn't that a good thing?" Greg asked.

"Yes. The world should be connected," Dex said. "The problem, in practical terms, is that many people who are barely surviving see a lot of the privileged on social media. With a few exceptions, our media rarely has much to offer about those in need. What they are exposed to, over and over again, is mindless reality programming, sitcoms, and action dramas. Your show *Vectors* gets broadcast all over the world, even in the poorest countries, to people living on the edge. Americans are four percent of the world's population, but we use twenty-five percent of the world's resources. The people in these failing states know that. They get it. They see it reflected all day, every day on the internet. In these poor places, even people in survival mode can often find ways to access the media."

Dex turned again to the audience and said, "Put yourselves in the place of those people. Raise your hand if you think American-style social media sends the right message to people suffering in the poorest places."

No hands were raised.

"Even those people who are indifferent to the massive scale of human suffering in the world must recognize it's in their own self-interest to get ahead of this problem. If we lose this battle, those of us lucky enough to live in the developed world may find ourselves in serious conflict with billions of disenfranchised people."

Dex stopped for a moment to collect his thoughts.

Greg could see the audience was with him.

"We're facing many, many existential challenges. They feed on each other," Dex said. "Overpopulation, climate change, extreme weather events, food insecurity, deforestation, desertification, every kind of resource scarcity, industrial toxins, communicable disease, media disinformation, all of these threats are global in scale and coming to a head now, early in the twenty-first century. If we, as a species, don't learn to live within our means, sooner or later, human society will collapse, as happened to the reindeer on Saint Matthews Island."

"What should a company like Starling be doing?" Greg said.

"Information and awareness are critical," Dex said. "First, we have to take these unprecedented, civilization-scale challenges seriously. Then, media companies like Starling need to be honest brokers. People need to believe you are giving them the truth. There was a time when newspapers, magazines, radio, and television treated their readers, their listeners, their viewers as their customers. This is the way journalism is supposed to be practiced. If you're going to serve the people honorably and effectively, you have to go back to treating the public as your customers. They have to come first. The common good has to come first."

"Big step," Greg said. "We can do it, but we also have to show our shareholders that the bottom line will be respected."

"You know what," Dex said, "if you tell the world you're doing it, then you deliver on your promise, the people will reward you by tuning in your webpages and buying your newspapers. The advertisers can't ignore that. They'll stick with you because the people will be with you."

Greg turned to his employees. "We have to reinvent ourselves. We have to be an honest broker of information. We need our audience to trust us. We haven't pursued the truth enough in the past. That's on me. I was wrong. I came a long way to get to the place I'm at today. The high road is full of obstacles. It's not easy or comfortable to travel. It wasn't a road I ever expected to be on. If I can change, this company can change."

Somebody in the audience shouted out, "What about the Gulfstream?"

"You heard about that," Greg responded. His plan to get rid of the jet had been complicated by a major mechanical problem that had cropped up a few days earlier.

"I love that plane," Greg said. "Giving it up is hard to do. Why am I doing it? A friend told me how much carbon pollution I was personally responsible for when I used it. It's in the shop right now. When it's ready to fly again, we'll be getting rid of it."

Greg noticed that Michael was standing to the side of the stage. He was talking on his cell phone.

"We expect to be making a lot of changes in the coming months," Greg said. "There will be some sacrifices."

Greg stopped when he saw that Michael had put away his cell phone and was approaching him on the stage.

"Excuse me for a moment," Greg said to his employee audience.

Michael came up to Greg, leaned close, and whispered urgently, "Andre is in the building."

CHAPTER 37

A NDRE AND TWO OF HIS lawyers were rising rapidly on an express elevator in the Starling Worldwide building. The doors opened on the fifty-third floor. Andre went to Mindy, the receptionist. He looked her over with a blank expression and made a mental note to have her replaced by someone younger and more attractive.

"I'm here to see my uncle," Andre said.

"He's on his way up, sir," the receptionist said. "Can I get you something to drink?"

Andre ignored the woman and headed into Greg's private office, with his lawyers trailing behind. Andre hated the dark wood paneling on the walls and the gray patterned carpeting. The place was bland. The kind of authority it projected was stale. Everything would have to go. Andre wanted nothing left that would remind him of his soon-to-be predecessor. After the takeover was completed, there would be a makeover. He wanted a nautical theme to showcase his ocean racing. He'd already commissioned a quarter scale replica of *La Mer Cinq* for display in the Starling Building's lobby.

Andre settled into the chair behind Greg's desk. There was a folder on the desk. Andre opened it and was surprised to see it was Greg's action plan for reinventing the company.

At that moment, Greg appeared at the door, with Michael close behind.

"Already moving in," Greg said, sarcastically.

Andre eyed his uncle with a confident grin.

"You've got a lot of nerve walking in here like you own the place," Greg said.

Andre remained in Greg's seat. He patted the folder with the action plan. "Impressive."

"You're in my seat," Greg said.

Andre stayed put and raised the provocation ante by picking up Greg's file and stuffing it into his open briefcase.

"You can't be dumb enough to think you're walking out with that," Greg said.

One of Andre's lawyers leaned close and whispered into his ear. Reluctantly, Andre put the file back on the desk where he found it.

Andre leaned back in the chair and glared coolly at Greg.

The lawyer put a legal document into Andre's hand. Andre pushed it across the desk toward Greg.

Greg made no move to pick it up. Instead, he picked up the folder with the action plan and handed it to Michael.

"Wait outside," Greg said to Michael, who quickly turned and left.

Andre motioned for his two attorneys to leave the office.

Greg walked to the pair of sofas in the office's informal meeting area and sat down. Andre picked the legal document up from the desk, walked over, and sat on the opposite sofa, facing Greg.

"Why are you here?" Greg said, with unmistakable contempt.

"You could've been cool," Andre said. "You could have made it easy on everyone."

Greg eyed Andre coldly. "Why are you here?"

"We can do this the easy way, or the hard way," Andre said. Andre tossed the legal document down on the coffee table. "Game over, Uncle."

Greg glanced at the document.

"You actually thought you'd get away with this green goody bullshit?" Andre said. "You really thought you'd get a pass on that?"

Greg's expression turned to a defiant smile. "You can try, but you won't be able to kill it."

"So sure of that, are you?" Andre said. "The board has asked for an emergency meeting. You're gone as of tomorrow."

It was a move Greg had not anticipated.

Andre pointed at the legal document on the coffee table. "Signed and certified by the requisite number of directors."

Greg picked up the document and scanned it.

"You're required under the charter to comply and call the meeting," Andre said.

Greg was disgusted.

"Unless you're into humiliation, the easy way out is still open," Andre said.

Greg got to his feet. He stared coldly at Andre. "Are we done?"

Andre sat in place for another moment, then got to his feet, calmly acknowledged Greg with a nod, then headed for the door. He couldn't help what he was feeling. Greg had fucked him over repeatedly. Even if the guy was his uncle, Andre was looking forward to seeing him put out of the building for all the world to see.

———◆———

Greg called Michael back into his office.

"The board has been called to an emergency meeting," Greg said.

"When?" Michael said.

"Tomorrow at two," Greg said. "He has the votes."

"What can we do?"

"It's in the bylaws," Greg said. "We can't stop it."

Greg thought for a moment, then said, "I'm sure you're concerned about your own future. If this turns out badly, the next step for me will be to set up a foundation. You and the M&A team will be a part of it, assuming you want to be, same salary and benefits."

"Everyone will appreciate that, sir," Michael said.

"We haven't lost yet," Greg said. "Andre's got the board locked up. We need to focus on the shareholders."

"Whatever we can do," Michael said.

"As of tomorrow, I expect to be gone. Between now and then, we need to do what we can. The employees' forum we just had?"

"Already available on the in-house website."

"Put it up on our news websites," Greg said. "Give it to YouTube and any other site on the net where we can place it. We also need press releases. We want the world to know what's happening here. We position

Andre as the instigator. We paint this as a classic confrontation. It's our new way that balances revenue with ethical public service, versus the old way, driven entirely by profit. We need to connect with the progressive bloggers."

"I'll get the team together in the conference room," Michael said.

"Have some food brought in," Greg said. "We've got less than twenty-four hours."

Michael left to round up the M&A team.

Greg looked at his watch. It was nearly noon. Daria was supposed to be getting back to Prague late last night from her long weekend with Angelika in Schalchen. He called her on her cell phone. She was in her office.

"Back at work?" Greg said when he heard her voice.

"Yes," she answered. "So much to do."

Greg filled Daria in on Andre's unexpected visit and the dim prospects for hanging on as CEO of Starling after the next day. He knew she was feeling guilty about what had happened to him. As he'd done several times before, he assured her that he was responsible for his own decisions, and that he wouldn't do anything different if he could do it over.

"I'm alerting the bureau chief in Hamburg," Greg said into the phone. "Just to be safe, we want all the *Bright Eve* video material in post-production to be out of their hands and on the way back to you by close of business tomorrow."

"You think that's necessary?" Daria said.

"I do," Greg said.

"You're certain this will happen?"

"Certain about the board vote," Greg said. "A dismissal action against the CEO has to be ratified by the shareholders."

"To go quietly might not be so bad," Daria said.

"Would you do that?"

The phone was silent for a few seconds, then Daria said, "No."

"My team loves a challenge, and they think they're invincible," Greg said.

"You think you can win?"

"Long shot," Greg said. "However it turns out, our imprint will last."

At that point, their conversation turned to other things. Daria asked about living in New York. Greg took that to mean she was at least thinking about the prospect of a life with him.

After a few more moments of mostly sweet talk, they ended the call. However it went with Starling, there would still be Greg's unfinished personal business with Daria.

He started working on an email to the company's Hamburg bureau chief. As he was typing on his computer, his thoughts went to this father. Had he been wrong not to go to New Zealand to make his case with Poppy? He thought about it another moment, then decided he was not going to revisit that decision. Poppy was caught in the middle. Greg wasn't willing to get into an ugly tug-of-war with Lydia and Andre over Poppy's affection. If Greg was going to prevail over his half-sister and his narcissistic nephew, he would have to do it without Poppy's support.

Greg saw his M&A team passing by his open office door on the way to the conference room. He got up to join them. He was less than a day from losing his job, but he wasn't feeling down. Without a doubt, it was the fight of his life, and the cards were stacked heavily against him. Despite that, he still liked his chances.

CHAPTER 38

A T SUNRISE THE NEXT MORNING, video trucks belonging to all the major TV networks, except Starling, were crammed into the limited curb space available on Park Avenue in front of Greg's apartment building.

Greg eluded the media by ducking out the building's back service entrance. He hurried on foot to a newsstand two blocks away. He bought one copy each of the city's four major newspapers plus three other national papers, then hailed a cab.

En route to the downtown office, he went through the papers and found that all had his likely ouster as the lead in their business sections. The spin on every story was critical of the company and very particularly of him personally. He wasn't surprised. The media companies behind these newspapers were big-league competitors, seeking advantage. Where he was concerned, they were going for the jugular. If they'd thought he stood a chance of hanging on, they would've muted their analysis and reported their stories more respectfully. In every instance, Andre was presented as some kind of brash business hotshot, a colorful, rising star, heavily into fast boats and a busy social life.

Fortunately for Greg, there was another side to the public discourse. It was on the internet. Coverage was spreading virally across the blogs and the journalistically vital news and investigative websites on the net. They were reporting the story as Greg had hoped, like it was a struggle between the old way that was bad, which Andre represented, and the new, ethically transcendent way that Greg represented.

At the Starling Building, a horde of reporters, photographers, and TV and radio news crews surrounded Greg as soon as he stepped out of the cab. He was peppered by questions from all directions. He put on a cheery face and ignored the verbal assault. He tried to look confident as the media mob got their photos.

A squad of company security people came out of the building and cleared the way for Greg to get inside.

When he arrived in the executive conference room on the fifty-third floor, Greg found Michael and the M&A team already there.

"What do we know?" Greg said to Michael.

"We're trading six points above yesterday's close," Michael said. "Heavy volume."

"Question is, what's driving it?" Greg said.

The company's stock had lost fourteen percent of value since Greg had announced his intent to turn Starling green. In Greg's mind, six points up since morning trading began could be seen two ways. The first linked the market rally to the prospect of him being replaced as Starling CEO. But there was also a real chance that at least some of the gain was coming from people who were buying the stock to express support for Greg's bold new vision for the company.

Whatever the cause of the market rally, for Greg, the critical task at the moment was to keep his team enthusiastic and motivated. He got their attention, then spoke up. "You have been outstanding these past few days. You took a simple mandate and turned it into a tangible green strategy for Starling. In the best of worlds, we win this battle. In the best of worlds, we become a good corporate citizen and earn the public's trust. In the best of worlds, we become the example our competitors are forced to emulate."

Michael and the M&A team applauded Greg enthusiastically.

Suddenly, Greg had an inspiration.

"Good citizenship versus business as usual," he said. "That's our frame. Greg Hammond versus Andre Akers is good corporate citizenship versus business as usual. That's how we play this out. We're about doing the right thing. Andre is entirely about serving himself and the bottom line."

The team members couldn't contain themselves. They started chattering and sharing ideas. Greg loved their enthusiasm. He glanced at his watch, then spoke up again. "We're still in charge, for at least another five hours. Let's get this out. Press releases, and anything else we can think of."

"You should make a statement, sir," Michael said.

"Let's do it," Greg said. "Get a video crew up here. Everything we do needs to be finished and out the door before the board meeting."

————◆————

The media mobbed Andre when he arrived at the Starling Building, accompanied by his lawyer entourage, at 2:10 p.m. Smiling broadly, he waved to the cameras. He knew he cut an impressive figure with his neatly trimmed mane of blond hair and his perfectly tailored charcoal suit. He loved the spotlight. He relished the idea of becoming one of New York City's big dogs, partying with the rich and famous in sports, politics, and entertainment. He already had one of Manhattan's most exclusive real estate agents looking for a pricey co-op near Central Park.

So what if the media was characterizing him as some kind of bachelor bad boy? He'd carried that reputation for years. It hadn't slowed him at all. In fact, with the ladies, it made it easier.

Andre entered the building's lobby. He was thinking about where he would take the company. First rule, don't mess with what's not broken. Starling was not going to change under his leadership. The emphasis was going to be on acquisitions and profitability. He knew what he wanted. It was about setting the direction and having competent and loyal managers make it happen. Andre was convinced he could maintain his edgy lifestyle while running Starling Worldwide. There would still be time for Antibes and racing *La Mer Cinq* in the summer months. He would be calling the shots, and he would make damned sure his schedule included plenty of play time.

After a quick trip up the elevator, Andre arrived with his lawyers at the company's sleek, marble-paneled boardroom on the fifty-second floor. Twelve of the company's directors, all of them drawn from the highest echelons of business and finance, were present. They welcomed

Andre with a lot of backslapping and gladhanding. He soaked it up like a conquering gladiator.

Though he wasn't on the board, Andre's substantial stock ownership in the company and the likelihood of his ascendancy to the chairman's suite had made it easy to get the emergency meeting organized. Four directors had begged off, all claiming scheduling conflicts. Andre would deal with them later. For now, he basked in the friendly gladhanding and good wishes. The board members who'd shown up had made the calculation. They were with him unquestionably. He had the votes needed to dismiss Greg, and also to have himself designated as his uncle's replacement.

Greg could have kept his dignity if he'd just gone with the flow. His time on stage was up. Now, it was time to make way for Andre.

Just after the digital clock on the wall clicked over to 2:30, Greg appeared in the boardroom with his assistant, Michael.

Greg didn't bother to greet the gathering of board members, all of whom had at one time been his friends and allies. He went to his place at the head of the table and called the meeting to order.

"Per the rules set forth in the Starling corporate charter, this emergency meeting of the Starling Media Corporation Board of Directors has been called to act on a petition for the dismissal of the chairman and chief executive officer," Greg said. "I'm sure you are all familiar with the arguments made for this petition. I ask that the written material put forth in support of the petition be placed into the meeting record in lieu of being read aloud."

The motion was made, seconded, and passed unanimously.

"We all know why we're here," Greg said. "As a point of personal privilege, I ask two things. First, you hear my position on this issue as presented in a six-minute statement that has just now been released to the media and posted on the company website. Second, if the petition for dismissal is sustained, I remind the board that a full validation by the shareholders, conducted by an independent arbiter, is required, as set out in the company bylaws. Anybody have anything to say at this point?"

No one spoke up. The tension in the room was palpable.

Andre sat back in his chair, smirking. Better to stay quiet and let his uncle play out his last hand.

Greg signaled to Michael, who launched a video on the room's wall-mounted display. It was very slickly done with lots of quality video images of collapsing glaciers, deforestation, desiccated landscapes, and hordes of third-world slum dwellers laid in over Greg's comments. The conflict, according to Greg, came down most basically to finding common ground that gets all people past the polarization. Greg Hammond, being the good corporate citizen, focused on serving the best interests of humanity. Andre was nothing like that. Andre's motives were wrapped in empty calories designed to maximize profit and shareholder value, and his own inflated ego.

Andre wasn't surprised by the video's dismissive slant. He also wasn't concerned. He had a lock on the vote. This kind of play on emotion would have no impact.

When the video ended, Greg spoke up again. "Any comment at this point?"

No one said a word.

Greg continued, "The approach we've taken is not only the right thing to do, it is the only wise course. There's no other way to get ahead of the problems we face as a human civilization."

Andre scoffed.

Greg glared at him scornfully.

Andre said, "I'm sorry it's come to this."

He wasn't sorry at all. He just wanted an expression of sympathy included in the meeting record.

"I ask for a motion on the petition," Greg said.

The motion was moved, seconded, and passed.

At that point, without another word, Greg got up from his chair and left.

The board's vice chairman took over the meeting. Andre was quickly nominated and confirmed as the company's acting CEO, pending ratification of the board's decision by the shareholders.

The whole thing took less than twenty minutes. It was almost too easy. Andre phoned his mother to give her the news.

⸻❖⸻

By 3:00 p.m., Greg was being driven home by Michael in a company car. The trunk was loaded with five boxes of items Greg had not wanted to leave behind, including his laptop computer.

An hour after he was back in his Park Avenue apartment, Greg got a call from Carl Samuelson, the company's chief counsel. The shareholder validation vote would be conducted a week from today in the ballroom at the Plaza Hotel. Shareholders could appear in person to vote, or they could have their votes recorded by proxy through another shareholder.

Carl was angry about Greg's dismissal. He was ready to resign himself. Greg talked him out of it. He reminded Carl that even if he wasn't there anymore, he was still the company's largest single shareholder. Carl would be a badly needed voice of reason if the shareholders sustained the board's decision and Andre was confirmed as Starling's Chairman and CEO.

After the call with Carl ended, Greg dialed Daria's cell number. It was late in the evening in Prague. He got her at home. He filled her in on what had happened.

He didn't want to waste time on regrets. He quickly moved to a more positive subject. "As of this morning, the Whio Foundation is an officially registered nonprofit charitable corporation in the state of New York."

They'd agreed earlier on the name. It was an outgrowth of the little blue plastic duck Nani had been holding tightly in the hospital in Tesfa. It reminded Greg of the blue duck, a web-footed species that was indigenous to swift rivers in New Zealand. The name for the blue duck in Māori was *whio*.

"We're working on transferring the initial two hundred million dollars into Whio's accounts," Greg said.

"You must not give up this fight with the shareholders," Daria said.

"Even if we don't win, the seeds will have spread," Greg said.

"You can still win this," Daria said. "The key is your father."

"Not an option," Greg said.

"Why not?"

"Lydia's living in the same house," Greg said. "If I go there, Poppy will end up in the middle. I can't do that to him."

"You don't think you could change his mind?"

"If I tried, she'd push right back," Greg said. "Nothing I've done with my life would have happened if it hadn't been for Poppy. I can't do that to him. The stress could kill him."

"Could his mind be changed?" Daria said.

"Maybe, if Lydia wasn't there," Greg said. "You have to remember, she's been with him pretty much every day since he had his stroke. She's had a lot of time to fill his head with poison."

"What if she weren't there?"

"She is there."

"Could you get her away from there?"

"Not if I go anywhere near him."

"What if you don't leave New York?"

"He's had a stroke. The only effective way to communicate with him is to be there with him."

"I understand," Daria said. "I am only asking is there some way to get Lydia away from your father for a few days."

"You mean if I stayed in New York?"

"Yes."

"How does that help if I'm not there to talk to him?"

"Does it have to be you who talks to him?"

"If not me, then whom?"

"If this could happen," Daria said, "I have my secret weapon."

CHAPTER 39

LYDIA HAD GOOD CARDS. SHE was becoming annoyed with the slow play of her partner. They were at one of six bridge tables set up in the sunroom at Shamrock. At each table, four ladies were intensely focused on the cards they were holding.

The cell phone in the pocket of Lydia's slacks began to vibrate. It was the third time in the last twenty minutes. When her table finished the hand they were playing, she excused herself and went outside onto the veranda. She pulled out the cell phone and saw the calls had all come from Andre, who was in New York, serving as Starling's acting Chairman and CEO.

Lydia punched in the speed dial number for Andre. Moments later, she had him on the line.

"Why are you calling me?" she said. "I told you I'm hosting Bridge Club this evening."

"Greg's challenging the proxies," Andre said.

"He can do that?" Lydia said.

"It's a legal maneuver," Andre said. "My guys say it won't hold up, but it could complicate things."

"So, let the lawyers figure it out."

"You need to come to New York."

"I can't do that."

"There's a chance the proxies won't be validated."

"You have people who can fix those things," Lydia said.

"Mother, this is the biggest thing that's ever happened to me. You need to be here. I want you to be here."

"You know I can't leave," Lydia said. "Somebody needs to be here. We can't have Greg showing up, trying to change Poppy's mind."

"Greg's in New York," Andre said. "He's not going down there now. Not enough time."

"You're sure he's still in New York?"

"I've got people watching every move he makes," Andre said. "He's not going anywhere."

"My table is waiting," Lydia said.

"This is a big deal," Andre said. "You need to be here."

"I need to get back to my game."

"The lawyers say you should be here," said Andre.

"I'll think about it," Lydia said.

"Mother."

"Call you later," Lydia said. Then she ended the call.

The main reason she hadn't gone to New York was she didn't want Greg sneaking in and changing Poppy's mind. It wasn't that she didn't want to go. The prospect of basking in the New York limelight was exciting. She'd thought about it a lot. The society scene, not just in Christchurch, but in New Zealand in general was minor league compared to the high life in New York. Only a couple of cities in the world came even close to New York. London, Paris, and Los Angeles came to mind. Lydia had already checked into the harness horse activity in New York. There was a long-established racing tradition in and around the city. If she did decide to relocate there, that part of her life could be transitioned easily.

Greg had been a workaholic. He'd never been much of a factor in the New York social scene. Andre would be better at it, but Lydia knew he'd still focus most of his down time on his addiction to young women. Somebody had to be there to represent the family's social obligations. Andre was about to take over the empire. She was his mother. She was the new matriarch. That would include real social power. She imagined herself at the center of a great salon gathering, surrounded by New York's beautiful people, all eager to curry favor and friendship.

Lydia activated her cell phone and selected Andre's number. He was on the line a moment later.

"You know exactly where Greg is?" Lydia said.

"Yes, Mother," Andre said.

"You're sure?"

"I am. He flies out now, he'd miss the vote."

Lydia was giddy. The most exciting time of her life was unfolding.

"I want people to know I've arrived," Lydia said.

"They'll know," Andre said. "I've got that covered."

"There's a hotel near Greg's co-op," Lydia said. "You know it?"

"Yes."

"Book a suite," Lydia said. "Hairdresser, nails—you know what I like."

"Don't worry," Andre said. "You'll be taken care of."

Lydia glanced inside the house through the nearest window. She could see the other bridge players watching her. She spoke into the phone. "Greg makes a move—"

"I assure you, he's not going anywhere."

"Call me tonight," Lydia said, just before breaking the connection. She moved off to where she couldn't be seen. She lit a cigarette and smiled. She didn't mind keeping her cronies waiting. In New Zealand society, she was already A-list. Upping the ante was a regular part of the social game with this crowd.

She finished her cigarette, then threw it down. She thought about her half-brother as she squashed the discarded butt with her foot. Greg was finished. The spotlight was shifting to Andre and to her.

Lydia smiled. Her time had finally come. She had to tell her bridge crowd. She hurried and rejoined them and began gushing about New York, about her elevated social obligations, and about the rich and famous people she expected would become her friends.

⸺⬥⸺

Eddie was with Poppy the next morning when Lydia came to see him.

"Poppy," Lydia said, "I'm going to New York to be with Andre when he officially takes over next week."

Poppy took her hand.

"I know you're upset," she said. "I really am sorry it's come to this."

Poppy had tears streaming from his eyes. He was obviously deeply distressed about the rift that divided the people closest to him.

"It'll be okay," Lydia said. "Andre will be great. You'll be proud of him. Greg's already announced he's launching a new foundation. He's going to be fine."

Lydia hugged Poppy.

"The staff knows how to reach me if anything comes up," Lydia said. "I'll see you in a week or so."

Eddie had volunteered to take Lydia to the airport. He'd always tried to maintain a neutral attitude toward the things she did. It hadn't been easy. In fact, he'd never liked her. She was loud and insensitive, and totally full of herself. She was expert at pretending concern for the old man.

Eddie knew better. He'd overheard the snide comments she'd made about him to Andre.

And he didn't like the way they'd shafted Greg. He didn't like it one bit.

After he dropped Lydia off at the airport, Eddie parked the car in the lot. He hadn't told her about the guest who was coming for a stay at Shamrock. He hadn't told Big Boss about her either. The lady was due on the 11:00 a.m. flight from Auckland. Her name was Angelika Grünberg.

CHAPTER 40

FLYING THROUGH HALF THE WORLD'S time zones had nearly exhausted Angelika. Fortunately, she'd landed in New Zealand early the previous morning. She'd spent the first night in Auckland, giving her at least a little time to recover from having her body clock turned upside down.

She walked briskly through the airport terminal at Christchurch to the baggage claim, retrieved her luggage, and headed outside. She spotted a tall Māori man right where she'd been told to look.

"Eddie?" Angelika called out.

"That's me," he said with a smile.

They were quickly away from the airport, driving south on Route One, headed for Kakapo Bay and Shamrock.

"So, you've been with Jack Hammond a long time?" Angelika said.

"Almost forty years," Eddie said.

"You know everything about him?"

"Pretty much," Eddie responded.

"He's a good man?"

"Mostly."

"Honest?"

"For sure."

"Can I change his mind?"

Eddie chuckled. "If not you, then who?"

Angelika smiled. She wasn't sure what to expect with Jack Hammond. He had a reputation for being hardheaded and conservative on most things. All she'd heard suggested, he was also honorable and decent.

"I was told he's lost his appetite for women."

"Just since the stroke," Eddie said.

"Why?"

Eddie was reluctant to answer.

"You mind if I ask questions?" Angelika said.

"He's embarrassed," Eddie said. "He hates what happened to him."

"Does he have a girlfriend?"

"No," Eddie said.

"What about friends?"

"Lots of friends," Eddie said. "They don't come around."

"Why not?"

"He's depressed," Eddie said. "He doesn't encourage visitors."

"When was the last time he was with a woman?"

Eddie hesitated to answer.

"You don't like talking about him?"

"He trusts me."

"I understand," Angelika said. "I ask you to trust me."

She could see he wasn't entirely convinced.

"I'm here to help Greg," Angelika said. "I must know these things."

"Before the stroke."

"You would know?"

"Yes," Eddie said.

"A long time."

"Long time."

"He was once very interested in sex, yes?"

"Always."

"Lot of girlfriends?"

"Yes," Eddie said. "Except when he was married to Greg's mother."

"After that?"

"Sure."

"So, he still likes to be with a woman?"

Eddie laughed. "If the woman is you, I have to say, yes."

When they arrived at Shamrock, the housekeeper was the only person in the house other than old Jack. She seemed to know why Angelika was there and was happy to see her.

"Where is he?" Eddie asked the housekeeper.

"Still in his room," said the housekeeper. "Looking very gloomy."

"I'll take you to meet him," Eddie said to Angelika.

"First, I will have a shower and change my clothes," Angelika said. "There is a place I can do this?"

Eddie and the housekeeper led Angelika upstairs to a guest bedroom with a breathtaking ocean view.

Angelika looked at Eddie and the housekeeper with a cheery expression. "Okay, so now, we make our plan. This is okay?"

"Whatever we can do," Eddie said.

Angelika put her hand on Eddie's massive shoulder. "You go to Jack. Tell him a lady has come to visit. Maybe you can say some things, get him a little excited."

Eddie beamed. "I can do that."

Angelika then turned to the housekeeper. "Something light to eat would be good, soup and salad. No meat—tasty, but not sweet. This is possible?"

The housekeeper smiled and nodded. "In the dining room or out on the veranda?"

"The weather is nice, warm," Angelika said. "Outside would be good."

Angelika looked at her watch and said, "It's now 12:15. I'll meet him for this lunch at one."

Just before 1:00 p.m., Angelika headed downstairs. She'd changed into a white-and-pale-yellow sundress that showed some cleavage and accentuated her still-slim, very attractive shape. She was also wearing some of Daria's lavender-scented Great Incitement fragrance. She hoped it would have the same effect on the father as it had on the son.

She was amused by the irony that she was about to employ a variation of the game her beloved bonobos had been using on the river shores of the Congo for generation after generation. These close human relatives were not shy about their sexuality. They used sex eagerly and often to resolve disputes and keep the peace. Daria had also employed her sexuality on multiple occasions to serve a greater good. Now, it was Angelika's turn. She had no misgivings. With so much at stake and so little time left before the shareholder vote, she had to get Jack Hammond's attention. She had to act quickly. She had to create a bond between them. She had no illusions it would be easy to change Jack Hammond's mind. What Angelika wanted was for him to take her seriously and listen thoughtfully. She had to make him listen. Connecting with him intimately was the quickest path to an open and receptive mind.

Out on the veranda, a light breeze was blowing in from the bay. Angelika marveled at Shamrock's picture-perfect landscaping and its magnificent view of Kakapo Bay.

Eddie soon appeared with Jack Hammond. He was more attractive than Angelika had thought he would be. Clean-shaven and dressed nicely in casual slacks and an open-collared sport shirt, the old man was walking well. It appeared he had full use of his left arm. His right arm still had a tremor, but he seemed to have regained some use of it. The right side of his face still drooped slightly.

Angelika smiled and said, "I am Angelika Grünberg."

She took his left hand and held it gently.

"Such a beautiful place," she said. "I'm so happy to visit you here."

Jack made no attempt to say anything, but he was smiling. Eddie had apparently said the right things.

The light lunch Angelika had requested was in place on the table. She and Jack sat down across from each other.

"I am a new stockholder," said Angelika. "Just the other day I purchased seventy-five thousand of your company's shares. This would be about six million in US dollars. For me, a bargain. Already, the stock value has increased."

Over lunch, Angelika charmed Jack with talk about herself, how she met her deceased husband, how she was left a widow with so much money. Then she talked about her friend Daria, about their adventure in the Congo with the bonobos, about the bonobo exhibit she helped to build at the zoo in Munich. She spoke in glowing terms about the wonderful things Daria was doing.

Jack didn't seem to catch on that this Daria was the one connected to his own son.

Angelika decided to wait for the right moment before saying more about Daria.

Angelika liked Jack Hammond. For the moment, she was happy just to see him enjoying her company.

"You don't want to talk?" Angelika said. "You're embarrassed because of the stroke?"

Jack nodded.

"You don't like to sound foolish?"

Jack nodded again.

"You shouldn't worry about how it sounds," Angelika said. "Maybe your speech will come back, if you make an effort."

Jack seemed to agree with her.

"We try a little now, and see how it goes," Angelika said.

Jack gestured that he was willing to try.

"I make the sound of a letter. You repeat… A."

Jack made a guttural sound. It was slurred, but it was understandable as an A.

"Good," Angelika said. "You see? You can do it."

For the next ten minutes, Angelika coached Jack, encouraging him to emulate her as she went through the alphabet. Some letters were harder for him than others, but he managed to make a sound that was discernible for each of the letters.

"This is good," she said. "Very good. We'll stop now. A little at a time is best. We try more later. Okay?"

Jack smiled, then he stuttered a bit and managed to blurt out a slurred version of the word, "Okay."

Angelika was delighted. "See what happens when you try?"

Jack was obviously very pleased with himself.

"Now," Angelika said, "I like to see the place where you sleep. Can you show me?"

Jack seemed surprised by the request but nodded agreeably. He got up from the table, took her hand, and led her into the house.

Angelika made eye contact with Eddie and the housekeeper, who were just inside the kitchen. She smiled and mouthed the words, "Thank you."

Jack led Angelika up the staircase to the second floor, then down the corridor, and into his airy suite of rooms that overlooked the bay through large windows.

Angelika flashed a lusty smile at him as she closed the door behind them. "Now, we have some private time."

A broad grin spread across Jack's face.

Angelika led him to the bed and sat him down on it. "We can have a little rest."

She knelt down and began to remove his shoes. "Only yesterday, I have come from Europe. I am feeling jet lag. Rest in the afternoon is always good, you agree?"

Jack nodded. He seemed to like the direction things were headed.

Angelika unbuckled his trousers and helped him out of them. Then she unbuttoned his shirt. In another moment, he was wearing only boxer briefs and socks.

She saw he had a stiff erection. She smiled seductively and moved in very close to him. She let him get a good whiff of her wonderful fragrance, then she leaned in, cupped his cheeks in her hands, and pecked him on the lips.

A big smile spread across Jack's face.

"It seems you are happy I am here."

Jack nodded.

Angelika was pleased. "Now, lie back on the bed."

Jack eagerly complied.

Angelika stood a few feet from the bed and began to swing her hips sensuously. She slipped out of her high-heeled shoes. The classy sundress she was wearing had buttons on the front from top to bottom. She unbuttoned them slowly, one by one.

Jack's eyes were glued to her.

She teased with the dress, opening it, giving him little peeks. Then, she turned her back to him. Slowly, she allowed the dress to slip off her shoulders to the floor. All that remained was a strapless black bra and matching garter belt holding up dark nylons.

She turned around and saw Jack's stiffness pushing at his shorts. She loved that her body could generate this reaction from a man.

"You want to touch?" she said, with a silky lilt in her voice.

Jack nodded.

Angelika moved to the bed and stretched out beside him. He put his hand on her hip and caressed her bottom.

She pecked him on the mouth then said, "So eager. Still the tiger."

Jack playfully made a '*grrrr*' sound.

Angelika laughed. She kissed him again, then said, "Before we go further, I ask you to do something for me."

He was all ears.

"You will listen to what I have to say?" Angelika said.

Jack nodded.

"I have your promise?"

Jack nodded again.

"Okay, so, your son, Greg, he is my friend," Angelika said.

She displayed the gold chain and the bonobo pendant around her neck. "He has given me this wonderful gift."

Jack's face tightened. He seemed to have the wrong idea.

"Just friend, not lover," Angelika said, with a smile. "He is together with my dearest friend."

Jack suddenly had a look of recognition.

"Yes," she said. "My friend I told you about, this wonderful, good woman I told you about, your son loves her. She also loves him. If you ask me, I think one day they will be married."

Jack seemed uncertain how to react.

"Maybe, one day, they give you a grandchild."

Jack appeared to like that idea.

Angelika sat up. She straddled him and began caressing his body.

Jack smiled. His attention was riveted on her.

Angelika moved down close to him. "I have some things to say. Again, I ask your promise. You listen. You keep an open mind. You can do that?"

Jack didn't hesitate. He forced out the word, "Y-y-yesss."

Angelika's eyes lit up. "That was good. We will work on this, okay?"

She noticed Jack staring at her lacey black bra. "You like this off?"

Jack nodded eagerly.

Angelika unhooked the strapless garment and tossed it aside.

Jack stroked her breasts, which were small and firm.

Angelika closed her eyes and enjoyed his touch. Then, she saw that Jack had lost himself in his own moment of pleasure. Angelika leaned close and kissed him on the forehead. She liked him. Now that she had his full attention, now that she'd had these moments to spend time with Jack Hammond, she sensed she had a chance to win him over.

CHAPTER 41

IN ROOM 1114 AT THE Sheraton Towers in Times Square, Daria was in the shower, thinking about Greg. It was midafternoon, the second Tuesday in July. The moment of reckoning had arrived. In another hour, the Starling shareholder vote would begin.

She hadn't told Greg she was coming to New York. Until now, it had been important that he keep all his attention on building shareholder support for his ambitious vision for Starling.

A few blocks away, at the Plaza Hotel, company shareholders would cast their votes starting at 4:00 p.m. The late hour was out of deference to the substantial number of shareholders observing from New Zealand, where the company got its start. It was early morning over there.

Daria stepped out of the shower and toweled herself off. She picked up the remote and flipped through the channels. The fate of Starling was front and center. All the networks except Starling were cutting away regularly to live, on-the-scene reports on the impending shareholder vote.

Daria found the coverage blatantly biased. Andre was presented favorably, as a youthful media innovator. In contrast, Greg was ridiculed as a dinosaur entrenched in tired tradition. It was amazing how perceptions could be twisted and reality could be distorted in the modern media.

She stopped cycling the TV remote at breaking news on a local broadcast. A protest had broken out across the street from the Plaza. Several thousand people were gathered by the pond in Central Park, raising hell about the big corporate media, while specifically opposing Andre's takeover at Starling. Daria was thrilled. At least some people recognized what was at stake.

Back in the bathroom, Daria ran a brush through her hair, then applied moisturizer to her face. She'd hoped things would go better with Angelika. Before leaving Prague, she'd received an email. Angelika had been with Greg's father for several days, but thus far, there'd been no change of heart. Angelika had been encouraging, but her journey to New Zealand had never been more than a long shot. If something good were going to come of it, Daria assumed she'd have heard by now.

After applying a hint of eyeliner, she took her time putting on her favorite muted red lipstick.

With the shareholder vote about to begin, there was no longer any reason for Daria to stay out of Greg's way. She wanted to be with him. From the things he'd said, she knew the vote by the directors the previous week had been an extreme humiliation. The vote today would likely be his final repudiation. It was such a shame. So much good could be accomplished by a global media company that was truly committed to fostering a dialogue on the world's long list of planet-scale problems. Greg was the rare alpha male who'd found the will to transform himself. He should be rewarded for his courage. Instead, it would be more humiliation. She hoped he would be happy she was there to stand by him when it happened.

Room service arrived with her first meal of the day. Daria threw on a robe and accepted it from the waiter. She thought about Greg as she worked on a bowl of sliced fruit, some yogurt, and a glass of soymilk. She'd tried to resist her feelings. She was done with that. She loved him and was ready and eager to give herself wholly and completely to a life with him. She believed his passion for her was forged out of the respect he had for the person she was and the life she had chosen. He'd not only talked the talk, he had walked the walk. He'd taken the risk and was prepared to accept the sacrifice of losing his career and the business he built as a consequence of reinventing himself. No person could ask another to do more. Daria hoped the affirmation of her love would compensate him in some way for the defeat he seemed destined for this day.

There was another reason for Daria to be present at the shareholders' meeting. She'd become a shareholder herself. The week before, at Angelika's suggestion, Daria had purchased two thousand shares of Starling Worldwide common stock. She would vote on those shares today. She was also holding proxies for the seventy-five thousand shares Angelika had bought. There were millions of shares of common stock outstanding, so it was more symbolic than anything else. Still, it might make a difference if, somehow, the vote ended up being close.

She glanced at her cell phone and saw it was 3:42 p.m. Time to go. She went to the classy, blue-accented, white summer dress laid out on the bed. She put it on and latched the accessory belt around her waist. Dark-blue heels that perfectly complemented her dress came last.

Daria checked herself one last time in the mirror. She was about to leave when she remembered a final touch. She pulled out a small dispenser of Great Incitement. Normally, at professional meetings, she didn't wear a fragrance. Today, it was for Greg. She sprayed it lightly on her neck and wrists, then headed for the door.

She took the elevator down, crossed the hotel lobby, and exited a side door onto 53rd Street. She walked east two blocks to 5th Avenue, then headed uptown. The wide sidewalk was packed with pedestrians passing to and fro. The bright summer sun was mostly blocked by the shadows of the tall office buildings lining both sides of the street.

The Plaza Hotel was six blocks ahead, at 59th Street. Even from that distance, Daria couldn't miss the gigantic banner hanging from an office building across from the hotel. It was a huge, vertical graphic rendering of *La Mer Cinq*, Andre's racing boat, in the Starling Colors, black and gold. A jam of taxis, trucks, and cars were moving slowly, headed downtown on 5th Avenue. As Daria crossed 57th, she saw a van carrying a TV news crew approaching. Suddenly, the van pulled into a nearby loading zone. A reporter and his news camera crew jumped out. They rushed to her side and began to walk along with her.

"Are you Daria Kocánová?" said the young reporter.

Daria smiled, said nothing, and kept walking.

CHAPTER 42

ANDRE LOVED THE ADULATION. EVERYBODY wanted to talk to him. He was in the largest, most lavish suite in the Plaza Hotel, rubbing elbows with the city's elite. At least fifty people, including many of the company's directors, and a number of invited dignitaries from Wall Street and Manhattan's media communities, were present. The suite currently served as a VIP reception and holding room for the shareholder vote. Four flat-screen televisions, set to one side of the suite's main salon, were showing the afternoon news broadcasts from the various networks.

After becoming interim CEO, Andre had wasted no time. Eight of his senior people from Starling Asia were now in New York, managing the transition. The chopping block was out. Dozens of termination notices would go out the next morning. Among them were all former members of Greg's M&A team, who were currently employed in executive positions with Starling. The list to be fired also included the head of Starling's Hamburg news bureau that had extended post-production assistance to Greg's girlfriend.

Andre had talked to the producers of *Vectors*. The show would be back in production as of tomorrow. He liked their work. So did the company's big business customers. Andre wanted more primetime action programming. There was even talk of building an action-adventure series around an ocean racing team that doubled as terrorist busters. Andre loved the tie-in with *La Mer Cinq*.

Andre was eager to impose his own indelible stamp on Starling Worldwide. He would put the focus back on growing the company's profitability. Screw the common good bullshit his uncle was preaching.

Saving the world was not in the CEO job description. The focus would return to building shareholder value.

Greg was off the deep end with his world-coming-to-an-end, alarmist crap. He'd stirred up as much trouble as possible. Andre was prepared to return the favor. True, Greg was still the largest shareholder in the company. As soon as the vote was in and Andre's leadership was affirmed, he would approve a clever accounting maneuver designed to undermine Greg's stake in the company. Once he was vulnerable, he'd be offered a buyout too good to ignore. In a way, it would be like a hostile takeover, the kind of aggressive gambit Greg had pulled off successfully many times in the past. Once Greg's stake was sufficiently diluted, he would become unofficially persona non grata. Andre relished the prospect of denying his uncle access to any and all Starling facilities.

In a month, everything would be in order. Once his own people were firmly in place in New York, he intended to return to Antibes to catch up with the young ladies of summer. Morty and Bernard were still in France, still having a good time. Andre wasn't about to let them have the field to themselves any longer than necessary. The company's G650 jet would be in the shop for another three weeks. The boys at Erskine and Hyndes had done a little too good a job of putting the plane out of service. The damage to the landing gear would cost a couple hundred thousand to repair. No matter. It had stopped Greg from unloading the jet. Once it was back in service, Andre intended to make good use of it. He imagined three-day work weeks in New York, with the rest of his time in Antibes.

He glanced at his watch and saw it was nearly 4:00 p.m. One of the TV monitors was linked to a closed-circuit camera inside the ballroom where the voting would take place. Andre focused on it and saw the shareholders were starting to register.

Greg's insistence on going strictly by the rules in the company bylaws had made this process much more aggravating than it needed to be. The whole thing could've been handled by mail. Greg had insisted it be done in person or by proxy. He'd also insisted on hiring Liebert, Mars, and Caldwell, a law firm that specialized in shareholder vote oversight. Because of that, every shareholder, even those with one share, had a right to register and vote in person. All of Greg's grandstanding the past week had accomplished one thing. The place was crawling with tree-huggers, who'd bought one or a few shares of stock in the company. They were there to make a public show of voting their shares for Greg. As if it mattered. The deal was done. All the loser shares amounted to squat compared to the votes committed to Andre. No way could Greg win. He was done. His stupid games had only added a few wrinkles to the process.

Extra security had been hired. A shareholder had only to show proof of identity and they would get a punch card ballot that showed how many shares they were voting. The card could be punched, yes or no. A yes vote ratified the board's decision and affirmed Andre's appointment as the company's new CEO. The small shareholders would be done voting within the next hour or so. After that, Andre and his mother would go to the ballroom. They would end the process when they voted their shares and the proxy shares from Poppy. The whole thing would be wrapped up in time for Andre and his mother to host a lavish private dinner for loyal company directors and other VIPs.

The progressive blowhards on the internet had managed to stir up a fair amount of public sentiment in Greg's favor. Because of that, the Erskine and Hyndes portfolio had been expanded to take on two new tasks. The first was a campaign to undermine Greg's sudden popularity with the public. The second was an effort designed to shift Starling's image back to the right, where it had been before Greg had gone off the deep end.

Andre wondered where his mother was. She was staying at her exclusive hotel on the Upper East Side. He expected her to show up anytime. No doubt, she'd find a way to make some kind of grand entrance.

After taking a moment to greet a couple of newly arrived VIP guests, Andre glanced back at the TV monitors. The closed-circuit view of the ballroom showed the voting process going as smoothly as could be expected.

Something caught Andre's eye. It was on one of the monitors tuned to a live local TV news feed. It showed a very attractive young woman walking along the street with a news crew following her. *Damn,* thought Andre, *that's Greg's girlfriend, Daria.*

According to the reporter on the scene, she was less than a block away, headed for the hotel.

What was her game? Andre knew Greg was waiting the process out in a smaller suite two floors down. Why was his lady out on the street by herself? It was easy to understand why Greg was so hung up on this babe. She was fine, and the way she walked… It wasn't swagger, and it wasn't what you see with hotties interested in drawing attention to themselves. It was the kind of self-confident stride you'd expect from someone who had it together.

At that moment, Andre had to give his attention back to greeting more arriving VIP guests. Ten minutes later, he stole another glance at the TV monitors. He saw that Daria was now in the ballroom where the voting was taking place. She was waiting in line to register. She must have become a shareholder. Greg was nowhere to be seen. Maybe there'd been a falling out.

Maybe she'd dumped him when he was knocked off his big-shot pedestal.

Andre felt a stir in his loins. This was a lady he had a need to sample. How sweet it would be if, in addition to taking Greg's job, Andre had a taste of his girlfriend as well. *Why not?* he thought. He watched her on the monitor a moment longer, then made up his mind. If he was going to make a run at Greg's babe, the time was now.

Andre excused himself and left the room. Two minutes later, he stepped off the elevator in the hotel's lobby and headed directly for the ballroom. Once inside, he ignored the people who approached to talk to him, and also some nasty chatter from the loser shareholders. He spotted Daria across the room in a line of people waiting to vote. He went directly to her.

"Excuse me," he said when he came up to her. "Your name is Daria, right?"

She turned and looked at him. He could tell she knew who he was, but she said nothing.

He smiled and switched on the charm. "You don't have to stand in line. Come upstairs, and you can wait in the chairman's suite. Vote later with us."

"Why should I do that?" Daria said.

She was playing hard to get. He'd seen this attitude so many times. You could wear this kind of woman down. Be persistent. Heap on the bullshit. A lot of times, the hardest ones to get were also the most satisfying. And, in this case, there was added incentive.

"Actually, I was hoping to have a word with you," Andre said.

Daria's eyes narrowed. She was not looking happy.

Andre would not be deterred. He pointed to an area of the room that was unoccupied.

"Could we just step over there for a moment?"

Daria said nothing.

"Just for a moment."

"I don't want to lose my place in line," she said.

"If you want to come back, I'm sure these people will hold your place."

Andre looked at the people in line behind Daria. "Am I right? You'll let her back in, right?"

The people in line agreed to let her back in.

"See?" said Andre. "No problem."

Daria reluctantly stepped out of line. He led her to the place where they wouldn't be overheard.

"You are Andre?" Daria said.

"I'm Andre."

"I know about you."

"You don't know me. You shouldn't judge me."

"I know how you treat women," Daria said.

"I'm a man," Andre said. "In my situation, I get a lot of attention."

"You play dirty."

"I play to win."

"Why are you talking to me?"

"I saw you. I was thinking, *This is a very impressive woman. My uncle is nowhere around.* I tell myself, maybe this lady is open to other possibilities."

"You want to add me to your collection?"

Andre pretended to be wounded by her remark.

"Why should I be interested in you?" Daria said.

"You're a shareholder. We should be friends."

Daria glared at him with piercing eyes.

Andre smiled and reached for her hand. She avoided his touch.

"Sleep with your uncle's woman," Daria said. "What better way to hurt him?"

This is one sassy bitch, thought Andre.

She began to mock him. "It takes a lot of man to satisfy me."

Her attitude annoyed him.

She put a hand on his chest and backed him into the wall just behind him. She got right in his face.

"You know," Daria said, almost whispering. "You know it would be so good... so very good for you."

A big grin spread across Andre's face. That was more like it.

"I'm just as sure that for me, sex with you would be a disappointment, a very big disappointment. It would be all about you. All... about...you."

Andre noticed that many of the people in the room were staring at him and Daria. He leaned in close to her, and said, "Lady, you are totally hot."

Daria clenched her right hand to a fist and extended an insulting middle finger. She waved it in Andre's face, then turned and walked away.

Andre heard cheers and enthusiastic applause from many shareholders waiting in line. It was humiliating, beyond anything Andre could remember. He made a vow. Tomorrow morning, his first call would be to Erskine and Hyndes. Their new assignment: shred this bitch's reputation. On her knees, that's where he wanted her.

His cell phone went off. He pulled it from his pocket. It was his mother.

"I'm on the way," Lydia said.

Andre's face twisted to an angry frown.

"Are you there?" Lydia said.

"Yes, Mother."

"The entrance," Lydia said. "Ten minutes."

"Just come to the suite, Mother," he said, with too much sarcasm in his voice.

"Be there," Lydia fired back at him. "And don't embarrass me. This isn't the South of France. Act like you belong here."

Andre broke the phone connection. Then, he noticed that many people in the room were looking at him. He felt like a fool. Rage began to boil over. He headed for the nearest exit.

CHAPTER 43

Thousands were gathered by the pond in Central Park, across from the Plaza Hotel, thousands who were fervently standing up for Greg and his ambitious green agenda for Starling.

Greg was watching from a window of the modest suite he'd rented at the Plaza. The massive display of support was exhilarating. In the past, when the public had shown up in response to his presence, they'd come to condemn, not to praise. It felt good to be appreciated this way.

Greg knew that Angelika was in New Zealand with his father. Daria had told him about their plan to intervene with Jack Hammond. Greg had seen no harm in it. He'd used a lawsuit as a ruse to lure Lydia to New York. He also had arranged with Eddie to facilitate Angelika's visit to Shamrock. It was worth a try, despite the fact that Greg thought there was almost no chance of regaining his father's support. Even if Angelika were to find a way to change the old man's mind, he could not speak, and he was not in New York.

Greg was ready to accept exile from the business he'd built into a global empire. He just wanted it to be over so he could focus on finalizing his merger with Daria Kocánová.

The only others in the suite with Greg were Michael and members of the M&A team. There were no big shots from Wall Street, no big-name politicians, no socialites, and no celebrities. Greg found it amusing. The elite who formerly had been eager to curry favor were nowhere to be seen this day.

Then, he saw Michael coming toward him with a tablet. "Sir, you gotta see this."

Greg took the tablet, which was displaying video from the hotel ballroom, where the shareholder vote was underway.

Michael touched the screen, pointing at a woman in a white dress who was registering to vote.

Greg focused. The woman looked like… "Daria?"

"It's her," Michael said.

"She's in Prague," Greg said. At least, that's where she'd said she would be when they'd spoken yesterday.

"That's her," Michael said. "I called down. She's registered as a shareholder."

Greg had to go to her. He turned to leave.

"Hang on, sir," Michael said. "Gotta see the best part."

Greg turned his attention back to the recorded video on the tablet screen. He watched Daria get in line with other shareholders who were voting. It appeared the people in the line around her had recognized her. They were engaged in friendly chatter with her.

"It gets better," said Michael. He fast-forwarded the video to where Andre appeared on-screen.

Greg was stunned. His eyes were riveted to the video as Andre approached Daria.

"How did you get this?" Greg said.

"You've got a friend in the production truck outside," Michael said. "He forwarded this video file."

A moment later, on the video, Daria left the line of shareholders and went off to the side with Andre.

Greg couldn't believe what he was seeing. He was getting angrier by the moment. The video cut to another camera angle.

"The guys in the truck saw this," Michael said. "They switched to another camera they could operate remotely."

The camera centered on Andre and Daria and zoomed in close.

Greg's eyes grew wide. Andre was hitting on her. The guy was eight inches taller than her, looming over her. She was not intimidated. Damn, she was right in his face, backing him into the wall.

The entire M&A team was huddled around the tablet.

Greg could hardly contain himself.

On the screen, after one last remark, Daria shoved her middle finger in Andre's face, then walked away.

Greg clenched a fist, threw it over his head, and let out a howl. He was the kid who'd just seen his hero hit the winning basket. He had to go. He had to be with her.

He took off out the door and sprinted to the elevator.

Less than three minutes later, Greg was in the ballroom. He spotted Daria in line. He rushed to her.

Daria's face lit up when she saw Greg approaching.

He rushed up and embraced her.

People nearby cheered.

"I saw what you did with Andre," Greg said.

"How do you know this?"

Greg pointed to one of the video cameras mounted on a tall pole.

Daria understood. She smiled, leaned close, and whispered, "Your nephew is an asshole."

Greg laughed and nodded. Then, very happily, he said, "You're here."

Daria smiled. "I could not miss this."

"How'd you get in?"

"I am a shareholder," Daria said.

Greg was delighted. "Since when?"

"Since five days ago," Daria said. "Angelika also."

Daria held up the voting punch cards she had for Angelika and for herself. "I must vote."

Greg pulled his voting punch cards from his inside jacket pocket. "Me too."

"You have many friends across the street," Daria said. "We vote, then we go to them."

That was great with Greg.

Daria began introducing him to the people she'd met while standing in line.

Awesome, thought Greg. *She's just awesome.* He noticed her fragrance. He leaned close to her, took in a deep breath, and thought how much he loved this girl, while savoring the wonderful, lavender way she smelled.

Lydia was pissed. She was alone in the back of a stretch limousine stuck in a jam of taxis, cars, and airport vans at the Plaza Hotel's entrance. She could see Andre and a mob of TV crews waiting there. She could've stepped out and walked the rest of the way, but that would spoil the moment. Her mind was racing. As she waited, fantasy took over. She saw herself stepping from the limousine. She saw Andre greeting her. She saw TV cameras and photographers pushing in on them, recording them, broadcasting them to the world. It was so, so exciting. Lydia was ready for her close-up, ready to be recognized as the newest granddame of New York society.

Finally, the limo reached the hotel's grand entrance. Andre was waiting.

The moment was at hand. *Savor it. Bask in it,* Lydia told herself. *The spotlight is yours.*

The hotel's doorman opened the limousine's passenger door. He helped Lydia out of the vehicle. With the photographers snapping away, she smiled and touched cheeks with her son.

She soaked up the adulation.

Suddenly, there was a commotion inside the hotel. Somebody was coming out. The photographers and video crews shifted their attention to the hotel doors.

An instant later, Greg and Daria exited, hand in hand. A small mob of enthusiastic supporters was with them.

Lydia made eye contact with Greg. He acknowledged her, smiling like he was the day's big winner.

Lydia scowled. Then she saw one photographer was still snapping pictures of her. Immediately, she forced a smile. She watched as the mass of photographers and video crews left her to follow Greg and Daria away from the hotel.

Lydia felt humiliated. She struggled to mask her rage. She glared at Andre, then grabbed his arm and hurried him toward the hotel's revolving entry door.

At the corner of West 59th and 5th Avenue, Greg waited with Daria for the light to change. He was thinking about Lydia and Andre. He was surprised to see them standing outside when he and Daria emerged from the hotel. He had every reason to be angry with them, especially given Andre's outrageously boorish behavior with Daria only a short time ago. But Daria hadn't needed any help. She'd taken Andre down firmly and unequivocally on her own. Greg couldn't get over it. He was sure the video of Daria ripping Andre would become a monster hit on YouTube.

Greg had a right to be furious with Lydia and Andre over losing control of Starling. He had the right, but they were not worth the waste of emotional energy.

Andre and Lydia might win today, but they would never be satisfied. No matter how much they had, it would never be enough. They would always think they were entitled to more. Greg knew such feelings could devour a person. He'd been there. No, he wasn't going to expend any more energy being angry with Lydia and Andre. More than anything, what he felt for them was pity.

Over the past weekend, while browsing the internet in his Park Avenue apartment, Greg found an essay that focused on the ethical philosophy of Aristotle. Here was a Greek philosopher who lived 2,500 years ago, a man who'd been a student of Plato and was the teacher of Alexander the Great. Aristotle, one of early history's greatest scholars, wrote about every subject conceivable in his time.

Greg hadn't expected to find meaning in the words of the ancient sage. But what Aristotle said about life had struck a chord. Happiness was the highest order of being, according to the immortal Greek thinker, and the way to achieve happiness was to live virtuously, guided by truth. Virtue was an ideal, a standard that required a moral compass unfettered by corrupt rationalization.

That was Daria's secret. That was why she was so strong. That was why she was so totally together and happy. She didn't fool herself. She was compassionate because it was the right way to be. She was determined to make the world better because it was the decent thing to do. She had the ability to cut through the bull and find the truth. Then, she became truth's stalwart, unflinching champion.

Greg admired her. He loved her because she was the perfect example of virtue. His greatest desire was to emulate her. He wanted so much to be worthy of her love.

The light turned green. Greg and Daria hurried across 59th, into Central Park. They were greeted like conquering heroes. They waded into the crowd, shared handshakes and hugs, and took time to talk to people. For Greg, it was exhilarating. For the longest time, he'd been a corporate high achiever. Here he was on the day that could, probably would, mark the loss of all his corporate power. But he wasn't depressed, not at all. On the contrary, to be recognized and appreciated, as was happening at this moment, to be sharing this wonderful experience with Daria, it truly felt like he was in touch with the highest way of being.

CHAPTER 44

"HE HAD TO BRING HIS girlfriend," Lydia said, making no effort to conceal her resentment.

"He didn't bring her," Andre said. "She came alone."

Mother and son had just arrived in the VIP Suite. The company directors and other guests had already left for the ballroom, where the ratification vote was progressing. One of the suite's broadcast video monitors was showing a live TV news feed of Greg and Daria in Central Park, engaging the crowds gathered to protest the takeover at Starling.

In a rage, Lydia kicked the leg of the closest table, knocking a tray of food to the floor.

"Why is that woman even here?"

"She's a stockholder," Andre said.

"So?" Lydia said. "This isn't her day. It's your day. It's my day."

"She's voting a big block of proxy shares."

"For whom?"

Andre called to his assistant, who was on the other side of the room. "The lady is voting somebody's shares, who is it?"

The assistant took a moment to pull up the information on his computer, then he said, "Angelika Grünberg, from Germany."

"You know that name?" Lydia said to Andre.

"That's her rich bitch girlfriend," he said.

This was all supposed to be so perfect, Lydia thought. Greg's grandstanding wasn't going to mean anything in the end. Once the votes were tallied, Greg would be out. Andre would be running the show.

Lydia admitted to herself, she hadn't always believed Andre would get this far. Despite all the help he'd received along the way, she'd wondered many times if he could make it the last mile without screwing it up. No question, there were two different personalities trapped in Andre's body. One was the aggressive, business-minded competitor, but the other was the swaggering stud determined to bed all the girls. Fortunately, it seemed, on this occasion at least, the adult side had won out.

Despite Greg's best efforts to spoil the moment for them, it would all be over very soon.

The entire day had been scripted. The little people would cast their votes. Then, the directors and VIP shareholders would cast their votes, and Andre and Lydia would come last. They would make their grand entrance. They would cast their votes. They would deliver Poppy's proxy. The result would become official. They would celebrate with the leaders of New York society at a dinner in the hotel's grandest banquet room. Most of all, that dinner was what she was looking forward to.

It would be her personal coming out in the most exclusive social circle in all the world.

At that moment, Lydia craved a smoke. She dug a cigarette out of her purse and lit up.

A waiter approached immediately. "Pardon me, Madame. Smoking isn't allowed in this suite."

Lydia glared at the waiter and took a drag on the cigarette.

"Madame," the waiter said. "Please."

Lydia sucked in another lungful of smoke, then squashed the cigarette on the waiter's tray.

Just then, the live TV news broadcast switched to a breaking story. It was the video of Andre hitting on Daria.

Andre groaned and cursed under his breath.

Lydia was stunned. She gave the video her full attention.

When it was over, Lydia glared coldly at Andre.

"She hit on me," Andre pleaded.

Lydia kicked him hard in the shin.

"That's what happened."

"You expect me to buy that?"

She kicked him again.

"Stop," Andre said.

She delivered another kick to Andre's shin.

"Damn. I said stop."

She kicked out at him again. Andre avoided it. He got behind her, grabbed her arms, and held on. She kicked and struggled to break free.

Her cell phone went off. Andre released her. She checked the phone's screen and saw it was the family estate's Filipino gardener.

Lydia answered. "Why are you calling?"

"Miss Lydia, you said I get five hundred dollars if I saw something," the gardener said. "You remember?"

"Yes, I remember," Lydia said. "What did you see?"

"A lady has come here."

"Who?" Lydia demanded.

"A lady," the gardener said. "I came to work today. I saw her. I think she's been here since you left."

"You don't know who she is?" Lydia said.

"No," the gardener said. "You said if I saw something, I get five hundred dollars."

Lydia cut off the call. She ripped through her speed dial list. She found the number for Poppy's caretaker, Eddie. Moments later, he was on the line.

"What's going on?" Lydia said into the phone.

"Is this Miss Lydia?" Eddie said.

"You know damned well who it is," Lydia said. "Who's in the house with you?"

"Nobody with me."

"There's a woman in that house who doesn't belong."

"The lady is not with me," Eddie said.

"I want her out," Lydia said. "Get her out, now."

"Can't do that, Miss Lydia."

"You can! You will!" Lydia said. "I told you no visitors!"

"She's with Big Boss, not me," Eddie said.

"With Poppy?"

"Yeah."

"Who is she?" Lydia said. "Do I know her?"

"I think not."

"Is she sleeping with him?" Lydia said.

"Not my business."

"Make it your business."

"I can tell you this, Boss is a happy man."

"I want that woman out of the house!"

"I can tell you some other good news," Eddie said. "Boss is starting to talk."

"Since when?"

"Since this good lady came here," Eddie said.

"I want her out!" Lydia said. "Put her out right now!"

"Can't do that, Miss Lydia," Eddie said.

"You will do it!"

"I work for Big Boss," Eddie said. "He wants her to stay."

"Who is this person?" Lydia said. "Who is she?"

"Very nice lady," Eddie said.

"Her name?" Lydia said. "What is her name?"

The connection went dead.

"What's wrong?" Andre asked.

Lydia ignored him. She had to know who was with Poppy.

"What's the problem?" Andre asked.

"There's a woman in the house with Poppy."

"Who?"

Lydia ignored him. She went through her phone's directory until she found the cell number for Florencia, Shamrock's young housemaid. She would talk. Lydia would make her talk. Seconds later, she had Florencia on the line.

"Who's in the house with Poppy?" Lydia shouted.

The response could barely be heard.

"I don't know."

"Tell me her name."

"I don't know her name."

Lydia knew Florencia. She was too timid to lie. "Where's Poppy?"

"Outside."

"With this lady?"

"Yes."

"Where's Eddie?"

"Outside with them."

"Are you upstairs?"

"Yes."

"Go to Poppy's room."

"Yes," said Florencia.

Seconds later, she spoke up again. "I'm in his room."

"Is the lady's luggage there?"

"Yes."

"Go to it."

A moment passed, then Florencia said, "I'm there."

"Is there an identity tag?"

"Yes."

"Read me the name."

Several moments of silence passed.

Lydia paced restlessly. "Come on. Come on."

Then Florencia returned. "Okay."

"What's the name?" Lydia demanded.

"I can't pronounce it," Florencia said.

"Spell it."

"A-N-G-E-L-I-K-A."

The recognition light went off in Lydia's head.

"Last name."

"G-R-U-N-B—"

"Grünberg?"

"Yes."

"From Germany?"

"Yes."

Panic swept over Lydia. She killed the call and turned to Andre. "Poppy's proxy. Where is it?"

Andre touched the chest pocket of his suit coat. "Right here."

Lydia grabbed his arm and pulled him toward the door. "Let's go!"

"What are you doing?"

Lydia kicked him again on the shin. "Now!"

They rushed out of the room, headed for the elevators.

⬥

Greg and Daria crossed 59th and headed for the hotel. They entered through a brilliantly polished brass-and-glass revolving door. As they started across the lobby, they saw Lydia and Andre burst out of a guest elevator and rush off toward the ballroom, where company shareholders were still voting.

Greg sensed something was up. He grabbed Daria's hand. They hurried off in pursuit.

A moment later, Daria's cell phone rang. She answered the call, listened a moment, then handed the phone to Greg.

"It's Angelika," Daria said.

Greg stopped and put the phone to his ear.

"Some lawyers are in the hotel's lobby," Angelika said through the phone. "They represent your father. They need to get into that meeting."

"Why?"

"He has changed his mind," Angelika said.

Greg was stunned. "Say again."

"Your father has changed his mind. He's with you," Angelika said. "You must get his lawyers admitted to that meeting."

Greg looked ahead and saw three men in suits arguing with the security people at the ballroom entrance. He hurried that way. When he got there, he gave his attention to the two security officers who were denying the lawyers' entry. Lydia and Andre were right there, blocking the lawyers from access to the ballroom.

Greg focused on the trio of lawyers. "Are you here for my father?"

"These men do not represent my grandfather," Andre shouted at the security officers. "They are not authorized to enter this room."

"Do you have proof you're on retainer to Jack Hammond?" Greg asked the lawyers.

One of the lawyers handed Greg a copy of a faxed letter. Greg began a quick scan through it.

Lydia said to Andre, "Get inside and vote."

He hesitated.

She kicked him on the shin. "Go!"

Andre hurried inside and headed for the table where the ballots were being accepted.

Greg knew if Andre got Poppy's proxy into the record, it would be over. Once cast, the company bylaws did not allow votes, by proxy or otherwise, to be changed.

Greg held on to the letter and told the lawyers, "Wait here."

Lydia blocked the doorway. Greg tried to get past her. She shoved him back.

"What do you think you're doing?" Greg said.

"You got to Poppy," Lydia said.

Greg tried again to go around Lydia. Again, she blocked his way.

"You think you're so smart," Lydia said.

Greg turned to the security guards. "You see this?"

The security guards were phoning their supervisor. Greg saw they would be no help.

Lydia picked up a metal easel and waved it threateningly. Then, she lashed out with her foot and kicked Greg on the shin.

He looked at the guards. They did nothing.

Greg tore the easel away from Lydia.

Then, Daria stepped between him and his unhinged sister.

Lydia tried to go around her to get at Greg, but Daria blocked her way and said, "Enough from you."

Lydia directed a kick toward Daria. She side-stepped it. Then she reached out, pinched Lydia's nose between her fingers, and steered her out of Greg's way.

Across the room, Andre was aggressively pushing his way past other shareholders waiting in line at the voting table.

Greg rushed up. "These people were here first."

Andre shoved him aside to get to the election judge, who was just behind the table.

"I am the CEO of this company," Andre said to the judge. "I want my votes and my proxy's counted now."

Greg got the judge's attention and displayed the letter the lawyers had given him.

"I have a faxed letter from my father. He's petitioning to vacate the proxy and cast his votes himself."

"He can't do that," Andre said. "He's not here."

Greg handed the letter to the judge, who quickly turned away to confer with his associates.

"You have no right to prevent me from casting my votes," Andre shouted at the judge.

Greg glared at Andre. "You have no right to bypass the line."

Andre ignored Greg. His attention was focused on the judge.

"I am the chairman of this company! I demand the right to vote my shares!"

The judge didn't like Andre's bluster.

"All shares are created equal, Mr. Akers."

Andre was livid. "This is my company!"

The judge motioned for help from two uniformed security men.

"I'll have your ass for this," Andre said to the judge.

The judge ignored the threat. After another quick scan of the letter, he turned to Greg.

"Your father is Jack Hammond?"

"Yes."

"It seems he wants to cast his votes himself," the judge said.

"He can't do that," Andre said. "He's in New Zealand."

"Is that true?" the judge said to Greg.

"His lawyers can explain his intentions," Greg said. "Can you talk to them?"

The election judge took a moment to consider the request, then said, "Have them come forward."

"They've been barred from the room," Greg said.

The judge signaled the security officers at the door. They allowed the three lawyers to enter.

The judge took the lawyers aside and conferred with them.

Andre moved close to Greg and shoved him. "You're not getting away with this."

Greg stood his ground. "We'll see."

The judge came back to Greg and Andre. "The petition is allowed into the record."

"You can't do that," shouted Lydia, who was now at Andre's side.

"I have my grandfather's notarized proxy," Andre said. "I have the legal right to vote his shares."

The judge responded, "The shareholder has the right to vacate his proxy in person."

"He's not here!" Andre insisted. "He can't do that if he's not here!"

"We have our client live over the internet," said one of Jack's lawyers. He produced a tablet computer showing a real-time video image of Poppy sitting in a chair at Shamrock on the veranda overlooking Kakapo Bay.

Lydia lunged for the tablet. Daria blocked her from getting to it.

The judge looked at Jack's lawyers. "Can we hook this up to our video feed?"

A moment later, the tablet was connected to a digital system that displayed a live, larger-than-life video image of Jack Hammond on the tall wall screen behind them.

"This is an outrage!" Lydia said. "He's had a stroke! He can't tell you what he wants!"

"Can he hear us?" the judge asked the lawyers.

"He can," said the lawyer operating the tablet.

"Mr. Hammond," the judge said.

Everyone in the Plaza Hotel's ballroom could see Jack Hammond on the wall video display, as he acknowledged the judge with a smile and a nod.

"Do you wish to vacate the proxy your grandson is holding?" the judge said.

Again, Jack nodded affirmatively.

"Can you say that?" the judge said.

Jack spoke up tentatively, but intelligibly, "Y-y-yess."

"Yes, you wish to nullify the proxy?" the judge said.

"Y-y-yess, n-n-nullfffy," Jack said.

Greg was stunned. Tears of joy welled up in his eyes. His father was talking. He was talking.

"I s-s-suppporrt m-m-my sssson," Jack said.

"You vote against the directors' decision to remove Gregory Hammond as company CEO?" the judge said.

"AAgggainnnsst," Jack said.

"You vote to retain Greg Hammond as CEO of Starling Worldwide?"

"Vvvotttte ffforrr Gggrreggg."

A large portion of the people in the ballroom were small shareholders who supported Greg and his bold ambition. They erupted with cheers and thunderous applause.

Greg and Daria embraced. They cheered and applauded with the crowd. Greg couldn't believe what he'd just heard. They'd won. They'd won the war for control.

On the live video image on the wall screen, Jack was beaming. Angelika could be seen moving into the frame. She kissed Jack on the cheek. Then, she smiled and waved to the camera.

It was the most thrilling moment of Greg's life. Seeing his father talking, and seeing him happy—what an awesome, unexpected gift.

Greg felt reborn. He thought about the tremendous media power at his disposal. Daria had convinced him that honest communication was critical to meeting the unprecedented challenges threatening life on Earth. The media was the nervous system of humanity. Sincere, transparent, unbiased communication was an absolute imperative. From now on, that's exactly what the public would get from Starling Worldwide.

He wrapped his arms around Daria and held her tight. What an extraordinary human being. She'd taught him so much about courage and conviction, and most of all, about compassion. Together, they had the means to affect change on a grand global scale. It was heady stuff. Greg couldn't wait to get on with the rest of his life, a life renewed, a life bursting with possibility with him and Daria Kocánová standing side by side.

---

*"Never doubt that a small group of thoughtful
and committed citizens can change the world.
Indeed, it's the only thing that ever has."*

—Margaret Mead, Anthropologist

AUTHOR'S NOTES

The inspiration for *Virtue* came from many people. Three in particular are reflected directly in the story.

The healing presence of Marc Wren is fiction, but his selfless nobility was motivated by the extraordinary dedication of the late, real-life physician, Paul Farmer. The actual story of Dr. Farmer's inspiring work in Haiti and other places came about through his wonderful, life-affirming organization, Partners in Health (www.pih.org). Paul Farmer's story of unswerving commitment is told brilliantly by author Tracy Kidder in his best-selling book, Mountains Beyond Mountains, Random House, 2004.

The compassion and commitment reflected in the Daria Kocánová character was inspired principally by the distinguished author and humanist Riane Eisler. Having written extensively on the cultural evolution of gender relationships, Dr. Eisler calls for a caring, cooperative 'Partnership Way' between women and men to shape a planetary future that is life-affirming and sustainable. Riane Eisler's website is The Center for Partnership Systems.

Daria Kocánová's work with bonobos in the story was inspired by Jane Goodall and her studies of Chimpanzee behavior at Gombe stream in Tanzania.

The issue of female genital cutting featured in *Virtue* has affected hundreds of millions of women, a great many of them on the

African continent. Tostan (www.tostan.org) and the Orchid Project (http://www.orchidproject.org) are two organizations doing particularly impressive work on FGC. Their approach is grounded in cultural sensitivity, education, and the empowerment of women. I admire the good people associated with these two organizations. I urge those who are inspired by *Virtue* to stand with African women on the FGC issue. Visit the websites for Tostan and The Orchid Project and support their noble efforts.

Others whose wisdom influenced the characters and the story in *Virtue* include Carl Sagan, Paul Hawken, Muhammad Yunus, Paul Ehrlich, Jane Goodall, Elisabet Sahtouris, Julian Cribb, and EO Wilson. I have learned so much from these distinguished pathfinders.

I cannot say enough about the constant inspiration and encouragement I receive from Michael Charles Tobias and Jane Gray Morrison. It has been my honor to stand with them for nearly three decades as they compassionately serve humanity and all life on Earth.

http://www.dancingstarfoundation.org

Finally, I want to express my deep appreciation to my closest confidante, my wife, Jennifer, for her love, her partnership, her encouragement, and her enduring support.

Geoffrey Holland

https://www.virtueisgreen.com/